To Mary,

INJUNCTION

by

J. S. MATLIN

With very best wishes

Copyright© 2023 J. S. Matlin

J & S Publishing

J. S. Matlin has asserted his right under the Copyright Designs and Patent Act, 1988, to be identified as the author of this work.

All rights reserved include the right to reproduce this book, or portions thereof in any form. No part of this text may be reproduced, transmitted, downloaded, decompiled, reverse engineered or stored, in any form or introduced into any information and retrieval system, in any form or by any means, whether electronic or mechanical, without the express written permission of the author.

A number of historical figures appear as characters in this story. However, this book is a work of fiction. References to real people, events, establishments, organizations or locales are intended only to provide a sense of authenticity and are used fictitiously.

All other characters and all incidents and dialogue are drawn from the author's imagination and are not to be construed as real.

dearjsm@uwclub.net

ISBN: 9798391199380

Injunction

An injunction is a court order restraining a person, firm or corporation from beginning or continuing improperly or illegally an action which threatens or invades the legal rights of another.

J S Matlin

To Linda

For fifty years my severest critic

and my best friend

Already published by J. S. Matlin

Truth to Power.

Smoking Gun.

Trade Off.

End Game.

Awaiting Publication

Fall Guy.

List of Characters:

Arthur Hawkins.	
Harry Hawkins:	Father.
Tilly Hawkins:	Mother.
Eddie Grey:	Gym owner and Coach.
Mr. Harris:	Newsagent.
Maisie Duckworth:	Girl-friend and first love.
Theresa March:	Matron at Mary Grey's Care Home.
Big Sam Mullins:	Bookie.
Charlie Pearce	Author.
Elle Pearce:	Wife.
Lizzie Pearce:	Daughter.
Harry Pearce:	Son.
Amber Pearce:	Daughter.
Mrs. James:	Housekeeper.
Hardy Burgess:	Solicitor: Senior Partner, Ventriss, Phillips.
James Turner:	Solicitor: Partner, Ventriss, Phillips.
Lilian Collier:	Secretary to Hardy Burgess.
John Davis:	Assistant.
Jackie Swain:	Assistant.
Harry Noble:	Specialist driver.
Miriam Smith, Q.C:	Barrister for Pearce.
Barry:	Clerk.
Fay Reynolds:	Junior Barrister.
Judge Judith Benton:	Queen's Bench Judge.
Miles Shackford, QC:	Attorney General.

Peregrine Vaughan: Television journalist.
Maxwell Rankin: Proprietor: *The Daily Sentinel*.
Martin Richmond: Editor-in-Chief: *The Daily Sentinel*.
Mark Maynard QC: Barrister: *The Daily Sentinel*.

Douglas Bunn   Barrister.
Rachel Hawks.   Barrister.

Barry Barratt: Reporter – *Daily Sentinel*.
Johnny Flag: Photographer – *Daily Sentinel*.
Paul Spencer: Legal Adviser – *Daily Sentinel*.
William Tovey: Solicitor and Partner at Houseman, Tovey and Letts.

John Baker: Bank of Illinois.
Gerry Watkins: Money man to Rankin.
Jillian Holder: Advertising wunderkind to Rankin.
Connie Strauss: Gossip/celebrity writer on *Daily Sentinel*.
Bill Jones (TYW):   Gofer at *Daily Sentinel*.
Minnie Carter: Private Investigator.

Eric Buddell: Clerk/Manager GI Insurance Co.
Gerry Rhodes: Junior Minister in Treasury.
Freddie Styles: Co-worker at General Insurance.
Harvey Williams: Member of the Bass Lloyd's Syndicate.
Ronnie Bass: Leading Underwriter at Lloyd's Syndicate.
Henry Aitken: Administrator and Underwriter.

James Morton: Plastic Surgeon.

Prologue.

Arthur Hawkins never forgot World Cup final day, 30th July, 1966. Pretty well the whole of England held its collective breath as Alf Ramsey's boys beat the Germans. But Arthur remembered the day for a very different reason. His mother died.

Tilly Hawkins had no remarkable qualities, wasn't particularly good looking, nor was she a dab hand in the kitchen. Put simply, she was mum. She got Arthur dressed for school, made him his packed lunch and was home when he returned. "Glass of milk and a bicky, Arfa?"

In the first ten years of Arthur's life, mum had been ever-present but suddenly she wasn't there. It would just be 'Arry, his dad, and 'Arfa'. Arthur didn't really know his father. Harry Hawkins was a working-class bloke who laboured on the docks at Rotherhithe, where they lived on the ground floor of their rented, terraced house.

Every week, 'Arry brought home his pay packet which he gave to Tilly. He'd have a night in the pub once a week and twice a month he'd go out with his mates to The Social Club to have a few beers and play snooker or darts. Arthur remembered being taken on day trips to the seaside now and then. And one year they stayed five days at a B & B in Clacton. Luxury!

Harry and Tilly were products of their age. They just rubbed along, leading their lives in the house. Arthur knew there was no spare money but when you're young, these things don't signify. None of the other kids living in his street had much. They made their own fun.

Injunction

The day Tilly died started well. The sun was shining, hardly a cloud in the sky and Arthur wanted to go outside and play. But breakfast didn't happen. Tilly yelled for 'Arry and was taken to hospital in an ambulance. Arthur knew he was getting a baby brother or sister. He heard the word 'premature' spoken by the ambulance man but had no idea what it meant.

Arthur went next door to the Bye's house. He didn't much like it there. It smelled of boiled cabbage. Mrs Bye was a jolly lady but ready to take a carpet-beater to her children if needed, and Arthur too, for that matter. Tony Bye was Arthur's best friend. That morning, Mrs. Bye gave Arthur a bowl of cereal and allowed him and Tony to play in the street. All the talk was about the World Cup final. Nobody had a television set, so everyone listened to the match on the radio.

At about 4.30 that afternoon, Harry came home. He was pale and walked very slowly, as if the weight of the world was on his shoulders. Nobody was outside the house. Everyone was indoors, listening to the commentary. Harry knocked on the Bye's door and quietly whispered to Mrs. Bye who went to fetch Arthur. On seeing Arthur, Harry hugged him. This was unusual.

"Dad, I can't breathe. Let me go."

In the hallway of the Bye house, Harry could not contain himself. He released Arthur, fell to his knees sobbing, with his head in his hands. Arthur was dumbfounded. He had never seen his father cry before, let alone descend into such misery. Harry pulled himself together.

"Let's go next door, son."

"What about the football?"

"I have something important to tell you."

Once they were home, Harry asked, "Want a glass of milk?" Arthur nodded. Had Harry looked properly at Arthur, he would have seen a very frightened little boy. Arthur sat at his place in the kitchen. Harry brought over the milk.

"Arfa, I've some very sad news. I don't know how to tell you this, son. Mum died and so did your baby brother." Harry paused, trying not to cry. "So, from now on, it's going to be just you and me. I'm so sorry."

Arthur stared at the glass of milk. He said nothing for a while. "I don't understand. Isn't mum coming home tonight? Will she be back tomorrow?"

"No, Arfa. She's gone. She's not coming back. But she told me to tell you she's sorry and that she loved you very much. You and me, we will have to do our best without her."

Harry burst into tears again and left the kitchen. Arthur was numb. He just didn't understand. Would he see his mum again? He, too, started to cry.

The funeral took place a week later. A few neighbours and friends attended. Both Harry's and Tilly's parents were dead, there were no siblings, no cousins, no uncles and aunts. That was that. Tilly's clothes and knick-knacks were soon removed and sold or given to the Salvation Army.

Harry and Arthur fended for themselves. It wasn't that Harry was cold to Arthur and unemotional. Like many men of his generation, Harry had been brought up not to show his feelings. He clothed and fed his son and made sure he went to school but that was that. They talked little.

Within months of Tilly's death, the Bye family moved to Birmingham. Mr. Bye was offered a job in a Lucas factory making car headlights. Arthur lost touch with Tony but he wasn't the kind to make friends easily. He felt so lonely.

His looks didn't help. He had stick out ears, a bulbous nose and protruding chin. His ugliness made him a target of the kind of verbal cruelty that schoolboys call 'just a bit of banter.' "Big conk" was often said to his face. He was pilloried as a 'mummy's boy,' another unkindness. Little wonder he was quiet and withdrawn.

He was bullied physically at school. Small and weak, he had nobody to protect him and there was no point complaining to the teachers. They would do nothing. Arthur became resigned to the fact that school was just a part of life to be endured.

One day when Arthur was twelve, he arrived home with his school jacket torn, scratches and bruises on his face and knees and a painful wrist, which had been turned forcefully by a much bigger boy. Harry was home. When he saw his son, he became angry.

"Who did this to you? Why did you let another boy beat you up? Why didn't you fight back?"

"There were three of them, Dad, all bigger than me. They've had it in for me all year. I take different routes home to keep clear of them. I can run faster than they do but sometimes it's no use. Today, they were waiting for me. I didn't see them till it was too late. I tried to fight back but...." Arthur started to cry.

"Cryin' won't help, nor will snivellin'. You have to toughen up."

That night, Arthur cried himself to sleep. Next morning was a Saturday and Harry woke Arthur early. "You're comin' with me."

They walked for 20 minutes, arriving at a doorway that announced itself as 'The East End Gym. Boxing, Judo and Martial Arts.' Arthur didn't want to go in. He was beyond scared but he had no choice. He and Harry climbed a flight of stairs into a large open space, full of gym equipment and a boxing ring. Harry introduced himself to Eddie Grey, the owner, who coached and trained youngsters as well as aspiring boxers. Arthur was told to sit as the two adults talked. Then Harry came back to Arthur.

"I'm leavin'. I'll be back in two hours. Now you do everyfin' what Mr. Grey tells yer."

Grey came over to Arthur. "Where's your kit?"

"Sorry, sir. Don't have any kit with me. I didn't know I was coming here. Dad didn't tell me."

Grey, in his fifties and a grandfather, realised this was not a time for shouting and screaming.

"Okay, let's find some kit for you. Once you've changed, we'll have a little chat. You can tell me what's been going on with you at school. Then we'll work out a way to get you fighting fit. Alright?"

Arthur was unused to kindness. His eyes teared up as he mumbled, "thank you." Grey tousled Arthur's hair and gave him a friendly pat on his back. Five minutes later, Arthur appeared wearing shorts and a T-shirt which was much too big. He had a pair of old, ill-fitting plimsolls on his feet.

"Artie, what sports do you do at school?"

"None really. I play football in the playground. We get PT once a week. I'm not much good at either."

"Right, we'll start from scratch. I want you to work weights. To begin with, they will be light. I'll show you the technique. Every two weeks, we'll increase the weight a bit. To get fitter, you need to run. When you get home from school, I want you to go out running for fifteen minutes. That's the first week. I want you to increase the time by five minutes every week until you can run for an hour."

"Yes, sir. My wrist got hurt yesterday. Don't know if I can work weights today."

"That's okay and it's Mr. Grey or boss."

"Yes sir, erm, Mr. Boss."

Grey laughed. "Lord, you are a nervous Nelly."

"Do I do boxing?"

"Not yet. You're not fit or strong enough. Now, your Dad told me you're being bullied at school. We'll start on self-defence next week and when I think you're ready, I'll teach you judo. It might suit you better than boxing. It will help you see off those bullies."

Arthur nodded. "Good," said Grey. "Now let's get you started on an exercise bike."

When Harry returned to the gym, he watched his son work. On the way home, there was little conversation. It was limited to "how was it?" and "okay." Arthur asked if he could have new gym shoes and training kit to wear. Harry got him some second hand gear.

Over the weeks, Arthur's fitness and strength improved, as did his self-defence skills. Soon enough he was running an hour a day after school. Physically, he was changing before his father's eyes. Muscles on his torso, legs and arms demonstrated the difference. He was also growing taller. He was no longer a weed.

One day in May, Arthur found himself trapped by two of the bullies who often tormented him. They caught him crossing waste ground near his home. One bully was behind him, the other in front. Instead of running, he stood his ground.

"Make it a fair fight. One at a time," Arthur shouted.

The larger boy, three inches taller and twenty pounds heavier than Arthur, nodded as he took seniority rights. He replied, "your funeral." Arthur removed his jacket and tie and rolled up his shirt sleeves. The boy charged at Arthur who neatly side-stepped him, tripping him onto the rubble, causing grazes to hands and face. The bully got up, red in the face and angry, and charged again. He got the same treatment but this time Arthur jumped on his back, kneeling on either side of the boy's chest. He grabbed the bully's left arm which he put in a lock, twisting his wrist. The boy squealed in pain.

"Get off me. Get off. You're hurting me."

Arthur pulled back the bully's head and slammed it down into gravel, drawing blood as the bully squealed with pain. "Don't like it, do you? It's only what you've done to me."

The other boy moved in. Arthur stood and faced him, fists held high as Mr. Grey had taught him. The boy showed fear. Arthur smiled as he moved close. At that, the boy ran, shouting, "Leave me alone." Arthur hoped the boy had peed his pants.

The first boy was standing. His face was a picture of blood, anger and fear. He held his bad wrist in his other hand. He was clearly in pain. "You broke my wrist. I'll get you for this, 'Awkins."

Arthur laughed. "Fine, come and get me. Your back-up isn't much use is he?" Arthur grabbed the bully's wrist and bent it again. The boy screamed in pain. "Let me go. Let me go."

"It's not broken, you big girl. I'll let go when you give me back all the money you and your mate have stolen from me."

Arthur eased his grip on the bully's arm, then suddenly gave it another twist. The boy yelled and started to cry. Arthur let the boy's arm go and punched him in the face with the knuckle of his middle finger slightly raised. One of the boys at Mr. Grey's gym had taught him the move. The boy's nose broke and more blood spouted.

"Give me your money." The bully got some notes and coins from his pockets and gave them to Arthur, who counted it. "You and your mate still owe me six quid and change. We'll call it seven quid. Pay me by next week or else you'll get more of this."

Part I.

The Claim – 2006.

Chapter One.

"What?"

"I'll repeat." The voice was part American drawl, part panic. "Do I have to put up with a crowd hanging around my front door? Don't I have a legal right to privacy?"

"Charles, I heard the questions," replied Hardy Burgess. "I'm just not awake. What time is it?" Burgess sat up in bed, put on his spectacles and wondered why as he hadn't anything to read.

"Ten to seven."

Burgess sighed. "Charles, this is an uncivilised hour to be asking questions. What's going on?"

"I've got about thirty journalists camped in the road outside my house. Claire and the kids are scared stiff."

"It's not even seven o'clock in the morning," Burgess moaned. "Christ! Charles, are you calling me from your mobile?"

"Yes. So what?"

"Don't use it. And that goes for all your family. Turn all mobiles off now. These phones can be hacked, conversations overheard."

Burgess yawned audibly. "Give me an hour to get to the office. I'll round up some people. Make sure your land line stays clear. I'll call you as soon as I can."

There was a pause and an "okay" from Charles Pearce.

Hardy Burgess was a bachelor in his fifties, a man whose ways were set in granite. He lived in a spacious mansion flat in Mount Street, Mayfair. His early morning routine was fixed. He detested any variation. He arose at 7.30 am, showered and dressed. Breakfast, prepared by his housekeeper, was at 7.55 am sharp. He read *The Times* and eased himself into the day. At 8.25 am, he either took a brisk walk to his office in Berkeley Square, arriving by 8.34 am or his chauffeur would drive him if it was raining or very cold.

Burgess was a lawyer for authors, publishers, literary agents, people like that. He could handle all sorts of issues from contracts to defamation. Whilst he would not profess to be an expert on social media, he advised government committees on media law. As one of the senior partners of Ventriss, Phillips & Partners, he commanded much respect within the legal profession, not to mention high fees from his clients.

On arrival at the office, Burgess would have a coffee while he meandered into the day, looking over messages and reading e-mails and post. This morning would be different. His routine would be totally out of shape. From home, he telephoned Lilian Collier, his secretary. Dispensing with any pleasantries, he told her, "I need the media litigation team in the office soonest. I want you here too. Take a cab and tell everyone to do the same. Clear my diary for the day. Check Harry Noble's availability. We'll need extra security at the office."

Lilian knew that when the boss was in this mood, her best course was to do exactly as he said. Don't ask questions. Normally, it would take her over an hour to reach the office. A cab might cut thirty minutes off the journey. She made some calls and rushed out of her flat.

Shortly after 7.45, Hardy Burgess entered V P House, his firm's Georgian building. Ventriss, Phillips & Partners owned three adjoining houses on the Square. The interior bore little relation to the exterior. The former had been gutted and now housed thirty four thousand square feet of modern, air-conditioned office space.

Burgess took the lift to the top floor. His vast office had triple glazed windows, overlooking the Square. The decor was traditional, neutral colour walls, landscapes, portraits and law cartoons on the walls, oak bookshelves and desk, padded chairs and a deep blue carpet. It suited him. He wore Savile Row uniform. He was a handsome man. People who didn't know him wondered why he was not married, often adding two and two and making seven. He liked women but not sufficiently to make a lasting commitment.

Ten minutes after Burgess arrived, Lilian put her head around his door. Lilian had worked for Burgess for more than twenty years. They had a rhythm together, always professional.

"Morning, Mr. Burgess. Coffee?"

"Thank you, Lilian. Did you get hold of the team?"

"I did. They should be here in a few minutes. And I have ordered extra security too."

Injunction

"Get Charles Pearce on the land line for me, would you please?" He paused before paying a compliment. "Thank you for getting in quickly so. I suspect it's going to be one of those days."

Three minutes later, a steaming mug of coffee and three media team members arrived in unison.

"Good morning to you all. Please sit. We have to move quickly. Our client, Charles Pearce, the novelist, and his family cannot move from their house without running a gauntlet of reporters. Charles estimates there are some thirty people camped in the road outside his house. I have nothing else yet. I terminated our very brief call because Charles was on a mobile. I've told him not to use it and make sure nobody else in the house uses one."

Hardy's red phone rang. "It's Mr. Pearce for you," he heard Lilian say.

Burgess began. "Charles, I apologise for being so abrupt this morning but mobiles just aren't safe. Our experts have advised us not to use them if any part of a conversation might be confidential."

"Understood."

"I have my team listening in. Please would you start from the beginning?"

"Did you watch television last night? I was on the Peregrine Vaughan show."

"Vaughan? That gutter-snipe. What possessed you?"

"My publishers. They thought it was a good idea. When Vaughan asked questions about my private life, there was a bit of a conflab. He had agreed not to do this and I caught him in a big fat lie. I had him on tape agreeing not to ask me that kind of stuff. I walked off the show in mid-broadcast. If you watch a recording, you'll see it all. Around half past six this morning, my phone started ringing. Then the front door bell was pressed continually. The children ran into our bedroom; they were very scared. Claire and I calmed them down as best we could. I called the police and got nowhere, so I called you."

"I see. I sympathise. It must be very unpleasant."

"We are under siege here. We are prisoners in our own home and I want these people removed. Did I say I called the police? They said if these people weren't committing a crime, there was nothing they could do."

"Charles, if you want an injunction to remove these people, we'll need you to come to our offices. There is a process we have to follow. It involves you providing evidence and seeing a judge. It will be awkward if you can't come to us. How long do you think it would take you to get here?"

"Oh, that I could, but we really are under siege. The front gate is blocked. There is no rear exit for a car. To leave, I would have to run the gauntlet of these media vultures. Claire wants to go out to do some shopping and we need to get the children to school but if she tries to get her car onto the road, she will be stopped. She's scared she will knock somebody down."

"You're right about the police. They will consider this a private matter and unless there's a crime, they can't intervene."

"Can we do our interview over Skype?" asked Charles.

"I don't know how secure this type of communication would be. Since you may need to go before a judge to get the injunction, we really need you here. Skype is new and I suspect the technology is as risky as a mobile. What's happening to you is called doorstepping, from which you are entitled to legal protection. I regret that the sole course open to people in your position is to take out an injunction against the media to clear them from your home. If the press remains on the public highway, the police have no right to remove them, unless the press are committing a crime. Loitering isn't a crime if there is no intent."

"So what can be done?"

"We can get a car to you. We use a driver, Harry Noble for this sort of thing. He'll come to you. He is familiar with these situations. Back in the day, he was a professional rally driver. All being well, he'll be at your home within the hour. He'd have you here in good time."

"Okay. Let's do it."

"When he gets to your house, here's what I suggest you do." Hardy gave the instructions.

"Charles, do you have a video camera at home?"

"I don't but Lizzie does."

"How old is she?"

"Fourteen."

"She's with you there?"

"Of course. The children will be here today unless the press moves out."

"May I speak with her?"

Lizzie came to the phone. "Lizzie, I'm Hardy Burgess, your father's lawyer. I'd like you to do something for me."

"Okay."

"Please would you sit upstairs in a room that overlooks the front of the house but make sure you can't easily be seen. I want you to video anyone who passes through the front gate onto your drive or front garden. If you see anyone doing things they shouldn't, like throwing refuse into the front garden or weeing on the flowers, stuff like that, please get it on video. If anyone comes to the front door, video it if you can. Do you want to ask me anything?"

"I think I understand. Will this help Daddy?"

"Yes. Very much. Now here is my telephone number if you need me for anything. Any time. Please don't use a mobile. May I speak to Daddy again?"

Burgess read a message handed to him by Lilian.

"Charles, Harry Noble is on his way to you. Call if you need me. When Noble gets to you, you know what to do. Do you want us to arrange security for you at home?"

"I don't think so. The worst they do is ring the door bell and cat call."

"Okay. Good luck. One final thing. Apart from you, your wife and children, is anyone else in your home?"

"Our housekeeper, Mrs. James."

"Okay, all of you sit tight. It may take quite a while to remove the press but it will happen, hopefully by tonight or tomorrow morning. In the meantime, keep everyone out of the line of sight. Not Lizzie, though. Her role is important."

Hardy said goodbye and spoke to his team.

"We need to line up counsel. This one has Miriam Smith's name on it." Burgess turned to one of his assistants. "John, call Smith's clerk and check her availability today. I expect we will want to see Benton late this afternoon or tonight." Judith Benton was the High Court media judge. "Have Smith's clerk alert the judge's clerk about this." John left to attend to these tasks.

"Let me think out loud," Hardy continued. "Pearce's statement is crucial, of course. While we're waiting, we should watch the Peregrine Vaughan programme to see what this is all about? I assume it's on You Tube. Who's got a lap-top?"

An assistant placed a lap-top computer on the conference table. Hardy stared as pictures flashed on the screen. The assistant clicked on a succession of icons and prompts and 'You Tube' appeared. He then searched 'Peregrine Vaughan + Charles Pearce.' A new picture flashed up on the screen. He clicked on the start icon.

Vaughan: "I'd like to welcome my guest tonight, the best-selling author, Charles Pearce. May I call you Charlie?"

Pearce: "Charlie's fine."

Vaughan: "What's it like to be a best-selling author? You're not in the traditional mode are you? You don't do book signings, you don't give talks and you grant very few interviews.
"But you have all the trappings. I mean the grand house, luxury motor cars, a boat on the Thames, a place in Cornwall, and lots of money in the bank."

Pearce: "Writing isn't easy, at least not for me. You don't just sit at a keyboard and watch as the words magically appear on a screen. A lot of research is needed. If you write a historic novel, the history needs to be as accurate as possible. Much thought goes into a plot. Characters have to be created, analysed and critiqued. Often, I write for days, only to scrap everything because it is just not good enough. Trial and error. It can be a frustrating life. But I don't deny I have enjoyed huge success."

Vaughan: "What about limiting your exposure to the public? No book signings and the like? This is 2006. Doesn't your public have rights?

Pearce: "I accept the public has an interest but a long time ago I decided to restrict my availability. If an autographed copy of one of my books is wanted, publishers always hold a stock that I've signed. I don't give talks because I find them uncomfortable. For example, what do I say if I get challenged about why a character behaves in a particular way? The real answer is that it's my story and my decision but can I say that? The same applies to interviews. I think the expression is, "out of my comfort zone."

Vaughan: "Don't your readers deserve better? Aren't they entitled to more?"

Pearce: "I don't think so. My readers read my books. If they want more from me, I'm sorry but it's not on offer. Never was and never will be. What is on offer is a good story, or at least I hope so. Let me ask, are your *Daily Sentinel* readers entitled to more from you than your public persona?"

Vaughan: "They get it in my television shows."

Pearce: "But they don't get you, do they? I mean Perry Vaughan, the man. Do you tell them where you live and in what style? How would you feel if you had to answer these questions? You're as much in the public eye as me, if not more so."

Vaughan: "I'll answer if you will. But let's start with you. Your first book was published about eighteen years ago. What were you doing before then?"

There was a long pause.

Pearce: "Mr. Vaughan, we agreed I would not be asked this kind of question."

Vaughan: [Leering] "What do you have to hide? What don't you want the public to know? Why can't the people who pay to read your books and watch your movies know more about you? What are you concealing from them and this audience?"

Pearce: [Reaches into the inside pocket of his jacket and removes a sheet of paper with writing on it.] "Mr. Vaughan, let me remind you of our agreement about this interview. [Reads] 'Mr. Vaughan promises to limit his questions in a television interview to Mr. Pearce's books and films, his methods of writing, how he creates characters and plots. Questions about Mr. Pearce's earnings from book sales and film and video rights are acceptable. Mr. Vaughan promises not to ask anything whatsoever about Mr. Pearce's private life.' Mr. Vaughan, you signed this letter only two days ago."

Vaughan: "Please show me this letter. [Pause] Well, that's not my signature. I have no idea who signed this. Was it you?"

Pearce: [Reaches again into a jacket pocket and produces a mobile phone.] "Could I have a microphone? Thank you." [A conversation between Vaughan and Pearce ensues.]

Pearce: 'So, we are agreed. Nothing at all about my private life. You will restrict your questions to my books and films and my earnings from them. I prepared a letter before I came here. Will you sign it?'

Vaughan: [Pause] 'Alright, I'll sign, for what it's worth.'

Pearce: 'What does that mean?'

Vaughan: 'If you ever produce the letter, I'll deny that's my signature.'

Injunction

Pearce: "So, what do you have to say for yourself now, Mr. Vaughan? You're a liar. I'm not staying here a moment longer. You call yourself a journalist? If journalists are bottom-feeding slugs, then you're a journalist. My apologies, ladies and gentlemen." [Pearce removes his microphone and walks off stage, to applause from the audience.]

The computer was logged off. One of the team expressed the feelings of the room. "No wonder the press is camped on Pearce's doorstep. They don't like it when one of their own is exposed as a cheat and a liar. Perry got served royally."

Lilian put her head round the door. "Thought you would like to know, Harry called. He's collected Mr. Pearce. Expects to be here in about 45 minutes."

"Thank you. Did the extra security arrive here? I want them at the front and back entrances." Lilian nodded.

Hardy cleared his throat. "Let's see if we all agree on the law relating to door-stepping. The European Convention on Human Rights was codified into The Human Rights Act of 1998. The important provision for our purposes is Article 8. People have the right for their family, private life and home to be respected. However, the press have an exemption under Article 10 which gives the media the right to freedom of expression. This phrase has not been defined in law. So the law is not straightforward. I suggest we keep an open mind until we have all the facts."

"Have Pearce's rights actually been infringed?" asked John. "The media have camped near his home on a private road. Under the law, does this make a difference? Mind you, if incursions have been made into the grounds of the house with people ringing the door bell, this will make a difference. He'll have a case."

"Yes, thank you, John," Hardy responded, while thinking, 'sometimes he can be too academic.' "We'll find out more when Pearce gets here. So far as I am aware, the law makes no distinction between public and private roads. From what we have heard, Charles and his family have a good case. One thing is certain. You people will have a busy day. Lilian, please make sure we have a conference room and lay on lunch."

As always in these situations, Hardy Burgess offered a prayer of gratitude for the calm, unpressured way in which his secretary handled things. 'Yes, it's just a room and a few sandwiches and drinks but she never flaps,' he reminded himself.

The team withdrew. Hardy sat back in his ample, cream leather office chair. He shut his eyes and tried to draw in strength for the day's battles to come.

Chapter Two.

Harry Noble tried to pull his car into the drive of the Pearce mansion. He was met by a phalanx of photographers pushing their cameras at every dark tinted window of his dark blue Jaguar XK, 4.2 litre V8. He slowed the car so that nobody got hurt but placed his left hand on the steering wheel, honking the horn perpetually. As he reached the open gates, people inched out of his way. In the drive, he carried out a hand-brake turn expertly, steering the car so that the passenger door opened directly to the front door of the house. A figure exited with a coat over his head. He jumped into the passenger seat and Noble moved the Jag towards the gates. His way was blocked.

Harry Noble leant again on his steering well but the throng of photo-journalists and reporters would not budge. Instead, they yelled questions at the passenger as some tried to open the locked passenger door. Noble reversed the Jaguar to the front door, the passenger opened the car door and ran back inside the house. Noble drove away. The press, knowing there was no passenger, didn't block his way. As he exited the gates, a loud cheer could be heard. Lizzie videoed the whole episode.

Three quarters of a mile down the road, Noble stopped the car. Charles Pearce came out from behind a hedge into the road and got into the Jag.

"Okay, Mr. Pearce, next stop Berkeley Square."

"My God, is it always like this?" asked Charles.

"I've known worse," Noble replied, "but there are always ways to beat the press. Now relax and enjoy the ride. I'll keep to the back roads for a bit. Fasten your seat belt. I drive quickly."

At 11.24 that morning, Charles Pearce walked into the rear entrance of the Ventriss, Phillips building. He was relieved that no journalists were lurking. He made his way to Reception where John Davis was waiting for him.

"Mr. Pearce. I'm John Davis. I am one of your legal team. Mr. Burgess and the others are waiting for you."

"Thank you. Are these men for me?" he asked, pointing at security people.

"We added some people for today just in case but so far, so good."

Pearce was escorted to the lift and taken to the top floor. Hardy was waiting for him at the door of Conference Room 2.

"Quite a morning, Charles."

"You can say that again." Pearce looked aghast at the number of people in the room. "Hardy, how much is all this going to cost me?"

"A small fortune but as you have a large one, does it matter? Let's not worry about money. If this thing goes the way we hope, a high percentage of our fees will be paid by the media. Now let me introduce you. You've met John Davis. This is Jackie Swain. John and Jackie will be doing a lot of running around for you."

Charles, a few years younger than Burgess, was looking grey. Hardly surprising. He was an inch or so shorter than Burgess and slimmer. He had clear blue eyes, an aquiline nose and a chin that stuck out a tad. He was dressed casually, a light blue Ralph Lauren shirt underneath a navy blue cashmere sweater, beige chinos and casual slip-ons.

Hardy invited all to sit. Lilian entered and provided teas, coffees and soft drinks. Pearce asked for a strong builders. Lilian didn't need an explanation to produce the required cup of tea.

"I need to call Claire to tell her I'm safe."

"Use this one," said Hardy, pointing at a phone on a side table. "Don't mention where you are, just in case."

Charles spoke briefly. Claire sounded angry but Hardy wasn't concerned. After the morning the Pearce family had endured, there was bound to be tension.

Hardy went to work. "Charles, we've watched your interview with Peregrine Vaughan. The media has taken offence at the perceived attack on one of their own so they've door-stepped you. I'll explain the law, so far as it applies to your case. I'll have to ask a lot of questions, some of which you may find excessive but this is the way the injunction process works. Then John will take your witness statement and I'll cover what members of your family tell me. When this is done, we'll assess if we have the evidence to go to the next stage."

"What is the next stage?"

"I'll come to that but let me first explain the law to you."

Hardy gave a slightly more detailed version of the law which he had set out for the team.

"After we have collected the evidence, the next stage is to meet with a barrister who will represent you in court. I recommend Miriam Smith Q.C. She is bright, smart and the judges like her. She is an acknowledged expert in the field. If Smith is satisfied with the merits of your case, she will go to the media judge later today and, hopefully, get an interim injunction. It's interim because the defendants will have had no chance to tell the judge their side.

"If the judge grants the interim injunction, John and Jackie will come into their own. John will be serving injunction papers on all the reporters and photo-journalists at your house, while Jackie will do the same thing for all editors at their places of business. Later today, as the case develops, I'll go into more detail, especially what happens after the interim injunction is granted. Do you understand so far?"

"That's a lot to take in. I'd like to speak with you alone."

The others stepped outside the Conference Room. Charles showed his frustration.

"I'm not happy. I feel you are making decisions for me before I can understand my options. Interim injunctions, full injunctions, where does this go?"

"If you don't take out the injunction, you can ignore the journos at your house and wait them out. I don't know how long they will stay there but this has become a story about the media as well as you. The press is tenacious. They won't give up easily."

"Is there no way we can negotiate our way out of this?"

"I don't see how. By going on the Perry Vaughan show, you let the genie out of the bottle. Your self-imposed privacy shield disappeared. You made it open season for any journalist to pry into your past. You could try stonewalling but to what end? The journos will not let this go. Only you know what they might find but we'll be talking soon enough about your past. Any negotiated deal would require you to open up about your private life. If you decide on the injunction route, you will be seeking an equitable remedy and there is a legal maxim that those who go to equity must come with clean hands. In other words, you have to tell all, first to me, then Mrs. Smith and, if asked, the judge."

"I can't avoid this?"

"No, it's a requirement. Also, by appearing on Vaughan's show, you poked the bear with a sharp stick. The media will keep up their demands for information whether you get an injunction or not. But to get the injunction, it's important that you tell us everything about your past that might be to your detriment. Without this information, it would be like fighting with one arm behind our backs."

"Hardy, you've just rammed me with metaphors. Maybe you should be the writer."

"Why on earth didn't you talk to me before you went on that show?"

Charles sighed. "Like I said, pressure from publishers and my own screw up. Too late to fix it now."

"This is as good a time as any for you to talk to me about the life of Charles Pearce. We've never had the dark night of the soul talk, have we? We need to do this now."

"What do you want from me?"

"Let's start with what I know about you. You are an American citizen. You grew up in California, in a Los Angeles suburb. You graduated college and worked in advertising until you were thirty. Your parents died when you were twenty-nine. They left you independently wealthy. You soon decided to give up your career and you travelled the world. I don't know exactly where you went and for how long. I know in 1987, you took classes at University of Minnesota, where you met Claire, and Macalester University. You started to write and your first novel caught fire.

"You published your second novel in the 1990s before you moved to England. We met when you settled here. I have been your lawyer for fifteen or more years. During this time, you've published seven more novels. I know nothing about your personal life in England except your immediate family and where you live. Certainly, I am unaware of anything about you which might be defined as unorthodox, let alone scandalous. Have I got it right so far?"

"Yes."

"If there is anything to your detriment in your private life, I assume it would emanate from America. Is there anything I need to know? Whatever you tell me is in confidence. I cannot disclose any information to anyone without your permission. Once I know all there is to know about you, I'll be in a better position to advise you whether or not to start legal proceedings."

Charles thought for a while. "Is working on an advertising campaign for women's lingerie sufficiently salacious? Hardy, there is nothing in my past which, if found, would embarrass me or make me ashamed. You asked about my travels. I did indeed spend time going around the world. I ended up in the Twin Cities because I wanted to settle down and get a better education. That's where I met Claire."

"So why don't you tell the press about your private life? I distinguish this from your family life. I'm not suggesting you have a spread in Hello Magazine with glossy pictures of your home and Claire and the children by the swimming pool. Clearly, that's off limits. But I could arrange an interview with a friendly journalist who would write about your unremarkable life in America and your travels. What do you think? We'd get PR advice for you. It would take a day or two to get the story out but there are advantages. It might avoid litigation. The press will soon go hunting someone else."

Pearce sighed deeply. "Oh, that it were so simple. I dropped my guard for a moment and invited the hell that has followed. Hardy, I know the media will be after me till I crumble. A bland story like mine won't satisfy these ghouls. They'll dig and dig and when they find nothing, they'll invent. I suspect my best option is to go ahead and take my chances with the law."

"As you wish, Charles. It's your decision. I'm sorry if you got the impression I was driving you into legal action. I assure you this was not my intention. I wouldn't think the worse of you if you backed off. Litigation can be brutal."

"My mind's made up."

"Okay. Let's get people back in and get on with it."

Pearce told the team, "I can't have these journalists besieging me and my family. So, what's next?"

John Davis took over. "It might be best to take you through the legals again. Briefly, everybody should have respect for private life. This right is protected by statute. However, as a counter, the press and the media have a right to freedom of expression. The two rights have equal status and if a Court believes it is in the public interest to publish material, that belief will override privacy interests."

"So?" asked Charlie, "the right to privacy is not sacrosanct."

"It will be for us to show your private life has suffered and your right to privacy has been infringed. We don't have to worry today about the public interest issue. That comes later if, and only if, the press decides to fight the interim injunction. Then the burden is on the media to prove the public has a right to know about you. It must prove that door-stepping was a reasonable act on their part. If you were a cabinet minister, a film star, a famous actor or sportsman or someone continually in the public eye, it would be easier for the press.

"This case is different. I doubt the public has ever shown much interest in writers, except the dead ones. We'll argue that people don't want to know about the people who write, for example those who scripted shows like Men Behaving Badly and Red Dwarf. As I said, we may have to address the point down the line, unless there is something about you that the court should know right away."

Pearce looked at Hardy. "My private life is my own. I don't want my wife and children to live in the glare of publicity caused by me. Before I wrote my novels, nobody knew me. I was just one man among millions. I haven't appeared at book signings, rarely given library or literary talks, nor have I engaged in question and answer sessions at conferences. I have given one or two interviews but always on terms excluding my private life. I don't see myself as someone in public life. I am not a celebrity. I have not courted publicity in any way."

"Okay. Are you clear on the law?"

"I guess I'm as clear as anyone can be who doesn't have a legal qualification. What's next?"

Hardy took over. "Let's get started on the evidence. Why did you agree to the interview with Vaughan?"

"His people have been nagging my agents for months. Vaughan said he wanted to know about the man who is the writer. We kept telling him 'no'. Three weeks ago, my publishers got involved. They have my latest novel coming out in two months' time and thought it would be good publicity. In other words, they wanted pre-publication sales. They told me the Vaughan interview would be limited to my life as a writer, nothing else."

"Have you spoken with your publishers after last night?"

"Very briefly. I told them they failed to protect me. They said I had wrecked the launch of the new novel. They're in the wrong. There's no such thing as bad publicity. I suspect a major row is on its way. More work for you, Hardy."

Hardy nodded. "Okay, we can't look to them to provide help right now. When did you know the press was door-stepping you?"

"A little after six thirty this morning. There was a phone call. A journalist identified himself. He asked me why I stormed out of Vaughan's programme. I told him to watch the programme and put the phone down. Over the next few minutes, I had three more calls from reporters. Then I took the phone off the hook."

"Do you remember the names of the callers and the newspapers they were from?"

Pearce took a scrap of paper from a trouser pocket. He handed it to Burgess. "I thought this might be needed." Hardy read the names of four journalists and their newspaper titles. He noticed the name, Barry Barratt. He worked for *The Daily Sentinel*, the newspaper where Peregrine Vaughan was a columnist. He knew the names of two of the other three journalists. They worked for national newspapers.

"This is helpful. What next?"

"Claire and I sleep at the back of the house. Two children, Lizzie and Harry, have bedrooms overlooking the front. They both came into our bedroom to tell us they had been woken up by a commotion outside. I went to Lizzie's bedroom and saw a crowd of people outside the front gates. Some were blocking the road. Photographers brought short ladders and were taking pictures of the house. I saw one or two lenses pointed at Lizzie's bedroom windows. I took the children away and drew the curtains. Everybody, including Mrs. James, went downstairs to the kitchen, where we wouldn't be overlooked. I called the police who said they were unable to help. Then I called you."

"Remind me, how old is Lizzie?"

"Fourteen."

"What sort of girl is she? I mean is she shy, confident, good with people?"

"Why?"

"She has videoed things. She might have to give evidence down the line."

"She'll be fine. I'm biased but she really is a lovely teenager. Takes after her mother."

Lilian Collier, a mother of three herself whose children were almost out of the teenage angst era, couldn't restrain a smile as she set sandwiches on the table.

"I'd like to talk to Lizzie? Charles, would you mind calling her for me?"

Pearce pressed some numbers on the conference room phone. Claire answered. In reply to a question, he told her he was fine. He asked Lizzie to be put on. "Hi, darling. Please talk again with Mr. Burgess. He'll explain."

Hardy took the phone. "Hello, Lizzie. May I check a few things?"

"Yes." Lizzie's voice sounded strong.

"Have you been able to take videos of the people outside the house?"

"Yes. I have six videos for you."

"Do you know how to send them to me? I mean by e-mail."

Hardy thought he heard Lizzie snort.

"Of course."

"My e-mail address is hardy1@vp.co.uk Okay?"

"Yes. If you haven't received the emails in five minutes, please call me back."

"I will, Lizzie. Thank you. Please don't wipe the videos. They may be needed as evidence. And keep videoing. E-mail me every time you see anything new, especially if anyone crosses the front gates. I'll have my e-mail checked every few minutes."

"Okay, Mr. Burgess." Hardy passed the phone back to Pearce.

"Well done, Lizzie. May I speak to Mum again?" Claire came on the phone.

"Claire, looks like we have to go for the injunction."

The reply was inaudible to the room but the voice sounded frustrated.

"I know but it is what it is. We really don't have a choice. I'm going to have a long day here but I'll call when I can."

Hardy asked Jackie to check his e-mails and, as and when, to make copies of Lizzie's videos into DVDs. Hardy looked at his watch. "Let's have some lunch."

Lilian offered drinks as Hardy asked people to help themselves to food. He was ready for a smoked salmon sandwich. What he really wanted was a chilled Chablis to go with it but he contented himself with fizzy water, ice and a lime slice.

"So what's the next book about?" he asked Charlie.

"Big pharmaceutical is damaging the planet. An independent journalist gets hold of the story from a disgruntled employee but will he get the story published? And there's a bit of sex. I'm glad this is the final book of that three-book deal. I can relax a bit before the next one."

Charlie realised he was hungry. He had had no breakfast. He tucked into the sandwiches.

"Any chance of a beer, Hardy?"

"Not sure it's the best idea but if it's what you need. Anyone else?"

John and Jackie shook their heads. Hardy grinned. "Lilian, may I have a glass of Chablis."

Jackie bent her head to a laptop, clapped her hands and told the throng, "The videos are in. I'll make DVDs. We can watch on the TV."

Ten minutes later, heads were directed to the Conference Room television. The picture from the first video wasn't the best quality but it was clear. The camera was pointed at the Pearce front gates, which were open.

It would not be possible for people in the house to walk or drive out because of the crush of people blocking the way. John counted, saying 'thirty seven.' The picture moved to the front hedge adjoining the road. Ten or more photographers stood on ladders, pointing their cameras at the house. Voices could be heard, calling for "Charlie" or "Pearce" to come out and talk.

The first video ended and the second started. A man broke past the gates, coming to the front door. He rang the doorbell. Then he rang again. Then he called out, "Charlie Pearce, come out and talk. What are you hiding?"

The third video was similar to the first, except for the chanting. The camera pointed at the faces of the media. Many of them were laughing, giving an impression that it was a kind of game, until the aggression on the faces of some of those chanting was taken into account. They were an ugly mob.

The fourth video was similar to the second except this time three people came to the front door. One of them rang the front door bell, his finger resting on the call button without cessation. The other men were banging rhythmically on the door, calling, "Charlie Pearce, show your face" and laughing. Then they picked up some pebbles from the drive and threw them at the upstairs windows."

The fifth video showed the incident when Harry Noble drove up to the house but was prevented from leaving with his passenger. The film showed Harry reversing the car after failing to exit and the passenger running back into the house before Harry drove the Jag away.

"Who was the passenger?" Jackie asked.

"Mrs. James," Pearce replied.

The sixth video pictured a reporter walking through the front gates and moving to a flower bed to the right of the house. He unzipped his fly and urinated. Four other reporters followed his example."

John looked at Hardy. "The judge is going to love this. Harassment with a capital H."

"What do you mean?" asked Pearce.

"For a long time, members of the public had no effective protection from door-stepping or any recourse," John replied. "Complaints could be made to the Press Complaints Commission, who might decide to call editors to ask them to have their journalists moved on. However, as a result of the miners' strike in the 1980s, the government decided to legislate. It took a long time but the Protection from Harassment Act, 1997 protects individuals from this kind of behaviour. More than one incident is needed. Here we have evidence of stone throwing, persistent door-ringing, incessant phone calls and urination on flower beds inside your grounds. That's more than enough evidence."

"Will Lizzie have to give evidence?"

"No, not yet. Hardy will make a statement, explaining how the videos were obtained. This will be good enough for now. Possibly, Lizzie might have to appear in court later or swear an affidavit backing up the evidence but no need to stress about it. All we have to do for the present is e-mail the videos to Miriam Smith. With your statement and Lizzie's videos, I am sure she'll advise taking the injunction application to Judge Benton."

Hardy looked at his team. "I think we have enough to get started. I'll get Mr. Pearce's statement drafted. Jackie, you do the same for me. John, please check with Smith's clerk to see where the land lies." He checked his watch. 1.55 pm. "This shouldn't take much more than two hours, so let's say 5.00 pm for a consultation with Smith. We'll have to see the judge at her home tonight. Check on this too."

Hardy spoke to Pearce. "I suggest you speak to Claire. Warn her it will be a late night."

"Anything else?" Charlie's question was ironic.

"You might say your lawyers are confident of getting an injunction to remove the press from your home. Lilian, we need to book a people carrier for this afternoon and evening. Please make the arrangements."

Richard, the chief clerk at Miriam Smith's chambers, confirmed the consultation for 5:00 pm. The witness statements were approved with a few changes. Pearce and Burgess both signed. The statements were e-mailed to Miriam Smith, together with the videos. Pearce and his legal team arrived in Chambers shortly before 5 pm.

Pearce watched his legal team with a mixture of amusement and irritation. The law could be slow, tedious and mind numbing. The thoroughness, the attention to detail and the nit-picking were necessary perhaps but extremely annoying. This was not his world. Why had it taken the lawyers all day to deal with something that could have been summarised in two paragraphs? Pearce sighed inwardly and geared himself for the next episode.

Chapter Three.

Barristers' chambers are usually oases of peace but, at the same time, threatening. The large set, headed by Miriam Smith Q.C., consisted of five silks and twenty one juniors. It was a rare experience for Pearce to meet with barristers. On only two occasions over the past ten years had he sought their advice. One was a claim against him for plagiarism, which he won. The other was a dispute with publishers which was settled unsatisfactorily for both sides but Hardy had been persuasive. "I don't mind in the slightest if you continue the argument but you will be spending any gains on me."

Charles gazed around him and took in the plush, deep red carpet and beech veneer bookshelves filled with legal tomes, running the length of chambers. 'If only I knew a tenth of what is in those books,' he thought. 'Hell, I'm even thinking like a lawyer.'

A junior clerk escorted them to a waiting room while Burgess headed for the clerk's room. Soon after, he returned with the senior clerk, Richard. Barristers' clerks were known by their first names and addressed as such.

"Mr. Pearce, I've been looking forward to meeting you. I've read your books. They are terrific," Richard said.

"Thank you. Not sure about terrific but I'm a sucker for flattery." This was not false modesty. Pearce thought of himself as a lucky hack. "If you'll send the books to Mr. Burgess, I'll be happy to sign them for you."

At that moment, the junior clerk told them Mrs. Smith was ready. He escorted Pearce and the entourage to a large room, which befitted Smith's status as Head of Chambers. A bow window overlooked a garden square. The room was furnished with a vast mahogany desk, a comfy looking brown-stained Chesterfield chair behind it, three Queen Anne chairs in front and in one corner a conference table large enough to seat ten. Bookshelves, crammed full of law books, briefs and papers were on other walls. Pearce also noticed an open drinks cabinet.

Miriam Smith rose to meet them and addressed Pearce. "How do you do? I'm Miriam Smith. This is my junior, Fay Reynolds." The contrast between the two women could not have been more pronounced. Smith was an inch short of six feet, overweight and crammed into a black skirt and white shirt. Her face was unusual. A very high forehead, small, pointy eyes, a pug nose and full lips which made Charles feel uncomfortable for reasons he could not identify. She was neither ugly nor attractive. But her voice was like silk.

Fay Reynolds was short, with long blonde hair, a petite figure and a very pretty face with bright blue eyes. 'She would make a great night-club hostess,' Charles thought to himself. However, when she said "hello," her voice was high in the octaves, almost squeaky.

Charles was sensitive to atmospheres and felt a frisson, a chill between Smith and Burgess. 'What goes on here?' he asked himself. Smith offered drinks. The lawyers chose teas and coffees. Charlie needed a scotch and said so. "On the rocks, please." A clerk fixed the refreshments and left as everyone made themselves comfortable around the conference table. Smith started the conversation.

"I've reviewed the papers, including the You Tube video, the videos made by your daughter, Mr. Pearce, and the draft witness statements. I congratulate your legal team on putting the evidence together so quickly. I'm sure you have been advised of your legal rights and the likely outcomes if we seek an injunction but it's best I go over them with you. Injunctions are mere overtures to legal action." Pearce nodded his head.

Smith continued. "I'm sure you have received advice on the law, but at the risk of repetition, The Human Rights Act states all citizens have a right to privacy and everybody should have respect for private life. Counter to these rights is the media's right to freedom of expression. The test is whether the contents to be published are in the public interest. It's the so-called right to know.

"If we seek an injunction tonight, it will be ex parte. In English, this means the judge will hear only our side of the argument. Should the injunction be granted, those who are served with it will have the right to go to court and tell their side of the story. So far so good?"

Pearce nodded. Smith continued, "I have no doubt whatsoever that the judge will grant the ex parte injunction." Turning to Burgess, she added, "The judge will dispense with the niceties of sworn affidavits tonight if you undertake to have them sworn tomorrow. Are you happy for me to give your word, Mr. Burgess?"

"Of course."

"Now, Mr. Pearce, I have some questions."

"Fine. Please call me Charles?"

"I'm Miriam. Why do you feel it is so essential to protect your privacy? I'll be blunt. What do you have to hide?"

"As to your first question. I've always been a private person. For me, there is a principle at stake. My home life, my family, what I do in my own time away from writing, is no business of anyone else. This is not some abstract construct. If I play tennis or squash at my sports club, or play bridge with friends, what interest does the public have in knowing this? If I go shopping, why does the public have the right to know what I buy?

"Let me ask you something. You are an eminent Queen's Counsel. Does the public have the right to know about what you do outside the courts and these chambers? Things change if and when you become a High Court judge but the process of enquiry about you is well established. You are off limits.

"I've become a popular writer. I didn't expect to sell books in the thousands. I could stop writing today. I could write under a nom de plume or leave my work unpublished until I die. But this is not what I want. I don't court celebrity status, I don't appear at book festivals, literary conferences, book talks, signings and the like. I made an error appearing on the Peregrine Vaughan show but I thought I had an agreement which restricted his questions to areas where I was willing to talk. I saw red mist when he broke his word.

"As for your second question, am I hiding things? I have no trouble with disclosing the financial deals connected to my writing. I pay all taxes due from my earnings. My investments are straightforward. I've no off-shore trusts or assets. I have accounts in America and pay tax on my earnings there. I don't get involved in tax avoidance schemes. My accountants will confirm all of this if need be."

Pearce stopped, picked up his ornately cut glass tumbler and took a hefty draught. "I understand," said Smith. "The Inland Revenue has all the financial information but, of course, it is confidential."

"Yes, but I have nothing to hide about my financial affairs. As for my early life, there's nothing of which I'm ashamed. Mind you, it was pretty boring. So my answer to your second question: I have nothing to hide."

"Why not talk about your private life to the media, get it out of the way and move on?"

Pearce's face hardened. In a low voice, he replied, "Surely this is why we are here, to stop the press hounding me for information to which it has no entitlement. If I follow your chain of thought, what happens when the press are not satisfied with the truth? You know exactly what they would do. Print lies and invite me to sue. I'd be back where I started."

"Keep calm, Charles," said Hardy. "Mrs. Smith is just testing you. She is looking down the road to a full hearing and the legal action which will follow from the injunction."

"What? I don't understand. Please explain this to me." Pearce was nonplussed.

Smith resumed. "Let's assume the judge grants the injunction tonight. If it is contested at an on notice hearing, that's when both sides argue their cases, and assuming you win again, the injunction will have an element of permanence.

"But that is not the end of the case. You have to bring proceedings against the media for breach of privacy and harassment in support of the injunction. These proceedings will have to be litigated, fought in court, unless they are settled. The process will take at least a year, maybe two, during which you'll have the protection of the injunction. If you win your case, you will be awarded damages and the injunction will be made permanent."

Charles looked at Hardy. "You didn't explain this. What am I letting myself in for?"

Hardy responded quietly. "Your instructions were to have the journalists removed from your house and I concentrated on this. Perhaps I didn't cover every aspect as fully as I should have but we've had very little time."

"Little time?" replied Pearce. "I've been with you all bloody day."

Hardy sighed. "Charles, let's say a French newspaper prints something about you which, had the paper been English, would be a breach of the injunction. We can't stop publication unless we get an injunction in France. Same point applies in every foreign jurisdiction where there is publication about you and this includes Scotland. We haven't covered this kind of variable either."

Charles shook his head. "Am I wasting my time here? Am I getting into a hurricane of a law suit that never ends?"

Fay Reynolds spoke. "I don't think so, Mr. Pearce. I agree with you that privacy is important. Our courts also agree. As you have nothing to hide, I see no reason why you should not protect yourself. I think you are doing the right thing."

Miriam Smith was not concerned by the interruption. She liked her juniors to speak their minds. "I agree with Ms. Reynolds. Let's take it one step at a time. I have a duty to advise you about the negatives as well as the positives.

"You are seeking an equitable remedy from the courts. Accordingly, you must come with clean hands. This means you need to make full and frank disclosure about anything the court ought to know about you and your private life. If there is anything in your past which is unlawful or which right-thinking members of society would find offensive or just plain wrong, you need to tell us. We will not judge you or think the worse of you. We are your lawyers. It is our job to advise you to the best of our ability. You need to understand that if there is something in your past which comes out before the case is over and you have not told us, you will put yourself at a huge disadvantage."

Pearce took a deep breath. "Mr. Burgess covered this with me earlier today. I repeat, I have done nothing illegal. I have no convictions for any crimes except minor driving offences. What about the other test, the right-thinking members of society? What exactly does that mean?"

"It would include, for example, an extra-marital affair or something of a sexual nature which was, shall we say, unorthodox. It might be conduct like failing to pay a lost wager or shop-lifting as a result of a mental illness. And it might not be your own conduct. Say there was something in your wife's past which she wants kept secret. If such a thing was disclosed during the hearing and you hadn't mentioned it, the court could take an adverse view."

Pearce sat stone-faced for a minute or so. Through gritted teeth, he replied, "there is nothing I have to tell you."

"Okay. Let's move on. To get an injunction, you need legal grounds to base your case. Here, there are breaches of privacy and harassment. The court will not grant the injunction unless legal proceedings are formally commenced against members of the media. Proceedings start with a High Court writ. If the injunction is granted, the case will have to be pursued by you. If not, the injunction will be lifted. So, it's Hobson's choice."

"So I have no choice at all, do I? Now I understand. Let's keep going while I mull this new information over."

"Good enough but you don't have long. When we meet the judge, it will be a condition of the injunction that your solicitors give an undertaking to commence proceedings tomorrow."

Smith went to her desk and picked up the phone. "Richard, please come in?" Richard entered in seconds. Smith collected a sheaf of papers.

"Please would you copy these papers and DVDs and forward them to Judge Benton's clerk? I'll prepare a handwritten note for you to attach. Would you ask the judge's clerk if it would be convenient to see Judge Benton tonight? If so, what time and where will suit her? There will be seven of us."

"Of course, Mrs. Smith. Will there be anything else?"

"I don't think so"

Smith moved to her desk and wrote a note for the judge. The others stayed seated at the Conference table. After five minutes, with an "excuse me", Smith left the room. She returned swiftly, saying the judge will see them at eight that night. "She lives in Epping. Mr. Burgess, please arrange transport. Fay, we had better get a draft Order ready."

Fay looked up. "How about this? 'The privacy of Charles Pearce of, I'll need his address, has been invaded by the conduct of journalists, photo-journalists and other members of the media. Mr. Pearce is also being harassed at his home by said journalists, photo-journalists and media members. Therefore the conduct of said journalists, photo-journalists and members of the media should be prohibited pending the outcome of trial or further interlocutory application. For the avoidance of doubt, any journalist, photo-journalist or member of the media found within a radius of one mile from, we'll insert the address, on matters related to the subject matter of this injunction, will be in breach of this injunction.' What do you think?"

"Not sure the judge will allow the radius rider but we can try. Please get the writ drafted. Sue for distress on grounds of breach of privacy and harassment. Damages at large. Just Mr. Pearce. We can always add Dr Pearce and the children later as claimants."

Pearce listened. He might not be the most knowledgeable on legal matters but he got the gist of what was said. If all went well, the journalists would be gone later tonight or by the next morning and he'd be suing the newspapers for damages to compensate him for what they had done. He felt adrenalin leaving his body. This often happened after he had spent too long writing. He knew he needed some air. He excused himself and walked out of Chambers.

"Pity I stopped smoking," he said to nobody in particular. "I could use one right now."

He went back inside to the clerk's room. "May I use a phone?" he asked. He spoke with Claire for a minute or two, giving her the headlines of the day and what would happen next. Her responses sounded wooden.

Returning to Smith's room, Hardy told him, "We'll leave in about three quarters of an hour." I've ordered a roast beef sandwich for you and a cup of tea. Don't want you smelling of alcohol when you meet the judge."

"Am I crazy to do this, Hardy? I know we've been over this but these journos will eventually get bored and leave, won't they?"

"If you've got cold feet, I completely understand. But the national papers are interested in you now and they won't be shaken off. Eventually the door-stepping will stop but that doesn't mean you won't be investigated. By taking out the injunction, you'll get these people away from your front door and put the media on the back foot."

"I feel I've little choice. If I don't take action, those bloody people will be at my house day after day, scaring Claire and the children, not to mention making the neighbours' lives a misery. Okay, Hardy, my wobble's over. Let's get this done."

Chapter Four.

A few minutes before eight o'clock that evening, a people carrier pulled into the drive of Lady Justice Judith Benton's home. She lived in a Tudor-style mansion in a smart residential area of Epping. Pearce admired the house, although his first thought was uncharitable. 'Lawyers live well off the misery of people like me.' Miriam Smith led the way. This was not her first visit to the judge's home.

A manservant opened the front door. "The judge is expecting you. Please follow me." Judge Benton was seated at the head of the dining room table. There were eight empty chairs, enough for the crowd. The judge gestured to Smith to sit next to her.

"Good evening, everyone. We can dispense with introductions. Miriam, I've read your papers. This is a clear case of harassment. I will grant the injunction. May I speak direct with your client?"

Pearce thought he should stand. Judge Benton motioned to him to resume his seat.

"Mr. Pearce, the evidence you've provided is sufficient for me to grant the interim injunction. I assume you've been advised that those served with the injunction can challenge it? Indeed, I fully expect to see you in court in the next few days."

"Yes, M'lady." Pearce had been coached on how to address the judge.

"And you've been advised about making full and frank disclosure."

"I have, M'lady."

"There is nothing you want to add to your witness statement."

"No, M'lady."

"Very well. Miriam, do you have a draft Order for me to sign?"

"Yes, judge." The Order drafted by Fay Reynolds was passed to Benton. She read it quickly. "I'm not sure about the one mile radius but I understand the rationale. Cameras with long-distance lenses easily defy injunctions. Rather than use the distance test, should I not expressly ban the media from taking any photographs by the use of cameras, mobile phones or any other electronic devices?"

Miriam paused to think. "We'd like both," she replied. "The radius issue arises because Mr. Pearce lives on a private road which is more than a mile long."

"So be it but with the proviso that if a journalist encroaches the one mile radius because there is another, unrelated story and the journalist does nothing to infringe this injunction, he or she will not be in breach. I'll grant the Order on these terms. I'll sign it once you make the appropriate changes."

As Fay wrote, Judge Benton asked Hardy Burgess for the necessary assurances and undertakings in having affidavits sworn and the writ issued. Hardy assented. Fay passed the draft Order to Miriam who read it quickly and passed it to the Judge, who scanned it and signed. She also affixed a Court seal. "There," she said, "all done."

The group rose to leave. "Might I talk with Mr. Pearce?" the judge asked. "If you don't mind, in private."

The lawyers left the room reluctantly. This judge's request was unorthodox but she would have her reasons. The judge motioned to Charles to sit next to her.

"I didn't want the others to hear this. I've read your books and I'm a fan but I need to stay impartial. I will treat you as I would anyone else. However, would you mind signing these books for me?"

Pearce was amused to see the judge blush. "Delighted, M'lady. Shall I sign 'To x' with best wishes and add my name?" he replied as the judge carried several hard-back books to the table.

"That's fine. Sign it to Judith, please."

Once in the people carrier, Hardy could not resist asking, "What was that about?"

Charles replied, "I'm shocked you would ask. A gentleman never talks."

Hardy had already checked with Charles if it was okay for him to stay at the Pearce home overnight. "I need to see if any journalists break the injunction. If they do, woe betide their future before Mrs. Justice Benton."

Charles asked if he could borrow a mobile. He called Claire. "I have to be discreet. All done. I'll explain when I get home." He paused to let Claire speak. "No, I just had a sandwich. Anything will do. You know Hardy will be staying with us."

The others didn't hear Claire's sigh. "Okay, we'll talk when I get back." Charlie ended the call with, "an hour or so."

"Trouble in paradise?" grinned Hardy. "Don't worry, it's just stress."

"I know."

The barristers returned to Chambers. Hardy's team would take a taxi to the Berkley Square office to prepare the documents needed to serve the injunctions. It would be a long night. Journalists from eighteen national and local newspapers had been identified, as well as a further fifteen from the internet media and twelve freelance photo-journalists. All would have to be served with certified copies of the Injunction Order.

Before Hardy's team left, Charles asked them to wait a moment. "I've been remiss. I haven't said thank you. To put it mildly, I've not been at my best today. I've been short tempered, grumpy and withdrawn. My excuse is shock to find I'd become the target of a hostile media. But all of you have helped me without reproach. I'm grateful for that. Thank heavens it's over for today."

Miriam Smith replied. "All of us understand the pressure you're under. We're used to it. You're not. Today was just the beginning but we all look forward to meeting the real Charles Pearce. Goodnight, Mr. Pearce. Mr. Burgess, my clerk tells me some things have arrived for you from your office. Come with me."

"Of course," Hardy replied. "James, why don't you take everyone to The George before you go back to the office?"

Hardy followed Miriam to her room. Without a word, she handed him a suitcase. Hardy knew it would contain a suit, shirt, tie, underwear and toiletries, as well as something casual for the evening and he offered a silent vote of thanks for the efficient Lilian who, early in their working relationship, encouraged him to keep such items in the office in case of emergency. Nevertheless, Hardy would have preferred to have returned to the Mount Street apartment. He liked his creature comforts.

Miriam turned to face Hardy. She was angry. "Why did you instruct me in this case? Have you forgotten our agreement or do you just not care?"

"Miri, I told you at the time, there could never be a binding agreement. You and I can't avoid each other. The cab rank principle applies. I instructed you because you are the best silk for this case. I'm doing what I have to do."

"There are other good silks. Why didn't you instruct one of them? I know you, Hardy. What's in this for you?"

"I don't want a good silk. I want the best. That's you. I have no ulterior motive."

"Do you know how hard today has been for me? I haven't seen you in weeks. And then you descend, almost without warning." Miriam's face was contorted.

"Miri, I'm sorry. Our affair was wonderful but we had to stop. Both of us were jeopardising our careers, you far more than me."

"So you were being noble by ending it!" The sarcasm bit into Hardy's conscience. "It hurt you more than me, did it? You are such a bastard."

"I wasn't the adulterer. You were. If we had been discovered, your husband's political career would have been damaged, probably holed below the water line. God knows what your Inn would have done to you. You don't have the protection of being a man. Your career might have been in ruins."

"You're fooling yourself. James and I were over long before you and I got together. I'll have a decree nisi soon enough. The Bar might have applied double standards but, like you said, I'm the best. I'd have survived."

"It would never have worked, Miri. You knew about my commitment issues. I was up front with you from the start."

Miriam broke a long silence. "You'd better go back to your people."

"How will this work now? I need you on top form. I want to win."

"We'll both be professional. But you hurt me, Hardy. It hasn't gone away. I detest you."

Hardy picked up his bag and left. He felt a sense of relief as he closed Miriam's door, coupled with unease about her anger towards him.

The Peugeot people carrier took Pearce and Burgess to the Pearce home. After what had happened during the day, Pearce hoped the journalists would have dispersed. He was wrong. About thirty people were there, crowding around the Peugeot as it pulled through the gates. The driver was not fussed and parked close to the front door.

Once inside, Hardy was pleased to see Claire again. They had been acquainted for several years. Claire showed Hardy to his room. "Why don't you freshen up?" Claire suggested. "The room has an en-suite. We'll be in the kitchen when you come down."

Within minutes, Hardy had freshened up. In a casual outfit, he went towards the kitchen. He saw Charlie had changed clothes He could also see a worried look on Charlie's face. Claire was tearing into him. He heard her say, "You are such a fool. You'll see. It will all come crashing down about our heads."

Hardy coughed as he strolled towards the kitchen. Charlie had a resigned look on his face. Claire looked sad. Her eyes were bleary and Hardy noticed a bottle of Sauvignon Blanc on the kitchen table.

"You must be hungry," Claire said. "I have a lamb casserole for you. Ready in ten minutes. Have a drink? I'll have one too. Charlie, there's another Sauvignon Blanc in the fridge. I've opened a Fleurie for you and Hardy"

Charlie poured the Fleurie for Hardy and himself and refilled Claire's glass. As Claire put out cutlery and serviettes, Hardy explained to her what had happened that day. Charlie was impressed by his lawyer's ability to include everything important without descending into legal language.

"So, when will the crowd outside leave?" asked Claire.

"Hopefully, as soon as they and their newspapers and organizations are served with the injunction. After I've eaten, I'll talk to the people left outside.

"I'll tell them about the injunction. If they still remain here, papers will be served on them as soon as my office brings them. It's up to the door-steppers to decide if they want to defy a High Court injunction. If they do, we'll have them before the judge soon enough. I assure you it will be an experience they won't forget."

Claire checked the stove and called, "Food's ready." Charlie helped her serve. Afterwards, Claire removed the empty plates and offered dessert.

"Just a coffee for me, thanks," Hardy answered.

"Cognac, malt whisky?" Charlie offered. Hardy declined. "I need to keep a clear head."

Hardy's mobile rang. "Hi, Jackie, how are things?"

Her response was brief. "I've e-mailed the newspapers. They will be served with hard copies soon enough. All the major daily and Sunday titles and some of the media outlets will be visited. Not sure about the freelance photo-journalists yet."

"Well, make yourself sure about the freelancers. Everyone must be served. Have John bring forty copies of the injunction here as soon as he can."

Within the hour, John arrived. He received the usual greeting from the fifteen or so journalists who lingered outside the house gates. When Hardy and John served the injunction papers, some of those served refused to give their names. John took pictures with his mobile.

"Fun, isn't it, having your picture taken when you don't want it?" He received scowls and the expected 'fuck off,' in exchange. This was recorded.

Inside the house, Hardy booted up his lap top and compiled a spread-sheet of organizations and people served, the time and place of service and the response, if any. He e-mailed the list to Miriam Smith, Fay Reynolds and Jackie. Interestingly, four of the people who remained outside the house were from daily newspapers whose editors had been served earlier that evening. All were now in breach of the injunction.

Hardy realised John was waiting. "We'll have an early start tomorrow. We'll be back in court soon enough. If newspapers are going to defy the injunction, there will be fireworks. Let's get you a cup of tea before you go home. Thanks for today."

Hardy sat with Charlie. "I couldn't help overhear Claire talking to you before dinner. Why is she so worried? What does she think will come out?"

Charlie reddened. "We all have things in our past that we'd prefer to forget. Before we got married, both of us had relationships. I had more than one torrid affair. Some of the women may have been married. It was a long time ago. I'm not going to talk about Claire's life to you. It's not in issue."

"I see. Well, it might be and you might have to but I'm calling it a day. I need to be up early. Early tomorrow morning, I'll want to see who is still here. If any journos remain or return to the house and if their titles have been served, they will be taking a giant risk. Contempt of court is a serious thing."

Chapter Five.

On Arthur Hawkins' thirteenth birthday, his father greeted him with a birthday card and a ten shilling note.

"Appy birfday, son."

"Cor, thanks Dad."

"Time to make some changes. There'll be no more pocket money. You need to earn. I've had a word with Mr. Harris at the newsagents. He'll give you a trial deliverin' newspapers on Tuesdays, Thursdays and Saturdays. You have to be at the newsagents by 6.30 sharp. Mr. Harris says your round will take an hour and a bit, so when you finish, go straight to school. You'll need to get up before six. Here's an alarm clock for you. And you will make your breakfast just like now but earlier. Hope you realise I'm treatin' you like a man."

Arthur mumbled "okay" out of politeness. His self-confidence was low. How would he manage all this? He took himself off to see Mr. Harris and got his orders for the following Tuesday. Later that day, Arthur arrived at the gym. Grey stopped what he was doing and grinned at Arthur, saying "Happy Birthday. I've got something for you. Come with me."

Arthur followed Mr. Grey to a storeroom where a tarpaulin was removed to reveal a rusty bicycle. "What do you think?"

"Blimey, Mr. Grey. A bike, for me? Thank you."

"It's in need of some TLC. We'll work on it together. After school and training on Saturdays. How's the money situation?"

Arthur told Grey about the newspaper round. "I'm almost okay, with what Mr. Harris will pay me but I'll be skint by the end of the week."

"How about doing some work for me? The place could use a regular tidy up. Want to work an hour or so on Saturdays after training? I'll pay you ten bob an hour." This was not only generous but it would also make a huge difference to Arthur's finances.

Soon, Arthur owned a shiny, reconditioned bike. It speeded up his paper round. Getting to school on time was no longer a problem. Mr. Grey threw in a sturdy padlock. Given half a chance, the boys at school would steal the bike and sell it for five bob. Fortunately, Arthur was not the only boy to ride to school. Jealousy was spread wide.

For the rest of Arthur's schooldays, nobody bullied him. Word had got around that 'Arfa 'Awkins was not one to mess with. Arthur liked his new found fitness. He kept up his running and the gym work with Mr. Grey. Unlike most of Arthur's school teachers, Mr. Grey encouraged him, not just with the gym and self-defence but also with his school work.

Arthur was no academic. He had little enthusiasm for science or geography but he enjoyed history and reading stories and he understood arithmetic better than most of his year. He found something special in numbers. They never lied or changed and they didn't cheat. Algebra, geometry and logarithms, he got them. They were his friends.

Every week, Arthur went to the local library. The librarian took a shine to him and helped him choose two books each week that he could take home. She started him on Swallows and Amazons and Treasure Island. After a while, Arthur moved on to stories like Gulliver's Travels. He loved the plots, the acts of heroes, the devilry of villains and the way words brought out feelings. The librarian appreciated how Arthur was scrupulous in returning books on time. He was a boy who had few books of his own. His father regarded them as frivolities, not worth buying.

Arthur moved to a secondary modern school, a bus ride away from home. Mr. Harris adapted the paper round so Arthur could do his work and get to the bus on time.

Suddenly, he found he was one of nearly a thousand kids, most of them lost and killing time till they left school to have rubbish jobs, maybe rubbish lives. In Arthur's year there were two hundred pupils. There was a girl in his class, Maisie Duckworth. Arthur had a crush on her but he had no idea what to do about it. He could not bring himself to talk about her, even to Mr. Grey. He was too embarrassed. His father noticed nothing but Eddie did.

"What's up, Arthur," Mr. Grey asked at the end of a training session. "You've been miles away today."

"Nothing, Mr. Grey."

"Pull the other one. I reckon either something has happened to you at school that's worrying you or maybe it's a girl?"

Arthur blushed. "Things are alright at school."

"So, it's a girl. Nothing wrong in that. Do you two talk lots? Do you treat her nice? Have you kissed her?"

"No!" Arthur half shouted. "Sorry, Mr. Grey." Arthur paused for a moment. "To tell the truth, I haven't even talked to her. I wouldn't know what to say."

Mr. Grey knew not to laugh. "Arthur, you're growing up." He moved close and put his arm around the boy. "First love is always difficult. Might I suggest something? When you see her next, just ask her if she would like to talk. Suggest you have a coke after school. There must be a café nearby." Arthur nodded. "Then take it from there. Ask her what she likes and doesn't like. Compare thoughts about teachers, classes, other school things. But let her do a lot of the talking. Girls like good listeners."

"Look at me, Mr. Grey. My Dad always says I'm no oil painting. Why would she be interested in me?"

"Girls don't care that much about looks. Look at me!"
Grey pointed to his broken nose and puffy eyes. "Mary still likes my looks. There's so many other things that are important. Girls like boys who are interesting and who treat them well and sometimes have the devil in them. What's the worst thing that can happen? You ask to meet up and she says no. Are you any worse off than now?"

Arthur could not pluck up the courage. In fact it took him a whole term to speak to Maisie. By then, he'd grown three inches and his voice was now a man's. At the start of the autumn term, he finally plucked up the courage to speak to Maisie but his words came out mumbled and as a whisper. Before Arthur could speak again, two of Maisie's girl-friends joined her. Arthur turned away, crushed. But two weeks later during break, Arthur saw Maisie sitting alone on a bench in the playground. Taking a deep breath, he walked over to her.

"Hello, I'm Arthur."

"I know. I've shared classes with you for more than a year!" Maisie giggled.

"What are you reading?" asked Arthur.

"Jane Eyre."

"What's it about?"

Maisie took a minute or two to tell the story as far as she had read it.

"Sounds so sad."

"Do you like reading, Arthur?"

"Yes. Adventure stories and maths problems."

"Maths problems? That's a new one."

At that moment, a bell rang loudly. Break was over.

"Maisie, could we, ehm, meet after school? We could go to Jack's Café for a coke."

Maisie thought for a moment. "I can't today but maybe tomorrow. I need to ask mum. If she says okay, then I'd like to."

As Maisie left, Arthur wondered to himself what life would be like to have a parent that cared for you so much that you would ask permission to meet a boy after school. He felt his life hinged on Maisie's mum. His entire future was in her hands. He could think of nothing else. He hardly slept that night. The next morning, walking into class, he saw Maisie. A sixth sense told him to wait and let her come to him. The lesson started. Suddenly, the boy sitting next to him passed a note. Placing his hands under the desk, Arthur read: "Mum said it's okay." Arthur looked up and turned his head towards Maisie's desk. She smiled at him.

After school, Maisie and Arthur sat at a corner table at Jack's Café, sipping their Coca-Colas. Other pupils stopped there after school. Some boys started to laugh and point at Arthur, making 'ooh' noises.

"Ignore them," Maisie told him. "They're just jealous."

"Of me?" Arthur blurted out the response.

"Yes, you. I think you're interesting. How many boys do you know who read maths books for fun?"

Arthur laughed. "I suppose. Look, I don't like it here much. Could we go somewhere else next time? How about Saturday afternoon in Barber Park? By the pond."

"Not the morning?"

"Sorry, no can do. I go training on Saturday morning and I work for an hour afterwards at the gym. Mr. Grey would have my guts for garters if I didn't show up."

"Training? For what? And who is Mr. Grey?"

Arthur felt a new kind of confidence. "Meet me on Saturday at the park at two o'clock and I'll tell you," he smiled.

Maisie did not live far from Arthur so they took the bus together. Arthur walked Maisie home. Maisie stopped at her front door. "This is me. My dad's still at work but mum's home. Come in and say hello," Maisie told Arthur, whose new found confidence disappeared like a rabbit chased down a burrow. Maisie insisted.

"Mum, I'm home," she called.

"'Allo darlin'," came a voice from deep in the house. "In the kitchen."

The two walked along a corridor to the kitchen. "Mum, this is Arthur."

A slender woman in her forties looked at Arthur as she wiped her hands on an apron. "Hello Arthur."

Arthur thrust his right hand out, mumbling, "Hello, Mrs. Duckworth. Nice to meet you." Arthur felt panic. He was unprepared. "I just brought Maisie home. I have to get home myself. Don't want my dad to worry."

"Okay, luvvy. See you next time."

Maisie walked Arthur to the front door. "Arthur, you're trembling. Why?"

Arthur hung his head. He whispered, "Sorry."

"My mum is one of the sweetest people you'll ever meet. And so are you. See you at school tomorrow. And Saturday will be fine."

On Saturday, Arthur was in a haze. He did his paper round, trained at the gym, did his work afterwards and dressed to meet Maisie. He had kept his eyes on the gym's clock. It hardly seemed to move. But after what felt like a week, it was time for him to go. He said goodbye to Mr. Grey, got on his bike and cycled to Barber Park. At the pond, he checked his watch. Ten minutes to two. He found a bench and sat, watching the path Maisie would take. He kept checking his watch. At two o'clock, Maisie hadn't arrived. Five minutes later, she still wasn't there. At ten past two, Arthur felt so deflated. She wasn't coming. At quarter past two, he gave up. 'Should I go home via the route that Maisie would take, just in case? Or should I just go straight home?' he asked himself. He was crushed.

Then he felt a movement behind him. Cool hands covered his eyes. "Am I very late? Sorry. I'm not good at keeping time."

"I was about to go. I thought you'd stood me up."

Maisie walked around the bench and looked him in the eye. "Arthur Hawkins, what a thing to say! I'd never do that. I'd tell you if I didn't want to see you."

"Sorry. Hey, why should I apologise? You're the one who's late."

"I did say sorry. Let's start again."

Arthur melted when he saw Maisie's smile. Sitting at a table outside the park café, Arthur asked, "So how shall we start again?"

"At the beginning." Maisie put her right hand forward. "How do you do? I'm Maisie Duckworth."

Over the ensuing weeks, Arthur forgot what it was like to be alone and friendless. Maisie took him out of his shell and made him speak his thoughts. She introduced him to pop music and showed him how to handle himself with people of his own age.

Maisie was popular. She took him to youth clubs and taught him how to dance to the sounds of The Rolling Stones and The Who. Arthur didn't have much of a sense of rhythm but finally Arthur the Hermit disappeared.

Harry Hawkins didn't notice his son growing up. Probably, he didn't care. He no longer had the discipline of a wife to curb his excesses. He drank away too much of his pay packet. He hardly spoke to his son. Arthur might as well not have existed. As a consequence, Arthur did not feel he could bring Maisie back to the house to meet Harry.

Maisie became the centre of Arthur's life. He was naïve and respected Maisie far too much to try anything. Anyway, Maisie told him very clearly that she wasn't ready for sex. One night shortly before Arthur's fifteenth birthday, they talked.

"What shall we do to celebrate your birthday?" asked Maisie.

"Whatever you want."

"It's your birthday."

"What I'd like to do is what you want."

"You are difficult, Arthur Hawkins. Have you thought about next year?"

"I don't know. Not really."

"Well, you should. There's so much going on now. Loads of jobs out there. We can do whatever we want. New buildings going up everywhere. New gadgets for houses. And all kinds of studies to follow at university. I've decided to try to get into Uni. What do you think?"

"Maisie, I'm happy for you. You'll be great at university. But I'm only fourteen. I don't know about the world. The only times I've been to the West End are with you. And I haven't thought about exams, let alone university. You're clever. I'm not."

"This is the Arthur I used to know. Talking himself down. You are clever. You come top of maths all the time. And I believe in you."

"I don't know what that means. Anyway, what would my dad say?"

Arthur soon found out. On the evening before Arthur's fifteenth birthday, Harry sat him down.

"Son, tomorrow you'll be fifteen. You need to get into the world."

"What do you mean?"

"Time for you to leave school. Start work. I've got you a labourin' job at the docks. It pays £8 a week. Once you're in, it will lead to somethin' better, more money. You might even work with me one day."

Arthur was shocked. No discussion, no argument. Harry Hawkins' word was law. But Arthur had gumption now. He stood up for himself.

"Dad, I don't want to do this. I'm thinking about taking exams, getting qualifications, even going to university."

His father glared at him. "What's goin' on inside your head? University? That's not for the likes of you. You'll do as I say. No argument. I'm not workin' my guts out so you can stay at school, all pampered and then take yourself off to some poncy university where you'll learn nuffin' useful. Not likely."

"I don't want to be a labourer."

"Why not? It's honest work. You're too good for it, are ya'?"

"I want something different. What's wrong with that?"

Harry stood, shouting at his son. "If you don't do as I say, I ain't goin' to support you. You can get out of this house. Look after yourself. Who do you think you are? Are you special? I don't think so. University? You make me laugh. I'm goin' for a drink and you ain't invited."

Arthur was scared. What choice did he have? Kids from the East End left school at fifteen. If he was kicked out of his father's home, where would he live? How would he look after himself? He hoped Harry would forget and calm down.

Arthur's birthday fell on a Saturday. He did his paper round and went to the gym. Mr. Grey gave him a birthday card. "There's a little something in there for you."

"Thank you, Mr. Grey." He opened the card and a five pound note fell out. Arthur felt tears start to fall. "Why can't my father be like you," he whispered.

"Come into the office," he told Arthur. Once seated, Mr. Grey asked, "Now what's wrong?"

Arthur spilled out his guts. How Harry rarely talked, how he was so remote and uncompromising, how Arthur had been put into an impossible position and his dilemma: stay at home, do a job he didn't want and succumb to Harry's orders or leave home, live on the streets and starve. Either way, no more education, something he now wanted badly.

Grey was a compassionate man. "Mary and I have a spare room. Your father's not a nice man these days. It might be best for you to get out for a while. You can stay with me and Mary and pay rent when you get a job. I'm sorry but I have no right to keep you in school. Do you really think you can pass all those exams? I know you're good at maths and you like books but what else can you do?"

Arthur shrugged his shoulders.

"Have you thought about getting a proper job? What would you like to do?"

"I don't know. It's all a bit sudden."

"I have people working in insurance companies who come here to train. They tell me they need young people who are good at number work. I could speak to someone about you. What do you think?"

"Thank you. I'm really grateful to you and Mrs. Grey. I'd better speak to dad first. He might change his mind."

Later that day, Arthur had a furious row with his father. It ended with Arthur telling his father he'd leave the house. "You're kicking me out. That's your privilege. Mum would have fought you tooth and nail. And you know it. I'm not taking that job you arranged. I don't want it because it has no future."

Harry got very angry and screamed back. He swore at Arthur, calling him ungrateful. "You just take, never give. Your mother would be ashamed of you. Get out, get out now." Harry's parting words to his son were, "I'm goin' for a drink. Be gone by the time I get home. Lock up and put your keys through the letter box."

Arthur could not believe how nasty his father had been, how cruel. He had no choice but to pack his meagre belongings and leave. He left a note for Harry about where he could be found. Later that night, Harry read the note and ripped it up, got out a bottle of scotch and drank himself into oblivion.

An agitated Arthur arrived at the Greys' house. The door was opened by Mary who took Arthur into her arms. "Don't worry, love," she said, "it will be alright. We'll help you."

The next day, Arthur cycled to the Duckworths. Maisie was in.

"Can we talk? Shall we go to the park?"

Arthur was invited for lunch. He thanked Mrs Duckworth but said he was expected at home. She didn't realise this meant the Greys, not his father's home. At the park, Arthur cried as everything came out. Maisie was horrified. Arthur eventually pulled himself together.

"Maisie, if I don't stay on at school and go to university, will I be a big disappointment to you? Will you still speak to me?"

Maisie put her arms around him. "I'll always be your friend, Arthur."

But a sixth sense told Arthur life would get in the way. If he was not to be with Maisie through school and university, their relationship would not last. This proved to be right. Two months later, Maisie's family moved to a new high rise apartment block three miles away. There was no break up between Arthur and Maisie, just a drifting apart. Arthur was hurt more than he could imagine.

Chapter Six.

The Daily Sentinel moved from Fleet Street more than twenty years previously. Its proprietor, Maxwell Rankin, followed the trend of major newspaper titles and transferred the business, lock and stock, to a purpose-built structure in Stratford, East London where rents were low. Journalists now used computers to write their stories which they e-mailed to their editors and sub-editors. New printing presses were digital. Copy typing and hot metal were in the past. The terror of the print unions was a distant memory for Rankin and his fellow owners. But 18 months back, Rankin moved the newspaper to the Victoria area of town. He felt the need to be closer to the centre of political power.

Rankin was keenly aware of his role when it came to the direction of *The Sentinel* and what was published. He rarely demanded particular stories and if he did, it was usually with a gentle hint over drinks or dinner. Mind you, his editors knew their place too. While he allowed *The Sentinel's* editor-in-chief, Martin Foster, pretty well full licence, Rankin was hands on in certain respects. Foster was crystal clear about the editorial policy he was to follow.

Martin Foster was in his late fifties, neither trim nor fit. His baggy, rheumy eyes told the story of a man devoted to his work. Editing a major newspaper often required an eighteen hour day. Foster did not have private wealth. There was still quite a bit owing on his mortgage. As a result of a divorce six years before, he lost his share of the marital home. He bought a small flat in Pimlico, so he was close to the office. He earned good money at *The Sentinel* but a lot was spent maintaining his ex-wife and children. Another few years of gainful employment were needed to pay off his mortgage and other debts.

Foster decided long ago it was in his best interests to do Rankin's bidding. If it wasn't in line with his own thinking, he would compromise. Eventually, he'd retire to a place on the coast, sail a small boat and enjoy good times but he still loved the newspaper business. There was a good ten years in his engine if he was lucky.

Despite his servile attitude towards Rankin, Foster maintained a fiercely independent streak, especially over press rights. When he was shown the Pearce injunction, he saw red mist. It was axiomatic that when his newspaper was attacked, he retaliated. While he pondered the available aggressive retaliation, Rankin walked into his office unannounced. Max was not one for ceremony.

"What's going on tonight, Martin?"

Rankin was a big man, six feet plus, thirty pounds overweight, sallow skin, sagging brown eyes under which were vast bags, a big nose and a bushy moustache. He was virtually bald with tufts of hair on the sides of his head. He was the wealthy version of Worzel Gummidge.

Foster didn't know Rankin's age. He guessed him to be a man in his mid-sixties but he was probably ten years younger. Rankin spoke with a transatlantic accent, evidence of years spent in Canada and America. He had a deep and booming voice. You always knew when Max Rankin was in a room.

Rankin was accustomed to having his way. As chief executive and majority shareholder of Media Universal, a conglomerate of newspapers, magazines and television and radio stations, he had invested in the emerging social media market and benefited. He had businesses in most western democracies, as well as the Far East. He shunned the Middle East, Africa and Communist bloc countries. "Don't trust those fuckers. They'll smile at you while they steal your business and money whenever they feel like it."

Media Universal shares were quoted on the New York and London Stock Exchanges but the public held less than a third. Two thirds were held either by Rankin himself or through family trusts. As a result, nobody with an interest in MU could tell Rankin what to do. If MU looked likely to break monopoly or anti-trust rules, the politicians made sure Rankin was warned. He did not have to go to them. He was a truly powerful man and politicians and bankers knew it.

Rankin married three times before he was forty, had seven children by his wives and who knew how many other offspring. He was a ladies' man but without any understanding of the warmth and kindness needed to develop a lasting relationship. Three sons and a daughter already worked for MU in the New York and Paris offices.

Foster responded. "Politicians doing what politicians do, so by now they're tucked up in bed...or at home. America is stirring up the Iran/Iraq war. There's more political fallout after Blair's sacking of Charles Clarke. The new A 380 Airbus will fly tomorrow from Berlin to Heathrow. If you like a bit of gossip, there are rumours that Paul McCartney and Heather Mills are splitting up. And we were served with an injunction about an hour ago."

The editor-in-chief waited for his boss's reaction. Rankin fixed Foster with a stare. "Not much to keep us warm tonight except the McCartney-Mills story. Will you publish yet? And what's the injunction about?"

"Too soon on McCartney-Mills. If we get that one wrong, there would be a lot of trouble, the sort we don't need unless you fancy a multi-millionaire rock star's libel action. The injunction's an odd one. Did you watch Perry Vaughan's show two nights ago?"

"No. Should I have done? Vaughan's one of ours, isn't he? Can't say I like his column that much. There's too much about him and how clever he is."

"Have you heard of Charles Pearce?"

"Name rings a bell. Go on."

"He's a successful novelist who rarely gives interviews and when he does, he never discloses anything about his private life. Perry persuaded Pearce's publishers to get Pearce on the show. Pearce agreed only if there were restrictions on questions. Nothing on his private life. Take a seat, Max. I'll play the interview. It's not long. You should see it."

Foster logged his computer onto the internet and found the You Tube app. Soon the interview was on screen. Rankin watched in amazement.

"Perry got hung out to dry. He deserved it. So what's happened?"

"Journalism happened. The public has the right to know about people who are in the public eye. Pearce's books sell in the millions so the public has an interest in him. In a nutshell, the media door-stepped Pearce. Now he's got an injunction requiring the journos and photographers to move one mile from the Pearce house."

"Have we obeyed, moved away?"

"Not yet. I only got served a short while ago. Look Max, we're in the right here. We should not be restrained when there's a story to uncover, as there clearly is. I've pretty well decided to keep our people at Pearce's home."

"Who have we got there?"

"Barry Barratt. You know him? And a photographer, Johnny Flag. He joined us three weeks ago."

"Defying a court injunction isn't the cleverest decision, Martin. What does legal say?"

"Our legal eagle's immediate advice was we will be in contempt if we don't obey the injunction. He is studying the court papers now. I expect he'll worry about jail time for our journos if they refuse to obey the injunction. Fines for the newspaper, too. But our readers will love the defiance, a newspaper sticking up for the rights of the common man. The story will run for days. Just think of the increased circulation, not to mention advertising revenues. The important thing is, morally and legally we are in the right."

Rankin sat back in a chair and thought.

"Martin, I'm not happy about this. I want us to talk with legal as soon as we can. Refusing to obey a High Court judge will cause a brouhaha. I can't think The Board will approve. We'll be breaking the law. There's a barrel-load of lawyers on the Board as well as a new chairman. He's conservative. I'd better talk to him before we take this on."

Foster dialed a number. "Paul, get your arse into my office. Now."

Within three minutes, Paul Spencer arrived, holding a bundle of legal papers. A man in his early thirties, sandy hair, tired eyes, he did not cut an encouraging figure. However, he had a double first from Cambridge and was a specialist on media law.

"Paul, have you met Maxwell Rankin?"

"Right," started Rankin. "Martin wants *The Sentinel* to defy this Pearce injunction. What happens if we do? What are our options, legally speaking?"

Spencer took a beat. His anxiety bore through as if he was drilling the Channel Tunnel sideways.

"I've only just finished reading the court papers. If a newspaper defies an injunction without lawful cause, there are very serious consequences. Heavy fines and possibly custodial sentences for contempt. Reliance on rights under Article 10 of the Human Rights Act will not work as an argument for such defiance. The injunction must be obeyed. Its merits can be argued in court and that hearing will take place within days. My advice is to have our people leave the Pearce house immediately."

Foster showed his dislike of what he heard. "Aren't our rights under Article 10 equal to Pearce's under Article 8? Isn't this sufficient reason for us to have our people at Pearce's home?"

Spencer took his time. "First, I have not seen any evidence to support a claim that there are overriding Article 10 rights. What exactly are they in this case? How would the public's right to know apply? Second, you are misunderstanding the process. Pearce's lawyers have persuaded a judge that Article 8 rights have been infringed. We have the right to contest the decision in court. We don't have a legal right to stay at the Pearce house and defy the injunction."

Rankin had heard enough. He was a man with a short fuse and he exploded. "Good grief, I'm not here for an effing law lecture. What is all this Article 8 and Article 10 bollocks?"

Spencer showed some metal. "It isn't bollocks unless you have no respect for the law. The Human Rights Act governs the rights and responsibilities of newspapers. The media has the right of freedom of expression and to argue public interest as a contra to privacy rights of an individual."

"All I want to know is will we win?"

"Mr. Rankin, how can I say? I don't know the facts and Mr. Foster hasn't told me about the evidence he is relying on to argue public interest. Let us assume Mr. Foster has the facts on his side and evidence to support the facts; if so, we will have a good case.

"However, I cannot stress enough that we don't have the right to ignore a High Court injunction. If you don't want to accept my advice, let me instruct an experienced barrister for you. The newspaper will need expert legal advice anyway if you decide to contest the injunction. Mark Maynard, QC, would be my choice.

"I repeat, until I know the facts, I cannot possibly say whether *The Sentinel* would win a public interest argument. Let me make this crystal clear. If *The Sentinel* refuses to obey the injunction tonight, if it refuses to follow the accepted legal process and wait for the full hearing to argue the case, the judge will come down on the newspaper like the proverbial ton of bricks. Moreover, if the newspaper conspires with other newspapers to defy the injunction and the judge finds there has been a conspiracy, there could also be jail sentences for aggravated contempt."

Neither Foster nor Rankin liked what they heard. "You don't say 'we' or 'us.' Are you not with us?" Foster was angry.

"I am your lawyer. My job is to give you best legal advice. But please understand I cannot and will not be party to a serious, flagrant breach of the law. I am your employee so you can sack me but I have a higher duty to the court. If I advise against a course of action and you ignore my advice, that's your privilege but I will not be seen to condone your action."

Foster and Rankin looked at each other. Neither was used to being addressed like this, especially by an employee.

Spencer didn't stop. "I might add you haven't told me why Pearce's private life is so clearly within the public interest. For example, has he cheated on his taxes? For that matter, has he cheated on his wife? Is he a child beater? I need to know what evidence you have about him so Counsel is properly briefed."

"Okay, let's calm down," said Rankin. "What kind of fines might we be looking at if we ignore the injunction?"

Spencer took a breath. This was new territory for him. "I can't say. I have known the media judge to fine heavily for contempt, £20,000 or £25,000 in serious cases. I hate to say it but it may depend on what the judge has for breakfast. She will be furious that her injunction has been ignored. It would be seen as an act close to revolution or treason. The fines might be in six figures."

Foster guffawed. Max turned to him, glared and said gruffly, "I'm not happy about this, Martin, not happy at all. Call Barratt and Flag off. We can always send them back to the house in the morning. Spencer, when can we see this barrister, Maynard?"

"I'll get on it first thing", said Spencer. "We'll have to go to him. I doubt he'll come here. Will you both be coming? What time will suit?"

"Early as you can," said Foster.

At 10.45 the next morning, Rankin, Foster and Spencer sat in chambers with Mark Maynard Q.C. and his junior, Tom Phelps. Maynard, in his fifties, stood a little over five feet. He was pudgy and balding. He was not the best dressed of men. The collar of his jacket showed signs of dandruff. Maynard wasn't bothered by niceties. He was an expert in his field. He was the author of several law books on defamation. Phelps, ten years his junior, was stooped, with a Roman nose and eyes close together, a modern-day Uriah Heep.

Maynard spoke, his voice full of confidence and authority. "I have read the papers and talked with Mr. Spencer. I cannot support *The Sentinel's* defiance of the injunction and having its people camp out at the Pearce house. Your newspaper can contest the injunction but cannot ignore it. Continued defiance will lead to severe penalties. However, if you truly believe Mr. Pearce has something to hide and provided you have strong evidence to support this contention, the case changes. With that evidence, we will argue the public interest point at a hearing that will take place within days and seek to have the injunction lifted.

"In the meantime, it is my strongest advice that you must not keep your journalists at the Pearce house. If you do, there will be a severe penalty to them, your newspaper and yourselves. Now, exactly what evidence have you got to support public interest?"

Foster spoke. "We don't exactly have hard evidence yet but why would a man go to such lengths to preserve his privacy if he has nothing to hide? We've had little time for research. I gather Pearce came to UK about fifteen years ago with his wife and baby daughter. Their son and second daughter were born here. We know Pearce had two successful novels under his belt before he left the USA. Since then he has published six or seven more. His books sell well and some were adapted for motion pictures. One book was made into a television series. He is probably a very wealthy man. I can't say whether he pays all his taxes. To the outside world, he may appear a model citizen but there is something in his past he is desperate to hide.

"Isn't it strange we can find little or nothing about Pearce's life in USA? We have him in Los Angeles in 1987 but have found nothing before then. That year, he moved to Minnesota where he met his wife. They lived in Minneapolis until 1989 or 1990, then they moved to England. Maybe Pearce changed his identity? Whatever happened to him before 1987, he wants to hide it."

Maynard shook his head. "This is not evidence, Mr. Foster. Your beliefs count for nothing and I cannot take them to the judge in an Article 10 argument. Bluntly, you have nothing except guesswork. If you contest the injunction based on hunches and innuendos, you will lose."

"What if we instruct you to argue the case anyway?" asked Foster. "Our enquiry agents in America are looking into things. We are waiting to see what they can dig up. And we will keep our people at the Pearce house."

Maynard stared into the distance as he thought. "Such a course would be most unwise but if I am so instructed, I'll follow those instructions. However, I cannot be held responsible for the punishment meted out to *The Sentinel* and its employees as a result. I will need you to sign a note that you are continuing the door-stepping against my advice."

"Bloody hell," Foster exploded, "talk about self-protection. It feels like we are going into a fight with one hand tied behind our backs."

"Mr. Foster, you, Mr. Rankin and Mr. Spencer are free to seek alternative advice. I can try to make bricks from straw in court but I tell you here and now, the judge will have none of it. I am obliged to give you best advice. I have done so and I am obliged follow the Bar's Code of Conduct in these circumstances. If you choose to ignore my strong advice, why should I get into hot water with the court and the Bar when I have told you in the plainest language not to take that course of action?"

Foster looked at Paul Spencer. "Do we get another mouthpiece?" Spencer shook his head. "Right, we stay with you, Mr. Maynard. We want time to think. Spencer will let you know what we decide."

Back at *The Sentinel,* Foster sat in Rankin's plush office.

"So, Max," asked Foster, "made up your mind?"

"Not yet. I want you to speak to the editors of the other nationals to see if they will stand with us. If sufficient numbers are on board, I'll give you my final thoughts then. However, I want to make it crystal clear that this decision is yours. You are the editor-in-chief. If there is support from other titles and you want to defy the injunction, I'll probably back you."

"Okay. I'll get on with it."

"One more thing, Martin. You may be making the most fucking awful decision that Fleet Street has ever seen. I don't like defying the law. What you have to do is get the Pearce investigation up to speed. Top priority. You have a budget of £100,000. Get it done. I happen to think you're right. There is a great story here if we can find it."

*****

Hardy Burgess set his wristwatch alarm for 6.30 am. His bedroom overlooked the front of the house. He heard people chatting outside but the thirty or more from the day before had now dwindled to just a few. He showered, dressed and made his way to the kitchen. Charlie, Claire and Lizzie were waiting for him.

"This is odd," said Claire. "There were only four people when we got down here but now there are sixteen or more. I counted just now. What's going on? Hardy, tea or coffee? How do you like your eggs?"

"Scrambled, please and tea. I counted nine when I got up. I suspect that Fleet Street has decided to go to war. Let's have breakfast. Then we'll put our plan into action."

An hour later, Claire and Harry, Lizzie's brother, emerged with trays bearing mugs of tea and coffee for the door-steppers. Hardy went to everyone in turn, asked them to identify themselves and served injunction papers, even if it was for a second time. Lizzie followed behind him, taking a video. Once all journos were served, the video was e-mailed to Miriam Smith who passed a copy to Judge Benton's clerk.

Within a short time, the judge passed a message to Miriam Smith that she wanted a hearing the next day with all door-steppers and their editors present. She insisted that those served with the injunction who had either not left or had returned to the Pearce house be put on written notice of the hearing and be told to attend court to justify their behaviour. She wanted it made crystal clear that the national newspapers would be expected to account for their conduct in open court.

Hardy's team went into action. Hardy called Lilian Collier to clear his diary for that day and the next. He knew there would be fireworks.

Chapter Seven.

The Royal Courts of Justice building in the Strand is vast. It occupies an entire block. It is almost as wide as it is long. Known simply as 'The Law Courts,' it was built in Gothic style and opened by Queen Victoria. The building's design is intended to intimidate, as if judges and barristers, dressed in wigs and robes, were not enough to scare the pants off anyone.

Court 13 on the Queen's Bench corridor was a regulation-size large room. On high, there was a wide judge's bench, capable of seating seven judges, although today there would be only one. There were long, leather covered benches for the lawyers and the public. There were press benches to the side, almost underneath the judges' bench. The carpet was purple. The judge's chair was upholstered in the same colour.

The legal teams of those litigants required to appear reached their seats by the side doors of the Court. The claimant's team sat to the judge's right and defendants' team on the left. Seats were on hinges, covered in purple shaded leather. Charlie felt discomfited by his surroundings. His nerves eased a bit when he heard the wooden doors to the court squeak when opened and slammed on closing. Sometimes, humour comes from the oddest circumstance.

Court 13 was the domain of Her Honour, Judge Judith Benton, Q.C., the media judge. After a successful career at the bar, Judge Benton was highly respected. In legal circles, she was tipped for early promotion to the appellate court. She was also known to be irascible on occasion and extremely polite on others. Those who appeared before her never knew which Judge Judy they would get.

By 10.25 on the morning of the hearing, the Court was overflowing. On the right hand side, Burgess, with his firm's team and Charlie Pearce, sat in front of Miriam Smith. Fay Reynolds sat on the bench behind her leader.

The other side of the benches were crammed with barristers and solicitors representing the media people and organizations who had been parties in the door-stepping escapade. With their solicitors sat proprietors, editors and journalists. The press bench was completely full, as was the public gallery.

At 10.30, the court usher called "all rise" as the judge entered. She sat in her huge chair. Hardy noticed the anxiety in Charlie's eyes. "Don't worry," he whispered, "this place is designed to frighten."

"It's succeeding," came the response.

Judge Benton's expression was stern. She nodded to the lawyers who bowed their heads and nodded back. Pearce saw the whimsical side of this tradition. He wondered if he was watching a Japanese bowing ceremony.

"Mrs. Smith," asked the judge, "are you ready?"

"Yes, M'lady."

"Mr. Maynard?"

"Yes, M'lady."

This exercise was repeated several times with the rest of the barristers.

"Mrs. Smith, what would you like to tell me?"

Expertly, Smith took the judge speedily through the events of the past two days, ending with the defiance of the injunction. She introduced into evidence blown up photographs of the journalists who stayed at the Pearce house after the injunction was served, naming all of them and the newspaper or media titles they represented. Judge Benton asked whether any of those photographed and named contested the evidence. None did.

The judge moved on speedily. "I propose to deal with the mamas and papas people first." These were the few independent media people, those who blogged or posted stories on the web and had failed to obey the injunction. Their barrister, Douglas Bunn, was an inexperienced junior. The judge realised he was the best these defendants could afford. Bunn rose to address the judge.

"I appear for these respondents, M'lady. None of my clients intended to break the law. The simple fact is that they have little or no experience of traditional journalism and did not understand the meaning and effect of the injunction. They have asked me to apologise sincerely and unreservedly to the court. I am instructed to give an undertaking on their behalf that in future, they will follow this and any other injunction to the letter. None of my clients have been involved in legal proceedings like these before. I ask you to deal with them leniently."

"Mr. Bunn, persuasively put but can your clients not read? Are they masquerading as journalists? I doubt it. I believe they understood the full import of my injunction but decided to break the law. I repeat, they defied an injunction, Mr. Bunn. However, I accept these are first offences so I will limit the fines to £2,500 each, payable within seven days. I will not grant any extension of time for payment. Furthermore, should any of your clients come before me again in similar circumstances, I will not be so lenient."

Next up were three photo-journalists who had re-appeared at the Pearce house the previous day. Their barrister, Rachel Hawks, put forward a similar mitigation argument. Whilst all, photo-journalists were freelance, two had a close relationship with reputable newspapers. The judge addressed Mrs. Hawks.

"Your clients are experienced photo-journalists. Despite what you say, I have to cast doubt on their veracity and sincerity. I believe they knew exactly what they were doing. A photo of Mr. Pearce or his family could fetch many thousands of pounds. They let their bank accounts rule their heads.

"There is no doubt they were properly served with injunction documents. Their careers in journalism will have told them that injunctions cannot and must not be defied. Yet they did defy it. Each will be fined £10,000. The fine is payable within seven days. No time extensions."

Max Rankin's eyebrows rose. He looked at Martin Foster, as if to say 'you've cooked our goose. It's going to be roasted to a cinder.'

The judge continued apace. "Now we have four national newspapers, their proprietors, editors and journalists. Mr. Maynard, I believe you are instructed by all these defendants."

"Yes, M'lady. I am instructed that there is a fundamental issue in this case, the right of the public to know. When a celebrity is paid huge sums of money for his work, there is a public interest. Mr. Pearce receives vast amounts from his writing. He is in the public eye as a best-selling author."

"Mr. Maynard, you may be under the impression that I will give you more than the usual latitude this morning. You know perfectly well this is neither the time nor place for you to argue the merits of your defence. We are here to determine punishment to be meted to your clients for defying a court injunction. They broke the law, knowingly and, it seems, without regard for the consequences. Please restrict your remarks to this issue, not the merits of the injunction."

"M'lady, I must protest. Surely, what is at the very nub of this case is the personal life of Charles Pearce, something he is determined to protect at all costs. We have evidence..."

"Mr. Maynard, cease. I repeat, your argument on merits must wait for the full hearing. I granted an ex-parte injunction for good reason. Mr. Pearce and his family were being door-stepped by your clients and many others.
"I don't understand why you ignore my point. You know perfectly well today's hearing is not the forum for the argument you seek to promote. I want you to address the reasons why your clients should not be severely punished for breaking the law. If you are unwilling or unable to do this, then I must ask you to be seated!"

"M'lady, may I be permitted to take instructions?"

"That would be a good idea."

Maynard leaned towards Rankin, Foster and the other proprietors and editors. Solicitors joined them.

"As I advised and feared, we are done for. I'll do my best with mitigation but you are about to get slammed. I told you in the clearest terms that arguments on the merits would not be heard. If I try again, the judge will probably cite me for contempt."

Rankin hurrumphed. He pursed his lips, turned to Foster and whispered, "Your fucking judgment has got us into this." He nodded his head towards Maynard, as did the other proprietors. "Okay, time to get shagged. Do what you can."

Maynard addressed the judge. "M'lady, my clients accept unreservedly what you say. I am instructed to apologise sincerely on their behalves. As you will understand, they strongly believe that their rights under Article 10 of the Human Rights Act must be preserved and that the freedom of the press cannot be suppressed." The judge frowned but resisted a comment when she heard Maynard add, "These arguments will be presented at the full hearing."

"What do you say about the defiance of the injunction? Do you deny collusion between four of this country's national newspapers to ignore an injunction and break the law?"

Maynard paused. "I am not aware of any collusion, M'lady. But what this case shows is the tension between two distinct provisions of the Human Rights Act. My clients believed they were protecting, and were entitled to protect, the rights granted to them by law."

Judge Benton nodded her head. "Very well. Do you have anything else?"

"No, M'lady."

Mrs. Smith, do you have anything further to tell me?" Miriam shook her head. "Very well, I'll take a short recess to review my decision."

The judge rose, as did all in Court 13. After the judge exited, barristers, solicitors and clients entered into animated conversations. Pearce asked Miriam Smith, "What happens next?"

"My bet is that everything, including the kitchen sink, will be thrown at the four national newspapers. I expect the judge decided what she would do before she arrived in court but she likes to create a little drama. You will come off well this morning but don't forget, this is just the first round. When the full hearing takes place, these newspapers will pile on you with everything they have."

Ten minutes later, the usher returned, calling for silence. Judge Benton entered. Pearce had to control his nervous giggling as the nodding and bowing ritual was repeated before all were seated.

"Mr. Maynard." Maynard stood. "Years ago, Lord Denning, as Master of the Rolls, told Sam Silkin, the Attorney General: 'Be you ever so high, the law is above you.' If the law is not paramount, the rules of society collapse. The fourth estate serves a valuable and important need in our society. It holds the three other estates to scrutiny and criticism. In exchange, it enjoys many rights and privileges, with which come responsibilities and obligations.

"There can be no doubt that the fourth estate must obey the law. Over the past two days, your clients have shown disrespect and contempt for our laws by wilfully ignoring an injunction that was properly obtained.

"Mr. Maynard sought to argue that no notice need be taken of the injunction because the claimant has something to hide. If the proprietors and editors believe they have evidence against the claimant, they are free to publish it. The injunction does not silence the press. However the injunction restricts your clients' methods of confronting and intimidating the claimant and his family. Disputing the validity of the injunction at this stage can neither be permitted nor ignored.

"This is what bothers me most. Intimidation was used against the claimant in an attempt to force disclosure of information. Fear and harassment were the tactics. In our society, this cannot be tolerated. The injunction was intended to prevent further harassment. Your clients chose to disobey. They thought they were above the law." Judge Benton paused, then added, "I am here to tell them they are not. The journalists and photo-journalists who returned to the Pearce house after the injunction was served will be fined £25,000 each. The editors and individual proprietors who broke the injunction will each be fined £100,000 and sentenced to six months imprisonment but the prison sentence will be suspended for two years. Should any of these defendants commit a similar offence within that time, this custodial sentence will take effect.

"Finally, I address the newspaper titles themselves. I find the conduct sufficiently heinous as to warrant a fine that will ensure those who run such enterprises will think carefully before repeating it. Each are fined £500,000."

As each punishment was handed down, the buzz in the court became louder and louder. At the last fine, the gasps were clearly audible. There was a call for silence as the judge banged her gavel.

"Should any of the defendants breach the ex-parte injunction again, the fines will double for each day the breach occurs and custodial sentences will be imposed. I want the journalism industry to understand in the clearest terms there are consequences for purposely breaking the law."

Maynard rose. "M'lady, my clients will appeal the fines and custodial sentences which, in my experience, are unconscionable. Will you grant a stay pending the appeal?"

"Yes, so long as the appeal is lodged within seven days. If it is not, I expect payment to be made immediately thereafter. Mr. Maynard, if your clients wish to contest the injunction itself, I will hear arguments in ten days' time. Mrs. Smith, is this acceptable?"

"Yes, M'lady."

"Mr. Maynard, any evidence needs to be with me and the claimant 48 hours before the hearing, failing which I won't allow its introduction."

"Yes, M'lady."

The judge rose and swept out of court. Opposing barristers nodded to each other and left court with solicitors and clients in their wake. At the back of the court, Maynard addressed his legal team and clients. "Let's all go back to chambers. We need to talk."

In court, Smith spoke with Pearce. "Let's see what evidence they produce. If positions were reversed, I'd let the injunction stand and take my chances in the hearing of the harassment case." They shook hands. "Charles, it has been a pleasure. No doubt, we will meet soon."

Smith left court ignoring Burgess. Fay Reynolds followed the party line. "So far, so good," she told Charlie. "My bet is the other side will keep their powder dry for the time being." She left, seeking to catch up with her leader.

*****

At Maynard's chambers, the clients were shaken. "I know it's early but I could do with a scotch," said Foster. "Good idea," said Rankin. The other newspapermen asked for the same or gins and vodkas. The newspaper world is renowned for hard-drinking at unsociable hours but eleven o'clock in the morning was a tad early.

"Are these fines enforceable?" asked one of the proprietors.

Maynard, seated at his desk, put his chin in his hands. "You were in contempt. The law states that a judge may impose such fines or jail sentences as he or she sees fit for someone found guilty of contempt of court. The punishment is within the judge's discretion. However, I have not experienced such high fines before. Your solicitors should get moving with an appeal."

One of the proprietors responded, "Yes, yes, but what about the money? I'm not worried about the prison sentence. I know I shan't repeat the conduct."

"I'll do some research and advise your solicitors. You must appreciate your conduct was verging on the criminal. The Attorney General has the right to intervene and bring criminal proceedings against all of you. I doubt he will but it is in your interests to behave impeccably from now on. I suggest you focus on how to defeat the injunction itself. Concentrate your efforts on getting the evidence."

"Mr. Maynard, you said nothing to us before about the Attorney General. I don't quite follow," said Foster.

"The Attorney General has an overriding discretion to investigate any criminal act. Because of the notoriety of your actions, he could get involved but I don't think he will because of the political implications. The injunction stops you from invading the privacy of Mr. Pearce and prevents the media from harassing him. It is silent about what you can publish about him. If you discover anything detrimental, you are not prohibited from publication, subject to defamation laws. My advice is to let the injunction stand.

"Ask yourselves, how have you benefited from doorstepping? You have seen today the consequences of disobedience, not to mention ignoring my advice. By not challenging the injunction, it will be a strong argument to the Court of Appeal that you respect the law and have obeyed it, apart from this rare departure. I would argue the fines are penal, extortionist and should be reduced. As I said, this needs research."

"But," said Foster. "There's always a but."

"There are no buts. Let me take you through the process again. Mr. Pearce has brought an action against you for distress because you have breached his rights of privacy. This is separate from the injunction. Your defence to his law suit will be that your conduct was reasonable within the law, that's the Article 10 defence. There is overriding public interest in a famous author. It will take quite a while for the case to come to court, maybe a year to eighteen months. In that time, you can collect evidence about Mr. Pearce and his private life. The more salacious the better. You need to be able to show to the court that Mr. Pearce has a lot to hide."

"What if nothing is found?" asked a proprietor.

"The court is concerned with facts, not unsupported allegations. If you don't find the evidence, my advice would be for you to settle. Damages will be low, especially in comparison to today's fines."

Rankin snorted in disgust. "Settle? Mr. Maynard, who do you think you're dealing with? What do you think we do? We are fighters for truth. *The Sentinel* does not quit, it does not turn the other cheek."

Rankin spoke to the throng. "Don't know about you lot but I'm totally hacked off with lawyers and the law. No disrespect, Mr. Maynard. I'm going to The George for few pints. Then, when I'm pissed, I'm going to get more pissed. I've had more than enough of the British legal system."

Part II.

The Counter-Claim. 2006-7.
Chapter Eight.

A week passed. Paul Spencer, on behalf of *The Sentinel,* its proprietor and editor-in-chief and its journalists, lodged an appeal with the Court of Appeal against the fines and sentences meted out by Judge Benton. Other titles and proprietors also filed their appeals through different lawyers. They now wanted separation from *The Sentinel* to be visible.

The advice from Maynard was inconclusive. The Court of Appeal had no sentencing guidelines to follow. Judge Benton had wide discretion on contempt of court issues. After the consultation with Maynard, Rankin expressed sarcasm. "That's two grand more down the drain on someone who has no fucking idea!"

Maynard thought Pearce's people were very unlikely to take part in the Court of Appeal hearing. "Only the defendants will appear. Pearce has no interest in joining an argument about reduction of fines, et cetera. I see no risk in the court increasing fines. It will cost you little in legal fees in comparison to savings that might be made. Say you achieved a 20% reduction in fines, the appeal would be worthwhile financially. So, do you want to take a gamble?"

Rankin said he wanted to think it over. Foster wanted to go ahead with the appeal but he knew better than to press the boss right away. The next day, Foster changed his mind. He wanted a decision from Rankin. He chose the worst time.

At a board meeting that morning, Rankin was flayed by his fellow directors. Arguments abounded but Rankin held 42% of the Ordinary shares of MU and 90% of Preference shares. Overall he held more than 75% of the voting rights. He had control. He was bomb-proof.

Consequently, he didn't appreciate being scolded by the non-executive directors 'for behaving like a cowboy' and 'showing appalling judgment in breaking a court order and the law of the land.'

The chairman was particularly caustic, especially when Rankin reminded him he had been consulted. "Yes, you talked to me, Max but you didn't listen."

Some members of the board favoured a resolution designed to prevent a re-occurrence of what had happened by requiring decisions which might break a court order to be referred to the board first. Usually, Rankin dealt with these situations with aplomb but he lost his cool at this last suggestion.

"What do all of you think we do here? We are not some stuffy financial services company, regulated up to the ears, although I'm pretty sure those people break the law every day. We are one of this country's great institutions. Our nearest rival in importance is *The Times* and no newspaper has a bigger circulation than we do. We have a reputation for holding people's feet to the fire. Politicians, big businessmen, captains of industry, leading actors, film stars and sportsmen quake if we get them in our sights. And now you want to handcuff the very people who make the important decisions which keep us in business? Do any of you think you have a journalist's ability to decide what to publish and how? These decisions are taken by our editor-in-chief and his teams, not the stuffed shirts around this table.

"I was aware of our barrister's advice before we challenged the injunction. We thought it was worth a try. We were wrong. But you need to realise this is how newspapers work. Yes, we made a mistake. And we will pay for it. We are making another major mistake which none of you have picked up on. We have only one newspaperman on this Board. That's me. The rest of you are accountants, lawyers, bankers and professional non-executives. None of you has a day's experience running a newspaper. Yet some of you think you should have the final say on what to publish and what action to take. I will not have my editors restricted on what they can or cannot do.

"Editors make these decisions, not you. If you don't like it, resign, go. Get out. This meeting is closed. I am going to ponder on this company's constitution and expertise of this board and whether it's up to snuff. None of your seats are safe."

Rankin stormed out of the Board Room and returned to his office. 'Who the hell do these fucking people think they are?' he thought. 'This is my newspaper. They are just hacks, ciphers, sitting on their arses to satisfy City regulators when all they do is take a fee for doing bugger all. This has to change.'

Max Rankin was a dangerous man to cross. His rise to fame and power had been well publicised in unauthorised biographies. Max neither courted publicity, nor did he shrink from it. Many newspapers wrote about 'Rankin, The News Mogul.' *The Sentinel* was just one of the many media outlets he owned.

*****

Max Rankin grew up in Ottowa. His father owned two local newspapers which made decent money. When Rankin was nineteen, his father died. Rankin changed his plans for further education and took over the newspapers, with his mother's support. Rankin had a good head for business. With his mother at his side as guarantor, he negotiated a loan from the First Bank of Canada to buy more newspapers. When Rankin was twenty one, his mother signed over the shares of the Ottowa newspapers to him outright.

Rankin borrowed more to propel his buying spree. Soon he owned newspapers in Montreal, Toronto, and other Canadian cities. Business was good until 1981 when the Canadian economy went into recession.

Advertising revenues shrank, circulations fell and the profit and loss sheet of The Rankin Group, the holding company, went speedily from black to bright red. Whilst First Bank was sympathetic, they warned they would call in their loans if the following quarter's figures did not show a strong improvement.

Rankin's father often took his son on trips to the USA, usually Minneapolis and Chicago. Max met prominent businessmen and bankers. When Rankin found himself in difficulties with First Bank, he went to Chicago to meet John Baker, CEO and major shareholder of The Commercial Bank of Illinois. Baker agreed to lend The Rankin Group sufficient funds to repay the Canadian bankers, while providing enough working capital to trade out of difficulty.

Rankin's plans to deal with the recession included cutting staff to the bone, centralising a number of group operations and edging his newspapers towards the lowest common denominator. His papers would appeal to centrist and conservative attitudes. The progressive, crusading days of The Rankin Group were over. Several journalists left the newspapers on principle.

Within eighteen months, the recession faded and the Rankin Group roared back like a lion. Rankin was fond of the story where First Bank of Canada approached him, 'cap in hand,' as he liked to tell it, with offers of new loans. Rankin showed First Bank the door. His eyes were focused on bigger things.

The Commercial Bank of Illinois was the principal lender to a group of Midwest American newspapers. The owners were getting old and wanted to sell. Baker thought The Rankin Group would be a good fit. It took six weeks for Rankin to close the deal. He now wanted to find east and west coast titles too. He didn't mind 'the fit' this time. He was happy with garish tabloids, as well as conservative broadsheets. And Baker was happy to back Rankin.

Rankin often spoke of the newspaper business as simplicity itself. On the debit side, a title needed a building, a printing press and staff, especially journalists, who got stories. On the credit side, the title attracted advertisers and readers.

The more readers you got, the more space advertisers would buy and the more you could charge them. Rankin concentrated on circulation as much as content, knowing that advertisers and revenue would follow.

Rankin needed good people around him. He discovered a financial genius working at one of the Midwest titles. The man could read balance sheets and profit and loss accounts and tear them apart as if they were tissue paper. He joined The Rankin Group executive board.

Fifteen years ago, Rankin changed The Rankin Group name to Media Universal. He built strong teams. His executive people were acknowledged editors, experienced journalists and advertising specialists. Max gave his people authority and room to grow. He put up with non-executives. After all, he was the supreme pragmatist.

When he was in his late twenties, Rankin cut quite the figure. He was tall, well built, good looking in his way and a magnet for women. As the coming man, he frequented the club scene in New York and London. No waiting in line for Max. He was a celebrity, reported as much in the gossip columns as the business pages.

Rankin realised that citizenship might be an obstacle to his ambitions. Canada was a backwater. Using persuasive skills, he obtained American and British passports by the time he was thirty. MU paid tax in so many countries that it seemed only right that he became a citizen of the world. He crossed the Atlantic often. Clearing passport control and customs speedily was a formality for one of his importance. MU bought a Cessna jet, enabling Rankin to travel in comfort and privacy, long or short haul, untramelled by the usual roughness and delays at airports.

For Rankin, business came first, second and third. It wasn't the money that drove him. He knew there was only so much you could spend to satisfy greed. He was content with two Rolls Royces, one in London, the other in New York. He didn't need a fleet of cars everywhere.

Rankin based himself in Manhattan in a luxurious triplex apartment in Beekman Place. He did not want homes in London, Paris or Los Angeles and the other major communication centres where he spent time. The penthouse suites in the best hotels were good enough for him. He wasn't rigid about real estate. He bought a villa in the hills above Antibes with unfettered views of the Mediterranean. There were also two homes in the Hamptons for two of his ex-wives and children.

Power propelled and motivated Rankin. The influence of newspapers, especially a title like *The Sentinel,* was like an aphrodisiac, irresistible to those who sought it. MU, with its radio and television stations and new social media outlets, made the corporation strong enough to persuade politicians, industrialists and businessmen, who thought they were all-powerful, to a different view. What Rankin loved was a request from a political leader to meet, especially when the politician came to him for advice, opinion or a favour.

It took Rankin more than twenty years to build this extraordinary empire. He was the most talked of man in the communications world, feared even by other newspaper titans.

*****

Foster sat in his office. Should he worry about his career? He had seen Max in a rage many a time but this was different. Max would judge him for his Pearce decision. If he got it wrong, would he be fired? At his age, it would be difficult to get another job that paid as well. 'Protect your back,' he told himself.

Foster opened his safe and withdrew a file headed "Max Rankin." He started to read the contents, prepared in strictest confidence for him by a private investigator. Unethical, for sure, but if discovered, Foster would say he was merely protecting the interests of the newspaper. He stopped reading and thought.

By and large, Max let his people get on with their jobs, so long as circulation numbers didn't drop. He was eagle-eyed on those numbers. If they slipped, a visit to Rankin's office was compulsory and explanations and solutions were demanded. Rankin would not tolerate what he regarded as failure.

Foster read on but paused after a few minutes. Instinctively, Max assumed that Pearce would be crushed like an ant. Max might blame himself for failing to pay sufficient attention to the lawyers, although he would never admit it, but for certain Foster would be put in the stocks. Within *The Sentinel*, this would be Foster's screw up. 'I need to worry,' he told himself.

Foster skimmed the rest of the report but re-read a passage. 'MU owes a large sum to a consortium of banks who have supported expansion of the group into new media, especially television news channels. We have been unable to secure exact details of the financing but it is believed Rankin himself stands as guarantor for MU. There are bound to be covenants by Rankin and the corporation concerning the group's share value. Should the share price fall below a minimum value as stipulated, the consortium would have the right to call the loan and take action against MU and Rankin.'

"I need to remember this," Foster told himself. He knew the firing of *The Sentinel's* editor would cause the share price to drop even if temporarily. Would Max take this risk?'

*****

Seated at a voluminous desk, Rankin buzzed his secretary. "Get Foster in here." Now or as soon as possible was not needed. When Foster arrived, Rankin stared at him. "I fucked up a little bit on the Pearce business, but you fucked up a lot, in spades. That Spencer fellow was a wet weekend, all law, nothing else."

Foster was affronted. "I accept you fucked up. I don't accept I did. I followed the editorial policy set by you. Let me remind you of that policy: 'There is no individual so important that will escape our magnifying glass. If there's something to be told, we will tell it.' I know Pearce is hiding something and so do you."

"What is he hiding? Is it an affair?"

"I don't think so. There's not a whiff of anything suspect about his marriage. It's something else, it's deep in his past and he's scared we'll discover what it is."

Max's attitude changed. "I'm not happy with you but I'm not going to fire you, at least not now. Mind you, you deserve it and you're making it worse by not accepting the lion's share of blame in this thing. You got carried away and it affected your judgment. Look what you've cost us in fines, not to mention legals. I have the board on my back and they're right for once, although I gave them a flea in their collective ears. So don't you dare tell me you didn't mess up! You didn't listen to that Maynard fellow. You've made a complete clusterfuck."

"Max, we're going to have to agree to disagree. If it helps, I'll accept I am equally responsible for the screw up. Apart from this dressing down, what else do you want to tell me? I'm busy."

"We need to beef things up for the future. Paul Spencer has to go. He's weak. When he told us not to defy the injunction, he wasn't a team player. Find someone else, someone better. Spencer might be a clever lawyer but he's not suited to this newspaper and our business. Find a legal who is."

Foster knew better than to argue.

"While you're at it, find outside lawyers for this case and a smarter barrister. Now what are you doing about this bugger, Pearce?"

"We have investigators looking into him and his background here and in the States. So far, nothing to report above what we already know. Pearce met his wife in Minnesota. They married there and moved to England eleven or twelve years ago.

"They live in some style in a place in Buckinghamshire. But there's got to be dirt on Pearce before he met his wife. I just know it. And admit it, you know it too. It's early days."

"Early days? Martin, that's not good enough. Our people have had this for several days and turned up bugger-all. How is this possible? Everyone has a past. These investigators have to go deeper. They are taking our money for nothing. If they don't get results in a few days, fire them. Start thinking outside the box. That woman who works here, the one who writes the gossip column. What's her name?"

"Connie, Connie Strauss."

"Yes, that's her. Sexy little thing. Get her on the story. Her job is to dig into the lives of celebrities and she often comes up with the goods. Listen to me carefully. I want results. Don't fart around on this one. It's top priority. We'll be laughing stocks if we don't expose Pearce. We can't have him beat *The Sentinel.* Keep me posted."

'Beat you, more like,' Foster thought as he returned to his office.

*****

Half an hour later, Connie Strauss sat in Foster's office. "What have you got?" asked Foster.

"Bit of arthritis in my left hand. Otherwise I'm fine."

"Very droll." Foster looked at Strauss. Late thirties, probably, but looking younger, jet black hair, almond eyes, pretty face, petite frame, great legs and a 'come hither' look but she was strictly 'no touch' in the male dominated *Sentinel.*

"You know what I mean. What stories have you got?"

"A married premier league footballer's squeeze on the side who has a kiss and tell story plus pictures. A film star dying of cancer. Otherwise usual celebrity stuff. Why?"

"Just doing what editors-in-chief do."

"I work through Eddie Phillips." Phillips was Connie's editor, in charge of home affairs. She occasionally reported to his senior, an executive editor, but never to the editor-in-chief.

"What do you know about Charlie Pearce?"

"Nothing more than what I've read in the paper."

"We know he's an American in his mid to late forties. We know he came to England about eleven or twelve years ago. But that's where it ends. We can find nothing much about his life before 1987. After that walk out on the Perry Vaughan show, I'm sure there's a big story behind this. He's got something he desperately wants to hide. I want to find it and give Pearce a bloody nose and worse."

"Why don't you give this to our investigative journalism team? Oh, you can't, you fired them."

"If you ever get to where I sit, you'll find out how hard these decisions are to make. IJ teams are bloody expensive with no guarantees of results. The board, not me, took the decision in what they termed 'the best interests of the business.' I fought it but lost. The IJ team produced nada for almost two years and Rankin had had enough."

"In the best interests of the newspaper?" Connie muttered. "Martin, that's tosh. As for your instructions, I'm not a gumshoe. Isn't that what they call private investigators? I persuade people to talk to me. I don't do sleuthing."

Foster was exasperated. "Connie, I've told you to get involved in a huge story. If you find what we need, you'll have the by-line. It will make you a very valuable property. So, just access the female Sherlock within you. This is not a request from me. It's a directive. Rankin wants you to do this. So stop the hard to get act."

Connie flashed an insincere, thank you smile at Foster, rose and replied, "Right away, boss" as she left his office. She stopped. "Martin, a question. How do you find someone who doesn't want to be found, or, more precisely, how do you trace someone who disappeared years ago?"

"This is why we've asked you to do this. You'll figure it out."

"Let me think this over. I'll have questions."

"Sure."

Back in her office, Connie took time to think. What did it matter that this was not her usual line of work? She was a journalist. She wrote stories. Connie e-mailed Foster, asking for private investigator reports and access to the investigators. She also asked for a budget. Here, Foster was generous. When the reports were delivered to her office that day, the contents weren't helpful.

A week later, Connie's enquiry remained in the long grass, Foster was frustrated and Rankin was perpetually angry with everyone. "Surely to God, how hard can it be to find out about Pearce?"

*****

On a July morning, Appeal Court 2 at the Law Courts was crowded and hot. The lawyers' benches were not so full this time. As expected, with the leave of the court, Charles Pearce was not participating in the newspapers' appeals against the fines and custodial sentences imposed by Judge Benton.

However, the government in the form of Miles Shackford, the Attorney General, had an interest. Law enforcement and criminal contempt were in his bailiwick. The press bench was full, as were three rows of benches occupied by the public.

Rankin had calmed down and decided not to replace the newspaper's legal team. He and Foster were in court to hear Mark Maynard, who had hardly begun to speak when he was interrupted by Lord Justice Boyd, one of the three appellate judges. Maynard was not put off. An experienced silk, he anticipated a forensic grilling.

"Are the facts disputed?" asked Boyd.

"No, my lord, but there are grounds to argue Judge Benton exceeded her powers in sentencing."

Within moments, Maynard felt he had been placed in a document shredder.

"Do you say the learned judge erred in the exercise of her discretion?"

"I do, my lord."

"On what basis? Surely, the essential point about the judge's powers is they are discretionary. Are you suggesting there was either a failure to follow guidelines, or something personal clouded the learned judge's mind? If so, the first argument must fail as Parliament has set no guidelines. So what do you say clouded the judge's mind?"

"My lord, there is another argument. Is it natural justice to impose such heavy punishments? Are they fair, are they reasonable? In a nutshell, my submission is they are not."

"You may or may not be correct but you know perfectly well, these are not matters for this court. They were for the judge at first instance. I and my brothers are bound to assume she took all relevant factors into account. Or do you say there was something personal? If so, what evidence do you have to support such a contention?"

Boyd was angry with Maynard and showed it. Maynard leaned down to Rankin and Foster sitting on the bench in front of him. "If you have no evidence of bias, we're done. We should give up." Rankin's face was white with anger. He shook his head.

Maynard breathed deeply. "My lord, we are making no such assertion. But may I ask you to look at precedent. In similar cases, the punishment meted out was materially different, the fines substantially lower. I am ready to cite the cases."

"I am sure you are but precedent does not help you. None of the cases you will cite have reached this court. Mr. Maynard, have you any other arguments?"

"No, my lord," said Maynard, shaking his head and resuming his seat.

Boyd asked Shackford. "Mr. Attorney, do you wish to address us?"

Shackford knew the appeal had failed. "No, my lords, save to respectfully remind you that there was a flagrant, deliberate breach of an injunction by members of the fourth estate. Some national newspapers acted above the law. It is axiomatic that the learned judge took everything into account when passing sentence."

The appeal judges did not retire. They whispered to each other for less than a minute. Lord Justice Boyd relaxed back in his chair and told the Court, "Appeal denied. Our written reasons will be published in due course."

Outside Court, Foster asked Maynard, "Is that it?"

"Yes, unless you want to take this to the House of Lords but we would have to seek leave for the Lords to hear the case. I doubt leave will be granted and, even if it was, I believe you'd lose. Put this one down to experience, gentlemen. You still have the hearing of Pearce's case for harassment to come. By then, you may have uncovered the evidence to beat him."

"So you're telling me we're stuffed." Rankin was seething. He was a very bad loser. "Easy for you to say fight another day. You don't have to pay the bloody fines. I'm off for a drink. Coming, Martin?"

And that was that. *The Sentinel* paid the fines, licked its wounds and continued its search for Charlie Pearce's hidden life. However, Martin Foster decided to take a final shot. Two days after the appeal decision, he wrote an editorial. By the time the paper's legal team pruned it, all intemperate language was removed:

The Daily Sentinel

28th July, 2006

Who Judges the Judges?

By Martin Foster.

Recently, this newspaper was punished for ignoring a High Court injunction. A genuine and sincere apology was made for our shortcomings. Nevertheless, unprecedented heavy fines and suspended prison sentences were meted out. The Court of Appeal has upheld the decision of the learned Judge Benton. In doing so, it became clear that when dealing with contempt of court issues, a judge at first instance has the widest discretion and Parliament has set no guidelines for judges to follow to limit such discretion. Normally, guidelines are set by Parliament to assist our courts in deciding whether punishment is fair and reasonable but we are faced with the fact that there are no such guidelines in cases of contempt.

Separation of powers between Parliament and the Judiciary lies at the heart of our governmental system. It is a bastion to protect the public from a ruling elite. But the Judiciary is an elite. Its members are not elected. It is accountable to no one but itself. Therefore, constitutional experts might well raise the question, does the Judiciary in the appellate courts serve the public as it should?

The legislative branch has a responsibility to protect the lives and wellbeing of its citizens. The duty of the courts is to apply the law. Cicero, arguably the finest lawyer of his day in Ancient Rome, said: "Let the safety, security and wellbeing of the people be the overriding law."

The Sentinel is bound to ask: Did the Appeal Court have this in mind in judging the acts of this newspaper? There seems to be a serious democratic deficit in persuasive engagement with the public. First, far from giving the impression that governmental and judicial elites are working together in all our interests, the Appeal Court often seems to point-score against the government on matters of great public concern. Second, while the judiciary does indeed publish its detailed judgments on every case, it seems indifferent to giving a suitably comprehensible account to the general public. This is a dereliction of its duty.

There are few things more important than people's confidence in the good sense of its legal system. 'Let justice be done, though the heavens fall in,' it is said. But if the consequence of justice being done is that the heavens do in fact fall, on whom do they fall? Should not the appellate judiciary look at its elite, oligarchic self and ask whom its justice is serving?

Chapter Nine.

In 2006, the newspaper world was for hard-headed men and women who vied with each other to produce the best-researched, best-written stories. Well, that's what they told themselves. Many a correspondent wanted to make himself or herself the talking point of the newspaper universe and often used a short cut or two in trying to bamboozle editors. It was a dog eat dog world.

Many British newspapers thinned down after the print revolution of the 1980s. The tyranny of the unions was broken, mainly thanks to Max Rankin, Rupert Murdoch and one or two other crusaders. Computer technology changed everything. By the turn of the 21st century, newspapers were run on business lines; no fat, everything geared to profit.

Yet occasionally you'd find sentimentality. A few people from the old days held onto their jobs. One such *Sentinel* employee, Bill Jones, survived because no one had the heart to let him go. Bill started as a runner in the 70s and, truth be told, he was and would always be just a gopher. He was known as 'Tell Yer What' at the newspaper because it was a phrase he used invariably. Almost every sentence he spoke started with those words.

Bill was one of those people whom it was impossible to dislike. He was a naïve, lovable, sweet man, now in his mid-fifties, who spent his working day at *The Sentinel* and the rest of his time at home with his wife, Dulcie, and their dogs. He had no ambitions, a man content to fumble his way through life.

Tell Yer What appeared on Martin Foster's radar when cost-cutting was needed. Foster was in a quandary. Newspapers were no longer a place for hangers-on. People who did not contribute had to go. But Bill was liked by all. Making him redundant might well have proved more expensive in staff resentment. Truth be told, Foster had a weakness. TYW survived.

TYW was allotted a number of low-skill tasks, mostly fetching and carrying, but he was as honest as they come so he was of use when documents and messages were too personal to be given to outside couriers. On one occasion, he was sent to New York to deliver some highly confidential documents to Max Rankin. On his return, TYW could not stop talking about his trip. The Empire State and all the sights had made their mark. And this was a man who thought the height of leisure was the beach at Clacton-on-Sea.

For the sake of appearances, TYW was made the sub-editor of a *Sentinel* international edition which was sold mainly to ex-pats and holiday makers in Malta, the Balearics and the Canary Islands. TYW glowed with pride when he was told of this 'promotion.' By his terms, he had made it in the business. He would delight in telling people, "I help edit an international magazine."

Connie Strauss asked TYW to see her. "I want you to go to this address," she said, handing him a note, "and collect a package for me." TYW had a huge soft spot for Connie and would do anything for her.

"Tell yer what, Miss, I'll do this right away."

Within two hours, TYW was back in Connie's office, handing her a large envelope. "Here y'are, Miss Strauss. If you don't mind me asking, what's this all about?"

"Keep this to yourself." Connie knew from times past that TYW was no blabbermouth. Connie opened the envelope and took out some photographs.

"These are some pictures taken early this morning," she explained.

TYW looked and shook his head. "Who's that?"

"The wife of a cabinet minister. She has been playing away, husband found out and gave her a hiding, bad enough to put her in hospital. The pictures show her coming out of the Westminster Clinic."

TYW looked, shrugged his shoulders and started to leave but he couldn't help looking at papers on Connie's desk.

"Who's that?"

"Charlie Pearce. He's a famous novelist."

"What's the story?"

"He's the one who got an injunction against the paper a month ago."

"Why are you involved? Is he a celebrity?"

"Yes and no. He wants to keep his private life private. We are trying to find out about him. We have found nothing at all on him until about twenty years ago. He's American. We want to know what he was doing before 1987."

"Is that odd?"

"Yes because in America, like here, there are records of your birth, school reports, social security numbers, stuff like that but our people haven't found much yet. We have the standard information but nothing else. It's weird. Pearce has no usual trail."

"Give us a look at that photo."

Connie did so and waited. Eventually, TYW shrugged, said "nah," and left. TYW was a man of few words because he rarely had anything to say. He just kept himself to himself. But TYW was dogged. He would gnaw at a problem, even if it took him a long time to find the solution. Hence, the next day, he returned to see Connie.

"That photo, Miss Strauss, could I see it again?"

"Which photo, Bill?"

"The one of that writer bloke. Forgotten his name."

"Ah, Charlie Pearce." Connie rumbled through papers on her desk and with a 'voila' produced a photo.

"Nah, not Voiler, Miss, his name's Pearce. Give it here, please."

Bill looked at the photo. As he stared, horizontal wrinkles formed between his eyes. He turned to Connie.

"Not sure."

"Not sure of what, Bill?"

"Not sure if it's Arfa."

"Who's Arfa?"

"Sorry, not Arfa, Arthur."

"Who is Arthur?" Connie tried hard not to laugh.

"Arthur Hawkins. When I was growing up, Arfa lived around the corner from me. He was younger than me so I ignored him most of the time. Don't look like him much. His face has changed a lot but his eyes still look the same. It could be him."

"What else can you tell me?"

"Not much. The Hawkins' kept themselves to themselves. It was just Arfa and his Dad. Tell yer what, for a while, Arfa had a girlfriend. Can't remember her name. Pretty thing. One other thing. Arfa got a reputation of being tough, you know, handy with his fists. He could take care of himself. Other boys steered clear of 'im. I fink he got a job in the City. Never saw him after he left school."

Connie wanted to know more but pressurising TYW would not work. He would clam up. "Thank you, Bill. If you remember anything else, would you let me know?"

"Okay. One thing, Miss. This bloke Pearce, if he wants to keep his life to himself, why would you want to find out things? I never understand why it's our job to hurt people."

"Well, the public has a right to know things."

"I keep hearing people say that but does this Pearce bloke have a wife, does he have kids? If you find out bad things about him and put them in the paper, won't you hurt his family? How is that right? They did nothing."

Connie did not reply straight away. She was taken aback by his perceptive, ethical observations. Eventually, she told TYW, "That's life. It's what's called collateral damage. But it is far too soon to worry about Pearce's privacy. We know so little about him."

Chapter Ten.

In the week after Arthur was thrown out of his home, the school received a note from Harry Hawkins, withdrawing his son from the education system. Eddie Grey networked. Arthur was invited to an interview with The General Insurance Company of Great Britain at their head office in Lime Street in the City of London.

Eddie and Mary prepared Arthur for the interview. Arthur's only suit, an ill-fitting brown pin stripe, was cleaned. The trousers were too short. Mary lengthened them but they still stopped an inch from the top of his shoes. His hair was slicked back which emphasised his sticky-out ears. His shirt had frayed cuffs. He tried to pull down the suit jacket sleeves to hide the cuffs but that didn't work. Frankly, he looked more like an urchin out of a Dickens novel than a future City worker. But it was the best he could do.

Arthur arrived early for his interview. He was sent to the basement of the building. There were five other boys his age waiting to be seen. A man appeared in the corridor and barked, "Harris." One of the boys stood and was shown into a room. Twenty minutes or so later, he exited and the same man barked, "Hawkins." Arthur stood and entered a room. He offered his right hand to the barking man, who ignored it.

"Sit." Arthur sat at a desk. "On the desk there is a page with columns of figures. Add them up."

Arthur looked at the page. There were three columns of numbers. The first had one number followed by a decimal point and one more number. The second had two numbers, a decimal point and two more numbers. The third column had three numbers, a decimal point and three more numbers. It took Arthur eight minutes to complete the task. He handed the paper to the barking man.

"You can't have finished yet, Hawkins."

Arthur watched the man's eyebrows rise as he checked Arthur's work. He dialled a number. Arthur heard him say, "I have one you should see." There was a pause. "He completed the exercise in less than half the usual time. The answers are correct." He put the phone down. "Wait outside. Someone's coming to collect you."

Arthur was confident he'd done nothing wrong but he sat in a state of nervousness. A woman in her fifties appeared. Her hair was tied in a bun. She wore a white blouse and a charcoal grey pencil skirt. Her face might have been pretty once but now she looked pinched and severe.

"Arthur Hawkins?"

"Yes, Miss."

"Follow me."

The woman led Arthur to a lift and took him to the third floor, along a thick carpeted corridor. Wooden office doors with brass handles on either side proliferated. She stopped at a door with a sign. 'Clerk Manager.' She knocked, a voice said "enter" and in they went.

"This is Arthur Hawkins, Mr. Buddell."

Buddell nodded and dismissed the woman politely.

"Arthur Hawkins, yes?" Arthur nodded. "My name is Mr. Buddell. This company employs many clerks. They have all kinds of jobs from filing, making copies of documents and other duties needed in the insurance business. We have clerks who check figures. This company writes thousands of insurance policies every week. We have to tabulate and check the figures. We always have openings for young men like yourself to carry out this task. What do you think?"

Arthur hadn't a clue about what he thought. The job sounded dreary, monotonous and boring but it was figure work. Maybe there was something in it for him. "I'm not sure, sir. It's all happening a bit quick for me."

"Oh? What were you expecting?"

"Don't know, really. Had to leave school and I need a job. So it's good you might want me to work for you. Would I work in this building?"

"No. We have an office in Whitechapel for clerical work."

Buddell, deep down a kind man, realised Arthur was a bit shell-shocked. "Shall I tell you a bit more about the job? You'd work from nine in the morning till five thirty at night, Mondays to Fridays. We also work a half day on Saturdays. You will have 15 minute tea breaks in the morning and afternoon and 45 minutes for lunch. Your job will be to check and tally columns of figures sent from our city and regional offices. You will have sheets of policy details including premiums and you add up the premiums and cover amounts to give management people accurate totals of the business we are writing."

Arthur look blankly at Buddell. "Sorry, sir, but what are policies and premiums and cover? I don't know nothing about insurance."

"I see. A policy is a document under which this company agrees to insure a person or a company or a firm. The document sets out precise terms of what is insured. It might be a driver and his motor car, or a house or flat, or even someone's health. If the driver is hurt or his car is damaged in an accident, if the house or flat is damaged, say in a fire, or if a person is ill and needs health care, we pay the bills. If during the length of the policy there are no claims, we keep the premium paid to us. Of course, the insurance business is far more complex but you will learn it as you go along."

Arthur concentrated. "I think I understand. It's like putting a bet on a horse. If your horse wins, the bookie pays out. If you lose, the bookie keeps your stake."

Buddell smiled. "I suppose you could think of insurance in that way but keep it to yourself. You'd upset a lot of people here if you shared that view.

"Now, what I haven't told you is what you get for your work. We'd start you off at £17 a week. That's £884 a year before income tax. We also give luncheon vouchers. There is a canteen in our Whitechapel building where you can exchange the vouchers at lunchtime. You get paid for all the bank holidays. You are also entitled to two weeks paid holiday a year. What do you think?"

Arthur currently earned £2 a week from his paper round and another £1 from Mr. Grey. He would have to give up both jobs but he would still be £14 a week better off. After tax and contributing £3 a week for his rent and keep, he would still be way ahead. And maybe the work wouldn't be too boring. He could cycle to work, too. Rotherhithe to Whitechapel was doable.

"It sounds alright, Mr Buddell. Yes, I like it. Is there a place I can leave my bike where it won't get nicked?"

"Yes. Lots of people cycle to work."

"What happens next?"

"You go home, talk it over with your parents and if they are happy, let me know. I'll send you all the details." Buddell rose to say goodbye. Arthur stayed seated.

"My mother died a few years ago and my father and I don't speak any more. I don't live at home."

Buddell sat back. He asked Arthur to explain so Arthur told him the story.

"Would you like to have stayed at school?"

"After all the kerfuffle, I don't think so. I want to try the job. Sounds good to me."

Buddell took out a business card. "Ask Mr. Grey to call me. If he and I can resolve things, and I expect we can, you'll have a job with General Insurance, starting on Monday. Good luck Arthur."

Buddell and Grey spoke the next day. A form was sent to Grey who met with Harry Hawkins. The form was signed. The following Monday, Arthur started his career at The General Insurance Company of Great Britain.

*****

Arthur arrived at GI's Whitechapel building that first Monday, wearing his awful brown pin stripe. He felt uncomfortable until he saw others dressed just as shabbily. Mary said she would take him to Petticoat Lane that weekend to find him a better fitting suit, as well as some new shirts and ties. Arthur worried he couldn't afford it but Mary told him that she and Eddie would advance him the money and he could repay them from his wages.

The large building in Whitechapel was gloomy-looking. Arthur padlocked his bike at the rear with many others. He was directed to Room 205 on the second floor. It was cavernous with rows and rows of desks, more than a hundred of them. He soon got used to being seated for seven hours every day. His room was just one of many spaces where figure and clerical work was done. He found the routine mind-numbing. When he finished a sheet of work, he walked to the front of the room, handed it over to a supervisor who gave him another sheet to complete. Despite the monotony of the tasks, Arthur didn't mind. He enjoyed working with figures.

The room was warm, so by the afternoon it was hard to concentrate but Arthur prided himself on his accuracy. Before handing in a sheet, he always checked his figures. Rarely did he find an error. And he was quick. This didn't go un-noticed.

At lunch and tea breaks, Arthur sat on his own. He shared the canteen with hundreds of clerks but mone wanted to socialise with the awkward new boy. Arthur felt it was like being back at school but he was in the real world now. He tried to start conversations with one or two of his co-workers but they weren't interested. He didn't understand why until three weeks into his job.

One night as he was unlocking the padlock on his bike, he was called out. "Oy, new boy. What's yer name?"

"Arthur Hawkins. Who are you?" Arthur put himself on guard. He had dealt with enough bullies in his time. He was relieved to find the person was neither hostile nor about to make his life hard.

"I'm Freddie Styles. I work in the same room as you. You seem to be on your own a lot. Want a drink? Let's go to The Grapes."

"How old are you?"

"Eighteen but they don't mind in this part of the City."

"Well, I'm fifteen and I doubt I'd get in. And if I did, I'd get chucked out. We could go to a café."

"I'd prefer a pint but alright."

Over coffee, the two started finding out about each other. Arthur soon realized that Freddie knew a lot about the business.

"Why insurance, Arthur?" Freddie asked.

"I have someone who looks out for me. He got me an interview. I'm good with numbers and that got me in here."

"What do you know about insurance?"

"Not much. People insure houses and cars and we take their money. We pay out if there's a claim and pocket the dosh if there isn't."

"It's a lot more complicated than that. General Insurance is a tariff insurance company. That means the amount of premium charged is set from data in tariff tables calculated by rating organizations.
"In other words, it's not a free for all. The business is regulated. However, if you need to have a risk insured that's unusual or outside the scope of tariff insurers, you take it to Lloyd's. You've heard of Lloyd's?"

Arthur shook his head. Freddie continued. "Blimey, you really don't know much. Shall I tell you about it?" Arthur nodded his head.

"Lloyd's is a group of independent insurers. They are not government regulated. If you are a member of Lloyd's, it means that insurance business is written on your behalf by whichever syndicate you join. Every syndicate has working and non-working members. The non-working ones are in the vast majority. They invest their money and take a share of profits but they take no part in running the business."

"This is really complicated. Want another coffee?"

"Okay. I'm at GI to learn the business from the inside. Soon I'm going to be moved to Claims, then Policies. In a year or two, I'll go to work for my dad. He has his own general insurance brokerage and he is a Lloyd's broker too."

Arthur looked blank. "Arthur, you do know what a brokerage is, don't you?"

"No. I know sweet nothing but I'd like to learn."

"A broker advises clients on insurance matters and arranges insurance cover on their behalf. He is paid a fixed percentage of the premium as a commission."

"So, say I have a house - that'll be the day – and I want to insure it, I go to a broker and he sorts out insurance and gets paid by the insurer."

"Yes, out of the premium you pay."

"Why can't I insure direct with GI?"

"You can but it won't be any cheaper and you may not get the exact policy you want. There are risks a tariff insurer does not take on, like a lot of marine and cargo insurance, aircraft insurance and the like. Here, you have to go to Lloyd's to get cover and you do it through a Lloyd's broker."

"Freddie, I really need to educate myself. Is there a book I can read?"

"I'll ask my dad but why don't you ask Mr. Buddell? Underneath all that gruff, he seems to be a fair bloke. Now, there is something I need to tell you." Freddie ploughed on. "You do the figure work faster than the rest of us. Some of the others say you are showing us up and you need to be brought down a peg or two."

"Do you think that?"

"I'm not bothered. Like I said, this is just a training ground for me. I'll be moving on soon. But you need to watch out for yourself."

Arthur checked his watch. "Thanks for telling me. Time for me to go. Good talking to you, Freddie."

They shook hands and went their separate ways. Two weeks later, Freddie was moved to Claims and they lost touch. Nobody else wanted to talk to Arthur, save for a cursory 'good morning' or 'good night.' Arthur wasn't bothered by Freddie's warning. 'Not my fault if I can do things faster,' Arthur told himself.

One evening, when Arthur took his bike from the rack to go home, he saw he had a puncture. He got the repair kit out of his saddle bag. Kneeling down to fix the tyre, he didn't see men coming from behind him. The first he knew was a slap on the back of his head. Quickly, he stood and faced his attackers.

"Hawkins," growled one of them, "you need to be taught a lesson."

Arthur adopted the stance drilled into him by Eddie Grey. "So, it's three against one, is it? Come on then."

The one who spoke came towards Arthur, fists clenched. Arthur was quick on his feet and he heeded Eddie's words. 'Disable the first one. Turn him round, kick him in the back of the knee so he drops. Twist one of his ankles and stomp on it. That will take him out.'

When Arthur made these manoeuvres, the man squealed in pain and writhed on the ground in agony. Arthur faced the other two attackers. They were no match for him. In no time they were both on the pavement, one nursing a sprained wrist, the other staunching blood from a broken nose and holding an eye which would blacken within minutes.

Arthur decided to carry his bike but as he walked away, two City of London policemen ran into the alley, surveyed the scene and apprehended Arthur.

"What's been going on here?" asked one of the policemen.

The man with the damaged ankle shouted, "He attacked me after work. He hates me." The one with the sprained wrist chimed in. "We didn't see him coming. He's had it in for us for weeks."

The policeman turned to Arthur. "Well, what do you have to say?"

"My bike had a puncture. I was fixing it. This one," pointing to ankle man, "attacked me from behind. The other two joined in. It was three against one. I do self-defence. I guess they don't."

An ambulance arrived. "We'll need to take these three to hospital," a medic told the policeman. "You can come with us. Talk to them once they're fixed up." One policeman went in the ambulance.

The remaining policeman told Arthur: "You're coming to the station with me. You're in trouble, lad. How old are you?"

"Fifteen."

"You should have someone with you at the station?"

"What did I do? All I did was defend myself against three blokes out to get me."

"We'll sort this out at the station."

Arthur gave the desk sergeant Eddie Grey's phone number. Grey arrived at Bishopsgate Police Station twenty minutes after Arthur. He was taken to the room where Arthur was held. They talked. Then another policeman came in. He told Arthur he was going to be cautioned, finger-printed and charged.

"Charged with what?" asked Grey.

"Occasioning actual bodily harm."

"He was attacked by three men older than him."

"There's not a scratch on your boy. The other three are all hurt, one of them badly."

"I've taught Arthur self-defence for more than six years. He could have done a lot more damage to those men if he wanted to. He only did enough to stop them hurting him. Three on one and you're charging him? Are you nuts?"

"I'll ignore that. You're upset, Mr. Grey. Now, Hawkins, let's get on with the formalities."

After Arthur was charged, Grey asked, "Can we go now?"

"Hawkins lives with you?"

"Yes."

"I shan't ask for bail. I suggest you get a solicitor for him. You can go. His bike is at the front desk."

Outside the station, Arthur was in a daze. "I don't understand. They attacked me. Why am I the one in trouble?"

"It's the law. We'll put things right. Those hoodlums will be in hot water soon enough."

After a sleepless night, a drawn, tense Arthur waited outside Mr. Buddell's room. Buddell arrived at 8.30 sharp. He was like clockwork.

"What is it, Hawkins?"

"Sorry to bother you, Mr. Buddell. Last night I was attacked by three men who work in the same room as me. I defended myself and I hurt them. If I hadn't done what I did, you would probably find me in hospital this morning. The police didn't believe me and have charged me. I wanted you to hear this from me, not someone else."

Buddell stared at Arthur. "Hawkins, I was at Dunkirk and fought in the D-Day landings. I now manage more than two thousand staff at GI. I know when people are lying. Now, look me in the eye and tell me exactly what happened."

Arthur spoke again. He kept his head up and talked directly to Buddell. His story didn't change. Buddell asked some clarifying questions. Arthur named two of his attackers and passed over the charge sheet. Buddell read it carefully, looked at Arthur and said, "Right, Hawkins. You stay right there."

Buddell called Bishopsgate Police asked for the desk sergeant. When Sergeant Hicks came on the line, Buddell started: "Sergeant, my name is Buddell. I want to talk to you about one of my employees, Arthur Hawkins." He gave the reference number on the charge sheet.

"Yes, Mr. Buddell?"

"I am a manager at General Insurance. The three oiks who were also involved in this incident, the people who attacked Hawkins, those you decided not to charge, also work at General Insurance."

"How can I help you?"

"I'm going to help you. If the police prosecute Hawkins, you will be making fools of yourselves. I know this boy. He is hard-working and responsible, a peaceful character. He spends some leisure time at a gym and he has been trained in self-defence. I know the owner of the gym, Edward Grey. He recommended Hawkins to us. I know for certain that Hawkins is not lying. What he did last night was in self-defence."

"Mr. Buddell," Hicks sighed, "How can you know for certain? You weren't there. You can give evidence at Hawkins' trial about his character but we have three injured men."

"Are you seriously suggesting that Hawkins, who is only fifteen, picked a fight with three innocent adults?"

"It's not me, Mr. Buddell, it's the arresting officer."

"Right. Let me tell you what General Insurance will do. First, the three men who attacked Hawkins will be sacked. This isn't the first time they've caused trouble. They have all had written warnings which will be produced to the Court. Second, we will put General Insurance's best legal team on Hawkins' defence. They'll make the police case fall apart."

Hicks paused to think. "I don't like threats, Mr. Buddell but I can tell you're upset. Let me talk with the arresting officer. I'll call you back."

Hicks took the phone number. He read the police papers and saw the logic of what he'd been told. He called the arresting officer, who he gently persuaded to consider changing his mind. Hicks called Buddell.

"Do you have time to come to Bishopsgate to talk this over?"

"No. Come and see me if you want. I'm at our Lime Street office."

By the end of the day, the police withdrew charges against Arthur and, in due course, prosecuted the three attackers. In time, they were all convicted, fined and sacked into the bargain. That should have been that. However, the story soon got out, especially when the absence of the three attackers was noticed. From then, nobody messed with Arthur, who received a promotion and a pay rise of another £5 a week but he remained a loner.

Arthur's new role found him supervising the work that his former colleagues did, as well as taking on other tedious, supervisory clerical work required in insurance companies. Mr. Buddell arranged for Arthur to be sent on a course to learn basic insurance law and business practices. Arthur immersed himself as best he could in the ways of Lloyd's without giving away where he hoped his life might lead. No need to alert GI to potential plans. The more he found out about Lloyd's, the more determined he was to work there one day. He quickly realised that for someone like him, Lloyd's was where he could make really good money.

When Arthur turned eighteen, he received yet another promotion and came to the notice of senior people at GI. A non-executive director, Harvey Williams, was also a working member of a Lloyd's syndicate which was always on the look-out for bright young men. Williams spoke to Ronnie Bass, the chief underwriter at Syndicate 4455. The conversation was brief.

"Ronnie, I've found a lively youngster for you. His name is Arthur Hawkins. You should meet him. I hope you appreciate the things I do for you."

"Harvey, your track record could use improvement. You've not sent a winner since the old queen died."

"Danny La Rue's dead?" Bass had to laugh at that one. "Hawkins joined GI three years ago. He's had one promotion after another. He's a wizard with figures. Don't ignore a gift horse, Ronnie. Just talk to him."

*****

Ronnie Bass ran his business like his life, hard-working, risk taking, fast, expensive and with time for enjoyment in extra-curricular activities, except the ladies. He was a family man. He had earned respect at Lloyd's because he ran a highly profitable syndicate. Lloyd's remained aristocratic by nature and many working members did not like Bass but not enough to cross him.

Bass had all the trappings. He was a seriously wealthy, self-made man. Bass had a house in Mayfair and a villa in the South of France. He drove himself to Lloyd's every day, either in his convertible Bentley Continental or his red Ferrari 308GTBi. He employed a chauffeur who drove the glamorous Mrs. Bass and their young children. Ronnie preferred to drive himself. He was allowed to park in a space allocated by Lloyd's close to its front door.

When Bass entertained, he threw cash around like confetti. But he was as shrewd as those he entertained. They paid him back tenfold in insurance premiums, share tips and the like. Bass was in his mid-forties, a large man, vertically and horizontally. He was no oil painting but his pretty wife and daughters adored him. He wore Savile Row suits, Jermyn Street shirts and ties, and shoes and boots came from John Lobb. He always looked smart but a cockney accent disclosed his upbringing. He didn't care. He would tell people who asked, 'I'm here to make money for lots of people including myself.'

*****

One bright March morning, Harvey Williams put his head round the door of Arthur's room at GI, which he shared with two others. "Gentlemen," he addressed the two, "could Mr. Hawkins and I be alone, please?" Williams had a reputation for charm and politeness but Arthur was not fooled. He knew fake and oily when he heard and saw it. His guard was up. But he was polite. After all, Williams was a GI director.

"How are you today, Mr. Hawkins?"

"Pretty busy, Mr. Williams. How may I assist you?"

"Right. I'll get straight to it. As you may know, I have an interest in a Lloyd's syndicate. The syndicate is expanding, quite quickly in fact, and writing more and more business. It needs someone with your back office capabilities to help keep things in order. May I ask, how old are you now?"

"I'm eighteen."

"And what does GI pay you?"

"Three and a half thousand a year."

"And Luncheon Vouchers?" Williams smiled.

"Yes, that's right." Arthur had to laugh.

"Well, the syndicate can do better. I've spoken to people at GI. They know they would not be able to match better terms that would be offered by the syndicate and they wouldn't stand in your way if you wanted to leave."

"You're going too fast for me. Are you saying I can leave here if I want and won't be stopped? And when you say better, what does that mean exactly?"

"Yes to the first question. GI will understand if you decide to leave. As to your second question, come and meet Ronnie Bass, the leading underwriter. He's the syndicate boss. There aren't hierarchies at Syndicate 4455 like here at GI. Ronnie hires and fires. If he likes you and if you like his terms, that will be it. I'll not negotiate for him but when I say 'a better offer,' I mean substantially better. Come to Lloyd's tomorrow at four o'clock. Have a coffee with Ronnie. What have you got to lose?"

"I'll have to clear it here."

"I already have. Did you know Lloyd's started in a City coffee shop back in the eighteenth century?"

"No, I didn't." In fact, Arthur did know but he wasn't going to reveal anything to Williams.

"What goes around, comes around."

The next afternoon, Arthur took a ten minute walk to the Lloyd's building in Lime Street. At the entrance, a man wearing a black top hat with gold braid around the rim, a red cloak with a wide black collar and white cotton gloves stood guard. The man's black shoes were polished so that you would see your reflection in the toecaps. The front door was opened for Arthur.

At Reception he asked for Ronnie Bass. Within minutes, Harvey Williams appeared. He gave Arthur a brief tour of the ground floor, showing him the Lutine Bell and the huge underwriting room where 'boxes' were arrayed. Underwriters sat in their booths as brokers hovered, seeking to get business written. He led Arthur through the Ellipse and to a private conference room on the second floor. There was a large, dark stained oak table, around which there were twenty matching handsome Regency-style chairs with seats covered in dark blue material. There were matching brown leather armchairs too with a small coffee table. The room had rich lemon wallpaper. A silver service was already placed on the coffee table. The place just shouted 'wealth.'

Bass strode into the room. Arthur would recall his entrance as more of an explosion. He sat himself down in an armchair opposite Arthur and spoke to Williams.

"So, this is the clever bloke who's going to sort us out?"

"Steady on, Ronnie," said Williams. "You'll scare the shit out of him."

Ronnie extended his right arm towards Arthur who gave him a strong handshake.

"Ronnie Bass. Does shit come out of you that easy, Arthur?"

Arthur laughed. "Depends, Mr. Bass. If I've had a spicy curry, yup!"

Bass smiled back. "Listen, I speak as I find. Can't be buggered with airs and graces. No time. Harvey, thanks for your help. I'll take it from here."

Arthur's face remained unmoved. Inside, he wondered about the relationship between the two men. Williams had been swatted like a fly. He left the room without a word.

"You know what we do here, Arthur?"

"I think so. Lloyd's has rules about the amount of business a syndicate can write. The more members you get, the more business you can write. You have a few working members but most are non-working. They pick up their share of profits once a year and leave you alone."

"Not a bad summary. Lot more to it than that, though. Tell me, what happens if a claim is made against a policy?"

"One of two things. You pay it or you contest it. If you pay, the amount of the pay-out might depend as much on the business you do for the claimants as the validity of the claim.

"If you deny the claim, the 'utmost good faith' rules often protect you. If the claimant has told you anything that isn't totally correct, you can avoid the policy terms. I assume that if the insured does a lot of business, you negotiate a deal."

"How do you feel about that?"

"Business is business. But sometimes I don't like what General Insurance does about claims. That's between us, please. Anyway, it's not what I do for them. I'm just back office admin."

"I hear you're good at figures and interpreting them."

"Yes."

Bass liked the confidence in Arthur's reply. He produced some sheets of figures. "Here are our management accounts from six months ago. What do you think?"

"I need a bit of time."

"You have five minutes."

Ronnie rang a bell. A waiter appeared. "George, fresh coffee, please. Arthur, you want anything?"

"No thanks, I'm okay."

George re-appeared with a pot and poured Bass's coffee. Bass checked his watch.

"Well?"

"Nothing much to worry about on the surface. What I don't see is a reserve for contingent claims. You have a three year run-off liability but you seem to be distributing funds like no tomorrow. Also, salaries seem high but that may be the market rate for working members. I don't know the Lloyd's industry norm."

"Anything else?"

"Mr. Bass, give me a break. I need more time and I would want to ask some questions. For a start, I'd like to talk with your head of finance. This is the best I can do in five minutes."

"I see. Do you think you can run our back office?"

"You mean handle the numbers and paperwork."

"That's right. The bloke doing it wants out and I don't like him much. He doesn't seem to have the right admin skills the job requires."

"I reckon I can help you out but I'd need more than five minutes to make an assessment."

"Fair enough. Let's see if you like my terms: Three months trial. I'll start you at £10k a year. After three months, if you're still here and we like one another, you'll get a one year contract at £12 grand. After that, there will be a pay rise each year, probably 10%, and you will get a discretionary bonus in August."

"Discretionary?" Arthur had never heard of such a thing. "What does that mean?"

"It depends if you and the syndicate have done well. The bonus for you would probably be an additional two month's wages. If you don't perform or if the syndicate has a bad year, no bonus. I have total discretion."

"Okay." Inside, Arthur was doing jumping jacks. Twelve grand a year. A fortune.

"There are a few perks, Arthur. You get a car after the probation period is over and private health insurance. Other things will come your way. What do you think?"

"No wonder GI can't match your terms. Where would I work?"

"I don't believe in putting our back office miles away. I want you on hand. We have an office at Baltic House in Leadenhall Street. The back door of the building opens into Lloyd's. I'll visit quite a bit in the first weeks. I like to be hands on. Once I know you're coping, there will be less visits."

"I need a little time to think it over."

"Of course you do. But I don't have that luxury. Harvey gave you his card. Call him by the end of the day with a yes or no. Tata."

Bass left the room. No shaking of hands, no see you again, no pleasantries. Arthur needed time just to catch his breath. He stayed in the room for a while. 'Come on, Arthur,' he told himself, 'what is there to think about? If things don't work out with Bass, GI will take you back, so will any other insurer."

Arthur left Lloyds, dashed back to his office and told people he was leaving early. He biked over to Eddie's gym. There, Eddie helped him to look at the upside and downside of the Bass proposal. Arthur soon realised he would be nuts not to accept. He called Williams. The deal was done. He wrote his notice letter to GI there and then.

Eddie asked Arthur to stay a while. "Mary and I have something to talk over with you. Tea will be ready soon. We'll talk then."

That night, Mary told Arthur, "Eddie's not well. He needs heart surgery. We're selling up. We've seen a bungalow in Margate. It's lovely. It has views of the English Channel. I'm sorry but it will soon be time for you to find your own place. We're going to miss you so much." Mary started to cry. Eddie came in.

"She told you?"

"Yes. I'm so sorry, Eddie. When is the surgery?"

"Soon. Listen, Arthur, we'll only be in Margate. Easy to get there with that car you're getting. One other thing. It's time you made peace with your dad."

"Has he contacted you?"

"No, he's a stubborn old goat. Be the big man, make the first move."

"Let me think it over. Once I'm okay in the new job, I expect I'll do as you say."

*****

Arthur's boss at GI sighed when he read the notice letter. He called Arthur in.

"Can't say I'm surprised. You have a lot of talent. Just watch yourself at Lloyd's. They like to talk about being upright and honest over there but there are a lot of bad 'uns."

Arthur cleared his desk. He was told to leave immediately, setting him free to start at the Bass syndicate the following week. His final act was to see Mr. Buddell, whom he thanked for giving him a start.

"No hard feelings I hope, sir."

"Good luck, Hawkins."

That was it. No handshake, no words of encouragement. There's really no sentiment in business, Arthur decided.

*****

Three weeks later, Eddie had heart by-pass surgery. Two months afterwards, the gym was sold, the Margate bungalow bought and the Greys moved from the East End. Arthur rented a first floor flat in Islington. He visited the Greys every month but the relationship was never the same. Eddie had retired from life. No longer would Arthur have a mentor close to him.

Shortly after the Greys moved, Mary telephoned Arthur. "I'm sorry to give you bad news but we've heard your father is very poorly. He's at the London Hospital in Whitechapel. You should go to see him."

"I should have taken Eddie's advice, shouldn't I?"

"Maybe but we understand why you didn't. It sounds serious."

"Okay, I'll go tonight."

Arthur dreaded the visit. How could he make peace with his father, after all that had happened? At the hospital reception, he was directed to the ward where Harry was being treated. It took a few minutes to locate it. He asked the ward sister for Harry.

"Are you a relative?"

"Yes, I'm his son."

"Oh, he hasn't mentioned you. He's over there. Bed 6."

"What's the matter with him?"

"Cirrhosis. His liver is badly diseased. I'm sorry but it's just a matter of time. There's nothing we can do for him except keep him comfortable."

Arthur had grown layers of skin since his father kicked him out. He had no emotions or feelings for anyone these days except Mary and Eddie. He was unshaken by the news of his father. But as he neared bed 6, what he saw shocked him; a shrivelled, jaundiced old man, lying in bed in a foetal position.

"Dad?"

"Who's that?" Harry moved onto his back, grimaced and squinted at the man standing by the bed. "Who are you?"

"It's Arthur, dad. I've come to see you."

"Took your time. If you're looking for a job, it's too bloody late."

Harry coughed hard and mucus escaped. Arthur found some tissues and cleaned him up.

"I have a job. I work at Lloyd's, the insurers."

"If you'd stayed with me, you'd probably be on twenty quid a week by now. But you were a silly bastard. Too late now, Arfa'."

Arthur was incensed. He lost his temper. "A grand a year! Well, for your information, I earn twelve times that much. Who's the silly bastard now? You were never much of a father, were you?"

Harry glared at Arthur, breathing heavily in an effort to respond. He died there and then. Arthur was shocked. He called for a nurse. She checked Harry's pulse and shook her head.

"We had a row. Was that why he died?"

"No, love, he was very sick. We were expecting him to pass today or tomorrow."

Arthur did the right thing. He organised the funeral and a wake. Six people attended including the Greys. "What a waste of a life," was all Arthur could think.

Chapter Eleven.

"Connie, nice to see you. Tell me you've got something."

"If anything comes out of this, Martin, Tell Yer What gets the lion's share of the credit. I don't have the proof yet but Pearce may be someone called Arthur Hawkins."

Foster looked up. Connie had his attention. "Arthur Hawkins. Who's he? And what has TYW go to do with it?"

"TYW might have recognised Pearce as someone he knew from school thirty or more years ago. I've looked into it. TYW's school was in the East End but it has moved. I spoke with the headmaster. I told him a porky that *The Sentinel* was looking into a story about East End schools and how they were modernising in a multi-cultural society. I wanted to research the changes since the 1960s and 70s and asked to look at the old school records."

"You fluttered your baby blues, flashed a little neckline and he was putty before he could say data protection."

"Martin, you are a disgusting man. Your imagination belongs in a gutter. How on earth did you get the job editing this precious rag?"

"Good question. Bribery, capitulation, arse-licking, the usual qualities required from a journalist. Back to topic, please."

"I told the headmaster that my uncle, Arthur Hawkins, went to the old school. He had died and I knew so little about him. I said he had probably left school around 1972. I asked if I might see the records for that year. It took a while but the headmaster produced them and he let me take copies. There's not much there but there is an old photo of Arthur."

"Did you show it to TYW?"

"Yes. He recognised 'Arfa' immediately. The records say Arthur was at the school from 1969 for three years. Nothing academic worth mentioning, except a strong aptitude for arithmetic. No black marks. There's nothing about achievements but under out-of-school activities, there's a note about self-defence."

"Have you passed this to our investigators?"

"I got all this late yesterday. Up to you to decide what you do with it. Your investigators have had the Pearce brief for ages. I've got further in a few weeks than they have in all their time on it. You might want to ask yourself what you're paying them for."

"They have a retainer from us. But I agree with you. They've not put much heart into this one. Do you have any ideas, suggestions?"

"Occasionally, I need someone to do a bit of sleuthing. I've used a woman, Ermintrood Carter who has a habit of getting results. I suggest we get her involved."

"Who? What sort of a name is Ermintrude?"

"Not rude. It's ROOD. She calls herself Minnie."

"Precious. Tell me, what has she done for you?"

"Verifying kiss and tell stories, checking on dirt that comes my way."

Foster thought a while. "Okay, ask her to come in and talk to us. Normally I'd say fine but Max has his knickers in a knot about expenses after those fines. It's best I see her before we take her on."

The next day, a large black lady sat with Foster and Connie. After refreshments were offered, Foster started the conversation.

"Connie tells me you're a capable sleuth."

In a soft Caribbean accent, Minnie replied, "I pride myself on getting results for my clients."

"Tell me about your work. What's your bread and butter?"

"Divorce, mostly, tracing assets. Some probate work, tracing people. And the stuff that Connie and others in your trade send my way. Nothing unusual."

"What about your methods? How do you get results?"

"Mr. Foster, if I asked you to reveal a source, you'd show me the door. My methods are my methods."

Foster shrugged and shook his head. "Okay, Miss Carter, were we to take you on, what would your terms be?"

"It's Mrs. Carter but I prefer Minnie. My agency charges a thousand a day. If we work more than half a day, that's counted as a day. Of course, expenses are additional, as is our retainer. As for the job, Connie has given me a broad outline but I'll need more from her if we agree terms. My retainer will be five thousand. I gather Mr. Pearce's trail starts in America some twenty years ago. If this trail needs to be investigated in America, it won't be me who follows it. I have people there who do this for me. In that event, I will negotiate revised terms with you."

Foster was still shaking his head. "Minnie, we don't usually pay retainers and if we do, they are taken into account when paying fees. I'm not happy with the daily rate. It's high for your industry. I'd agree £750. And why would you not go to the States?"

"Look at my face, Mr. Foster. In a lot of places over there, they don't like blacks, especially black women asking questions. I have enough of these kind of problems here, thank you. I don't need any more."

Foster relaxed. "Sorry," he smiled, "That was insensitive of me. How's this? Let's guarantee you a week's work, that's five working days. I'll round up the figure to £4,000. If you need more time and if you can justify the request, I'll agree £750 a day. Plus reasonable expenses, of course."

"Mr. Foster, my fees are on the high side because I get results. I'll agree the guarantee of four grand for a week but it's a grand a day after that. And I want the £4,000 up front."

Foster paused for thought, eventually replying, "Okay. Connie, get a letter of engagement agreed and I'll sign it off. I want you to report to Connie every day you work for us, in writing please. I'll get the funds to you later this week but I want you to start now."

Minnie agreed and left *The Sentinel* building with her engagement letter. She wanted to get straight down to work. Business had been a little slow of late. She was relieved to be earning good money. Back at her office, she waited for Connie's detailed brief which was couriered over by early afternoon. After reading it twice, she began the thought process. If the East End school had no knowledge of Arthur Hawkins after he left, where next? Maybe find the gym he went to where he learned self-defence. Scud work. Minnie sighed. Time for a tour of the British Library. Something to do tomorrow.

*****

Minnie went on line to search The British Library catalogue. She discovered that what she needed to read was held at The British Newspaper Library in Colindale. She headed there and poured over business directories for the 1960s and 70s, as well as the 80s and 90s. There were numerous gyms in London's East End. She used her mobile to photo their names and addresses. She did a similar exercise for the ordinary directories which had a business section. Many of the names she had found were duplicated. The next day would make her foot sore but she had no choice. It was the job.

That evening after dinner, Minnie made tea and spoiled herself with three custard creams. She got out an A to Z map of London's East End. She used her photocopier to make enlarged copies of some pages. She found the address where Arthur had lived and used it as the centre point. Then she drew concentric circles and marked the positions of the gyms. She would go first to gyms within a half mile, then a mile, then the rest.

She went upstairs to her flat. Minnie was divorced and both her children had left home but she was comforted by the snoring of her cat. She smiled to herself as she quoted from the last words of Gone with the Wind. "Minnie, tomorrow is another day."

*****

The following morning, Minnie was up early. She had considered hiring a driver but worried that *The Sentinel* would regard this as a luxury. So, after devouring a healthy breakfast, she put on her walking shoes and made her way by underground and bus to the first gym on her list. She spoke with the owner. He told her the gym had opened in 1992 and he had bought it five years later. As the day passed, Minnie drew blanks from eight more venues. She made careful notes. *The Sentinel* wanted detailed reports. This is what they would get. That night, Minnie faxed Connie with the results of the day's work.

The next day, there were six more possibilities to check. Minnie planned her route, which she reckoned needed a walk of between six and seven miles. It would take most of the day. None of the gyms had opened before 1975. Minnie came home tired but not despondent. This was the way investigations went. She was used to it. That night, Connie was sent another fax detailing Minnie's efforts. Minnie mentioned that her retainer cheque had not arrived.

The third day would require an even longer walk for Minnie. By this time, her feet were very sore and she considered taking the day off. Had she owned a car, life might have been easier but parking would probably be a nightmare.

She worked out some bus routes and calculated that the likely ten mile walk could be reduced by more than half. The morning was another waste of time. Nothing of interest. Minnie stopped for lunch at a Kentucky Fried Chicken. She knew it was bad for her but she needed comfort food. That afternoon she stopped at a building in Jubilee Street. The ground floor was a convenience store. To its side was an entrance to upper floors. There was a neon sign advertising a snooker club. Minnie entered the store and bought a chocolate bar. When she paid, she asked the man at the till if he was the owner.

"I am," replied the man.

"Do you have a moment?" Minnie showed her PI identity. "I'd like to ask you a few questions."

The man shrugged. He wasn't busy. "Okay." He called for his wife to watch the till and took Minnie to a back room.

"Would you like a cuppa?" he asked. "You look like you could use one."

He made tea. "Now, how can I help you?"

"I believe the upstairs premises used to be a gym."

"Yes. When I bought this business, the gym was there."

"When did you buy it?"

"A long time ago. 1978. August."

"Did you remember the owner of the gym?"

"Yes, Eddie Grey. Can't say I knew him well. In those days, people kept themselves to themselves. We didn't say much to each other. I was busy buying a business and get it on its feet. I suppose he was busy too but he was always polite."

"I see the place is now a snooker club. Do you remember when it changed?"

"Not exactly. I guess it was around 1980 or 81."

"Do you know why Mr. Grey left?"

"He needed to sell up. He wasn't well. I think he had heart problems."

"Do you know where he went?"

The man took a beat. "It wasn't just Grey. He had a wife, her name was Mary. I recall they went to the Kent coast, Margate, some place like that. It was a long time ago."

Minnie realised that there was little to be gained from asking more questions. She thanked the man for tea and his time. She left her business card, asking him to get in touch if he thought of anything else. She went upstairs to the snooker club. The manager was new and had no knowledge of previous ownership. He was reluctant to give her a number for the owners. She left her card but was not hopeful of hearing anything.

Minnie felt the adrenalin leave her. She noticed a minicab office about fifty yards away and decided to indulge in a cab ride home. Why not? This wasn't an expense that would be challenged.

Once home, she had no energy to cook. She ordered an Indian take away. Lamb Jalfrezi, pilau rice and popadums. When the food arrived, she opened a beer. She ate and drank slowly as the efforts of the past three days washed over her. She watched the BBC ten o'clock news. The weather forecast for the next day was awful. She decided to spend the day in the office. Margate could wait till Monday. She sent the habitual fax to Connie. It showed progress and mentioned the forthcoming Margate trip, as well as the continued lack of a *Sentinel* cheque. She took herself to bed, weary to the bone. She slept like the proverbial log.

The next morning, Minnie dressed and went to her office, which was a walk down a flight of stairs. She smiled to herself when she saw rain chucking down. She had a mountain of paperwork to do but first order of business was coffee, second, open the post. She was disappointed to see that *The Sentinel* cheque had still not arrived. She picked up the phone and reached Connie.

"This is Minnie. I'm not happy."

Connie ignored the moan. She wasn't in the mood. "Minnie. I've read your faxes. When are you going to Margate?"

"When I'm paid my retainer. Mr. Foster promised it would be paid straight away."

Connie was surprised. "I'm sorry. I expect it's just an administrative error. I'll look into it and call you back."

"I won't do any more work until it's paid."

"Minnie, I am truly sorry. I will get to the bottom of this."

Connie checked with accounts. She was livid to find no one had asked for a cheque. So far as she was concerned, newspapers don't break their word. She walked through Foster's outer office, hearing: 'Mr. Foster is in a meeting.' She ignored the secretary's warning. Foster was talking with a group of editors. He looked up as she entered the room.

"Connie, I'm a bit busy here. Come back in an hour."

"No, Martin. This is can't wait."

"Ladies and gents, please keep going. I'll be back when I've poured oil on Ms. Strauss's troubled waters."

The secretary was shooed out of her office. A furious Foster turned on Connie.

"Who the hell do you think you are? You don't barge into editorial meetings. I don't care what the circumstances may be."

"Martin, listen to me very carefully. I am an experienced journalist with great contacts. I rely on those contacts to secure stories this paper wants to publish. If my people get wind that I'm not a woman of her word, my reputation will be severely damaged and stories will be lost. So please explain to me why Minnie Carter hasn't been paid her retainer. The money was promised days ago. And don't try the administration error bullshit. I've checked. No payment has been authorised."

Foster reddened. "Ah. Yes. I should have mentioned. Max blocked the payment. I meant to tell you. It slipped my mind."

Injunction

"It slipped your mind? That's bollocks. You didn't dare tell me, you coward. The fuck Max did this! I can't believe you didn't tell me."

"I'm still trying to persuade him to pay."

"That's another lie. You are a useless piece of trash, Martin. You're weak, a jobsworth. You are no editor. If you were, you'd stand up to a chief executive who has no right to interfere with things like this. You can have my resignation. I won't work for worms like you and Rankin."

"You need to calm down. Leave it for a day or so. I'll try to fix it. When Max gets into these moods. He's impossible to handle. You wouldn't know how much I protect you and your colleagues from him."

"So you're going to go back to Max? Today, tomorrow, next week, next year? You want Pearce exposed but you won't spend a measly four grand to get it done? Fine. I'm going over your head."

Connie flew out of the room and made her way to the building's penthouse, where Rankin installed himself when he wasn't prowling the *Sentinel* building. She was met at the lift by Rankin's secretary.

"He's not here, Miss Strauss."

"Bullshit." So saying, Connie pushed the secretary aside and stormed into Rankin's office. The room was enormous with panoramic views over the City. It was intended to intimidate anyone who entered. Rankin sat at a huge desk. He looked up, saw the secretary and Connie and glared at both of them.

"My orders were not to be disturbed. Do you not understand English? Miss Strauss, I'm very busy. Go away."

The secretary left immediately. Connie Strauss stood her ground.

"I don't give a hoot for your orders, Max. When you do things that damage me and my reputation, I will be seen and heard. Why did you block Minnie Carter's payment cheque? Why even concern yourself with something so miniscule?"

"Since you insist on interrupting me and my deliberations on the future of Media Universal, tell me, who is Minnie Carter? I have many, many things that cross my desk needing my attention, Miss Strauss. What are you talking about?"

"How can such an important world figure like you have such an awful memory? Minnie Carter is the PI we engaged to look into the Charlie Pearce business. She has a cast iron contract from this newspaper. She is a little person with bills to pay. You think you can just ignore her. What do you care about consequences for her, right? And, I might add, for me? That's what I'm talking about."

"Ah, I remember. Mrs. Carter's fees are too high. This paper's not made of money, you know. Nor am I. Martin should not have done the deal."

"I don't believe it. You wasted a fortune on the Pearce investigation but that's irrelevant to you. *The Sentinel* has a cast-iron, written agreement with Mrs. Carter. You have no right to change it. If what you've done was ever published, *The Sentinel's* reputation would be trashed and mine too.

"I tell you, Max, if your refusal to pay gets out, and it will get out, that *The Sentinel* welches on deals, it will put you and *The Sentinel* in the worst possible light. Nor will I have you screwing with my good name. I won't stand for it. Either you write a cheque right now or you can have my resignation, effective immediately. And I will take this story about the way *The Sentinel* does business to my next employer."

"You can't do that. You have a contract with the paper and a duty of confidentiality."

"Then sue me. Minnie has a contract with *The Sentinel*. You ignored that. Why the hell did you bother with such a tiny thing? Are you bored? Don't you have enough to do, running the world?"

Max stood. He walked over to the window, looking at the view. He realised he had been hasty and made a mistake. He needed to bring the temperature down.

"Miss Strauss, you've never run a business, have you? Sometimes it's important to look at micro as well as the macro. This is why the shareholders of MU are happy. They know I look after the whole business. I like working the micro when I need to relax. Minnie's deal came to my notice. I didn't like it. End of. Now, do you really want to go to war with me? If you do, I'll bury you in legal stuff. Your life will rapidly become uncomfortable. This is not what I want, not for you or for me."

"I don't respond to threats, Max. My new employers will back me. They'll love exposing you as a bully and as a man who doesn't keep his word, one who cheats people."

Rankin went silent for thirty seconds. He was hurt by the last remark. But experience told him to placate the woman in front of him.

"Let's you and I take a pause. I don't want to lose you. I felt Mrs. Carter was being overpaid. I stopped her money. I meant to tell Martin to renegotiate. I apologise."

"Why on earth would you do this? You could not spend all the money you have if you lived to a thousand and bought a new Rolls Royce every week. Minnie Carter is worth every penny Martin agreed to pay her. Look at what she has achieved already. She has found where Hawkins lived, the gym he attended and where the owner moved when he retired. Three days of her time did all that. What did your investigators find? Nada! And what did that cost you and MU?"

Rankin breathed heavily. "You make a valid point."

"Stop messing around. Call accounts now, have them write her cheque and bring it here to you. I'll watch you sign it. Then give it to me. I'll make sure Minnie gets it today. If you do this, I'll stay. If you don't, I'll walk."

Rankin nodded. One of his better qualities was to know when to reverse a bad decision. He picked up his phone and spoke to his secretary. Four minutes later, a cheque appeared. Max signed it and gave it to Connie.

"Make sure you get a receipt."

"One more thing. Martin Foster is not good for this newspaper. He won't stand up to you when he needs to."

Max snorted. He knew Connie was right but she didn't appreciate Foster's many qualities. Why bother to explain. She was not editor material, not yet. But re-appraising the woman, Max found himself attracted to her.

"Wait on. Let's talk a minute. Where do your ambitions lie in this business?"

"Do what I'm doing. I'm happy, sort of, but not if your paper is going to pull stunts like this."

"That's been resolved. You're a good journalist, Connie. And I admire the way you stood up to me. I'm busy right now. Come back this evening. We'll have drinks and dinner and talk about newspapers."

Connie wanted to reply, 'fuck off, you lecher. Your reputation precedes you.' Instead, she said, "that's kind of you but I have a date tonight. Another time maybe."

Connie left Rankin's presence as soon as she could. Outside, she breathed a sigh of relief. No way was that bastard going to get her anywhere near his bedroom. She took a cab to Minnie's Islington address. Walking into the office, she saw Minnie behind a pile of files and papers. "Hi, Minnie, got something for you."

Minnie took the envelope. "Is this what I hope it is?"

"It surely is. Sorry you had the hassle. Admin cock up. In future, send your invoices to me. I'll make sure they're dealt with promptly. So, how's life?"

They chatted for a while over coffee. "I have to take a cab back to the office. Shall I drop you at the bank?"

"And maybe wait for me and bring me back. It's raining cats and dogs out there."

Chapter Twelve.

By Monday morning, the rain had stopped. Minnie took the tube to Kings Cross, walked to St. Pancras and got on a train to Margate. She headed for the Town Hall and Registry Office. She searched the Electoral Roll and found Mary's name but not Eddie's. Mary was listed as living at a nursing home. Minnie wrote the address down and headed for Births, Marriages and Deaths. After a little more than an hour she found Eddie Grey had died in 2001.

Minnie took a cab to the nursing home. It was a large Edwardian building overlooking the English Channel. At reception, Minnie picked up a brochure. There were rooms for fifty residents. It was not cheap. Even if Mary was on the lowest tariff, she'd be paying £400 a week. When the receptionist was free, Minnie asked to see Mary Grey.

"Are you a relative?"

"No, I'm not," Minnie smiled.

"A friend?"

"No, I am a Private Investigator. Here is my identity."

"I see. Is there a problem concerning Mrs. Grey?"

"No, no, nothing like that. I just want to ask her about the old days and a person she might have known."

"Let me call Matron."

Minnie expected to see a sixty-something woman, dressed in a starched nurse's uniform. To her surprise, Matron looked to be in her early forties, wearing a smart, black trouser suit and white polo neck top. Putting her right hand forward, she said, "I'm Theresa March, the matron. How can I help you?"

Minnie gave a brief resume. Ms. March nodded. "Let me talk to Mrs. Grey. If she's willing to see you, I won't object but I'll want to sit in. I don't want Mary agitated or upset in any way. She is a frail, elderly lady."

A few minutes later, Minnie was taken to a small lounge which overlooked a rose garden with the sea beyond. When Mary saw Minnie, she said, "good morning, dear. You want to know about the old days? My memory is not that good but let's try."

"Mrs. Grey, I want to ask you about someone I think you knew back in the 1960s and 70s."

"Who's that, dear?"

"Arthur Hawkins. Is the name familiar to you?"

"Arthur Hawkins? Arthur Hawkins?" Mary frowned and then a big smile crossed on her face. "Arty. Oh, he was a love. His father chucked him out when he was just a boy. He came to live with my Eddie and me. We never had kids. He was like a son to us. He was lovely"

"What do you remember about Arty?"

"Let me think. Well, he came to Eddie's gym when he was ten or eleven. Eddie trained him, knocked him into shape so to speak. He was always a polite boy. When he came to live with us after his father threw him out, he always helped me around the house, kept his room tidy, and did his own washing, that sort of thing. We wanted him to stay on at school but he said he had to go to work, earn his keep."

"Do you remember what job he did?"

"Hmm. I think I do. My Eddie knew somebody at an insurance company. Arty went for an interview and got the job."

"Do you remember which insurance company?"

"No, dear." Mary shook her head. "It was a big one in the City. That's all I know."

"How long did Arthur stay with you?"

"Till he was seventeen or eighteen, I think. Eddie became unwell and decided he had to sell the gym. We owned the whole property so he got a lot of money for it. We moved down here and loved it. I remember Arty coming to visit a few times but I suppose he got busy with his life and we lost touch. Eddie died a few years ago. I sold our bungalow and came here. They are so good to me." She reached out to Theresa and touched her hand.

Minnie's heart melted. This lovely elderly lady was ending her days in comfort, with capable and kind people taking care of her. She made a silent promise. 'If I find Arthur Hawkins, I'll do my best to get him to visit.'

She took Mary's hand and leant over, kissing the old lady on her forehead. "Mrs. Grey, thank you so much. You've been very helpful."

Ms. March escorted Minnie out. Minnie gave Miss March her card. "Should Mrs. Grey remember anything else, please would you call me?"

"She liked you. Come back if you want. But make it soon. We don't think she has long."

On the train ride back to St. Pancras, Minnie thought over the next moves. 'How many big insurance companies are there? What is big? How to access employee records? The Data Protection Act might get in the way? I need to talk to Connie, see if she can help.'

******

Contacts in the newspaper world are multifaceted and symbiotic. Newspapers need politicians for information as much as politicians need newspapers to get their stories out.
Two days after Connie spoke with him, Martin Foster had dinner with Gerry Rhodes, M.P., an old friend and now junior Treasury minister.

"Gerry, how about a brandy or a port?"

"Martin, I'll pass. It has been a lovely dinner but I'm due back at the House for a vote. Now, tell me what you really want?"

"Very well. In the 60s or 70s, a man called Arthur Hawkins went to work for a large City insurance company. That's all the facts I have except he seems to have grown up in the East End. We want to know what became of him. His tax records will say where he worked, what he did and when he fell off the radar."

"I can't do that! The Data Protection Act expressly forbids this kind of thing. If it came out, I'd get prosecuted, as you well know. I'd get tossed out of government and Parliament. I'm shocked you'd ask."

"I think you can do this for me, Gerry. My newspaper hasn't published stories about you but it could. Now, remind me, what was the name of the company you were involved with? Devon Financial Investments, wasn't it? In administration I believe and scapegoats being sought."

"I was a shareholder. I had nothing to do with running the company."

"Of course you didn't, Gerry. But, how should I put it, your good lady is in the sticky stuff up to her pretty neck. I could publish the story tomorrow. That would finish her off and I doubt you'd survive. So what's it going to be?"

Rhodes shook his head slowly. "I'll see what can be done. You are vermin. If I can do you a bad turn, I will. Drink your brandy, Martin. I hope it bloody chokes you."

*****

Martin Foster called Connie Strauss into his office. Over the past days, their relationship had deteriorated. It was now arctic.

"I think it's time we buried the hatchet, Connie. I accept I should have done better over that payment. Anyway, here's what we've got. A friend of mine gave us a little help. This information comes from the Inland Revenue. It's golden. Just don't ask how I got it."

Connie's journalistic instincts took over. Her anger at Foster subsided as she read the report. It confirmed that Arthur Hawkins had been employed for three years at The General Insurance Company. Then he moved to a syndicate at Lloyd's of London. In the 1980s, Hawkins changed his name by Deed Poll to Henry Aitken. By the mid-1980s, he was earning very large amounts. The report disclosed nothing untoward but in 1986, Hawkins/Aitken dropped off the radar. Simply, he disappeared. The report mentioned that the syndicate Hawkins/Aitken worked for was ensnared in financial scandals and prosecutions.

"I wonder why Hawkins change his name to Aitken," Connie asked. "Is Aitken in fact Pearce? If so, what evidence is there to support such an allegation? Why did Hawkins/Aitken drop off the radar? Maybe he did something at Lloyd's that he shouldn't have done. Weren't there some financial scandals about twenty years ago with hundreds of people going bankrupt? More research for me to do. Who do you know at Lloyd's who I can talk to about the 1980s? It's quite a while back."

"It was actually twenty six years ago. How old were you then?"

"Mind your own business."

"Okay." Martin failed to suppress a grin. "You and Minnie Carter have done great work. Keep going. I'll look into the Lloyd's thing for you."

"I'll talk to Minnie. I'm not sure she still wants our business."

"Don't tell me silver-tongued Strauss has lost her touch. Get Minnie back on board. I'll get another cheque for you to take with you."

Foster called accounts and had a cheque brought to him for £3,000. He signed it and gave it to Connie. "This gets us a few more days of Minnie's time. Get your skates on. The hearing of the Pearce injunction case is coming up."

Armed with the new information and the cheque, Connie called Minnie. They met that day. Using *The Sentinel* contacts at the Home Office, Connie discovered that a Henry Aitken had taken a British Airways flight to Miami in April, 1986 and had taken Air Canada to Vancouver in October the same year. After that, there was no trace of Aitken. According to the American investigators, a man named Charles Pearce had arrived in Minneapolis, Minnesota in October, 1987. If these men were one and the same, what had Hawkins/Aitken/Pearce done for the intervening eighteen months?

Minnie spoke to her American contacts. They got a little further with Pearce's background. They reported that somebody fitting Pearce's age and vague description had grown up in Culver City, Los Angeles. His life was unremarkable. He graduated from UCLA and got a job in advertising. When his parents died, he inherited a large sum. That was all so far. There was no apparent link between Hawkins/Aitken and Pearce.

The Home Office supplied copies of the passport photographs of both Hawkins and Aitken. They looked alike. No surprise there. It took a meeting between Max Rankin and the Canadian ambassador to confirm there was no record of Charles Pearce for the flight to Vancouver. The link between Aitken and Pearce remained elusive.

Max and the American ambassador were old friends. A copy of Pearce's American passport was made available. The photograph showed no close likeness between Aitken and Pearce. The latter's nose was straight not bulbous, the chin much less protruded, the ears were flat and the eyes seemed wider.

"Maybe he had plastic surgery?" suggested Minnie when she looked at the pictures.

"Maybe," Connie replied, "but how do we find this out? Where would he have had the surgery? There are plastic surgeons all over Canada and the United States. And they'll be bound by confidentiality"

Later, Minnie sat in her office. The phone rang. "Is that Mrs. Carter?"

"Yes, how may I help?"

"It's Theresa March from the Margate Nursing Home. You asked me to call if Mary remembered anything. I don't know how important this is but Mary told me something this morning. She remembered that one night when Arthur was in his teens, he was arrested by the police. Her husband went to the Bishopsgate Police Station to sort it out."

"Did she say anything else?"

"No. This happens with old people. Memory cannot be fathomed. Anyway, I hope this is helpful."

Minnie called the Bishopsgate nick. She was on first name terms with a desk sergeant. It took a week and a few pints but she was able to deliver a set of Arthur Hawkins' fingerprints to Connie.

Chapter Thirteen.

On his first day at Syndicate 4455, Arthur arrived at the Baltic House office at ten minutes to eight. To his surprise, several people were already working. A woman in her early twenties came over to him.

"May I help you?"

"I'm Arthur Hawkins."

"Oh, you're the new boss. I'm Avril. Shall I show you round, not that there's a lot to see? We start early to catch up with the stuff left over from the day before. We've got seven clerks and three secretaries doing accounts, plus you, of course. The ten of us occupy this big room. You have that office by the window."

"And this is just the accounting staff."

"Yes, policies, claims and investments are down the corridor."

"How much business is written in a day?"

"Could be anything between a hundred and two hundred policies and lines. Some are repeats but everything has to be processed."

"Don't you use computers? I can't see any."

"We have word processors to produce policies but otherwise we aren't really ready for the 1970s. To be honest, it's a bit Victorian."

"Thank you, Avril. When all the staff are in, I want you to gather them together. Have you got any sticky labels?" Avril nodded. "Have people's put their first names on them. I want one for me. It's Arthur."

Fifteen minutes later, Avril knocked on his door. "We're ready." She handed him a label which he stuck on his shirt.

Arthur came out, looked at his staff and smiled. "Good morning. My name is Arthur Hawkins. Call me Arthur. I'm the new chief in this room. Now, I've not worked before at Lloyd's so I have plenty to learn. But I have experience working at General Insurance and I know how a tariff company processes policies and claims and deals with its accounts. I also know numbers. I know there are things to learn but I want you to help me find them out. I'll spend today talking with each of you. I want to know what you do, what you think is expected from you and what you expect from me. I want this to be a good experience for all of us."

Arthur went round the room, shaking hands. After a ten minute chat, one by one, the accounts staff came to his office to talk with him. Quickly, he realised he was required to cope with a 20th century accounts department using 19th century methods. If computers were introduced, their cost would be covered in less than a year by making a secretary and two or three clerks redundant but he would need to engage an experienced computer processor. He hadn't anticipated finding this on his first morning. He asked himself, 'do other syndicates run in this antiquated way?'

At lunchtime, Arthur headed into Lloyd's as ordered by Ronnie Bass. He went to the syndicate box, a booth on the Lloyd's trading floor where Bass and his people worked. He waited till Bass spotted him. Bass told him, "I'm off for a pint and a bite. Join me."

At Old Tom's Bar in Leadenhall Market, they ordered pints and sandwiches and found a table. "Well, Arthur, how's your first morning?"

"Exciting and worrying, Mr. Bass. How has the syndicate survived with its antiquated accounting methods? Haven't you had advice from accountants that you are woefully out of date? For me, it will mean hours and hours of extra work if things are left like this. If you invest in a computer system, you'll save money in the medium and long run and you'll have much more accurate information a lot quicker."

Bass took a long swig at his pint but he paid attention. "Call me Ronnie. Now tell me what I should know in my language."

Arthur explained what he thought needed to be changed and how it would benefit the syndicate.

"What will it cost me?

"I'll work up some figures for you. I don't want to guess."

"How long to get it working?"

"I will have to make sure the computer programmes you buy will do the job you want. You'll need consultants and the syndicate auditors will need to sign the processes off. All syndicate transactions less than three years old will have to be put on the computer's database, as well as details of settled or outstanding claims. Once this is done, you'll have what you need for the accounting history. Then you can start processing existing work. We can hire in people on three month contracts to do the input work, as well as train the people you keep."

"Alright. Let's assume it gets done. When it's up and running, what does this get me?"

"Up to date, speedy information on premiums, gross and net profits, accurate and up-to-date cash positions, outstanding and settled claims, brokerage paid and any other financial and management accounting information you want to help you manage the business. The computer can be programmed to provide pie charts and graphs showing percentages and all sorts. It can also provide detailed information of exposure to particular risks. Basically, you can get from a computer all the information you want, provided it's programmed correctly."

Their sandwiches arrived. "Good timing, Arthur. You mention pies and, hey presto, the food appears!" They ate and drank in silence for a while. Bass bought a second pint for himself, a half for Arthur.

"Right. Get this computer stuff costed for me and tell me who stays and who goes. I need a price from consultants, as well as a budget for the people we need to get the computer up and running. I'll make up my mind when I see the whole picture."

Arthur was not used to decisions being made over a pint at lunchtime. So different from General Insurance. Bass resumed the conversation. "I started at Lloyd's just after the war. Things were so different then. All records were kept by hand. I can remember the quill pens, too."

Arthur laughed. "Quill pens. Ronnie, you're pulling the proverbial. But how did Lloyd's work?"

"Lots of clerks in back offices writing, typing and printing. Mind you, you wouldn't have a pie and a pint for lunch. The underwriters took a good two hours off and enjoyed three courses and a bottle or two of vino. Okay, let's go."

*****

It took a while for Arthur to get the costings and plans worked out and approved by accountants. It took Ronnie Bass less than an hour to look at the proposals and approve them. Implementation of the changes was swift. Arthur was fully occupied and it wasn't until ten months into the job that he had an opportunity to properly review current business.

Arthur decided to look at premium income himself to see how well the new system was integrated. He found an anomaly and on closer investigation, he was shocked. He discovered that the benefit of some policies was being transferred from Syndicate 4455 to another syndicate. When Arthur researched the other syndicate, he found it was owned by Ronnie Bass, Harvey Williams and two other working members of Syndicate 4455.

In other words, the premiums paid to Syndicate 4455 on particular policies, after paying brokerage, were moved on to a baby syndicate which had many fewer beneficiaries. It followed that the working names of Syndicate 4455 who were not in the baby syndicate, as well as all the non-working names of Syndicate 4455, were being cheated of benefits. Bass and his chums were creaming off premiums from profitable policies.

Arthur kept digging and the discoveries got even worse. He found that if a risk arose under a policy which had been transferred to the baby syndicate, the policy and the liability was transferred back to Syndicate 4455. Premiums were transferred back as well. It was as if the original transaction had never existed. Arthur checked with the claims department and found that all policies transferred back to 4455 were indeed the subject of claims. The claims aggregate liability was huge, in the hundreds of thousands of pounds. This was fraud, simple, effective and plain wrong.

Instead of telling Bass straight away, Arthur decided to put the documentary evidence together. He needed to consider his next moves very carefully. There were important questions to answer. Were Bass and the others actually committing criminal offences? Checking into the criminality aspect, Arthur found there was no clear legal guidance about fraud. He read Lloyd's rules and to his surprise, the use of baby syndicates was not outlawed. But was the way Bass and his friends worked the scam actually legal? Certainly it was morally wrong but Arthur knew he was no lawyer and could not be certain.

Arthur had nowhere to go to get advice. He was on his own. If he blew the whistle to the Lloyd's Committee, would they protect their own? Maybe some of them indulged in similar practices too? Would the police be interested and listen to a nineteen year old? He'd probably be sent packing. He knew no lawyers. Anyway, once he told Bass what he uncovered, Bass would find a way to clean up the accounts before any investigation was mounted. Arthur's dilemma boiled down to this: should he just stay quiet or face down Ronnie Bass?

When Arthur assessed his options, he reckoned that if he could discover precisely what was going on, he could also find a way to disguise it. How had the auditors missed what was going on? The scheme was in operation well before his employment began. Was someone at the auditors being bought off? One thing was certain, Arthur knew staying quiet wasn't an option.

After two weeks, Arthur collected his evidence; accounts records, copy policies, audit trails and the like. He telephoned the box. In moments, a gruff Ronnie came on the line.

"What do you want? I'm busy."

"It's important. I need to see you as soon as you're available."

"Sounds serious?"

"Enough for me to call you and ask to see you urgently."

"It'll have to wait till business is closed here. I'll see you in the Board Room at 4.30."

Arthur waited the hours, getting more and more nervous. The Board Room was on the fifth floor of Baltic House. Shortly before 4.30, Arthur made his way there with his evidence. He was fortified by the knowledge that he had incontrovertible proof of the baby syndicate scam. He had decided what he would say to Bass. He was resigned to the possibility that all could go wrong, in which event he'd be out of a job that night.

He knocked on the Board Room door. A voice called "enter." He opened the door and saw not only Ronnie Bass but Harvey Williams. Quickly, he adjusted his thinking. It was good Williams was there. Arthur had a game to play and Williams would be witness to it.

"So, what's so bloody urgent? You should know not to bother me when we're writing business." Bass was grumpy. It would not make the next few minutes any easier.

"I've found something. I'd like you to look at these papers. Had I known Mr. Williams was coming, I'd have brought an extra set for him."

Bass read the information; policy numbers, premiums, brief risk description. Some had been circled in red, others in blue.

"Alright, clever clogs, what am I looking at?"

"The items circled in blue are policies and premiums transferred to another syndicate owned by you, Mr. Williams and two other working members. I call it a baby or side syndicate. The items circled in red are those policies transferred back from the baby syndicate to 4455 after a claim arose."

"And?"

"The policies ringed in blue were all low risk. Although 4455 wrote the business, it enjoys no benefits from them. The premiums were passed to the baby syndicate. I found this within days of starting to analyse current business. I then looked at previous years. You'll see my report goes back two years. I have not yet looked back to beyond those two years. Haven't your auditors raised the anomaly with you? I don't understand how they missed it. I'm still new to Lloyd's. This may be standard practice here but it looks unorthodox. You needed to know what I discovered."

Bass looked at Williams. "Bloody hell, how did he find this? No one else has."

Williams made a hand gesture to Bass as if to say, 'Stay calm, I'll handle this.'

"Arthur," Williams started, "Lloyd's has a long tradition of helping the hard working members who have much to lose. You do know baby syndicates are not outside Lloyd's rules."

'Nor are they within the rules,' Arthur thought. 'They are just not mentioned.' He stayed silent. He waited to hear what Williams would come up with next.

"As for the transferring back of some policies, this is just re-insurance. You know, transferring some of the risk to re-insurance underwriters."

Arthur remained silent but in his mind he wanted to say, 'No it isn't. It's not re-insurance. It's not like laying off a bet. It's making 4455 liable for a risk which ought to belong to and paid by others.'

Ronnie Bass lost patience. "Alright Hawkins, you think you have me by the balls? Are you blackmailing me? What do you want?"

"I came here to tell you about what I found in your business accounts. If I can spot it, others will too unless you disguise it better. I thought it was sufficiently serious for me to report it to you straight away."

"Yes, yes, you're a boy scout. Stop fucking around. What do you want?"

Arthur felt the anger growing within him. "Ronnie, I've found a substantial and serious anomaly that you need to be aware of, although it seems you and Mr. Williams already knew. I don't *want* anything. And I resent your implication. I am just trying to do my job. If you don't want me to do my job, you can have my resignation."

For good measure, Arthur glared at Bass. Arthur was gambling. Would Bass factor in the need to keep Arthur quiet? Or would Bass and Williams fire him on the spot and threaten him, should he talk to people on the outside. Arthur stood up and walked towards the door.

"Where do you think you're going?" Bass growled. "I've had a difficult day. Things got heated. Now sit down. Let's have a drink." Williams went to the amply stocked bar and poured a whisky for Bass.

"You?" Bass said, pointing to Arthur.

"Just a glass of water, thanks."

"Have a proper drink, boy!" Bass was still worked up.

"Okay. Vodka and tonic. Lots of ice."

Seated around the table with drinks, Bass told Williams he would take it from here. Williams left without a fuss. Bass stared at Arthur.

"You've had quite a day. Shocked, were you?"

"I'm just trying to work out in my mind what this is all about."

"Didn't think much of that re-insurance point Harvey made, did you? I saw you wince. Don't play poker with me, boy, not till you've properly mastered the art. Call that a poker face?"

"Re-insurance is just a fancy name for 'laying off.' When I was a kid, I was a bookie's runner. I know stuff."

"Tell me more."

"In those days, betting shops and bookmaking were still illegal. I was nine when I started working for Big Sam. He was a well-known 'good sport' where I lived. That's what they called bookies in those days. When betting became legal, he said he was too old to open a shop. My guess was he had a police record and wouldn't get a licence.

"Anyway, he used kids like me because the police were unlikely to stop us. I got caught once by the cops but I was prepared. I had hidden pockets in my trousers to keep the betting slips and money. When I was searched, all the police found was a shopping list and money for groceries. They let me go with a clip around the ear.

"Sam taught me the betting business. I was good at numbers. I could work out the odds and what was due. I became his settler when his eyesight was failing. He died when I was eleven. End of my bookmaking career."

Bass laughed. "Do you think what we do here is gambling?"

"Not exactly but there are similarities."

"You win a lot more than you lose at Lloyd's. Now what do you want from me?"

"Ronnie, I'll say it again. I don't want anything. I'm just doing my job."

"That's a load of effing nonsense. Of course you want something. Everybody wants something. One thing is for sure. You're too good for the back office but I'd need a football team to replace you. I am going to think this through, have a word or two with colleagues and we'll talk on Monday. Meet me here at 8.30."

Arthur spent the weekend worrying. He presented himself on Monday morning, bang on time. Bass was on his own.

"Morning, Arthur. Want some breakfast?"

"Wouldn't say no."

"Scrambled eggs and bacon?"

The two men went to the dining room and chatted football while waiting for breakfast. Arthur's heart was beating fast but he wasn't going to show any nervousness to Bass. When the food arrived, they tucked in. Bass polished his off in three minutes and decided they would have coffee back in the Board Room.

Bass drank his cup in three gulps. "Arthur, you're a very bright young man. You are ideal for this business. You're smart with numbers, you know when to keep your mouth shut and I can teach you how to be a great poker player."

Arthur gave Bass a quizzical look.

"Don't try to kid me. I know people. That was one heck of a bluff on Friday. You're ideal material for an underwriter."

"I'd like the chance."

"I'm giving you a one-off opportunity to change your life. I'll lay it out for you. When I finish talking I'll give you ten minutes for a yes in principle. If it's no, you're fired. You'll get a leaving present in exchange for your silence."

"And if it's yes?"

"We're off to the races. Right. Let's start. What are you wearing?"

"Clothes?"

"Very funny. Rags more like. I'm sending you to Savile Row, Jermyn Street and St James' to get you properly outfitted. You can't be an underwriter in my syndicate looking like a scruff. You can charge what you buy to my account. Don't take the piss and spend too much. You have a ten grand budget. Get five suits, an overcoat, a raincoat, fifteen shirts and silk ties, smart cufflinks, four pairs of shoes and boots, ten pairs of silk socks and other paraphenalia. You can buy your own underwear. If you go over ten grand, you pay the balance.

"Next, you need a proper haircut. I'll send you to my barber at The Ritz. Looks are important in this business. If you look like a million dollars, people will think you have a million dollars. Shallow? Bloody right, but it works.

"Next, with respect, 'Arfa 'Awkins is not a good business name. I gather you have no brothers and sisters, no relations and your parents have died. You're a loner.

"I want you to change your name. It's perfectly legal. The syndicate's lawyers will register a Deed Poll and deal with the legalities. How about Henry Aitken for a name? Aristocratic sounding. We'll arrange new documents for you: passport, driving licence, that sort of thing."

Arthur nodded, slightly in shock. "What if anyone here asks about my new name?"

"Tell them to mind their own business or that you were adopted a while back and have decided to change your name back to what it was. You'll need to find your own replacement in accounts. You can promote in-house if you want but this is your problem. Just run any decision past me first.

"Now, most important, you'll join my syndicate and be with me in the box, morning and afternoon. It will take a year or more to get you up to speed. Your evenings won't be yours. You will go to night school to learn about insurance law and practice. The course is a year of solid work with exams at the end. Don't fail. I'll expect good reports. Remind me, how old are you?"

"I've just turned nineteen."

"Well the rest of this year and most of the next will be all work and no play, pretty well. But you'll find there are perks working for 4455. I suppose you'll want to be paid?"

"That would help." Arthur laughed, then held his breath. How big an investment was Bass making?

"I'll start you off at forty grand a year." Arthur kept a straight face. "That will go up after a year. In three years' time, you should be on a ton."

"A ton?"

"Hundred grand. You make big money in this business."

"I see. What's in this for you?"

"If you're earning a hundred grand, you'll be making half a million for me. I haven't finished. We'll put the money up to make you a working member of Lloyd's. You'll be able to write three tons of business and in a good year you'll get a twenty five or thirty thousand pound dividend.

"You'll have to pay tax, of course. You'll also have to go before the Lloyd's Members' Committee who will read the riot act to you about behaviour and the dangers of investing at Lloyd's. They will tell you all the risks you're taking on because you will have to accept an unlimited liability. Don't worry. It's a formality and I'll take you through stop-loss policies."

"What do you want from me?"

"You will sign an agreement which will tie you to my syndicate for seven years. It will have a confidentiality clause. If you leave and keep your mouth shut, no problem. If you leave and talk about things you shouldn't, you'll have big problems. Here is the contract. Have a lawyer look at it if you want but I won't accept any changes. I will expect you to work, work, work. And the work will be really intense. You don't make money sitting on your arse. There will be travel involved too. But we'll talk more about the details if you agree the deal."

Arthur took the document. He scanned it and saw the terms Ronnie mentioned, except the new clothes and change of identity. The document named him as Henry Aitken.

"Where do I sign?"

"Not yet. We have to get your Change of Name done first. This won't take long. All I need is a yes or no in principle. One last thing. I'm a Spurs fan through and through. I don't care who you support so long as it's not fucking Arsenal."

"You know I'm a Hammer."

"Poor you."

"Ronnie, I don't need time to think. Yes. I accept your offer."

A handshake worked for them both. Ronnie Bass was good as his word. Within two weeks, Henry Aitken looked the picture of elegance. A new hair style and smart clothes turned him into a James Bond figure, albeit with Boris Karloff looks, but you can't have everything. His Deed Poll was registered and new identity documents arrived. He moved from his dingy rented Islington flat to a one bedroom apartment with a view of Hampstead Heath, bought with a mortgage arranged by Harvey Williams.

The new Arthur, now called Henry by everyone, worked like the proverbial Trojan. He quickly promoted from within, letting him move from accounts. In the Lloyd's box, he was amazed by the never-ending footfall of brokers requiring Ronnie's attention. Six other underwriters did the business but it was Ronnie who made the final decision to put his name to a line and the amount of risk 4455 would accept. There was little research. Reliance was placed on brokers' honesty and the fall-back position of 'utmost good faith' which protected underwriters if incorrect information was given by a broker.

Henry's work included supervising the baby syndicate business and making it opaque. He didn't object. It was the price to pay for the advantages he'd been given. Was he bothered by conscience? 'If I'm worried about morality, I'll see a priest,' Henry told himself.

Where Henry was really useful to 4455 was in handling re-insurance. Ronnie passed this aspect over, a little at a time. When an insurer accepted a risk, he could 'sell' part of it to a re-insurer. If the risk arose, the insurer would look to the re-insurer to pay its portion of the claim.

Henry's mathematical skills, coupled with street smarts and the lessons learned years before with Big Sam, brought good results. Soon, 4455 was paying lower re-insurance premiums for laying off greater percentages of risk.

Ronnie could not understand how Henry got away with his deals. When he asked questions, Henry would grin at him and touch his nose with a forefinger. Soon enough, Ronnie stopped asking. In truth, Henry was a really good negotiator. Recognising how Henry was adding to the bottom line, Ronnie upped his annual salary to sixty thousand.

At night, the college course was interesting but tiring. Henry made sure to change into casual clothes before he left the office. He did not want to be seen as a City gent. He liked being just one of many students. He started to make friends and there were a few girls with whom he occasionally spent the evening and breakfast. He found the advice given to him all those years ago by Eddie Grey was right. 'Looks don't matter that much if you're a man. It's how you treat women that's important.'

Henry had plenty of cash. He got to like having a good night out every now and again but leisure time was precious. As Ronnie had told him, life was work, work, work. The only aspect of his life which gave Henry concern was the presence of Harvey Williams. He could not put his finger on exactly why Williams was a worry but the man was as greasy as they come. He was like a worm, wriggling his way into all aspects of 4455's business. He seemed to do little work but he was paid big money. Henry was sufficiently smart to keep his thoughts to himself.

***

Henry had been working in the 4455 box for five months when Bass told him, "Lunch. I want to get out of here. Ever been to Sweetings?" Henry shook his head. "It's a City institution. Time you went. You can't book and you rub shoulders with all sorts. Drop what you're doing. Let's go."

The walk took fifteen minutes. Bass set a good pace for a man of his age. Fortunately, Henry had kept to his exercise regime, although the hour runs had been cut to thirty minutes. At Sweetings, they found a cramped corner table.

"I'm hungry," Ronnie announced to the waiter. "I'll have the dressed crab and Dover sole with bubble and squeak. What about you, Henry?"

"Give us a chance. I don't know the menu." Half a minute later, Henry ordered smoked eel, haddock fillet and lobster mash. Bass scanned the wine list. The waiter hovered. "We'll have a bottle of the Chablis to wash it all down. Make sure it's well chilled"

The waiter soon returned and poured some wine for Bass to taste. He swigged it down and indicated to the waiter to pour. The waiter put the bottle in a wine cooler and left.

"Now, Henry, How's it going?"

"Good, I think. I like the work in the box but you know that. Night school isn't easy but I'm doing okay. Not much time for fun but this is what I signed up for."

"Anything worrying you? Anything you want to mention?"

'How does he know?' Henry thought. "Well there are a couple of things."

"Shoot. This is just between you and me."

"Harvey Williams. Is he spying on me?"

"Well he is and he isn't. I asked him to keep an eye on you and tell me if you get out of your depth. So far, he's happy."

"Why do you keep him around?"

"There's a lot for you to learn which isn't in books. Lloyd's is a posh boys' club. Until twenty years ago, my sort would not be allowed to run a box, let alone own one. It was full of Harvey Williams' types, people born into money, people who get other people to do the work, people who glide through life without a care for their fellow man or woman for that matter.

"But I need him around. He's very well connected in this business and he makes sure I'm doing what I need to do to avoid battles. Do you know the buzz word, 'interface'? Well, he's the interface between me and the Lloyd's committee, as well as 4455's aristocratic and old money members. He protects me from them so I can get on with the job and make people richer. But he can be a smarmy git."

"I think I understand."

"I'll call him off if he makes you that uncomfortable."

"It's just that every time I see Williams, I feel like taking a shower."

"Shall I tell him?"

They raised their glasses and clinked.

"You're doing well enough for me. I'll soon bring you into the inside. Get you closer to the business moves we need to make to keep our members happy."

"What do you mean, bringing me into the inside?"

"I'm not talking about that here. Over the next few weeks, we'll meet and I'll explain. Anything else on that mind of yours?"

Henry took a breath. "Now this is just my opinion but 4455 is way behind the times with administration. It's like you're fighting a war with swords when your enemy has automatic rifles and tanks. You need to computerise more than just the accounts."

The waiter brought their starters. "Another bottle, mate," said Bass, holding up the empty Chablis. "I think I'm going to need it. Computers again? Bloody hell, Henry!"

"You have to admit the computerised accounts bring accurate figures quickly and you're better placed to spot problems. But computers can help other parts of the business: policy terms, claims and producing documents. We will need a mainframe machine and software. The manufacturers will supply all this. I took a quick look into what Siemens can offer. It would cost between twenty and twenty five grand, plus consultants' fees and staff training. This is just a rough number."

"Not cheap."

"True. But it will repay you. You'd be better off by having computers in the box, linked to the mainframe computer. I want you to think about giving up the old-fashioned ways, running slips and all that. You will get quicker and more accurate returns and eliminate a lot of human error."

"Anything else? Want to spend another fifty grand on more modernisation?" This was said with as much humour as irony.

Injunction

"Yes." A look of surprise crossed Ronnie's face. "But not that much. The investment side of the business needs first aid. The Stock Exchange is moving rapidly into electronics and Lloyd's won't be far behind. I'd like to keep a watching brief. We have a lot of cash that needs better care. We keep large sums in reserves for up to three years."

"You have it all sorted, don't you."

"No, of course I don't. I know little about investment but I'd be happy to make it my business to find out, although I don't know where I'll find the time. There's a saying, 'if you're not ahead, you're behind.' Computers won't replace you and what you do but they will become more than a necessary aid. They will improve the bottom line. Take a look around you. See how many other syndicates are changing. You might not want to head the herd but you don't want to be left behind. What gets collected after the Lord Mayor's Show?"

"Horseshit! I take your point."

The waiter removed the starters and brought the mains.

"Send me a brief, Henry, and I'll think it over. Tuck in."

"There is just one more thing."

Ronnie glared. "What else! Blimey, you're going to make me lose my appetite."

"Lunch is on me."

Bass nearly choked. "This is an expensive place, Henry. Very nice of you to offer. I appreciate the gesture but I don't think so."

"You've been good to me and you've kept your word. I want to say thank you."

Bass shrugged his shoulders. "Your funeral. Not for me to tell you how to spend your money. Don't choke too much when you see the bill!"

After a steamed ginger pudding and custard for Bass and coffees for both, Henry paid the bill. Inwardly, he gulped when he read the bottom line but, like the top half of the proverbial swan, he looked totally calm.

It was a pleasant day, so they strolled back to Lloyd's. On the way, they passed a car showroom.

"Let's take a look, Henry."

The showroom was like Ali Baba's cave for Bass, a lover of fast and expensive cars. He pointed at a yellow Lamborghini and a blue Maserati and grinned like a tiger catching its prey.

"Anything catch your fancy, Henry?" he asked.

"That E-type Jag is a real beauty." It was a 3.4 litre, dark blue bodywork, cream leather upholstery and hood. "Takes your breath away."

Bass called a salesman over. "How much for this one, Albert?" he asked, pointing at the Jaguar.

As the salesman consulted a manual, Henry whispered, "How do you know his name?"

"I don't. All car salesmen are called Albert."

Albert quoted a price. Bass gave him a look. "I don't mind buying you breakfast and even lunch but I won't buy you the bloody restaurant. Knock twenty percent off and we have a deal."

"Excuse me, sir. Give me a moment."

'Albert' had a short, animated conversation with his manager and returned. "I can't do twenty percent but I can agree fifteen. Would that be acceptable?"

Bass grunted. "No, Albert, twenty or I walk."

Albert returned to his boss. After a brief animated chat, he returned. "That would be acceptable. How will you pay?"

Bass produced a credit card which he passed to Albert. "My friend here will collect the Jag from you. Put all the registration documents in his name. Give him your business card, Henry."

Henry turned to Bass, astonished. "What are you doing? I can't accept it."

"Don't be daft. Of course you can. And why shouldn't I buy you a car? You bought lunch!"

Chapter Fourteen.

The rest of the year passed quickly. Henry completed his night course, passed the exams and, at last, his nights were free. A new computer system was installed for all of 4455's business. Underwriting profits were up, helped by Henry's brilliance with re-insurance. Henry's salary rose accordingly. He was not rich but he felt incredibly wealthy by his standards.

Ronnie kept his promises and took Henry 'inside', explaining some of the inner-workings of 4455. Some of the moves shocked Henry but he took the view that business was business. No wonder people like Ronnie Bass got to be so wealthy if such Lloyd's practices were the norm for syndicates. Henry wanted to be one of these well-off people.

But Henry felt exhausted. He needed a break, a holiday. He asked Ronnie when it would be convenient for him to take some time off.

"Use my place on the Cote d'Azur. It's in the hills above Antibes, near a village called Saint Paul de Vence. Very quiet place, Henry. One or two wonderful restaurants to go to, although I have a chef. It's lovely there just now. Have a couple of weeks away. Take a friend with you, if you like."

"That's very kind." Bass never failed to surprise him. "What will I owe you, Ronnie?"

"More hard work when you get back. Good of you to offer but no money needed. I expect I'll be over for the weekends. Sometimes Mrs. Bass comes with the children. They love it there. I'll be entertaining clients. Usually, we're there from Friday afternoon to Sunday afternoon. You don't need to join in if you don't want to."

"Are you sure you won't mind me being there? I'll try not to get in the way."

"No problem. It's a big place. Do you sail?"

"You're joking. I'm an East End boy. All I sail is close to the wind! I get seasick in dry dock."

Ronnie laughed. "Sort out dates."

Henry agreed dates with Ronnie and took himself off to Carnaby Street. He bought summer gear. He loaded up on cotton trousers, casual shirts and beach shoes. He loved that street. The shops catered for people of his age. Mind you, the highlight was a tobacconist which sold pipes. The sign in the window advertised, "Virgins, £1, Rejects 50p."

Henry did his research on the Cote d'Azur. He wondered what Cannes and Juan Les Pins were like. Nice sounded old fashioned. Menton looked enticing, a fishing village with a pretty hotel. He'd rent a car and take a look.

Henry left London on a wet Tuesday. The flight to Nice was uneventful and he cleared customs by early afternoon. A driver was waiting to meet him. They drove towards Antibes, hugging the coast road. It was a warm sunny day and the car windows were open. The driver turned away from the coast up steep inclines and soon Henry was in the hills of Provence with all its spring colours and aromas.

In a half hour, the car drove through the medieval hill town of Saint Paul de Vence and deeper into the Provence countryside. After fifteen minutes, the car turned into a narrow road and at the end, the driver made a left turn, stopping at some wrought iron gates, where he pressed a buzzer, the gates opened and the car drove another half a mile to the doors of the Bass home. It wasn't a villa, it was a palace.

Henry alighted and reached in his pocket for some euros. "Combien, monsieur," he asked in his awful French. The drive replied in perfect English. "It has already been taken care of." Henry gave him a 20 euro note.

The front doors opened. A man wearing black trousers and a crisp white open neck shirt took his luggage and invited him to enter. Inside it was cool. The hall was cavernous.

"Monsieur Aitken, welcome. Let me show you to your room? May I get you some refreshment?"

"Thank you. Water is fine."

"Still or sparkling?"

"Sparkling, please. Lots of ice."

Injunction

The man spoke into the phone on the hall table. Then, carrying Henry's suitcase, he led the way up a circular staircase to the first floor and along a corridor, opening a door to a huge corner room. Henry gazed with astonishment at the seven foot wide bed, the attractive sitting area and fantastic views. There was a door to the en-suite bathroom. A tray with a glass, bottle of water, ice and lime slices was brought in.

"My name is Claude. Chloe asked me to say she will see you at tea time. Call for me if you need anything. My number is 14 on the intercom. Would you like to take a rest?" Henry nodded

Claude left and Henry poured himself a drink. 'How come fizzy water here tastes so good?' he asked himself. He unpacked, undressed and took a fifteen minute nap. Then he showered and changed into a lemon short-sleeved shirt and navy blue slacks. He walked downstairs where a woman was waiting for him.

"Hello. I'm Henry Aitken."

The woman looked into his eyes and smiled. Henry felt like he had been punched in the solar plexus. The air left his stomach and lungs. He looked again at the woman. She was the most beautiful lady he'd ever seen. Her skin was coffee-coloured and smooth.
Although dressed in flowing robes and head scarf, he could see she had a model's figure and her face was indescribably gorgeous. Straight nose, large green eyes, a cherub's generous mouth.

"My name is Chloe. I am the housekeeper for Mr. Bass. He has told me to do all I can to make you comfortable." Henry liked the way she spoke. English with a French accent. It was sexy.

"Shall we go to the terrace? We'll have tea." At the table, Chloe removed her head scarf. Henry couldn't help notice a scar over her left eye; it went with the deep scar he had already seen on her left cheek. For Henry, neither detracted from Chloe's beauty. It made her all the more magnetising.

After tea, Chloe took Henry on a tour. There were many reception rooms on the ground floor, including a snooker room and library. There was also a ballroom and three dining rooms, one huge, one for twenty or so and the third small and intimate. There was a conservatory. The gardens were beautifully maintained, with a tennis court and a kidney shaped swimming pool.

"Upstairs there are ten bedrooms, most like yours. You like this place?"

"It's fantastic. I haven't had a break since I don't know when. I can see why Mr. Bass suggested I come here to recharge my batteries."

"Mr. Bass explained to me." Chloe smiled at him. "I am at your disposal. I wish you to have the best stay with us."

Henry decided to have a swim and take it easy before dinner, which he was told would be at eight-thirty in the small dining room. He rose in good time, showered again, shaved and dressed in light blue slacks and a pink shirt. He sat on the bedroom's balcony, watching the setting sun. The views were staggering. The hills of Provence had so many folds and colours.

When Henry went downstairs, Chloe was waiting. She escorted him to the terrace where she offered a drink. "This is a Bellini. Champagne and peach juice." It was delicious. Ten minutes later, she checked her watch. "Dinner?"

"What are we having?"

"A French surprise. We'll go inside. The terrace gets a little too cool at this time of year."

Over the first course of seafood salad, Chloe said, "You are looking at my face, Monsieur Aitken."

Henry blushed. "Sorry, I didn't mean to stare. But you have such a beautiful face. And it's just Henry or Henri if you prefer."

"I saw you looking at these?" She stroked the scars on her eye and cheek. "I will tell you. My father did it."

Something told Henry not to react.

"I was born in Morocco. I grew up in a small town, Sidi Slimane. It's in the north, west of Fes. My father was keen for me to have an education and I was sent to Paris when I was fourteen. Before I left, my father scarred me. He told me I was too beautiful and men would want me for my looks and do bad things to me. If my face was spoiled, men would not be interested."

"It didn't work," said Henry. "To my eyes, the blemishes make you even more attractive, if that's possible."

"Ah, you're a flatterer, Henri. My father was wrong but it was his way of life."

The starters were cleared. "To follow," said Chloe, "we have one of our chef's specialities. He is from Brittany. He has made Poulet a la Bretonne. Chicken simmered in a cider sauce, crème fraiche and mustard. I hope you like it."

Henry tasted the dish. It was mouth-watering. "I can see two weeks here will damage my waistline."

"I saw you swimming. You'd have to eat one of the Provence hills to damage that physique."

The evening passed in a flash. Coffee on the terrace was the final touch. It was cool, not cold.

"Would you like a cognac, Henri?"

"No thanks. I'm not much of a drinker. Don't let me stop you."

"I won't. I do if Monsieur Bass is here. He likes me to have a nightcap with him."

There was a silence. "I don't want to put my foot in it but what exactly is your relationship with Mr. Bass?" asked Henry.

"Do I sleep with him? No. I'm very fond of Mrs. Bass and the children and Mr. Bass is not that sort of man. He is like my protector. Do I sleep with the friends he brings here? No, unless I want to. I am the housekeeper. My job is to make people who come here feel happy and important. Then Monsieur Bass does his deals."

"I didn't mean to offend you."

"You didn't. I have my agreement with Mr. Bass. In three years' time, I will cease to work here and go back to Paris. He will help me with my new business."

"I hope it all works out for you."

Henry detected a bit of a freeze but he was wrong. "I am ready for bed, Henri. Are you? Shall I come with you to show you the way?"

*****

Henry's holiday turned into something quite unexpected. He and Chloe spent their days taking in the sights of Provence, often lunching in quiet village cafes and restaurants. One day, Chloe drove Henry along the coast to Menton. They lunched at a small bistro on the beach. Henry thought it was paradise. The nights were spent in Henri's room where he found many delights. In bed, Chloe was everything he had ever wanted and more.

On the second weekend, Ronnie arrived with his wife, children and three other couples, one of whom had children of similar ages to Bass's. Chloe was totally professional. Henry respected her boundaries. On the Saturday night, when everyone had gone to bed, Ronnie and Henry talked.

"I need you back soon. We are looking at some things and I need your head for figures. You don't have to come back with me. Wednesday's fine."

"What's this about?"

"It will keep. How is your holiday?"

Henry stared at Ronnie for a few seconds. "As if you don't know."

"Chloe is a great girl. She tells me you are 'very fine.' But she is not for you. You cannot give her what she wants."

"What do you think she wants?"

"I don't think, I know. She wants money, lots of money. More than you have or are likely to have. Chloe hopes I'll bring an unattached multi-millionaire who will marry her. But she's realistic. We have a deal about her time here. My advice, Henry: enjoy her while you can but don't harbour any expectations of continuing a relationship. Just not going to happen."

"That ship sailed, Ronnie. I'm in love with her."

"That's unfortunate. Don't say I didn't warn you."

On Sunday night, Henry had the villa to himself again. He took Chloe to Colombe d'Or, a restaurant in Saint Paul de Vence. Artists like Picasso and Matisse had dined there and paid for their meals with etchings and paintings which had been framed and hung on the restaurant's walls. Over dessert, Henry declared his love to Chloe and asked about a future together.

Chloe let him down gently but she was frank. "If you had many millions to your name, it might be different but you don't. I am sorry, Henri. You are my sweet nounourse but nothing else."

"What's a nounourse?"

"I think you call it teddy bear. Let's part as friends? I hope we can."

Henry had been warned and was realistic. "I don't have a choice, do I?"

Injunction

"Henri, listen to me. We don't make love. We have sex. Very nice sex but just that. Fun. You won't believe me now but in a little while, you'll forget about me. I think what you've enjoyed is called a holiday fling. You are, what is the word, infatuated? Let's not make this thing bigger than it is."

Henry left a day early. He said goodbye to the staff, tipping them generously. He left a note for Chloe. "Thank you for the best days and nights I've ever had. If you ever need a friend, you know where to find me."

But he would never hear from Chloe again.

*****

Back at Lloyd's, Bass laid out his plans to Henry. "We have an opportunity to buy a private Swiss bank. I don't want our auditors looking at this. The deal is off-shore and off balance sheet. And my identity and those of my partners in the deal is a secret. You can come in if you want. We'll need about seventeen million dollars to get the deal done. I can divert most of the funds I need from premiums. I need you to go to Geneva, check the bank out and make sure we are not buying a pup. You need to go now."

"Ronnie, what about exchange control regulations? Isn't it against the law to deal in different currencies? And I'm an underwriter, not an accountant. This is a job for them."

"What's turned you into an abominable no-man? Find an accountant in Geneva to help you. I use a lawyer there, Alexandre Paty. Call him and get a recommendation. Use my name. Alexandre is nothing if not discreet. As for foreign exchange, we can divert funds from foreign clients.

"We'll use a Panamanian corporation as the buyer. No one will know the identity of the shareholders. Panamanian companies are owned through bearer shares. The certificates will be kept under lock and key. Now, I need you to make sure we are not buying a bank with rotten assets and big, unsustainable debts. I need this information by next week. This deal won't be available forever."

Henry immediately thought: 'This has Harvey Williams all over it. There's a smell here.' But all he said to Ronnie was, "Aren't you worried? I'll do my best to assess the risks but this is not what I do. I am not trained." Other questions like how much Ronnie's people were risking, remained unasked.

"I can cut you in for, let's say 3%. We'll work out the payment if and when the deal happens. What you need to do is the job I ask you to do."

Henry spent three days in Geneva. He found an accountant who investigated and told him pretty well everything checked out. Bank assets were sound and the loan book was strong, as far as the accountant could tell. There were potential bad debts of some half a million Swiss Francs, not a significant sum. On the day Henry returned, he handed Ronnie a hand-written report.

"Is this the only copy? Do I need to read all this? I just want to know, is this bank kosher? Yes or no?"

"You should read the report but essentially, yes, the bank is sound with small exceptions."

That was the last Henry heard about the bank deal until it was done. The day after closing, Ronnie gave Henry a share certificate.

"Have you got a Safe Deposit Box? If not get one. You can rent one at Selfridges. Keep this certificate safe. It entitles you to a 1% shareholding of the bank. My partners in the deal agree this is a suitable reward for your work. You can buy in another 2% if you want." Henry baulked when he heard the price. This was not for him.

Bass was talking. "Every now and again, I'll tell you what is going on and the dividend you're getting. You'll need a separate Swiss bank account. Alexandre will set one up for you. Never bring your dividend earnings from the bank on-shore. Nobody needs to know."

Ronnie and his partners used the bank for deals that were high risk. They gave themselves unsecured loans. Hefty fees were extracted for risky loans made by the bank to 'friends.' The Swiss authorities did nothing. Henry wondered what the senior staff at the Swiss bank thought and why local auditors weren't waving a red flag. But this was Swiss banking. Eight months later on a trip to Lausanne, Henry visited Alexandre who introduced him to the banker looking after his private account. He was amazed to find it had a credit balance of 150,000 Swiss Francs.

*****

Syndicate 4455 was often the beneficiary of tickets for sporting events, theatre and film premieres, gallery openings and the like. One night, Henry went to a private view in an art gallery on Albermarle Street. His host was happy to see him and introduced him to some guests. A woman came over to them.

"George," she addressed the gallery host, "please introduce me."

"Sonia, this is Henry Aitken. Henry, meet Sonia March. She is one of tonight's exhibiting artists."

George excused himself. As they talked, Henry started to like what he saw. Sonia was petite, probably in her early thirties, and cute. Her outfit was expensive but unsuited to one of her age. It was too young for her.

"So, Mr. Aitken. What do you think?"

Henry had had a glass or two. "I don't know much about artists but I know who I like."

"Haven't heard that one before. Very funny. Let's get out of here."

Outside, Henry hailed a cab. "Where to?" he asked. Sonia gave the cab driver an address in West Hampstead. Inside a terraced house, Henry clambered over easels, paint pots, brushes and incomplete works as he was led to a bedroom. Sonia took off her clothes. 'Oh, what the hell,' Henry said to himself. The sex was okay, or so Henry thought. But Sonia didn't care for after-play. She made it clear she wanted Henry to leave.

"May I have your phone number?" he asked.

"I don't think so," she answered. "I don't want a relationship with you or anyone else for that matter. Now and then I just want sex. Close the front door behind you."

Henry felt used and abused. He returned to his flat thoroughly discomfited.

Henry had the occasional affair. He went to a party after an opening night and talked with the ingénue. "I don't suppose anyone noticed me," she told Henry, who, to her feigned surprise, recited some of her lines. "I was captivated," Henry replied.

Within two days they were sleeping together. Every night after the play ended, Henry collected her and they had a late supper. Most nights they slept together. Ronnie noticed his employee was looking tired. "Shagging, are we?"

Henry grew to like this girl. One night, about seven weeks into their relationship, he arrived at the theatre to find her leaving arm-in-arm with an actor who was also in the play. When Henry caught up with her, she told him they were over. "Right there in the street. No apology, I was dumped flat," he told Bass.

"Don't worry boy. Your motto should be 'on to the next' so move on."

Henry wondered why women rejected him so often. He told himself not to try too hard, be relaxed, see what happens. Nothing much did. So he changed tactics, became a man around town, taking advantage of many invitations sent to the syndicate. He liked football games at Wembley and being entertained at Ascot, Lord's and Covent Garden. He wasn't so keen on Henley, Wimbledon and Twickenham. He became better at small talk and romanced a number of women. But still no spark. What he wanted was another Chloe.

Meanwhile, as he achieved more seniority at 4455, he took on some of Ronnie's responsibilities. He travelled extensively to Western Europe, America and Canada, meeting insurance people and prospective names. He was really good at his job. Premium income for Syndicate 4455 rose steadily, year on year. Three years running, his bonus was more than half a million pounds after tax. Why not? He was writing a lot of good business.

New non-working names wanted to join 4455. With their addition, more business could be written, more premiums, bigger profits. Henry was now acknowledged throughout Lloyd's as valuable property.

When Ronnie brought Henry inside, it was an eye-opener. True, there were many legitimate investments made by 4455. Thanks in part to Henry's insistence on computerisation, the syndicate's stock market portfolio was now worth many millions, as was the portfolio of real estate. However, Bass and his friends had a habit of using 4455 assets like they belonged to them alone. Baby syndicates were just the tip of the iceberg.

Henry was informed about 'the Binder', a Lloyd's subterfuge which permitted American high risk business to be underwritten by a third party broker on behalf of Lloyd's syndicates. 4455 took advantage. The Binder permitted premiums to be paid to the third party broker, which for 4455 was a company owned jointly by Bass and Williams. However, the premiums were not passed on in full to 4455. The broker "skimmed," taking more in brokerage than should have been permitted.

On his US trips, Henry was told to look out for any high risk business that might be passed through the Binder to the benefit of the Bass/Williams brokerage. Oddly, when Ronnie talked about 'skimming,' he saw nothing wrong. "We achieve very high premiums so why shouldn't we take extra fees. And anyway, the risks are re-insured. Our names are getting a double dip."

But so were Bass and Williams. They got profits from brokerage, as well as profits as working names at 4455. Quite why the 4455 auditors did not scream 'foul' amazed Henry. He knew the books disguised the skimming levels with accountancy sleight of hand. He wondered what the Bass/Williams combo had done to keep the auditors quiet.

One day, Henry asked Ronnie about some new loans.

"Loans? Henry, what are you talking about?"

"I can see a few of you on 4455 are taking loans from syndicate premium income. These loans seem to be interest free."

"Do you want an interest free loan, Henry?"

"I just want to know what's going on. I don't want a loan, thank you."

"Very well. These loans are called "black box bonuses." A few of us at 4455 are given a bonus but rather than just taking it in cash, we are allowed to borrow from syndicate premium income, interest free. Lloyd's rules don't prevent the practice. These bonuses are payments made only to senior underwriters but are disguised as loans to minimize exposure to income tax. 4455 didn't invent this scheme. Many syndicates do it for their senior people."

"What do you do with all this money, Ronnie?"

"I beg your pardon."

Henry knew he had gone too far but it was too late to retreat. "Do you just keep it in the bank? Is this spare cash from 4455 which it doesn't need? I don't understand."

"It's really none of your business what I do with my money. But you know so much these days. I used the latest loan to buy an office block in Southwark. It's an investment for my old age. You can do the same if you want. Take a loan and buy a property investment."

"Me, buy a two million quid building. I don't have that sort of money."

"Listen to me carefully. Have you got two or three hundred grand in the bank?"

"I might have. Why?"

"So say you're 1.7 mill short. You'd get a commercial loan for a million three."

"I suppose but where does the other four hundred grand come from?"

"A black box bonus. 4455 will lend you the four hundred grand out of premium income. It's a bonus but in the books, it's designated as a loan. That gives you a tax break. The one condition is that at the end of the financial year, you have to pay the loan back in full but the following day you can borrow it again. Our bank will do the necessary finance for this. It costs about a grand."

"Is this legal?"

"You always ask this, don't you? It's a grey area. Like I said, it's not against Lloyd's rules. The taxman might find it dodgy but how will he know? You borrowed the money and invested it."

Henry thought it over and decided that if you can't beat them, join them. Using the black box bonus scheme, he bought two office buildings, using Panamanian companies as the buyers of record. When the buildings were sold, he kept the profits off-shore. He paid no capital gains tax. It was a really neat scam, although an eagle-eyed Inland Revenue official could have made a case. But the Revenue never did as they never knew the ultimate beneficial owner of the Panamanian companies.

Henry also used the black box scheme to repay the mortgage on his Hampstead flat. He was astonished to find no questions asked by auditors. Ronnie rewarded his silence and discretion with extra bonuses and perks. Every now and then Henry remembered the job his father wanted him to take. 'I earn more here in a couple of days than I would have in a year had I given in to him,' he thought.

Lloyd's rules changed as the City of London embraced the Reagan/Thatcher Big Bang era but unscrupulous practices continued unchallenged. Oversight remained lax as Lloyd's continued to be run as if it was a private fiefdom.

For example, nothing prevented owners of Lloyd's syndicates from selling their ownership to third parties who were not Lloyd's people. Limited liability companies could now buy Lloyd's syndicates. When this happened, the non-working syndicate members were not released from personal and unlimited liability after any such a sale. Their risks increased exponentially.

Syndicates that looked attractive to large American brokerage firms were gobbled up and underwriters/owners received massive rewards. Non-working members of such syndicates were persuaded to approve the deals because of the additional capital that would be invested by the buyers, thus enabling syndicates to write more business.

No one in authority questioned the conflicts of interest that were bound to arise when a large overseas brokerage bought and owned a Lloyd's insurer. Henry felt Lloyd's had moved from a City gentleman's club into a saloon in America's Wild West.

Henry did well when 4455 was sold. By 1984, his annual salary had risen to four hundred thousand pounds to which would be added his annual bonus. He was paid more than one million pounds after tax by new owners of 4455 to sign a new five year employment agreement, which also guaranteed a minimum bonus equalling his annual salary. Heavens knew what Ronnie was paid for signing up. Henry was niggled that Harvey Williams continued to be rewarded for doing pretty well nothing but he rationalised his feelings by telling himself not to care what others earned.

Henry's bank account and assets had swollen to more than five million pounds. His small flat in Hampstead had been sold and he now owned a large mansion flat in South Street, Mayfair. The E-type Jaguar had gone and he drove a convertible, silver Jaguar XJS. He did not have a live-in housekeeper but he employed a lady who cleaned and cooked whenever he didn't dine out. It was a comfortable life but a lonely one. A lasting relationship with a member of the opposite sex still eluded him.

Injunction

Henry never returned to the Cote d'Azur villa. Too many raw memories. Instead, he vacationed in quiet spots in Mallorca, the Amalfi Coast and even the Seychelles. He was usually accompanied by a lady but only because he didn't want only his own company. Rarely was there a problem for him finding a companion. His money compensated for his looks.

At Lloyds, Henry's nagging doubts about the schemes used by 4455 hierarchy increased. Were they all living on borrowed time? Was Lloyd's rotten to the core? If he needed proof, he got it when Harvey Williams asked him to have a drink. In the Baltic House dining room, Harvey laid out plans for a new scheme.

"Henry, it works like this. We underwrite a risk that is bound to occur. For example, we'll accept a risk that a fleet of jet aeroplanes will not have engine trouble for a year. This is a risk that is almost bound to arise. Agreed? The risk will not be re-insured. The syndicate is liable for 100% of claims. When the risk arises, 4455 pays out in full."

"Harvey," he sighed, "what are you driving at?"

"The fleet of jets will be non-existent. The company owning the theoretical fleet will be a Panamanian company which we will own. The policy will be bought through our off-shore brokerage. The claims will be accepted and paid to the off-shore bank account of the Panamanian company. The Panamanian company will be quids in and no tax to pay. Cute isn't it?"

"Why tell me about this?"

"We want you to handle the underwriting."

Henry was horrified. There was no disguising a blatant fraud. Henry realised he needed to play for time and was non-committal. He told Williams he wanted to think about it. The next day, Henry talked to Ronnie to voice his concerns about the scam.

"He was careful to avoid any direct allegation of criminal illegality but if the reality of the deal was uncovered, there would surely be serious consequences for everyone involved, maybe prison. And where was Harvey Williams in the paper trail? Nowhere. Nor was Ronnie for that matter. The paper trail started and ended with Henry Aitken.

"I'll be alone in the firing line, Ronnie. Harvey won't, nor will you. You both have deniability. This one will be on my head alone. Looks to me that if the Fraud Squad ever came calling, I would be thrown to the wolves. You and Harvey could just walk away."

"You don't fancy this idea much, do you?" Ronnie was strong on irony.

"It's a needless risk, one easy to spot. You always justify this sort of thing by saying it's not against Lloyd's rules but so what? This one has a very bad smell. I'm not using the word fraud to you as I'm not a lawyer but if this deal was an animal, it would be a skunk that has let one go."

Henry shook his head as he continued. "Ronnie, you've made me wealthy and I'm grateful. I don't know what you're worth. Not my business. But why do you need to take risks like this just to get even richer? Please ask yourself, what do you gain and what might you lose if this one goes pear-shaped? Yes, you're damn right, I don't fancy it one bit. To be blunt, I won't handle the underwriting."

"I'll talk to Harvey." Henry heard nothing more but he noticed a frost with Williams. 'Am I bothered?' he asked himself. 'I don't need that bugger. In fact, if push gets to shove, I don't need any of them.'

Over the following days, Henry came to the conclusion that the behaviour of Bass/Williams and their friends was now out of control. They were reckless and dangerous. Did these people think they were untouchable? Henry decided he no longer wanted to be a part of Bass/Williams and their way of doing business.

Henry felt pangs of guilt about his participation in some of the scams and worried where trails of criminality led to him. Bass and Williams had been clever in disguising their roles. They might not even be targets of any police enquiry. What evidence or proof did he have that they were as guilty as him?

*****

Henry's worries that his liberty might be in serious jeopardy increased. He doubted he would persuade Bass/Williams to change their ways. If the poop hit the fan, he'd be covered in the stuff. He began to drink heavily. He found sleep elusive and when it came, he would wake up in the small hours, sweating. In the box, Bass noticed the change.

"Henry, you're not looking right. What's up?"

"Nothing. Just feeling a bit pressured."

"Why? Business is good. We're doing well. What's up, boy?"

"I'm running on empty, I guess."

"Take some time out. Want to go to the villa?"

"That's kind but I don't think seeing Chloe would help. I'll take a break though."

Henry took a week off on his own. He went to a favourite spot in Mallorca. At the Cala, the hills changed from grey to pink at sunset and the local restaurants were more than adequate. The locals knew him and made him welcome. He had time to think. His decision about the future was drastic. He would quit syndicate 4455. But he would have to leave without telling anyone and disappear. What was there to keep him in London? Did he need more money? No. Was his life empty? Undoubtedly. Would his life change if he lived abroad and what would that entail? He had no idea. There wasn't a soul in the world in whom he could confide.

If there was any doubt about his decision to go, it was dispelled three days after he returned from Mallorca. The head of the accounts department asked to see him urgently.

"Mr. Aitken, there are some movements on the accounts I don't understand."

Henry looked at the computer print-out and realised that the black box bonus scheme was the subject of the queries. Three entries had been made on the computer which should have been off the books.

"Don't worry, I'll take care of this. It's just an administrative error."

"So, nothing for me to do? Should I mention it to auditors?"

"No. No need to take it further but thank you for bringing this to my attention. I'll take it from here."

Henry knew how to manipulate the computer system and that evening, he accessed the relevant account and changed the entries. Having done so, he had left a fingerprint which, if the scam came to light, would bring it right to his doorstep. What a schoolboy error! Yes, it was definitely time to leave.

Henry checked in again with his conscience as he had in Mallorca. If he left England, would he ever be able to return? What did he owe the non-working 4455 members who had been cheated? Should he not go to the police, whistle-blow, own up to his own wrongdoings and face the music? For this, he would need to disclose the accounts. He could make print-outs out of hours but he might be discovered. And what if he did all this? His fingerprints were all over the 4455 scams. Bass, Williams and other beneficiaries of the chicanery were not implicated directly. 'If I was in America,' he told himself, 'I'd be called the fall guy. If any of this comes out, I'm toast. All roads lead to me.'

Henry saw clearly that by giving himself up and disclosing the evidence, all he would achieve was a jail sentence for himself while his collaborators would continue to live off the fat of Lloyd's land. So, doing the right thing, the proper thing was not an option. He asked himself, what would Eddie Grey say? He couldn't decide whether Eddie would tell him to own up to all or there was no point in hurting himself if he couldn't bring the whole 4455 house down.

Henry knew he needed to leave England and soon. He put his knowledge to good use. He contacted lawyers in Panama City and paid cash for an untraceable $1500 money order which he sent to the lawyers, giving them a post office box number and address for their reply. Six days later, he received corporate documentation for a Panamanian Company, Capital International SA. It included two blank Powers of Attorney and bearer share certificates.

He sold his share portfolios on the London and New York stock exchanges. He handed stockbrokers' cheques to Raglans, a City of London private bank where he held an account. He sold his Mayfair apartment. He lowered the price for a quick deal. He was pretty sure the estate agents bought it for themselves but banking fifteen thousand pounds less than its value was neither here nor there. He also sold his other property investments, in each case repaying the loans, including the black box bonus money. The net proceeds were deposited into his Raglans account.

He flew to Geneva, where he closed his private Swiss bank account. He removed the balance in cash after it was changed into US dollars. He closed his account at Barclays and took a Barclays bank draft to Raglans, having first drawn more sterling and US dollars in cash for himself. He instructed Raglans to buy Canadian Treasury Bills, emptying his account. He collected the Treasury Bills in person three days later. That same day he emptied his safe deposit box at Selfridges and terminated the rental agreement.

He bought a business class British Airways ticket for Miami, charging the cost to 4455. Over two days, he met business contacts and negotiated some insurance deals.

On the third day, he took a cab to Fort Lauderdale airport. He chartered a Cessna to take him to Grand Cayman and return him the same day. He paid the operators $15,000 in cash. No name given, no questions asked.

Arriving in Grand Cayman, he showed his passport. No record was taken. He headed to Albert Panton Street. At Renwick Bank, he met the Head Clerk, Hugo Lomax, a local man who took Henry through formalities. Introducing himself as Alexander Ross, Henry asked for an account to be opened in the name of Capital International S.A. Mr. Lomax asked for the corporate documents including a Power of Attorney in the name of Alexander Ross. They were handed over and copies were made. No ID for Ross himself was required.

Henry completed forms in the company's name and handed them over with the Canadian Treasury Bills. He instructed Lomax to sell the TBs and deposit the cash in US dollars and UK sterling into new savings accounts. Rates of interest and fees were agreed, as was the manner in which instructions to Renwick Bank would be given. As a customer, all he had to do was to quote a client code number and his instructions would be effected. Nothing in writing was needed.

Henry also rented a safe deposit box. He went through the administrative rigmarole of box-opening regulations, after which he emptied the contents of a brief case into it. It included uncut diamonds and a miniature Picasso drawing.

Henry was given the client code number by Lomax, as well as a receipt for the Treasury Bills. He needed to get back to London before he was missed so, tempted as he was to spend a few days experiencing the delights of the Caymans, he returned to the airport and four hours later his British Airways flight left Miami. Henry marvelled at how easy it was to make some ten million pounds disappear. Canadian Treasury Bills were not traceable.

*****

Back in London, Henry booked into a hotel in Knightsbridge. He found a telephone box and made a call to Renwick Bank, asking for Lomax. When Lomax came on the line, Henry quoted the client code, adding, "just checking the system."

"All okay, sir. Your deals are done. There is just over 5.5 mill in your sterling account and 6.7 mill in your US dollar account."

"Thank you, Hugo. I'll be in touch."

Henry now had to deal with other important questions. When should he leave, where should he go and what would he do when he left? The closest friend he had was Ronnie Bass, the man from whom he was escaping. There was nobody with whom he could share his plans.

Henry spent a day at the British Library and the American Embassy, gathering information. He soon had answers to all the questions except 'when'. This decision was taken out of his hands one morning in August. Three partners and staff from a firm of accountants arrived unannounced at the Baltic House office. 4455's new owners, a large American brokerage, were alarmed because of holes spotted in the syndicate accounts. Calls were made to the box and Ronnie was summoned to meet the accountants. Henry overheard the conversation and panicked. The fan was going to be hit big time. He could hear himself screaming inwardly, "leave, go, now."

Henry left the box, took a cab to his hotel, packed his bags and paid the bill. He took another cab to Heathrow. Henry found an Air Canada flight to Toronto, leaving in two hours. He bought an open return ticket in Business Class and paid cash. Should anyone try to trace his departure, he hoped they would conclude he would be returning.

Injunction

Henry found a bar in the airport lounge and sank a scotch. After what felt like hours, he heard his flight called. He felt his blood pressure rise as he boarded the jumbo jet. He half expected the police to burst into the flight cabin and haul him away. But nobody came.

The flight was uneventful. Arriving at Pearson International, he navigated passport control and customs without incident. A cab ride took him to One King West Hotel, a stone's throw from the railway station. The next day, rested and fed, Henry took a sleeper train to Vancouver. He was disappointed with the scenery. Daytime was spent travelling through forest, then dreary prairies and grasslands. The Great Plains were vast. But on the third morning, he saw the glories of the Canadian Rockies. He felt he was close enough to touch them. He went outside to stand on the caboose and breathe the air.

On arrival in Vancouver, Henry agreed a fare of $350 Canadian with a cab driver to take him to Seattle. At the border, he was required to show his passport, nothing else. He had entered the United States and nobody in London would have the slightest idea where he was. The cab driver took him to Seattle-Tacoma airport. He booked into one of the perimeter hotels for the night. When asked for a credit card, he plumped down $200 in cash.

The next day, he flew to San Francisco and took a room at an hotel near the Embarcadero. He telephoned a realtor and, in the name of Alexander Ross, arranged a booking the next day to see a fully furnished apartment in Taylor Street. After a viewing, Henry returned to the realtor and signed a year's lease for the apartment. He paid six months' rent and services in advance as well as a deposit, all in cash.

Once installed in Taylor Street, he called The Rosamund Plastic Surgery Clinic and booked an appointment with plastic surgeon, Dr James Morton, who was high on the list of those in his profession. Research at the American Embassy paid off. Meeting Dr Morton was a surprise. Henry had expected someone elderly, not a man just a few years older than himself.

"How can I help you, Mr. Ross?"

"I want to change my looks, doctor. My face is an invitation for women to indicate how much they feel sorry for me."

"I see. What exactly do you want me to do?"

"My ears stick out. I'd like them flat. My nose is bulbous. I'd like it to be Roman, pointed. I'd like my chin to be flatter, not protrude. And I don't want that awful birth mark on my cheek. Also I'd like my eyes to be bigger."

"Okay. All this is possible except for the eyes. They do not grow. They remain the same size for life. But I can do something with the eyelids to make them look wider. This will require four or five operations, weeks apart. It will be painful for you, although we'll do our best to manage the pain. And it will be expensive."

They talked a while. Henry like it that Morton was matter of fact, down to earth. Nothing phased him. Morton ended the consultation, saying, "If you want to go ahead, our accounts department will talk you through the finances."

"When can we start?"

Morton checked his diary. "I can do the first op, the ears and nose, in three weeks. We will have to do some tests first, just routine, nothing to concern you."

"Such as?"

"Bloods, heart check, that sort of thing. The work on your chin and eyes is more substantial. Separate operations. Once it's all finished, you'll need several months to recover. Some of the time will be spent with us at the Clinic but you will also need to convalesce, as well as have nursing at home." He paused to let Henry take all this in. "How do you feel? A lot to process. You should take time to think this over."

"No need. I want to go ahead. There's one other thing."

When Henry explained what he wanted, Morton replied, "no, that's not what I do. It borders on the unethical."

"If you won't help, I'll find someone who will. Wouldn't it be better and safer for you to do it? I'll pay extra."

Morton thought for a while. "Okay but I'll want you to sign a letter than I advised against this part of the procedure. And I will not accept payment for it."

"That's fine. Where do I find your accounts department?"

Morton picked up his phone and talked. He told Henry, "Mrs. Newbury in accounts is expecting you. Her office is on the first floor. On your left just before you leave the building."

Henry agreed a fee of $350,000 with Mrs. Newbury to include nursing at his apartment after he was discharged. He also agreed to deposit a further $25,000 to cover any additional expenses. He took the Clinic's bank details and told Mrs. Newbury the funds would be wired straight away.

*****

Just over a year later, Henry Aitken emerged looking nothing like the old Henry. He had endured much pain but it was now at a level with which he could cope. He grew a beard and moustache and let his hair grow long. Henry had a good ear for language. He practised hard on developing a Californian accent. It took a while but by the time his recovery was virtually complete, he could pass as a native of the Golden state.

Once he was confident enough to venture out on his own, he went to the San Francisco Public Library on Larkin Street. He looked through back issues of the newspapers for 1987. On the third day, he found what he wanted in *The Los Angeles Herald Examiner.* He photocopied an obituary page. The entry stated:

> *Charles Lionel Pearce, aged 30, of Culver City, California died on 17th March, 1987, as a result of a car accident. Mr. Pearce was a student at Culver City High School and graduated in 1978 from UCLA with a Business Studies degree. He had started a promising career in advertising. Mr. Pearce was an only child and unmarried. Both his parents predeceased him.*

There was more about Pearce's life, including some voluntary work. The obituary featured a picture from Pearce's high school days. Henry and Charles weren't exactly a match but both he and Pearce seemed to share similar height and build and their looks were such that they could pass for one another on a cursory glance.

Henry contacted both the high school and university, asking for copies of Pearce's transcripts. He visited both and paid the charges in cash in exchange for the documents. He frequented some bars in town. At 'The Barbary Coast', he met someone who said he knew someone able to provide forged documents like passports and social security cards. Money passed and he met the forger; more money passed and fourteen months after leaving London, Charles Pearce, previously Henry Aitken and Arthur Hawkins, was documented with an American passport and all other papers needed to back up his new identity.

Arthur/Henry might not have been an academic but he had acquired street smarts. He paid the forger to provide another passport which covered the period including the date of Pearce's death but prior to the start of his new passport. At more expense, he had entry stamps added for Sydney, Australia, Auckland, New Zealand, London, England, and several European ports of entry, as well as New Delhi, India. He plotted his travels around the world. Spending numerous days at the library, he detailed the sights and sounds of his fictional journeys.

He opened checking and savings accounts at a Wells Fargo branch and had $500,000 wired over by Renwick Bank. He received the usual bank documents including a Wells Fargo cheque book and credit card.

The new Charles Pearce needed to go where people would be least likely to look for him. Neither Henry nor Arthur before him had shown real interest in the academic life. Who would look for him in a college town?

Chapter Fifteen.

"Hardy." The voice on the phone was female. She slurred rather than called his name. He didn't recognise the caller immediately. He checked his watch. Almost two in the morning.

"Hold on." He sat up in bed. "Hello."

"Hardy, it's me." More slurred words. Then the penny dropped.

"Miri? Is that you?"

"Yes, it's me, Miri, and I'm drunk. Drunk as a skunk. What are you going to do about it?"

"Miri, what's this about? We've not seen each other for months."

"You saw me just a few days ago."

"You know what I mean. That was business."

"What do I have in my life except the law? What do I have to show for all this work? A broken marriage, no children, a life where nobody cares. And you, you hurt me like nobody else ever did. I've phoned to tell you I hate you."

Hardy was not an emotional man but he was disturbed when he heard Miriam sobbing.

"Miri, what do you want?"

"Come see me, please. Now. I need someone with me. If you don't come, I won't be accountable for my actions."

This was emotional blackmail. Hardy was tempted to tell Miriam to call the Samaritans. He would not be manipulated by a drunken woman.

"Miri, listen to me carefully. I won't come over. I want you to stop drinking and sober up. Drink water. Black coffee at this time of night is not good for you. Tomorrow morning, call me when you wake up. Then, maybe we can meet. Perhaps we'll have lunch on Saturday."

"That's just like you, Hardy. No feelings. Get the girlfriend off the phone so you can have a quiet life. You're the one responsible for me being like this."

"Miri, we were friends, then we had a relationship and it was marvellous while it lasted. You're making it much bigger than it really was. Let's meet this weekend. I always enjoy your company."

"You told me you loved my mind. I wanted you to love me. You didn't. You wouldn't. You're cruel, Hardy. You never give anything of yourself."

"Do you think you'll make me change, berating me like this? Sober up, we'll talk tomorrow. Good night, Miri."

Injunction

Hardy heard Miriam call him, "fucking bastard," as he put the phone down. They had known each other professionally for years and their affair had lasted almost a year. But so what? Did he owe her anything? They were both consenting adults. He had shown her a luxurious side of life. Best hotels and restaurants, finest champagne. And she knew all along he was not one to commit.

By the following afternoon, Hardy had not been called by Miriam. He rang chambers but was told she was in court and unavailable. He left a message. His call was not returned. He decided to lunch with someone else on Saturday. It took no time for him to find a different companion.

Chapter Sixteen.

Professor Claire Richardson took the familiar walk from her apartment on Melbourne Avenue to her office in Lind Hall on the University of Minnesota campus. This was her third year teaching English Literature at the U of M. At eleven o'clock sharp on October 5th, 1987, she strolled into Room 134 in Vincent Hall, her lecture theatre. Two years earlier, her first day of teaching at U of M had been a trial. Today was different. No longer did she have anxieties when lecturing to more than a hundred students. Confidence was her middle name.

She greeted the first years who filled the room. "I'm Professor Richardson. Welcome to the University of Minnesota and to this course on 19th century British novels. If this is not the course you signed up for, please leave now." Nobody moved. "Good. Your course outline will have told you that this year, we will cover works by Charles Dickens, Jane Austen, the Bronte sisters and others. This is great literature to look forward to."

Five minutes into her introductory talk, the lecture room door opened. A man wearing garish clothes entered. His trousers were orange, his T shirt was also orange but of a different shade. The outfit clashed. He wore sandals without socks. He had a full, unkempt beard and moustache and long hair. The overall impression was werewolf. The man raised his hand.

"Sorry to be late. Lost my way on campus."

"Mr., I don't know your name. I appreciate it if students arrive on time. Find a seat, please. Okay, now, where were we?"

Two hours later in the Vincent Hall cafeteria, Claire was seated on her own, reading and sipping coffee when the werewolf came to her table and sat, uninvited.

"Hi, Professor, I'm Charlie Pearce. I didn't get to town until early this morning. I'm trying to settle myself in but I didn't want to miss your lecture. I apologise for being late."

"Mr. Pearce. Apology accepted. But if you can't get to a lecture or seminar on time, just don't come."

"Noted. I will do my best to ensure it won't happen again."

"Thank you, Mr. Pearce. Might I ask you to leave me in peace?"

Two days later, Charlie appeared on time at Claire's lecture. He was dressed differently. He looked like an advertisement for expensive Italian casual wear. His hair was still long but smartly coiffed. The beard and moustache had been trimmed short and barbered. When Claire walked in, she couldn't fail to notice him. He sat in the front row. He had left a note on the desk:

'I would respectfully request a meeting to discuss literature and creative writing. Here is my cell number.

Regards, Charles Pearce.'

Claire noticed the neat handwriting. Maybe she had judged Mr. Pearce too quickly? Later that day she telephoned him.

"Mr. Pearce, I read your note. Why creative writing?"

"Good evening, professor. Could we meet? Talking over coffee or tea is much more civilised than the telephone."

"You're welcome to see me in office hours. Just fill in the form on my door."

"I see."

Claire relented. "I run a creative writing course, as I suspect you know. It's on Saturday mornings on the second floor of The Book House in Dinkytown. It's on 4th Street.
"May I ask, what's the fee?"

"No fee. The Book House sponsors me. The first session is this coming Saturday. We start at 10.30 and finish around 12.30. If you're interested, just turn up."

The call ended and Claire reflected on her turning Pearce down. She shrugged her shoulders. It was of little relevance.

On Saturday, Pearce arrived at The Book House before Claire. He sat patiently, notebook and pen ready. Fifteen students turned up, as well as ten older people, including three of Charlie's vintage. Claire arrived on time. She explained that she was not a writer herself but, in addition to her teaching, she helped authors by editing their work. She went round the class asking what they had written. At the coffee break, Charlie kept his distance.

When class resumed, there was a discussion about what to write. Charlie was astonished by the breadth of topics chosen. When it came to his turn, he had nothing to offer. "I'm still thinking about it."

Claire asked the class to work on a synopsis of a story for the following Saturday, as well as the story's first page. Charlie obliged with both. He wrote about a man who grew up poor, got lucky but needed to change his whole existence. Claire took the synopsis, saying she would read it for the following week. Then she asked him to read his first page. Nervously, Charlie read:

> *"It was a typical cold, wet November day on the South Side. Nothing remarkable about that. The clouds were low, shedding their wetness. The streets glistened and people occasionally slipped on the cobbles as they went on their way.*
> *Walkers shivered and tried to shake off the dripping rain. Some huddled in doorways, others went on their way with the collars of their raincoats turned up. Women wearing scarves would have to wring them out at their destinations.*
>
> *"The rain got heavier and heavier. Pity the poor souls who would have to venture out to work, to shop, to labour at the docks, toting soaking wet sacks from ships. Some lucky people had bicycles. Of course, they risked a skid and a tumble but it was worthwhile as they'd escaped the soaking sooner than the rest."*

"Has anyone got a comment for Mr. Pearce?" asked Claire.

A woman put her hand up. "Not so much comment but questions." She checked her notes. "Where is the South Side? Is there a purpose or point in describing a rainy day in such detail? And "went on their way" is repeated. I know you can't tell a story on page one but where is the story?"

"Mr. Pearce, any response?" asked Claire.

"The south side of Chicago. I'm describing the awful day my protagonist's younger brother was born and the day both the brother and their mother died."

"Okay," Claire intervened. "We are getting somewhere. And it's an easy fix. What all of you need to realise is that publishers won't publish a book that starts with heaps about the weather. What they want is words that jump off the page, words that will grip a reader and make him or her want to read more. Mr. Pearce, I'll gladly read your synopsis but you have to make the beginning really gripping. Maybe something like this."

'The November day my brother was born on the South Side of Chicago was foul. Cold, wet and unforgiving. But I won't remember that day for the weather. It will forever be imprinted on my brain because my baby brother and mother died.'

"See the difference?"

Charlie blushed with embarrassment. "So my stuff is awful?"

"How shall I put it? Let's say the writing left something to be desired. But you had the guts to read your words aloud and I like that. Your writing will improve. Now, who else will read?"

At the end of the session, Charlie left. He said nothing to Claire and his classmates. He stopped for a burger and headed for Walter Library. He took out a book on literary criticism. Later, he went to a coffee shop for a break. Then back to the Library. This was a pattern he had already established. He was determined to improve in every way, as he indulged his enjoyment of reading, wiping away his slackness of the past fifteen years.

At his apartment that night, he turned on his cell phone. There was a message from Claire.

"Mr. Pearce, Claire Richardson. Today was brutal for you. I've read your synopsis. Let's meet tomorrow. Stub & Herbs. It's at 227 SE Oak Street on the East Bank, 1.00pm. If this doesn't suit you, send me a text."

Charlie arrived at the diner on time. He spotted Claire examining the menu. He walked to her table.

"Hi."

"Hello, Mr. Pearce."

Claire couldn't help admiring today's outfit. Lilywhite shirt, black hipster jeans, black cowboy boots.

"You are quite the clothes horse."

"Just trying to fit in. You're the picture, professor."

Claire wore a long flowery frock which had the character of a painting. Charlie liked to flatter. There was something about this woman that infuriated him but he couldn't deny he was interested. She was worth the flattery. Maybe it was just chemistry.

"Shall we order? Do you know about this place, Mr. Pearce?"

"No."

"It's open seven days a week. You can get breakfast, lunch and dinner. It started in 1939. I thought you might like to experience a college institution. Welcome to Midwest cooking."

"What's good?"

"Pretty well everything. I like the red pepper hummus and Caesar salad. Take a look at the menu."

"I'm more of a carnivore." Charlie studied the choices. "I'll go for bacon cheese fries and the mushroom burger."

"I like the local beer. Summit Pale Ale. It's brewed in St. Paul. Want to try one?"

"When in Rome," Charlie nodded.

Quickly, two bottles appeared. "It's like a Czech beer," Claire told Charlie.

"You know your way around beers, Prof."

"Not as well as you, I suspect."

They both laughed as they sipped. The food arrived. Charlie was hungry and tucked in.

"Tell me about Charlie Pearce?"

"If you've read my synopsis, you'll know quite a bit about me but my life has not been quite as dramatic. What else do you want to know? I'd like to know about you. You go first."

"How well do you know England?"

"I've spent time there. Mostly in London. Why?"

"I'm English. I was born in Leeds. My father is a vicar. I went to the local grammar school."

Charlie frowned. "Is that like a high school for academics?"

"I suppose. Anyway, I stayed at school till I was eighteen. I wanted to go to University. My father agreed on condition that I went to Leeds University. I refused. I wanted to go to the University of East Anglia. It's in Norwich near the east coast. Its English course was one of the best in those days and I was ready to spread my wings.

"My father was so angry when I defied him and chose to leave Leeds. He has hardly spoken to me since. My mother writes to me but I have to reply to a post box address, not home. She thinks my father would destroy my letters if I sent them home. I have two younger sisters and my father worries they will follow my example and defy him too."

"That's quite something. It's almost Dickensian. Is there no hope of a reconciliation?"

"Not at the moment. And why should I make the first move? He was the one who wouldn't listen. He wanted to keep me locked away."

"I understand but surely you don't want to leave things like this?"

"No, of course not, but my father needs to practice what he preaches. His congregants get love, understanding and kindness. I get frost and condemnation. It's so hypocritical."

Charlie reckoned it was time to change the subject. "How did you get from East Anglia to Minneapolis?"

"I loved to read and study. I'm not a party girl. I got a first class degree, that's summa cum laude, and stayed on at UEA for my Masters. Then I moved to King's College, London, where I got my Ph.D. It wasn't easy. I had to work for a living while I studied. But it was worth it."

"What did you do?"

"Wait on tables, stack books in the library, tutor students, anything to get my rent paid and some food to eat. Now, I live in the lap of luxury by my standards. I don't have to worry anymore whether I can afford to buy a cupcake."

"What did you do for your doctorate?"

"Would you believe 19th century romantic novels?"

"And after?"

"I taught at King's for a bit but there was no permanent post for me. In fact it was hard to find a permanent job at an English university but I saw a position advertised here and came two years ago. This is my third year teaching at the U of M. I love it except in deep winter."

"What do you do for relaxation?"

"That's not why we are here, Mr. Pearce." By now they had finished their mains. "How about dessert?" Claire asked. "Normally I don't but the peach cobbler is fantastic."

"I seem to be back in Rome," Charlie replied. Desserts and coffees were served.

"Now," said Claire, "let's get to it. Your synopsis. It's good. I found it interesting. It's not for me to tell you how to shape your plot. That's your job. Mine would be to edit your writing should you want me to assist you.

"You should keep coming to the Saturday class and find out more about the do's and don'ts of writing, as well as picking up tips from your fellow classmates. The more you read and listen, the quicker your writing will improve."

Inwardly, Charlie breathed a sigh of relief. Quite why Claire's opinion was so important to him was a mystery. He was daunted by her. But if she was interested in his writing, he wanted her help.

"So what do I do?" Charlie asked.

"Take your synopsis and hone it. If it were me, when I was almost satisfied, say eighty percent, I'd start writing. You'll find the story will move away from the synopsis but that's okay. That's how it's meant to be. It takes a while to find a fit."

"And you'll edit my writing?"

"It won't be the type of editing you'd get from a publisher. It will be more of a discussion between us. Remember, this is your story, not mine."

"What do you charge for this service?"

Claire gave Charlie an old-fashioned look. "Mr. Pearce, I thought you understood. I am your teacher. I am paid by the University and The Book House pays me a fee for my class. I don't take money from students."

"I don't understand how this works. I didn't mean to offend you."

"No offence taken. And I'll pay the bill. I can't have students treating me to lunch. Good day."

Charlie rose as Claire left, leaving silence in her wake. He sat down, ordered another beer and a steak salad to take home for dinner. 'It's compensation for the short-tempered, irascible woman I dined with,' he told himself.

Over the weeks, Charlie read voraciously, did okay on his tests and got on with his studies. He saw Claire at lectures. They did not speak. In the creative writing meetings, she spoke with him politely but there was a freeze. Despite this, Charlie found himself becoming increasingly infatuated with Claire. But how could he break through the icefield that surrounded her?

In November, he began writing the novel. It had no title. "This will come to you," Claire explained after class one Saturday. "Call it anything. What about 'Piddlefoot'?"

"Piddlefoot?" Charlie laughed. A smile broke on Claire's face. Was the ice melting?

In December, Claire told Charlie she was going home to Leeds for Christmas. Her father was unwell. "It might be the last time I see him and I want to make peace before it's too late."

"For what it's worth, I applaud you for going. Is there anything I can do to help you?"

"Yes, write your novel."

Claire returned in January. Charlie had written about a third of his book. He eagerly awaited seeing her, not just because he wanted her opinion of his work. He missed her. At the first meeting of the creative writing class, he was astonished by her looks. Her hair was now short and styled in an elfin cut. It really suited her. She wore a figure hugging white sweater and black jeans tucked into calf-length boots. She had a body that was more than desirable and she was no longer shy about showing it.

After class he handed her the manuscript. "This is where I've got so far. How was Leeds?"

"Let's have a coffee. I'd rather not talk here. Annie's Parlor is just a short walk."

Once seated, Charlie asked, "So, Professor, how are you?"

"Okay, I guess. I made peace with my father. We had a week together catching up. He told me how proud he was of my work here. Sadly, just before New Year, he passed away. It was expected. But my mother has taken it hard. I didn't want to leave her but I have a career and a contract to honour. She understood. She hopes to visit in the spring. Now, how are you? What have you been doing?"

Charlie was surprised by the questions. Why would Claire care?

"I'm fine, thanks. I spent Christmas here. I immersed myself in reading and writing. See what you've done to me."

"People don't change other people. People change themselves."

"Do you really think so? Was Donne wrong? Man is not an island?"

"Good point. You've been reading. This topic is for late at night when we're a bit pissed."

"Pissed as in angry?"

"No, pissed as in drunk."

They talked for a while about university politics and national politics, too. Had Claire been able to vote, she would be a Democrat. Reagan and his trickle down economic policies were anathema to her. She was following the fortunes of a new man, Bill Clinton, who might be a force in 1992. She was resigned to Bush following his boss into the White House that year.

Food arrived, chicken noodle soup for both, followed by a grilled ham and cheese sandwich for Claire, a roast beef sandwich for Charlie.

Over coffee, Claire asked, "Do you vote?"

"I am so tied up these days in reading and writing. Politics is a bit of a mystery. I should take more of an interest. As for voting, no. Can't see the point."

Claire's look was incredulous. "Can't see the point! I know you have brains. You're not a moron. The men and women sent to Washington and State Congress in St Paul have a huge influence on how we live, how we help the poor and the old and children, how we dispense healthcare. These days, Republicans fail pretty well all the people except the super-rich. But you wouldn't know, would you? You don't vote. You're not interested in politics. That makes me rather annoyed."

Charlie snapped. "You are perfectly entitled to hold whatever political views you want and express them to whoever you wish but you have no right to judge me because I have scant interest. Maybe I should go to a current affairs group, read *The New York Times* and watch television news every night.

"But don't think for a moment that this country is controlled or managed by a handful of people who sit in Congress or the White House or State capitols or even on the Supreme Court. If this is what you really think, you're politically naïve."

"What are you talking about? Politicians rule. They serve the public supposedly. If you think they have no influence, who runs this country?"

"I wasn't talking influence. I was talking control. America is in the clutches of men who run big banks and financial institutions. Wall Street has much more clout and influence in a day's trading than Washington, D.C. or St. Paul has in six months."

Claire sat open-mouthed. "Prove it."

"Tell me, who funds America? Who pays the welfare bills and Medicare? Who pays for all our servicemen and the bloated government bureaucracies? Don't tell me the taxpayer. This government engages in deficit spending. In other words it pays out more dollars than it receives from the taxpayer, much more. How does government bridge the difference? Printing cash is high risk and bad economics because it is inflationary. So money is borrowed, mainly from the bond market or, as you would call it, Wall Street. It is Wall Street that keeps government in business and ensures the bills are paid. There's the proof. You're right, I'm not a moron but I'm starting to wonder about you."

Charlie took a $50 note from his wallet and slammed it on the table. "I don't care what this might look like. I refuse to let an opinionated, ignorant English woman subsidise me."

And he stormed out.

Claire was angry. No longer did people didn't talk to her like that but she liked this man. She shuddered at a ghastly memory, an experience when she was an undergraduate. Her tutor had romanced her, seduced her and taken everything she could give and then dropped her cold. She thought she was in love. She soon realised it was just infatuation on her part and shockingly awful behaviour on his.

Now, ten years later, she rarely had anything to do with men, except the occasional one-nighter when she just wanted sex. But for reasons she couldn't fathom, Charles Pearce was different and it troubled her that she was now the teacher.

The following Saturday, Charlie was absent from the creative writing class. Claire send him a text. "I've read your draft. We should discuss it." Charlie didn't reply. The next day, Claire repeated her text. This time Charlie answered with a brusque, "when and where?" Claire considered answering, 'Monday morning, my office after the lecture' but instead, she responded, "201, Melbourne Avenue, SE, Apartment C. And get here now!"

Thirty minutes later, Charlie parked his black Ford Mustang outside Claire's apartment. He rang Claire's doorbell. She opened the door. He admired her appearance, casual, white trousers and boots and a beige top.

"Peace offering," said Charlie as he gave Claire a bouquet of flowers and a bottle of red wine. Claire looked at the label. It was a Ravenswood Lodi Zinfandel, 1979.

"Are you trying to spoil me or get me drunk?"

"Neither. I happen to respect good wine."

"Thank you, Charlie."

Charlie's insides jumped. He could not remember Claire using his first name before. Claire offered him a comfortable armchair and brought him a glass of red.

"Let's talk about your book."

"You mean 'Piddlefoot'?"

"Yes." Claire laughed. "There's good and bad. What do you want first?"

"The good. Let me have a minute in the sun before I'm destroyed."

"Okay. You have a plot that moves along. I want to read more. You have interesting characters. I want to know more. I like the villains, the men who create financial nightmares just to line their pockets at the expense of the innocents. They lack conscience, making them magnetic. The way you write dialogue is excellent. It moves the story along at a cracking pace. That's the good."

"And the bad?"

"You seem to have written for an English audience. The phrases, the dialogue, all English. Why? This is an American book. Write for the American reader. If, a long way down the line, 'Piddlefoot' is published in the UK, you can adapt it. Next, the spelling and grammar is shocking, awful. If your book was presented in this form, any publishing house would reject it. This can be worked on but it would be too big a task for me.

"I have three other issues. First, the love interest has yet to appear but I'm curious why you are leaving it so late. In the synopsis, this was on the second page. Next, the story is events driven. You are short on motive as to why people are behaving in the way they do. Why are the villains so greedy? It can't just be for love of money. Why do they buy big houses, fancy cars, huge yachts, expensive jewellery? How do they escape the taxman? What do they do it for? You need to spell out motivation!"

Charlie was ready. "I think it's like a sickness, the money thing. They do it for the same reason men want to boast about their dicks." Claire looked away. "Maybe I should have found a better analogy. They want to show their peers that they have more, that they are number one. Also, they do it because they can. Does that make sense to you?"

"Yes but you need to put it on the page. Don't expect the reader to guess. They won't know. You have to show it. And how do these people treat their women? There's nothing about this so far."

Charlie took a big gulp of wine. "Wow! This writing business is brutal. Do you think Rudyard Kipling went through all this?"

"Are you comparing yourself to Kipling? Every budding author goes through this. It's your first book. It was never going to be perfect on day one."

"No," said Charlie. "But I have lots of other stories in my head."

"I'm sure you do but one at a time. You are undisciplined. You don't always spell accurately, and your grammar is sloppy. I haven't told you everything yet."

Charlie held out his glass. "I suspect I'm going to need a refill. Okay, get the axe out."

"You don't do feelings. If you don't write about feelings, your reader won't understand why your characters are motivated to do the things they do. You need to show what they feel and why. If you don't, there is no point in your going any further. Do you feel anything when you write?"

Charlie was outraged. "Just listen to yourself. You are judging me. Again! You have no right to do this."

"If you want me to help with your writing, I have every right. This is the book's major defect. You have to address it."

"Says, who? How many books have you written and published? Who made you queen of books?"

At this, Claire lost her temper. "For the past few months, you've been reading great novels. Take 'Pride and Prejudice.' What sort of a story would it be if Jane Austen excluded the feelings of Elizabeth and Darcy?"

Charlie shouted, "I don't know. I don't know how to write feelings." He lowered his voice. In almost a sob, he admitted, "I don't have feelings."

Claire was three inches shorter than Charlie. She stood before him on tip toes and eye-balled him. They both breathed heavily. Charlie clenched his lips. Claire raised her hand as if to slap Charlie but his reflexes were quick. He grabbed Claire's upper arm and stopped her. For a moment they stared at each other. Then Charlie kissed her. She kissed him back. Soon, they were making love.

Afterwards, as Charlie held Claire in his arms, she murmured, "good quarrel, nice finish. You're not a one trick pony, I hope."

Charlie laughed. "Give me a few minutes. I'm not as young as I was. Nor is my back for that matter. Could we move to somewhere a little more comfortable?"

*****

The next morning, Claire was distant. "What's the matter?" asked Charlie, gently.

"It's not you. We can't do this again."

"Why not? I'd enjoy a repeat performance."

"It's not you. But it is. Sorry. I'm not explaining this. You are my student. I cannot have relations with you. This is an absolute no-no for the university. If we continued and it was discovered, I would lose my job and worse. I would probably not get another college teaching position in America."

Charlie looked in Claire's eyes. "If I wasn't your student, would you explore a relationship with me? Is it just my being your student that's getting in the way?"

Claire murmured, "I think so."

Charlie paused. "So, let me think outside the box. Hypothetically, I could stop being your student. I'll take classes with another professor. Doesn't this solve the problem?"

"That won't work, Charlie. They are a pretty conservative bunch here. They would still see me as a professor sleeping with a student. I'd get punished just the same."

Charlie got up and walked round the bedroom. After a minute or two, he returned to the bed and eyeballed Claire. "Let me be crystal clear. I am completely nuts about you. You challenge me, you demand the best from me, you get me furious, you are uncompromising and you're totally gorgeous. I like being with you. I liked making love to you. I do not want us to end before we start. So, I'll leave the U of M."

"You'll leave here?"

"Only the university. Then I won't be your student. Problem fixed."

"No this doesn't solve anything. It might solve my college issue but what about your education? You need more knowledge, Charlie. I know you're street smart but your writing won't be good enough unless you deal with the academic side. I won't be the one who deprives you of what might be a great opportunity."

Charlie tried to suppress a laugh but failed. "The trouble with you academics is you think in straight lines. Is the U of M the only university in town? No! Why can't I move to Macalester? St. Paul is what, five miles from here? I have my wheels. Macalester's a liberal arts school so it's bound to have an English course. All I need to do is ask them to register me. Hey presto! And if they won't have me, there are other schools."

Claire tried to look stern but it didn't last. She burst into laughter. "You have a wicked, evil mind, Charles Pearce. But that would work."

"I do indeed have a wicked, evil mind. Come back to bed."

*****

Injunction

It was as simple as that. Charlie dropped out of the U of M and enrolled at Macalester. Claire and Charlie became an item. There was no gossip, as far as either of them knew. After all, Charlie was older than Claire. In the summer vacation, they moved from their respective apartments to a house on Como Lake in St Paul.

Claire's mother had delayed her visit and was not now due to arrive until October. "I don't know what she will think, us living together," Claire said.

"May I solve your concerns?"

"How? I don't want you to move out."

"Claire, your straight line thinking is so wearying. How can someone so clever have such pitiful imagination?"

Charlie knelt on one knee. "Marry me. I love you from here to Jupiter and back. You are The One for me. You always will be The One and you know it. Please say yes." Claire accepted with joy. She was totally in love with Charlie. They made plans to marry during Mrs. Richardson's visit.

But Charlie was troubled. He had never made a commitment like this before and he worried about living a lie with Claire. What if she found out about him and his nefarious actions at 4455? Would she shrug it off? No, Claire wouldn't. She would be cut into pieces by his dishonesty. But Charlie was terrified that by telling the truth, he would lose the one thing in his life he treasured above all. If the decision about leaving 4455 was hard, this was worse by a factor of a hundred.

One night, shortly before Mrs. Richardson's arrival, Charlie asked Claire to put everything to one side and sit with him.

"I need to tell you things which I know will upset you but I can't marry you without your knowing the whole truth about me. I mean everything. After I tell you these things, if you hate me, if you don't want to marry me, I'll understand, although it will break my heart in the worst way. I've struggled for weeks about this decision but my conscience won't let me marry you under false pretences."

Claire was alarmed. "What on earth are you talking about?"

"This is going to be very difficult but please hear me out before you say anything. When I've finished, I'll answer all your questions. Let's start at the beginning. I'm not Charlie Pearce."

"What! Who the hell are you?"

Over the next hour or so, Charlie told Claire about his childhood, living with the Greys, his years working for General Insurance and at Lloyd's, indeed everything that happened in his working life until he escaped from London. He also told Claire about his private life, excluding only his interlude with Chloe and other dalliances with the ladies. This was not something Claire needed to know in detail. Suffice it to say, Charlie spoke about relationships that always failed and how he believed he was never good enough until he met Claire.

He told her everything he had done at Syndicate 4455. He hid nothing as he made a clean breast of his wrongdoings. He explained why he left and how he did it. He showed Claire pictures of himself before and after surgery. Claire was stony-faced when she asked if it was still painful. Charlie said it wasn't and how it was worth it to remove visible evidence of his ugliness. Claire was dumbstruck.

Next, Charlie spelled out the misdeeds of Ronnie Bass, Harvey Williams and others as well as himself. He did not try to justify or minimise his role. He accepted he had been a willing participator in the scams, that he realised that some actions might have criminal consequences but he acknowledged he went along with them. He explained how he would have been made the scapegoat had he remained in London as the other wrongdoers would likely have got away scot-free.

Charlie told Claire about his leaving England in haste, what he did in the Caymans to keep his money, his change of identity and surgery and why he chose Minneapolis.

Finally, Charlie set out his finances for Claire. She gasped when she found out how rich he was. Claire said nothing till Charlie finished but the money thing put her over the edge.

"So much money? You're a thief."

"I know you will need time to process all this. I'm so sorry to dump it all on you. I was going to keep it to myself to the grave but I just can't do that to you. Please understand I love you too much to have you live a lie with me. It would have been easy to keep quiet but so wrong. I couldn't stand the thought that some day after we were married, everything would come out. Then what would you think of me? I hope what I've told you won't alter your feelings for me but I'll accept it if it does. I know I've hurt you but if you will let me, I'll spend the rest of my life making it right. I'm truly, truly sorry."

Claire had turned pale at the outset. Now she was white. Quietly, she told Charlie, "Sleep in the spare room tonight, Charlie, or whatever your name is. I need to be alone."

Charlie didn't argue. The next morning when Charlie woke up, Claire had left. No note from her. He skipped class at Macalester that day. He toyed with the idea of going to the U of M campus to find Claire but a sixth sense told him this was a bad idea. Best to wait out the storm.

Claire came home late. She had been drinking. All she said was, "I don't want to talk." She went to bed. Charlie sat on his own. 'What to do?' he asked himself. He remembered the words of Big Sam, the bookie he worked for when he was a boy. "If you don't know what to do, do nuffink." And that's what he did. He would just wait and hope.

Friday and Saturday passed without a word from Claire. On Sunday morning, he percolated a pot of coffee, grilled rashers of bacon, scrambled some eggs, toasted two bagels, poured two glasses of orange juice and waited. He hoped the aromas would bring Claire into the kitchen. He was right. Claire looked like she hadn't slept. He poured her a coffee, handed over bacon and eggs with a bagel, saying, "good morning."

"Good morning Charlie, or is it Henry or Arthur? What name are you using today?" Claire poured on the sarcasm.

"I don't blame you for being angry and disappointed in me. But I really want us to talk it through."

"What's there to talk about? You are a fraud, a cheat, a thief, a man who doesn't exist. Will you go back to England and give yourself up? Will you repay all the money you have stashed away in the Caymans? Will you make recompense to all the people you hurt? What about the Lloyd's Names who went bankrupt? And how will I ever believe anything you tell me? How can you expect us to have a life together after all this?"

"That's a lot of questions. Will I go back to England? No. Give myself up? To whom and for what? For your information, Ronnie Bass, Harvey Williams and the others were tried and acquitted of all charges at their criminal trials. How could I be guilty of a crime when they are not? As for the money I have in the Caymans, to whom should it be repaid? I earned most of it lawfully and I paid most of the taxes due. I didn't splash out on big houses and fast cars. Instead I owned one car at a time. I had a flat, a nice one, but not a huge house. That money was saved. I accept there were sharp practices and cheating from which I benefitted. I stayed quiet but I never broke any Lloyd's rules of which I'm aware, nor it seems did I break the criminal law. As I see it, the money is lawfully mine."

Charlie took a breath, gulped some coffee and continued as Claire just stared at him.

"You think compensation is due to the Lloyd's Names on our Syndicate. In the years we are talking about, the non-working Names all made good money. We did not write the kind of business that made long-term losses. We were not involved in asbestos underwriting or risks like that. Our Names were not required to put up more capital, unlike many other non-working Lloyd's Names. And you're wrong about one thing. To the best of my knowledge, none of our Names went bankrupt. Like I said, they made profits. True, their profits could have been greater.

"As for trusting me, I've told you pretty well everything about my life and my business affairs. All I omitted were the salacious details about my relationships with other women. Suffice it to say none of these relationships lasted. But if you want to know anything, anything at all, just ask. I'll answer all your questions."

"What do you mean by pretty well?"

"I had a brief affair when I stayed at Ronnie's place in the south of France. I fell totally in love and was badly hurt by the lady in question. I never saw her again. There have been other women but none with whom I had a real, meaningful relationship. Then I met you and my life changed. What else would you like to know?"

"Nothing. I don't want to know anything else."

"You asked a question, how will we have a life together? We could have a wonderful life because you must know beyond doubt that I am deeply in love with you and until two days ago, you loved me. I've laid bare all my secrets. The photo I showed you was me before plastic surgery. Be honest with me, isn't this man plug ugly? You might say this wouldn't have put you off but just look at it from where I stand. Before I had the surgery, every morning of my life I looked at this face when I shaved and was repulsed. Claire, my life is in your hands," he whispered. "And I swear to devote that life to working hard and putting everything right with us. Please don't throw away what we have. I don't think I'd recover."

"It's not that easy, Charlie."

"I know. I'm going out. I need some air. I'll leave you on your own to think."

*****

It took time for Claire to decide to take a chance on Charlie. She was swayed not so much by his laying bare his entire life but how much she loved him, despite everything. A week later, they sat together.

"I accept you should keep your American identity. You should keep up your studies at Macalester and we'll stay in St Paul or anywhere else in America, depending on where my career takes me. As for marriage, it depends."

"On what?"

"I want a clean slate. I want you to give away all the money in the Cayman Islands. I want a voice in the charities you choose. Your money, most of it also has to go. You can keep $250,000. And you have to concentrate on your writing. I think you have the makings of a novelist. I'll help you. You'll earn money honestly. Do you agree my terms?"

Charlie agreed with a massive inward gulp. What was the use of all that money if he didn't have the one person in the world he wanted? The deal - Claire in exchange for giving nearly all his money away – was not just necessary. It was worth it. Charlie came to see it as the deal of the century. Carefully, all the Cayman money was given away anonymously. The uncut diamonds and the Picasso were sold privately by Renwick Bank and the proceeds gifted. Charlie had a clean slate.

In October, Claire's mother and sisters came to the wedding. Charlie paid for business class flights. The next month, Claire despaired when George Bush was elected president. Charlie's view was, 'same old but with a recession.'

By spring, Charlie finished his first novel. Naturally it was no longer called 'Piddlefoot.' Instead it was named, *Progress*. A New York publisher loved the book. Over time, it sold in hardback in the tens of thousands and the American public bought more than a million paperbacks. Charlie travelled the States, giving talks and signing copies, something he never repeated. When she had time, Claire accompanied him. Hollywood came calling with an offer for the film rights. Within a year of publication, Charlie was back in the money. Two years later, his second novel was published to critical acclaim. He and Claire became parents to their daughter, Lizzie, named for Jane Austen's heroine.

When Lizzie was two, Claire told Charlie, "I would like Lizzie to grow up in England, be educated there and go to an English university. I know there's a risk for you going home but you don't have live in the States to write. And we can easily afford for me to be a full time mother."

"Can I think about it?"

"Yes, but you need to factor in something. Lizzie will have a brother or sister in a few months' time."

Although thrilled at the news of his burgeoning family, Charlie needed quite a bit of persuasion to leave America. England worried him, despite the fact that his tracks were covered. However, he was becoming less enthusiastic about the American way of life. George Bush's presidency started shambolically and the mood of the country wasn't right. The 1992 election for president would be a three-way fight with no obvious winner. It was time to leave. In October, 1992, the Pearce family moved to a rented apartment in Kensington.

It took time to find the house they wanted and a good school for Lizzie but they settled on an eight bedroom home in Penn, a village in Buckinghamshire. The house had all the comforts including a swimming pool, library and a tennis court, not to mention a splendid conservatory. One of the reception rooms was converted into a study/writing room for Charlie. This was true luxury for him. When it was finished, he brought Claire into the room.

"I'm thinking of where I started life. It was a tiny dump in the East End where there was no central heating. We ate in the kitchen and used an outdoor lavatory! I guess I've come quite a long way."

Despite his fame as an author, Charlie did his best to make sure he was left in peace. The Pearce family became respected members of the local community. Claire gave her time for good works in the village. Charlie would invariably contribute to local charities.

More novels were published, all best sellers. The Pearce family, now three children, settled into a happy, fulfilled life. As time passed, Charlie Pearce became relaxed about his past. He no longer feared discovery. Nor did Claire.

Part III.

Judgment - 2007.

Chapter Seventeen.

As the hearing day of the court case approached, tension mounted in the Pearce household. The children noticed that Daddy was quieter than usual. He took little notice of them, often locking himself away for hours in his study. He got annoyed if he was disturbed. He rarely read to them at night. He didn't ask about school or help with schoolwork. Claire did her best to explain that Daddy was under enormous stress and all would be well soon.

Claire, too, was under strain. She couldn't help reminding herself that her own life was at stake. What would happen if everything about Charlie came out? What might happen to the children? What about her friends, and the people in the village, everyone? Over the months, Claire found salvation in a New Zealand Sauvignon Blanc and other wines, as well as the nightly vodkas and tonics. She was on the brink of a breakdown but Charlie did not see it. He was too involved with his own worries and fears.

Following the injunction hearings, Claire's sobriety deteriorated badly and Mrs. James now drove the children to and from school. Behind a driving wheel, Claire had become a danger. Mrs. James found Claire unapproachable.

The last straw came ten days before the scheduled start date for the court case. When Mrs. James returned home from school with the children, she opened the front door and heard raised voices from the kitchen. She asked the children to go to their bedrooms and begin their homework and she would call them when tea was ready. She quickly made her way to the kitchen.

There she found Charlie holding his right cheek. Blood soaked through his fingers. Claire was holding a sharp knife.

"You are such a bastard," Claire yelled at Charlie. "I'm only giving you what you deserve."

"You cut me! You used a knife on me. Claire, why would you do that?"

"Only what you asked for. For months, you've put me through hell. The worry of this bloody case is killing me and it's so unnecessary. And you forget it's not just about you, no matter what you think. It's about the children. It's about me. And who can I talk to? Nobody. You don't listen to me. You escape to your study and leave me alone for hours on end."

At that, Claire burst into tears and ran out of the kitchen. Mrs. James went to a kitchen cabinet and took out a first aid kit.

"Let's take a look at that cheek, Mr. Pearce."

Charlie removed his hand. "It's only a scratch," he was told. Mrs. James cleaned the wound and dressed it. "No need for a doctor. You'll have a bit of a scar for a while. I need to fix the children's teas but I want you to sit with them while I talk to Mrs. Pearce. After that, you and I need to talk."

Charlie nodded. "I'll see you in my study, if that's okay."

Half an hour later, Mrs. James knocked on the study door. Charlie opened it.

"Come in, Mrs. James."

"After we talk, you need to come back to the kitchen. The children want to see you. And so does Claire. Now, it's not my place to ask why there's so much tension in this house. I know you have a court hearing soon. But you employ me to run your house. I can't do my job when there is so much disquiet, such a toxic atmosphere. My major concern is the children. You know how much I love them but I cannot take much more of this. It has to stop or I'll hand in my notice."

Charlie nodded. "You're totally right. Let me see what Claire and I can do. I agree the situation must change. We simply can't lose you. Right now, you are the glue for this family."

"Okay, please go to the children. I want to talk to you again once tea is over."

They went to the kitchen. Charlie hugged the children in turn. He kissed Claire on her cheek. He told them, "I've been on edge for a while and I've let my feelings override other things. I am sorry but from this moment, the old Daddy is back. This is a promise."

Claire was watching. Charlie went back to her and hugged her. "Everything will be okay," he told the children. "Mummy and I had a tiny row but it's all over. We love each other and we love you children more. Now, who wants ice cream and cake?"

Charlie busied himself finding a chocolate cake. Claire produced a tub of vanilla ice cream from the freezer. She also made a pot of tea for the adults. Charlie gulped his down as he ate a large piece of cake.

"Daddy, you have chocolate all over your face," giggled Amber.

"You haven't. Would you like some on yours? Hey, I can put some on my eye too."

Things calmed down in the kitchen. The children were all smiles. Daddy and Mummy were back. Charlie told make-believe stories about tea-time when he was young. Soon everyone was laughing as the atmosphere lightened. When tea was over, Claire turned to Mrs. James. "I'll clear up. I know you want to talk with Charlie."

Back in the study, Mrs. James sat opposite Charlie.

"Do you know how close I came to handing in my notice today?"

"I do."

"I've worked for you for almost nine years. I love being here. You know how much I care for the children. It's like they were my own. But the past few months have just been awful. You have been a recluse. Mrs. Pearce has a drinking problem which is getting severe. And today she used a knife on you. What has happened to both of you?"

"That court case coming up. It has taken its toll."

"Yes, it has. I understand pressure. But your behaviour, you and Mrs. Pearce, is much more than just pressure. You've fought court cases before while I've been here. They were nothing like this. Why is this one so different? I can only think you and Mrs. Pearce have a dark secret you're trying to hide. And if I can see it, so will others."

Charlie blinked hard. Before him sat a woman who was content to spend her life with a family not her own, taking care of their needs. But she had common sense and wisdom aplenty, perhaps more than he had given her credit for. He needed to listen to her carefully.

"We are old friends, Mrs. James. You're an important member of this family. I apologise for what you saw and heard today. I can't excuse it. But the pressures of this case are gigantic. I can't tell you more. All I would say is that my entire life is at stake."

"But in this home, you have created a massive boil. You need to lance it."

"Pardon?"

"Burst this boil. Make the case go away. I don't know much about these things but get your lawyers to find a way to end it. Don't go to court. Give a little, take a little.
"And you must take care of Mrs. Pearce. She needs far more help than both you and I can give her. She needs a refuge and counselling, professional help. I'll be here to look after you and the children. You have to concentrate on her."

Charlie nodded his head but stayed silent. He was ashamed he hadn't seen how bad a state Claire was in.

"I've spoken out of place, haven't I?" Suddenly Mrs. James's confidence evaporated.

"No, you haven't and even if you had, you're only telling me truths I need to hear. I'll speak to our GP first thing tomorrow. Get Claire to a specialist. I'll give as much time to her as I can. Settling the case is not in my hands. *The Sentinel* needs to agree. I'll call my lawyer tonight."

"Thank you, Mr. Pearce."

"No, thank you, Mrs. James. You have wisdom and it's a very valuable commodity right now."

*****

The Sentinel redoubled efforts to find evidence to link Hawkins/Aitken to Pearce. Enquiries in America always led to a dead end. Whatever Pearce had done, he appeared to have covered his tracks really well. Enquiry agents in Los Angeles visited Charlie's old home, his high school and his college. His picture was shown around. Nobody remembered him.

In London, Connie Strauss took up the baton. She visited General Insurance and Lloyd's. At GI, life had moved on. There were few employees who had been present twenty five years earlier. Those that were still there did not remember Arthur Hawkins. None recognised his photograph.

At Lloyd's, quite a few people knew the story of Syndicate 4455 but it was no longer in business. Connie found no-one at Lloyd's who had worked for 4455 and was still engaged by another syndicate. People remembered Ronnie Bass well. "He was larger than life," was the standard reply "but Henry Aitken? Yes, I remember the name. No, that's not him. Henry was an ugly bastard."

At Foster's insistence, Minnie Carter spent time in the East End where Arthur had grown up. Minnie came up with nothing. Minnie took a guess that Arthur/Henry had become a man about town and she tried art galleries and other places he might have frequented but nobody recalled him. Foster became more and more frustrated.

"Find the link, the smoking gun," he shouted at Connie one night. "We know Pearce is Hawkins."

"Maybe but can you prove it. And shouting at me doesn't help."

"Try harder."

*****

Hardy Burgess sat in a comfortable armchair in the Morning Room of the Oxford and Cambridge Club in Pall Mall. As an alumnus of Selwyn College, it was a privilege he relished. The food was acceptable, as was the company most of the time. He read his copy of *The Times*. He checked his watch. 1.05 pm. His guest would soon arrive, fashionably late. Two minutes later, William Tovey, a man of similar vintage to Hardy and senior partner of Houseman, Tovey and Letts, was escorted in.

Hardy stood "William, good to see you."

"Likewise, Hardy. The world seems to be treating you well."

A waiter approached. "What's your tipple?"

"G & T, please."

"Same for me, Harries," he said to the waiter. "Make them large ones. And would you bring us menus."

They both ordered smoked trout and roast beef. "Plain food, William, but honest. Shall we wash it down with a claret?"

"So, Hardy, what's happening in the law?"

For the next hour or so, the two men yacked about the practice of law, the nuisance of young partners, the hell and imposition of the internet and most things grumpy old lawyers moan about. For dessert, Hardy went for the Spotted Dick, Tovey the syrup pudding. Heaps of custard too; the fare of public schoolboys. After the dessert plates were emptied, Hardy said, "We should talk about the case. Shall we have coffee here? Port or cognac?"

A coffee pot with hot milk was produced, together with two large cognacs.

"I haven't much to say," replied Tovey.

"William, let me put cards on the table? What I am going to tell you has to go no further. I am betraying a confidence but I think it's for the greater good."

"I'll respect your confidence."

Hardy took a breath. "Would you agree that if you had anything detrimental on my client, you would have produced it by now? Otherwise you'd be in breach of the evidence rules. The judge will need a lot of convincing to let you bring in new evidence between now and the hearing."

"I don't disagree."

"If we went to trial and beat you and if, later, your people discovered something detrimental about my client, they would not be prevented from publishing what they find, subject to defamation laws."

"I agree."

"If the action is settled now with a permanent injunction for my client but maybe with a reduced radius of, say, half a mile and with my client waiving his claim for damages, is there still a problem? Is a deal on such terms possible?"

Tovey paused a while. "Personally, I don't see a problem but a deal now? My clients are pretty adamant. What about costs?"

"William, it's a drop hands situation. Each side bears their own costs."

"Might I ask why you are keen to settle now?"

"It's personal and this must stay between us." Tovey nodded his acceptance. "Mrs. Pearce is unwell. The pressures of the case, and the likelihood that she will have to give evidence, seem to have tipped her over the edge. She is in a clinic. Mr. Pearce believes her recovery will be quicker if she knows the case is over. He fears for her future health if he doesn't settle."

"Hardy, I'm sorry to hear about Mrs. Pearce but if you swear me to silence, I can't use her current state of health as justification for settling. Mind you, I'd be delighted to recommend the deal. I can't see any winners except you, me and the barristers."

"You'll take it to your clients?"

"Of course."

"I'll ask Mr. Pearce if he'll let you tell your clients of Dr Pearce's predicament. I know Max Rankin is all business but I assume he'll see business sense settling on these terms."

"You're probably right but Foster is cut from a different cloth. I truly think he believes the courts should play no part in protecting private citizens from the wrath of the press. I'm probably overstating it. I'll talk to Rankin, see what can be done. That cognac was good."

"Another?"

"Why not? We're a long time dead."

Twenty minutes later, the two men shook hands and parted company. Hardy looked at the bill, winced, signed it and decided to go back to Mount Street to sleep off lunch.

*****

Martin Foster sat in Max Rankin's office, waiting to hear developments. "I had a call from Bill Tovey. Pearce has blinked," Max explained.

"Tell me more."

"He is suggesting what Bill called a 'drop hands' deal. We end the litigation on terms that the injunction stays in place but with a reduced radius of half a mile. Pearce waives his claim for damages. We each pay our own costs. If we find anything out about Pearce at a later date, we are free to publish, subject to the defamation laws. I was told in strict confidence that the case has got to Pearce's wife and this is why he's willing to walk away."

"What do you think?"

"Does Tovey know about the link from Pearce to Henry Aitken and Arthur Hawkins?" asked Rankin.

"Of course he does. Those old fingerprints when Hawkins was nicked don't help. We have no comparison. Tovey advised the problem remains that we still have no solid evidence that Hawkins/Aitken/Pearce are one and the same person. And even if we get evidence which stands up in court, it may be too late to introduce it because of the court's rules. Pity because I feel sure we are really close to finding out what Pearce is trying to hide."

"Maybe we are nearly there but in law, it's the pregnant thing."

"Eh?"

"You're either pregnant or you're not. You can't be nearly pregnant."

"So, what are you saying, Max? What do you want to do?"

"Strictly, it's your decision. You're the editor."

Martin blew a raspberry. "Well, I need to think through what we have to gain and what we have to lose."

"No you don't. You weigh up this kind of thing off the top of your head."

"Okay. We gain by getting rid of a court case which we may lose. We cut off paying legals for a hearing. We can get on with the business of this newspaper. But we lose because our competitors will think we don't have the stomach to back our journalists and to expose a fake. And far worse, we give up on the public's right to know."

"That's not entirely right," Max retorted. "There is nothing to stop us continuing to dig into Pearce's background. If we find something after the case is settled, we're not prevented from publishing. So what are you saying to me, Martin?"

"Screw the business decision. Do the right thing for journalism. Fight on."

"What about Pearce's wife?"

"Collateral damage."

Rankin nodded slowly as he thought. "Okay, I'll back you but this time, it will be your head if you're wrong."

Hardy telephoned Charlie Pearce. "Sorry. Their lawyers saw good sense in a drop hands settlement but *The Sentinel* wants its day in court. I tried my best."

"I'll talk to Claire. I think that just trying to settle the case cheered her. Do we need her to give evidence?"

"That's up to Mrs. Smith but I doubt it. Lizzie's evidence will do the trick. Tell Claire from me not to worry."

"Thanks, Hardy. See you in court."

*****

"Miriam Smith here. How may I help you Mr. Burgess?"

Hardy wanted no games. "Miri, this is business. You have the brief. It will help Dr Pearce if you would decide whether you need her to give evidence. Suffice it to say she has been unwell and it will assist her recovery if she knew she did not have to go into the witness box."

"If Lizzie Pearce gives evidence, I don't see how it helps our case to add Dr Pearce. After all, what can she say that Lizzie can't?"

"I agree. Thank you."

"Hardy, the other night. I apologise. I'd had a terrible day. My ex was making trouble and a case went badly."

"Say no more. All forgotten. Except."

"Except what?"

"Let's have that Saturday lunch after this case is over."

"I'll think about it."

After the conversation ended, Hardy thought to himself, 'I'm betting you will.'

*****

The night before trial, Martin Foster sat with Bill Tovey.

"Martin, let's review what we have. We've evidence that Arthur Hawkins started work at General Insurance in the early 1970s. A few years later, he went to work at Lloyd's Syndicate 4455 and soon after, Hawkins changed his name by Deed Poll to Henry Aitken. We have no hard evidence that Aitken was complicit in the antics and financial wrongdoings of Syndicate 4455 but as the criminal prosecutions of the lead underwriter and other working names failed, nothing can be introduced about Aitken's alleged criminal activities. None of those prosecuted have been willing to provide evidence to incriminate Aitken.

"We also have evidence Aitken left England in 1986 shortly before Syndicate 4455 was placed under investigation. About a year later in 1987, Charles Pearce turns up in Minneapolis. Supposedly born and raised in California, he travelled the world and ended up in the American Midwest to start his studies at the University of Minnesota. Soon after, he changed schools to Macalester University in St. Paul."

"I wouldn't argue with your summary."

"So, the nexus between Aitken and Pearce is still missing. Let me be clear. If you don't have this link, we have no defence under Article 10."

"So you say but I have a plan."

"What do you mean, a plan?"

Foster tapped his nose with his index finger. "There are more things in heaven and earth, Horatio."

"Martin, this isn't a playground. Judge Benton will make mincemeat of you and *The Sentinel* if you try anything underhand. My strong advice is this. Either you get the evidence by tomorrow morning or settle. I suspect the terms previously suggested would be available. If you go into court with some half-baked scheme, you will lose.

"I need to add two more things. First, expect an e-mail from me very shortly repeating my summary of the evidence and my advice today. I don't care how important *The Sentinel* may be in your eyes. I'll not have my firm's reputation put in jeopardy, nor mine for that matter, by some asinine press antics. Second, if you think I'd let any client of my firm tap his nose and tell me to mind my own business, you're an idiot. Tell me now what you're planning or I'll call Max Rankin and tell him you are putting the newspaper in serious jeopardy, following which my firm will resign from the case."

"I'll get Max for you. Do you really think Max doesn't know what I'm planning?"

"Fine. You're a pair. Now, are you going to tell me what you're up to or not? If you don't, be in no doubt I will pull my firm out from the case. If this happens, Judge Benton will scream and yell and may make my firm's life difficult but she will also know I wouldn't take such action unless there was a serious problem. So what's it going to be?"

"Calm down, Bill. The private investigator we used has the fingerprints of Arthur Hawkins. The prints are authentic. They were obtained from the Bishopsgate police."

"I know this. So what. Those prints are not in evidence. We can't use them. Anyway, you don't have the fingerprints of Charles Pearce so what use is this?"

"Not yet. But we have a plan to get them tomorrow."

As Foster unveiled the plan, Tovey was horrified. "Listen, Martin, your plan is just wrong. Further, no reputable forensic firm would do this. This firm you've engaged, who are they? Do they know the circumstances? Is the scientist willing to give evidence? I need to take his statement. Why the hell didn't you tell me earlier when I might actually have been able to do something?"

"You are too timid. Once we prove the fingerprints of Hawkins and Pearce are identical, his case collapses."

"Pity you don't know any ethics, let alone rules of evidence. The judge will throw this out. I need to warn Maynard. He might withdraw. I don't think you and Max understand that what you're proposing to do is as unethical as it gets. I need to think over my firm's position."

When Tovey spoke to his partners, they came to a decision that a letter to the clients advising against the proposed course of action was sufficient. After all, why throw away a huge fee now!

Chapter Eighteen.

At 9.30 on the morning of the *Pearce v The Sentinel* harassment case, all was tranquil in the Queen's Bench corridor of the High Court of Justice. By 10.15, organised bedlam had taken over. Barristers and solicitors were toing and froing, clerks wheeled boxes of papers, legal tomes and law reports and litigants and witnesses were trying to find where they needed to be.

Outside Court 13, the two sides were separated by ten yards or so in distance but by an ocean when it came to resolution of the dispute. Many cases are settled literally at the doors of the law court. The lawyers, especially the barristers, are happy to do this. Their brief fees will be paid in full. A settlement ends concerns over win/loss ratios and even if the litigants don't think so, it's often a better result for them than they would get from a judge.

However, today there was no meeting ground in *Pearce v The Sentinel*. There was nothing to discuss outside Court 13. *The Sentinel* had decided to fight on principle for the public's right to know. Pearce had decided that he wanted his judgment and a permanent injunction, believing his opponents had no worthwhile evidence.

Miriam Smith QC, resplendent in her silk waistcoat and gown, arrived moments before Mark Maynard QC. They strode towards each other and wished each other good morning before returning to their respective teams. It is an odd custom at the bar that opposing barristers do not shake hands. The opposing solicitors merely nodded to one another. The litigants and witnesses looked anxious.

The Court 13 usher opened the doors at 10.20 and bade everyone enter. Charlie Pearce stayed with his legal team. Claire, recently returned from the clinic, decided to sit in the public gallery. Lizzie sat with her father. It was probable that one or both of them would be called to give evidence that day. At 10.30, Judge Judith Benton entered and took her seat.

"My apologies to Counsel in *Pearce v The Sentinel*. I have an emergency application. I'm told it will not take long." A barrister spoke to Judge Benton about an unrelated matter. Lizzie asked Charlie, "What's happening? When is our case starting?"

"I don't really know. Guess we have to be patient."

The emergency application concluded. Claire Pearce's reverie was broken when Judge Benton asked Miriam Smith, Q.C., "Mrs. Smith, are you ready?" Smith nodded.

"And you Mr. Maynard?"

"Yes, M'lady."

At 11.40 am, Miriam opened her case, introducing her client as a popular novelist whose privacy rights had been trampled on by the national press, in particular *The Daily Sentinel*. By 12.30, her opening statement was concluded. Maynard declined to make an opening statement. He would wait until the Pearce case was closed.

Smith asked Judge Benton for leave to introduce a video of the television interview Pearce gave to Peregrine Vaughan. Maynard did not object. The video ended at 12.50. The judge asked counsel, "Would this be a convenient place to stop?" The question was rhetorical. "We'll resume at 1:50 pm."

After lunch, the judge asked Miriam Smith, "Are you ready to call witnesses?"

"Yes, M'lady. I call Elizabeth Pearce."

Maynard looked surprised. He thought to himself, 'Why start with the daughter? Ah well, we'll find out soon enough.'

Lizzie left her father's side and walked to the witness box where she was sworn in. Judge Benton intervened. "Mrs. Smith, I'd like to ask one or two questions of this witness before you begin."

Miriam acquiesced. "Elizabeth, would you prefer it if I call you Lizzie?" asked the judge.

"Lizzie is fine."

"How old are you?"

"I'm fourteen."

"Has it been explained to you why you are here?"

"Yes."

"And you understand you have to answer questions truthfully, even if you think your father might not like your answers?"

"Yes."

The judge let Mrs. Smith start her examination.

"Lizzie, do you remember a morning last year when lots of strangers came to your house?"

Maynard resisted the impulse to object to such a leading question.

"Yes. My bedroom is at the front of our house. I heard noises from the road very early in the morning."

"Do you know how early that was?"

"A few minutes before six."

"How do you know that?"

"I checked the clock on my mobile phone."

"What did you do after you checked the time?"

"I went to the window to see what was going on. There were a lot of people there, standing outside the gates to the house."

"What happened?"

"I went to tell my parents."

"And after you told them?"

"My father got up, came to my room and saw for himself the crowd that was outside. I used my mobile to take a video."

"Were you told to do that?"

"No. It's the sort of thing I like to do. I'm kind of a video historian."

Smith addressed the judge. "I'd like to play the several videos taken by Lizzie that morning and place them in evidence."

Maynard did not object. The first video was screened. It showed people from the media milling outside the house, nothing more.

"Lizzie, how many videos did you take?"

"Eight."

"Did anyone tell you to take videos?"

"Tell – no. Mr. Burgess, Daddy's lawyer, spoke to me eventually and asked me to keep taking videos."

Smith addressed the judge. "M'lady, we have a compilation disc of the other videos. I would like to play them too and place them in evidence."

Again, Maynard did not object. The DVD was played. It showed many acts of incursion, persistent door-bell ringing and door-knocking, men urinating on flower beds within the gates to the house and cat calling. The DVD covered the efforts by Harry Noble to collect someone from the house and how the media crowded around the car and prevented it from leaving.

"Lizzie, did you take all these videos?"

"Yes."

"What did you think?"

"I was scared. I felt like I was a prisoner. After Daddy left, Mummy and Mrs. James kept us away from a lot of things. When I wasn't videoing, I stayed at the back of the house."

"Who is Mrs. James?"

"Our housekeeper."

"How are you now?"

"Okay, I guess. Things have not been quite the same at home since this happened."

"Thank you, Lizzie. Please wait there. Mr. Maynard may have some questions."

Mark Maynard rose. Cross-examination of a young teenager was problematical. Intimidation wouldn't be tolerated but kid gloves wouldn't work either.

"May I call you Lizzie? Was it fun, having a day off school that day?"

Lizzie thought before replying. "A bit, but I like school and I missed my friends."

"How were things at school after all this happened?"

"Some of the older ones made fun of me and my brother and sister. I was bullied. It wasn't nice. But eventually things died down."

"So everything is okay now?"

"At school, yes."

"What about at home?"

"I don't understand."

"Is everything back to normal at home?"

"It's not the same. Recently, things got a bit tense. I think my parents are worried about this case."

"In what way?"

Smith rose. "M'lady, how is this witness qualified to answer such a question? Her evidence relates solely to supporting the claim for harassment. What the witness's beliefs might be about her parents' state of mind is pure conjecture and irrelevant."

"Mr. Maynard, I agree with the objection. Do you have any questions concerning the videos?"

"Indeed I do. Lizzie, do the videos you took exactly represent the DVDs we have seen?"

"I think so. Sometimes a DVD might cut off a second or two before the end of a video. Otherwise, I don't know about any differences."

Immediately, Maynard regretted the question. Nothing further to be gained from such a line of questioning. Best to leave this witness alone.

"M'lady, I have no more questions."

Benton looked at the clock. "I think I will rise. We will resume at 10.30 tomorrow morning."

Lizzie left the witness box and went to Charlie, who embraced her. "You did so well. I'm very proud of you." By then, Claire had made her way to the well of the court and hugged Lizzie. She was cool towards Charlie, asking only, "shall we go home?"

"I just need to check with the lawyers."

Five minutes later, the Pearce car was whisking them away home.

*****

Next morning, Miriam Smith called Charles Pearce to give evidence. Charlie entered the witness box, swore the oath and waited for the first question. Miriam took him carefully through his history and that of his family. He spoke of the Californian upbringing, his time working in advertising in Los Angeles, the death of parents and inheritance, travels, and his move to America's Midwest. He then spoke of his time at the Universities of Minnesota and Macalester, his marriage to Claire and their move to England. He answered detailed questions about his desire for privacy and his reluctance to allow the public to know about his private life.

"I have disclosed more this morning than I have in the previous fifteen years."

"How do you feel about that?"

"Not happy but I guess it's the price for the privilege of living in England and for protecting my legal rights."

The judge checked the time. "I think we'll rise for lunch. One hour."

As Charlie left the witness box, a court usher passed him, reached into the witness box, poured water from a glass back into a jug and removed the glass. Oddly, the usher wore surgical gloves. Hastily, he left the Court and headed for the men's lavatory. There he placed the glass in a zip-lock bag, removed his usher's robe and put it in a shopping bag. Then Tell Yer What headed for a private forensic science firm in Holborn.

At 1.55 pm, the Court reconvened. Charlie Pearce returned to the witness box and resumed giving evidence.

"Mr. Pearce," Miriam asked, "you say you are a private man. What exactly do you mean by this?"

"By profession, I'm an author. From time to time, I'm in the public eye when I publish a new book. I'm willing to discuss my books with literary journalists. They are welcome to question me on all aspects of my writing life, including my earnings from it. However, I'm not willing to talk about my family, nor my friends, nor matters which are unrelated to my writing. To do so would be unfair to both my family and friends who want no part of the glare of publicity."

"I gather you don't give public readings and the like?"

Maynard rose. "M'lady, might I ask that my friend doesn't lead the witness?"

Smith replied. "I'll re-phrase my question. Do you give public readings?"

"No. My publishers are not happy about this because when they arrange events, the public knows I will not be present. Actors read extracts from my books. Publishers engage their services, as well as those of literary experts who talk about the books."

"Do you attend book signings?"

"No. I'm unwilling to do this, even when a new novel is published."

"Why not? Surely it would help advertise and sell your books?"

"If I did as you suggest, it would take too much of my time. A book signing tour of the United States usually takes the better part of two months. A book signing tour of the UK takes at least three weeks. I'm unwilling to spend this amount of time away from my family."

"Even though sales might increase significantly?"

"This can't be proved and, sparing my blushes, my books sell well enough. Time with my family is worth far more to me than money raised from signing books."

"I want to take you through the night of your interview on the Peregrine Vaughan show. When Mr. Vaughan broke his agreement with you, how did you feel?"

Mark Maynard rose. "M'lady, I must object. Mr. Vaughan is not a party to these proceedings and Mr. Pearce's feelings are surely irrelevant."

"No, Mr. Maynard, I'll allow it. Vaughan was the catalyst for the litigation. Mr. Pearce, you may answer."

"I was angry, furious, livid. I felt betrayed and I wanted to get out of the television studio as soon as I could. I had a written agreement with Vaughan. He knew questions about my private life were off limits. He rode roughshod over the deal. Reputable journalists don't do that sort of thing."

"Where did you go after you left the television studio?"

"Straight home."

"Was Mrs. Pearce at home when you arrived?"

"Yes."

"What did she say to you?"

"As I recall, she said 'I have a scotch waiting for you. It's a double.'"

There was laughter in Court. The judge couldn't suppress a smile.

"Were you disturbed that night?"

"No, we took our telephone off the hook and turned off our mobiles. But early next morning, around six o'clock, Lizzie came into our bedroom to tell me there was a noise outside in the road."

Miriam Smith took Charlie through the disturbances of the morning, Charlie's escape to London and the events of the day.

"Thinking back, when you recall the events of that morning, when you watch the videos, what were you feeling?"

"Extreme fury, total annoyance and anger, seeing my family being threatened by journalists."

"After you obtained the injunction from her ladyship to end the door-stepping, it was broken by *The Sentinel*. Were you surprised?"

"Shocked."

"Why?"

"Without wanting to sound pompous, this country is a nation of laws. I could not believe *The Sentinel* would defy the law."

"Apart from that breach, for which the Defendant and its employees were severely punished, has the injunction been observed?"

"Yes, so far as I am aware. Mind you, since the injunction was granted, my wife has been engaged in conversations in our village which she would have preferred to avoid. Also, all my children have been bullied at school."

"This must have been very disturbing for you."

"Of course. It's the worst experience of my life. Claire and I spoke to the schools and the bullying eased off. In the weeks after, life reverted to normal, although I am suffering writer's block. I don't know if this is linked to what happened last year."

"M'lady, I have no more questions."

"Mr. Maynard," asked the Judge, "are you ready to cross-examine?"

"Indeed, M'lady, but looking at the time, might I suggest that we start afresh tomorrow?"

It was 3.37 pm. "I agree. I know it's early but it would be unfair to let you have less than half an hour before stopping your cross. We'll adjourn until 10.30 tomorrow."

The parties returned to the respective barristers' chambers. Miriam Smith was content. "You gave evidence well, Charlie. Just to go over things for tomorrow, Maynard will do his best to give you a hard time. He'll ask questions about your background, your parents and your time at college and work. He'll want to know what you did after leaving Culver City until you turned up in the Twin Cities. He'll suggest you are exaggerating and overstating your feelings, especially your private life rights and the way your family suffered. Just stay calm and don't overstate."

"Understood."

On the way out, Hardy stopped Charlie. "Where was Claire today?"

"She's still under the weather so she gave court a miss."

"Is she getting better?"

"I hope so. Hard to tell. She has cut down the drinking but she is distant. When this is over, I'll take us all for a holiday, time to re-connect."

Hardy clapped Charlie on the shoulder as they said goodbye.

*****

In Mark Maynard's room, the atmosphere was different.

"I know we have allegations of Pearce's change of identity after shenanigans at Lloyd's but there is still no hard evidence. You have nobody to say Pearce is Hawkins/Aitken. Nobody at General Insurance remembers him. Lloyd's members and employees are no help. Mrs. Grey is dead.

"Mr. Rankin, Mr. Foster, please listen to me carefully. I will not introduce mere hunches. Unless you can prove, on balance of probabilities, that Hawkins/Aitken is Pearce, you have no foundation on which to base an Article 10 defence. And even if you get the evidence, the judge may refuse leave to introduce it at this late stage."

"Assume you'll have the evidence you want by morning," said Foster.

"Mr. Foster still thinks he will have fingerprint evidence to prove Pearce is Hawkins," explained Tovey. "Just so you know, one of *The Sentinel's* people boosted Pearce's water glass from the court at lunchtime. It goes without saying that I have advised Mr. Foster and Mr. Rankin that the judge will be highly critical of this subterfuge and, furthermore, no ethical forensic scientist would undertake the fingerprint evidence task, especially if they knew all the facts."

"Tovey, why is this the first I've heard of this?"

"I only found this out late last night. Even if there is evidence to establish Pearce is Hawkins/Aitken, I doubt the judge will allow it to be introduced now."

Maynard turned to the clients. "What you are doing is plain wrong. When the judge finds out, she may well throw the book at you. You would be well advised to re-address the settlement terms that were on offer last week. I doubt the judge will allow any new evidence, especially when the other side is being caught by surprise. Why did you not ask Pearce's lawyers for fingerprints, do things on the up?"

Max Rankin had remained quiet but he erupted. "Maynard, this isn't a game of cricket. We are not gentlemen here. This is the real world. Once we get fingerprint evidence that proves Pearce to be a liar, would the judge exclude it just because of rules? What about truth and justice? I expect you to fight this. Fight with every weapon at your disposal."

"This is completely unorthodox but I'll do my best. When may I expect to see a report from these forensic people?"

"Tomorrow."

"When tomorrow?"

"First thing, I hope."

Outside Maynard's chambers, Rankin told Foster, "your assumptions about the fingerprints had better be right or you can kiss goodbye to your career. Are we clear?"

Foster had had enough. Years of being bullied by the proprietor bubbled up. He looked Rankin in the eye.

"Max, I'm fed up with your threats. I'm only doing what you want me to do. Remember your instructions, 'destroy Pearce.' If we don't get the evidence, I'll resign but I'll want a decent pay-out or I might have to look very carefully at my rights to publish my own story and you will feature. If you give me terms I'm happy with, you can be assured of my silence. I'll need enough to pay off the mortgage, pay my pension up for the next few years and some dosh in the bank. Are *we* clear?"

"Just get the fucking evidence. Then you'll get all you want and you'll keep your job."

Chapter Nineteen.

At 10.15 the next day, the parties assembled outside Court 13. Maynard asked Foster, "Where's the evidence I was promised? I need you to understand beyond any doubt that I cannot and will not make allegations of the nature you assert if I can't prove them. The judge will have me up before the Bar Council if I suggest that Pearce is Hawkins/Aitken when there's no substantive evidence in support. I want to make this abundantly clear to you beyond doubt and I want confirmation that you and Mr. Rankin have been advised accordingly. Mr. Tovey, will you get this done now, please?"

Tovey nodded and asked his clients to sign a note he'd drafted. They didn't like it. For Rankin, it was, 'who is this person, Maynard?' Foster looked at his watch. Where was that report? At 10.30 am, Judge Benton took her seat and invited Maynard to commence his cross.

"Mr. Pearce, do you admit you are a public person?"

"No."

"You are the author of eight highly successful novels. Your name is known the length and breadth of the UK and America. How are you not a public person?"

"Actually, it's nine. I have published nine novels. Why does writing books make me a public person?"

"It is not for me to answer questions but I will make a suggestion. Are you not in the public eye because the public as a whole pays a great deal of money for your work? Hence is the public not entitled to know about you?"

"I have never denied I have become wealthy from my writing. But I suggest you are wealthy from your advocacy. Does that require you to allow the public to know about your private life?"

Maynard reddened. "Mr. Pearce, I repeat you are here to answer my questions. I'm not here to answer yours. Now, what about Hollywood? Have not seven of your books been adapted into motion pictures or television series? Does not that make you even more famous?"

"I don't think you understand the movie and television business, at least how it works in Hollywood. Through a myriad of agents, film studios and producers, an author might be offered payment for an option to adapt a novel into a motion picture or TV series. With a lot of luck and if the option gets exercised, the author is paid. But the author is not the script writer. The author gets a minor mention in the screen credits. The Hollywood movies and television don't add to my fame, to adopt your words. All I get is a credit, which lasts on screen for less than a second. I'd mention that two of my books became major movies but the script writers were awarded Oscars and BAFTAs, not me."

"Mr. Maynard," said the judge, "I think you've exhausted this line of questioning. Please move on."

"Where did you go to school?"

"Culver City High School."

"Where is that?"

"Hmm. Culver City?" There was laughter from the gallery. "It's in the suburbs of Los Angeles."

"How many pupils attended the school?"

Pearce took a beat before he answered, "About two thousand, I think."

"Would you find it strange that none of the teachers or students we interviewed remember you?"

"Not really. I left Culver High over thirty years ago. I've no idea who your people asked. However, my lawyers have disclosed my High School transcripts."

"You attended university at UCLA in Los Angeles. Did you live at home?"

"Yes."

"Why? Isn't it the tradition that undergraduates move away and live on campus?"

"My parents did not wish to indulge me by paying for accommodation. College tuition was expensive enough."

"Again, we have made enquiries at UCLA. Nobody remembers you. Can you explain why?"

"I graduated from UCLA more than twenty five years ago. As with high school, my lawyers have provided my university transcript."

"What were your parents' names?"

"George and Martha."

"When did you last speak to them?"

"More than twenty years ago."

"Are you estranged from them?"

Pearce paused for affect. Pursing his lips, he replied, "No, of course not. My father died from cancer in 1983. My mother passed the following year. I believe she died from a broken heart."

Maynard paused. He had missed this in his brief. "My apologies. I was unaware." He glared at the back of Tovey's head. "Were you working before your parents' death?"

"Yes."

"Doing what?"

"I was employed at an advertising agency, 'Brands.' I worked on the creative side, trying to improve brand recognition for clients."

"Where was your office?"

"Santa Monica. And before you tell me nobody who was there remembers me, I was laid off from the agency a week before mother died. Brands went bust."

The judge intervened. "Mr. Maynard, this is all fascinating but where does this walk down memory lane take us? Please move on."

"When did you leave Brands?"

"1984."

"What did you do then?"

"On my mother's death, I inherited a lot of money, sufficient to allow me to give up work. I travelled the world."

"Where did you go?"

"A lot of countries. I always wanted to see India. I stayed for a short while but could not get accustomed to the food. I moved on to Australia."

"I've seen passport stamps. You were in Australia for nearly two years. Where did you go?"

"I bought a camper van in Sydney. Loaded it up with all sorts including a mattress and a lot of water and drove around Australia. Mostly the coast. There's not much hospitable land in the interior."

"You did this for two years?"

"Yes. The circumference of Australia is about nine thousand miles. It is amazing. I stopped off at many places on route. I'd work a while, make friends with locals and live the slower pace of life. Maybe you should try it."

The judge showed her impatience. "Mr. Maynard. I cannot see how Mr. Pearce's travels are relevant to a harassment suit. Move on."

Maynard was struggling. He tapped William Tovey on the shoulder. "Where is that evidence I was promised?"

At that moment, Tell Yer What entered the Court and went to the bench where Tovey sat, whispering to him. In turn, Tovey turned to Maynard and gave a thumbs up sign.

"M'lady, may I ask for a short recess?" asked Maynard. "It seems new evidence has come to light and I would like to confer briefly with those instructing me."

Benton was unhappy. "This is both unorthodox and highly irregular. What is the nature of this evidence?"

"It goes to the veracity of the claimant. I'd prefer to say nothing more until I have had a chance to examine it in detail."

"Very well, you have fifteen minutes."

Outside court, Maynard quickly read the report from the fingerprint expert who stated that Arthur Hawkins/ Henry Aitken and Charlie Pearce might be one and the same person. There was a problem. Pearce had no discernible, clear fingerprints. The central part of all his fingers and thumbs had been burned off. There were prints of peripherals but very few. The likelihood of the three people being one and the same was put at "maybe 50%."

Maynard shouted at Tovey, "What sort of evidence is this?" He turned to Rankin and Foster. "Look at this? So much for your great theory. What do you expect me to tell the judge?"

"Lawyers make bricks from sand. Bluff."

Maynard was furious. "Mr. Foster, that sort of game may be played by your newspaper but what happens here isn't your game, nor do I follow your rules. In a court of law, you don't bluff. If I did, the Bar Council would have me on toast. As I've told you repeatedly, if this is the only identity evidence you can muster, you have no defence and your best course is to settle."

"No, no, no. Get back in court and do what we pay you for."

Maynard looked at Tovey. "Make a full note of this conversation and distribute it. I'll need to see this so-called expert. Please arrange this for the lunch recess."

Back in Court, Maynard puffed out his chest and placed his thumbs on the lapels of his silk gown.

"Mr. Pearce, have you been entirely honest with this court?"

"I believe so."

"You've not hidden anything?"

"No, not so far as I am aware."

"Are you sure?"

Judge Benton was furious. "Mr. Maynard, you have asked the same question three times and received the same answer. Move on. This is your final warning."

"Apologies, M'lady. Very well, Mr. Pearce, I suggest you are not Charles Pearce of Culver City. Am I wrong?"

"That's a double negative. What's your question?"

"Mr. Maynard," said Judge Benton. "Put a direct question."

"Mr. Pearce, who is Arthur Hawkins?"

Claire Pearce was in court. If Maynard had eyes in the back of his head, he would have seen Claire go as white as a truce flag as she slumped in her seat. Charlie's game was up. Charlie blinked and stuttered. "I don't, I don't understand."

"Then I'll put my question differently. I suggest you were born in 1956 in Tilbury and christened Arthur Hawkins, the son of Harry and Tilly Hawkins. In 1981 you changed your name by Deed Poll to Henry Aitken. In 1986 you disappeared from England and re-emerged in America as Charlie Pearce. Am I right?"

Miriam Smith stood. "M'lady, we are caught by surprise. Mr. Maynard has provided no documentary evidence to support these allegations. I don't know how he proposes to prove what he is asserting but he has kept us in the dark. I would ask you to end this line of questioning and reject the introduction of any new evidence. At such a late stage, this is contrary to all the rules of procedure."

The Judge asked, "Mr. Maynard, do you have evidence to prove these changes of identity?"

"I believe so. I received the final piece of evidence shortly before the recess. I will put documents into evidence now." The Court usher took a set of documents and handed them to the Judge. Maynard passed four sets to Miriam Smith for herself, her junior, solicitors and Charlie.

"Now, Mr. Pearce, or whatever your name is…"

"Hold fast, Mr. Maynard," said the Judge. "I want to review these documents. Mrs. Smith has a point. Under the rules, it is far too late in the day for you to introduce new evidence. If I understand things correctly, you have given no indication at all to Mrs. Smith and her client of your intentions. In this event, on what basis do the rules allow this new information into evidence?"

Maynard was ready. "M'lady, may I direct you to Rule 44 of the Civil Procedure Rules? You have an overriding discretion to admit evidence at this stage. The defence has not opened its case yet. You will see the defence now has documentation supporting the allegations. I submit they prove Mr. Pearce's true identity. It follows that he has lied to the court. In detail, there is evidence from the Metropolitan Police which comprises a set of fingerprints taken from one Arthur Hawkins when he was sixteen years old. I will seek leave to introduce fingerprint evidence concerning the Claimant. That evidence suggests there are significant similarities between the prints of Mr. Hawkins and Mr. Pearce."

Judge Benton looked at Miriam Smith. "What do you say?"

"It is unreasonable to expect any comment from me right away, M'lady. My client and I have been blind-sided. I cannot judge the evidence until I have a chance to review it. Also I want the opportunity to seek advice from a fingerprint expert. My client and I have been caught completely by surprise, something the rules of the Supreme Court are there to prevent. If you insist upon a submission from me now, I'd invite you in the strongest terms to reject this evidence forthwith."

"I want time to consider the position. I'll adjourn for the day. Mr. Maynard, should I decide to allow this new evidence, I will want to hear first from your fingerprint expert."

"M'lady, before you adjourn, may I please explain the documents?"

"Very well. What do you have?"
The first document in the bundle is the birth certificate of Arthur Hawkins. The second is the Deed Poll when Arthur Hawkins lawfully changed his name to Henry Aitken. The third is a set of fingerprint photographs. Those labelled "A" were taken yesterday. They belong to the Claimant. Those labelled "B" were taken at Bishopsgate Police Station in 1972. They belonged to one sixteen year old named Arthur Hawkins."

"Fingerprints taken yesterday? What does that mean? What were the circumstances?" asked Judge Benton.

"M'lady, I am instructed the prints were on a water glass used by Mr. Pearce when he was in the witness box."

Miriam Smith was on her feet. "Yes, Mrs. Smith, I know." Judge Benton was appalled. "Mr. Maynard, what game do you think you are playing? Prints were taken without Mr. Pearce's agreement, knowledge or consent. How does the court know that what you are presenting were not a set of random prints from a third party? This conduct is completely wrong and unacceptable. I am minded not to exercise my discretion in your clients' favour because of this shoddy behaviour."

"I have advised my clients," Maynard responded. "But I have a solution. Will Mr. Pearce willingly give a set of prints now?"

"No, he will not," retorted Smith.

"M'lady, I am instructed that a fingerprint expert will say that there is at least a 50% certainty that the prints of Hawkins are those of the Claimant. We have yet to find incontrovertible evidence of details of the change of identity from Aitken to Pearce but from our present enquiries, it is highly probable that Mr. Pearce's American passport is a forgery."

"Mrs. Smith, is there anything else you want to say?"

"My client and I have been completely taken by surprise. As I have said, I cannot judge the evidence until I have a chance to review it. I need to take instructions from Mr. Pearce and seek advice from a fingerprint expert. However, I would submit that days after this hearing commenced, it is unfair and unjust to allow the defence to proceed in this way. It is against the rules and the interests of justice. I invite you to reject this evidence forthwith, especially in view of the underhand way it was obtained."

"Thank you, Mrs. Smith. I'll now take time to consider the position. I want to see counsel and solicitors in my chambers in ten minutes."

Judge Benton retired to her room in the Judges Corridor, removed her wig and gown and asked her clerk for a pot of tea as she ruminated on the next moves. Was Pearce a fraud? If so, surely she should permit late introduction of evidence in the interests of justice. But what if Pearce was not Hawkins/Aitken? Was *The Sentinel* playing tricks? Should she not throw out the new evidence now and take her chances on an appeal?

There was a knock on the door. Smith, Maynard, their juniors and solicitors walked in. Chairs were found for them. Benton fixed all with a steely stare. She addressed counsel formally as Mrs. Smith and Mr. Maynard, an ominous sign.

"I know television dramas about the law like to have a gripping, last minute denouement but not in my court. Here we play to the rules, rules which, if I may remind you, strike fairness between both sides.

"Mr. Maynard, you and your clients have had months to prepare your defence. Yet here we are, it's one minute to midnight, and you spring this surprise. I want a detailed explanation. If I find anything untoward, I will not hesitate to report you to the Bar Council. Mr. Tovey, I am amazed to find your firm involved in this shoddy business. I will report you to the Law Society if your firm has not adhered to the law."

"I'm happy to provide a full explanation, judge" Maynard replied. "You'll find that both I and my instructing solicitors have behaved properly. May I proceed?"

The judge nodded her agreement.

Maynard continued. "Over the past months, we discovered that a person named Arthur Hawkins worked for Lloyd's of London. Hawkins changed his name by Deed Poll to Henry Aitken. In 1986, Aitken disappeared. A year later, Charles Pearce surfaced in America, to be precise in Minneapolis, Minnesota. It is my clients' contention that all three men are one and the same person. When Hawkins was sixteen, there was an issue relating to an assault. The Metropolitan Police have Hawkins' fingerprints on record.

"Yesterday, my clients secured a set of Mr. Pearce's fingerprints in an unorthodox manner, I admit, but it is our case that the prints on the glass belong to Mr. Pearce's. Our fingerprint expert provided his report only this morning when I was cross-examining Mr. Pearce. The report states that a direct match cannot be made because the pads on Pearce's fingers don't exist anymore. I don't know what occurred but the expert suggests the finger pads have been burnt.

"The expert has compared peripheral areas on Pearce's fingerprints with those of Hawkins and will state there are comparisons. He thinks there is a 50% chance of a match. This is the evidence we want to introduce. I acknowledge it is late in the day but are not the interests of justice served best if the true identity of the Claimant is disclosed?"

Judge Benton nodded. "Your final point may have merit but I am troubled by two factors: why has it taken so long to find this so-called evidence and why were Mr. Pearce's fingerprints surreptitiously obtained when a simple request would have achieved proper results?"

"Judge, when an individual wants to hide the truths of his life and disappears, it can be very difficult to find evidence. Pearce's fingerprints were obtained from a water glass he drank from in court. The person who took the glass was an employee of the defendants. There were eye witnesses to all of this and they are in this room."

"May I intervene, judge?" asked Miriam Smith. "Who is this expert of yours and was he told how the prints were obtained?"

"His name is Walters, Harry Walters and I gather he was told about how the glass was obtained." Tovey nodded.

Miriam Smith breathed deeply. She was incensed.

"Judge, my knowledge of fingerprint evidence tells me no reputable expert would accept this subterfuge. I am truly shocked and appalled. The defendants' actions are plain wrong and the court should not entertain them. Were you to accept fingerprint evidence at this very late stage, it would serve to encourage similar behaviour by other litigants, seeking to put the other side at a huge disadvantage."

"In principle, I agree with you but I have to look at the overall interests of justice."

"If you decide to allow introduction of this so-called evidence, I will want full details of Walters' qualifications and a comprehensive list of the questions he was asked to answer. And before my client's cross-examination continues, I would like the fingerprint issue resolved by you. If you decide against me, I'll want to introduce evidence to counter Mr. Maynard's so-called expert."

"Noted. My question to you, Mrs. Smith, is, based on the assumption that *The Sentinel's* evidence stands up. Is not Mr. Maynard right that the interests of justice are best served by testing it? If your client has led a life which he has hidden from the court, should he not be judged accordingly?"

"I would say the interests of justice are not being served if a litigant is permitted to catch his opponent by surprise. To use an American expression, the defence is a day late and a dollar short. To allow this evidence will encourage litigants to ignore the rules, which are in place for good reason. Also, even at this late stage, please take into account the suspect nature of this so-called fingerprint expert. He has accepted the glass in doubtful circumstances and expressed similarities of prints in percentage terms, which I believe a fingerprint expert does not do."

Benton paused for thought. "The hearing is adjourned for today. If I allow the introduction of new evidence, I'll adjourn until Monday to give the claimant time to research and introduce counter-evidence. If I decide against the respondent, we will resume tomorrow morning. In that event, Mr. Maynard, you may not cross on Mr. Pearce's identity based on fingerprints. Am I clear?" All nodded. "I'll give you my decision this afternoon."

In the corridor outside Court 13, Charlie and Claire sat. Both were apprehensive. When they saw the lawyers appear, they stood. Hardy and Miriam spoke to them in whispers. "We're adjourned for today," said Hardy. "Back tomorrow if the judge refuses to allow new evidence or on Monday if she does."

"What do you think?" Charlie asked Miriam.

"My best guess is we'll be adjourned until Monday. Why are you looking worried? There's nothing you want to tell us, is there? You are Charles Pearce, aren't you?" she smiled.

Claire spoke up. "It's the waiting. Maybe you don't realise quite how scary this place is for people like us. The pressure is gigantic. We've been living inside a pressure cooker since this whole business started."

Injunction

"I know but it is what it is. You've been in court before, Charles. Let's assume the judge gives this round to *The Sentinel*. I will need a fingerprint expert to rebut their evidence. Mr. Burgess, I have used Kate Thomas at Pains Forensic. She's good. We need this expedited."

Hardy noted the formality of address. He told himself, 'So I'm not forgiven yet' as he replied, "I agree. I'll get onto this just in case."

"What do Claire and I do?" asked Charlie.

"Go home and sit tight. Mr. Burgess will call you as soon as we know if we're back tomorrow or Monday."

As Charlie started to leave, Smith called him back. "Show me your hands, please. I want to see the tip of your fingers and thumbs."
Charlie did as asked. His finger pads were smooth, virtually void of any normal signs that could be used as prints. One or two fingers had pads which, on their extreme periphery, had wrinkles.

"How did this happen?" Smith asked.

"When I was fourteen, one of my hobbies was photography. I joined Culver High's Photography Club. I liked the whole process, taking pictures, developing film. One day I was careless. I was in the school dark room and instead of placing my pictures in the correct tray to develop them, I dipped them into a tray containing an acid chemical. The tray was clearly marked. As I said, carelessness. In an instant, the damage was done. I yelled out in pain, a teacher saw what had happened and took me to the Emergency Room. I was treated for third degree burns. Ever since, my finger and thumb pads have been numb."

Smith nodded, said her goodbyes and went on her way. Hardy said he would get in touch as soon as he heard anything. Charlie and Claire found their driver and made their way home. Charlie wanted to talk but Claire told him it was best not to speak. "The driver will hear," she whispered.

At home, Claire busied herself, making a light lunch. Then she exploded. "Oh God, Charlie, they've got you. What are we going to do?"

"Well, let's keep calm heads. The judge may not allow the new evidence and, even if she does, I have no discernible fingerprints. The plastic surgeon dealt with this. So, they haven't got me."

"You're taking a tremendous gamble. How will it look, what will happen to us, if you are proved to be a liar?"

"What options do I have? If I try to settle now, *The Sentinel* will refuse. They'll know they have me, even if they can't prove it. If I admit my past, I'll be pilloried. I'll be front page news for weeks. We'll be hounded again. The English love to build you up and knock you down. The tabloids will print anything that makes me look bad and *The Sentinel* will scream my guilt and their vindication as they parade my life at Lloyd's. I don't see I have a choice."

"You're ignoring the value of honesty. Other newspapers will want your story and will publish another side, a different side: how you wanted to get away from your past, how you gave all your money from your old life to charity, how you have led a blameless life for 20 years."

"I'll think it over. Claire, I know it's a nightmare but, we need to hold our nerve. One way or the other, it will end soon."

"No it won't. I'm telling you, they have you. Even if you win the case, this will go on and on. The press will keep going until they get the evidence. I can't live in this nightmare or its aftermath, nor will I let the children endure it. I say own up, take what's coming and rebuild our lives. That's what I want."

Charlie offered a kiss to Claire on her cheek. She turned her face from him. He retired to his study.

*****

At three o'clock, the Judge's clerk sent both sides a message that the judge would allow late introduction of evidence. She confirmed she would hear evidence from fingerprint experts before Pearce's cross examination resumed on Monday. Maynard didn't like it but, as he told Tovey, "If I object to this process, the judge may well say 'very well, I won't allow new evidence.' We'll have to do what she says."

Both Rankin and Foster were fine with the ruling. So far as they were concerned, Pearce was getting closer and closer to being exposed. In their euphoria, neither of them read the Walters report carefully.

Chapter Twenty.

The hearing resumed at 10.30 on Monday morning. Maynard addressed the judge. "M'lady, may I explain again the documents provided to you and my opponents last week and the evidence relating to Mr. Pearce's fingerprints?"

"No need but by Mr. Pearce's fingerprints, I assume you mean those taken last week by the removal of a water glass from this court?"

"Yes."

Miriam Smith was on her feet. The judge motioned her to sit. "Yes, Mrs. Smith, I know. Mr. Maynard, how do you argue the lawfulness of prints taken without Mr. Pearce's agreement or knowledge? How does the court know they were not a set of random prints?"

"If needed I can call the person who removed the glass. My instructing solicitor, Mr. Tovey, witnessed the actions. You may recall my solution was that Mr. Pearce provide a set of prints himself. My opponent rejected the proposal. I wonder what the claimant wants to hide. Our fingerprint expert will say that there is around a fifty percent certainty that the prints of Hawkins and Pearce have remarkable similarities."

"Very well," said Judge Benton. "Call your expert witness."

Harry Walters was sworn in. He was young, no more than 25 years old. He wore a brown herring bone jacket frayed at the sleeves and a white shirt whose collar tips curled. He had tousled brown hair and a face with a haunted look. He was nervous as a tic.

Maynard took him through the examination in chief. Walters' qualifications were briefly recited. Enlarged photographs were produced of the Pearce fingerprints. The central parts of each finger and thumb pad were plain skin, apparently caused from old burns. Walters would not offer an opinion as to whether the burns were accidental or not, nor how old they were. When Walters was asked to compare those prints with the ones from the Metropolitan Police, he was on firmer ground.

Using a pointer, he said, "Look at the similarities here, here and here. This leads me to the belief that Mr. Pearce and Mr. Hawkins may well be one and the same person."

"And this is your expert opinion?"

"Yes."

"How certain are you?"

"Pretty convinced."

"Put that as a percentage or fraction."

"I'd hesitate about doing that."

"Why not? You have done so in your report."

"Yes, but I was told that figure wouldn't be used in court. It was just for *Sentinel* people."

Smith rose but was waived away by the judge. "You'll have your turn soon."

"What figure did you give?"

"Fifty percent."

"You are saying there is a one in two chance that Mr. Hawkins and Mr. Pearce are the same person."

"Maybe."

Maynard knew Walters was about to be crucified in cross examination but he had fulfilled his duties to the court and the clients. Miriam Smith rose.

"Mr. Walters, you are here as an expert witness. How old are you?"

"Twenty five."

"You told the court you have a BSc in forensic science from the University of Wolverhampton. Was fingerprinting taught as a course module?"

"Not exactly."

"Well was it or wasn't it?"

"No but one of the professors ran optional sessions on fingerprint evidence."

"Were these sessions part of your degree?"

"No, not really."

"Why was that?"

Walters pursed his lips. "Fingerprinting is not accepted as an exact science."

"Indeed. Isn't it true that no reputable scientist in this field offers a figure or a percentage when identifying fingerprints? Does not an expert deal in probabilities based on scans?"

Walters grimaced. He shrugged his shoulders. He didn't respond.

"Mr. Walters, we need your answer as an expert."

"I did what I was told by Mr. Foster, to state a percentage figure in my report. I told him that wasn't the way but he insisted."

"Did I hear you correctly? Mr. Foster told you what to put in your report? Do you see him in this court?"

"Yes in that he asked me to put a percentage and yes, he's there," said Walters, pointing at Martin Foster.

"You work for Riley's Forensics?"

"Yes."

"How long have you worked there?"

"Nine months."

"Did any of your superiors know about your instructions from Mr. Foster?"

"Not exactly."

"What *exactly* does that mean?"

"I told my boss that *The Sentinel* wanted a job done but I didn't say anything about the details."

"How much did Mr. Foster offer to pay you?"

"A grand."

"A thousand pounds? That doesn't seem much. Were you paid personally?"

Walters looked very uncomfortable.

"We are waiting, Mr. Walters. And you are under oath."

"Mr. Foster gave me a thousand pounds."

"Did Riley's know this?"

Walters hesitated, then replied, "No."

"Why did Mr. Foster come to you?"

"He knows my family."

"And he paid you personally, not your employers, for the report?"

Walters nodded his head. The judge motioned Smith to move on.

"Let's get back to the fingerprints. Would you like to reconsider what is in your report? Are there in fact any similarities between the prints for Hawkins and the prints for Pearce?"

"Yes, there are."

"How many similarities for each finger and thumb?"

"On average two or three on some fingers."

"Some fingers? How many exactly?"

"Two fingers, one thumb."

"If you were to take my fingerprints and compare the periphery prints to those of Hawkins, would the number of similarities differ?"

"I don't know."

"Come now, you say you're an expert. Let me put the question differently. Isn't it fair to say that, based on the methods of your examination, Pearce's prints would match millions of people around the world?"

"Probably."

"How do you reconcile what you have just said with the evidence given a few minutes ago of a 50/50 chance of similarity?"

Walters hesitated. Finally, he said, "I can't."

"I have no further questions, M'lady."

Rankin looked at Foster, shaking his head. He placed his left index finger to his throat and made a slicing motion.

"I have no re-examination, M'lady," said Maynard. He knew the fingerprint evidence was destined for the dustbin.

"I would like to hear evidence from your expert, Mrs. Smith. Is she ready?"

"Yes, M'lady. However, might I suggest spending further time on this topic is unnecessary? It is my submission that the fingerprint evidence offered by the defence should be excluded."

"Nevertheless, I'd like to hear from your expert." Judge Benton had indeed made up her mind but she didn't want to give the defence any room for an appeal. Smith called Kate Thomas to the witness stand. After Mrs. Thomas was sworn in, Smith got down to business.

"May I ask for your qualifications?"

"I've been a director of Pains Forensics for fifteen years. I have a B.Sc. degree and a Ph.D. in handwriting and signatures from the University of Birmingham. I'm a member of the Royal Society of Chemistry and I'm a chartered member of the Royal Society."

"Are you an expert on fingerprinting?"

"To the extent that anyone can be an expert in this field, the answer is 'yes.' The difficulty is that fingerprinting is not accepted as an exact science. I can go into detail if needed."

"That won't be necessary. Have you examined the fingerprint copies offered by the defence?"

"I have."

"As an expert, is there a probability that the copies demonstrate that the prints are of the same person."

"No, I don't believe so. The photo on the right of the easel is hard to decipher because of burning to the finger pads. The prints have few similarities to the photo on the left. It would be foolhardy to say there was any certainty that they belong to one and the same person."

"The defendants' evidence is that there is a 50% similarity."

"No respectable firm of forensic scientists would suggest a percentage chance. I would dismiss it out of hand."

"As an expert?"

"Yes, within the limits I mentioned."

"Do you think the sets of prints you have seen belong to the same person?"

"I very much doubt it. True, there are similarities but this could be said if you looked at prints of millions of people."

"Thank you, Mrs. Thomas. Please wait there. The defence may want to ask questions."

Maynard spoke with Tovey. "This is hopeless. We are done on fingerprints. If I cross, it will just make things worse. For sure, the judge is against us and I won't shake Mrs. Thomas's evidence."

Rankin and Foster listened. Max was now resigned that the fingerprint evidence was holed below the waterline. He agreed with the advice. Foster wanted Maynard to be aggressive. "Throttle her. Get her."

"With what, a teddy bear? My advice is to let it go. I'll ask for an early adjournment so we can talk this through but I'm not going to cross. It's suicide."

"M'lady," Maynard addressed the judge, "I have no questions at this time. I need to take instructions. Might I suggest we adjourn for lunch early?"

"No, it's too early. I'll give you ten minutes."

Outside the court, Maynard, his legal team and the clients huddled. "You have to face facts. You have no solid fingerprint evidence that Hawkins/Aitken and Pearce are one and the same person. I don't dismiss that you're right but unless you can provide eye-witness or documentary evidence, you're done. Face it, you promised me evidence but you didn't deliver."

Foster looked angry but Rankin indicated all was done.

Maynard continued. "As I see it, you have two choices. One, I can go ahead with what I have without alleging the Hawkins/Aitken/Pearce nexus based on fingerprints. Instead, I will seek to justify actions at the Pearce house and conduct subsequent to that. However, you need to know you don't have the proof you need to succeed in an Article 10 defence and the Judge may get irritated. Or two, we can try to negotiate a settlement. Who knows, the terms suggested to Mr. Tovey a week ago may still be acceptable? And it doesn't stop you from continuing your investigation of Pearce once this trial is over. If and when you find evidence of his true identity, you are free to publish."

Rankin turned to Foster. "Your fuck up, Martin, your choice. Why did you instruct an idiot like Walters? You have made us look third rate."

Foster shrugged his shoulders. Underneath, Max was furious. "Come on Martin, decide. We are done for. Time to bail?"

"No, Max. I want to fight on. If we get a drubbing, we get a drubbing."

"Why should I take such a risk now?"

"Because we are newspapermen and this is what we do."

Back in court, Maynard waived cross-examination of Mrs. Thomas and continued Charlie's cross-examination.

"Why do you have no fingerprints worth mentioning?"

Charlie provided the word-for-word explanation he had given to Miriam Smith.

"You seem to remember the incident well."

"It was traumatic and frightening. It was also painful"

"Which hospital treated you?"

"Southern California Hospital."

"Where was that?"

"Culver City. Maybe a ten minute drive from high school."

"Were you an in-patient?"

"No."

"What was the name of the doctor who treated you?"

"I don't remember. It was more than thirty years ago."

"Did the hospital offer after care?"

"No, I went to our doctor's surgery near home. The dressings were changed by one of Dr Lieberman's nurses."

"If I told you that neither the hospital nor the surgery has any records of your emergency, would that surprise you?"

"No, of course not. This happened thirty or more years ago when there weren't computerised records. I have no idea what happened to hand-written records."

"Would you be willing to submit to a medical examination to determine how and when your injuries occurred?"

Miriam Smith stood. "I must object, M'lady. The defence has had several days to make such a request. They did not do so. The defence has no evidence to contradict Mr. Pearce's statements. They," she said, pointing at the opposition benches, "only want to delay the inevitable. They have no argument in law or in fact."

"I agree. Mr. Maynard, if you have any evidence to contradict Mr. Pearce's explanation, produce it now or cease this line of questioning."

Maynard decided to end the cross. There was no point asking Pearce what he did when he left America to go travelling. His clients had given him nothing to work with. *The Sentinel* wanted its day in court. Well, they could have it but not at the expense of making him look like a fool. The gossip from the hearing would soon make the rounds of the Inns of Court.

After lunch, Maynard opened the case for the defence, reminding the judge of the people's right to know and the protections offered by Article 10 of the Human Rights Act.

He called Max Rankin to the stand. After preliminaries to establish Rankin's credentials, he asked, "Was it you who decided that *The Sentinel* should defy the injunction?"

"Yes and no. As proprietor, my views are influential. I told my editor-in-chief I would back his decision but the final decision was Martin Foster's."

"Did it not trouble you that you were breaking the law?"

"Yes, of course, but there are occasions when, for journalists, truth trumps the law."

"Can you give me an example, separate from this case?"

"Let's assume my paper gains credible and indisputable evidence of wrongdoing by the Ministry of Defence where people have died as a result of a minister's negligence. Publishing an article would be a breach of a 'D' Notice but I would approve publication."

"You would defy the law?"

"Air and sunshine is the best disinfectant. The minister should be held to account."

"So it was a matter of principle, important principle, for your newspaper to defy the Pearce injunction?"

Miriam Smith stood, saying sarcastically, "I would prefer opposing counsel not to lead this witness. If Mr. Maynard wants to give evidence, I'd be happy to cross-examine him."

Judge Benton suppressed a grin. "Indeed. Re-phrase your question, please Mr. Maynard."

"Are there other occasions when the law should be defied?"

"There are principles which newspaper people regard as sacrosanct. For example, a journalist should never be required to reveal a source but the law takes a contrary view. This is a position often contested in the courts, sometimes with the result that a journalist is imprisoned for contempt of court. Likewise, an injunction that prevents a newspaper from questioning a public figure is unacceptable, as a matter of principle."

Miriam Smith mumbled, "What a surprise," loud enough for Judge Benton to hear. The judge frowned but said nothing.

"How do you justify door-stepping?"

"The public has the right to know. Sometimes, public figures will talk when confronted by determined reporters. It is often a difficult call but public interest trumps privacy rights in the eyes of the press and the public."

Maynard told the judge, "I have no further questions."

Smith rose to cross-examine. "Mr. Pearce has gone to great lengths to avoid being a public figure, as we have heard. Has he not the right?"

"That's a matter of opinion."

"What information did you possess about the private life of the claimant on the day after the injunction against your paper was granted?"

"He was hiding things about himself."

"That's not an answer to my question but let's follow your response. What things was he hiding?"

"I have no knowledge of details at that time."

"So, at this stage, were these vague 'things', as you term them, within the definition of information which needed to be published in the public interest?"

"These are matters for the editor-in-chief, not me."

"But if you didn't know details, how could you possibly determine what was being hidden? Do you regard 'things' which you cannot itemise as information? Isn't that just surmise or simply a guess, a hunch?"

"We knew Pearce had made millions from his writing. The public deserved to know more about him."

"My client made public his earnings from book sales and film rights every year. The public already knew."

Rankin did not respond.

"Isn't it the truth that your newspaper went on a crusade against Mr. Pearce, making the full resources of *The Sentinel* available to get him for the sole reason that he had refused to speak about his private life to your reporter, Perry Vaughan?"

"This is what newspapers do, expose the ills of society."

"So, when the door-stepping happened, *The Sentinel* had no information on Pearce to warrant an Article 10 defence because it had nothing to justify a right to know argument?"

"We knew he was hiding things, just not the precise details. We know it now. Hence we were justified in what we did."

"How would you feel if the newspapers behaved like this towards you?"

"They have."

"Indeed. How did it make you feel?"

"It's not a fair comparison. I'm not a public figure. I am a businessman, so I was cheesed off."

"Mr Rankin, that is preposterous. You are a self-proclaimed multi-millionaire, maybe a billionaire. You run a vast group of newspapers and media interests. You publish and sell all over the western world. Senior politicians and businessmen, presidents and prime ministers, make pilgrimages to your door. You are often in the society columns. You have a private jet and homes on different continents. And yet you say you are not in the public eye. If I called you a hypocrite, would I be on the mark?"

Rankin's face was scarlet with anger but he didn't reply.

Smith let out an audible sigh. "I'm done with this witness."

Maynard conferred with Tovey. If he called Martin Foster, Smith would put him through a cheese grater. Nothing would be gained from his evidence.

"That is the case for the defence, M'lady."

The judge looked surprised. Smith tapped Burgess on the shoulder. "No Vaughan, no Foster? They've caved."

Maynard and Smith made their closing arguments. Judge Benton said she would retire and give her verdict the next day.

****

That night, Charlie felt no elation. He'd won the legal case because the truth wasn't proved but he also knew that one day everything would come out. He would get damages now from *The Sentinel* but what good was money to him? He had all the money he ever wanted. If he was short of money, all he needed to do was publish a new book. Claire and the children would also get money awards but it would be no real compensation for them for all they had suffered. He was defeated, ashamed and wondering what he could do to recover his own self-respect, not to mention change his wife's low opinion of him.

At home, he could not bring himself to talk properly with Claire. He merely gave her a precis of the day's proceedings and that judgment would be given the next day. He asked her to come to court with him. She said she thought it was unlikely she would.

At *The Sentinel,* Rankin sat in his office with Martin Foster. "We're going down tomorrow, Martin, going down big. I've given you all the support I can manage but it's your wrong decisions, your shitty judgment that has got us where we are. All the way through this thing, we have been miles behind Pearce. I've got no choice but to fire you. Clear your desk now."

"I don't agree with your summation. And legally, the Board has the right to fire me. You don't. But I'll go quietly if you give me the terms I want."

"What do you want?"

"A year's salary in lieu of notice. And you pay the tax. My pension premiums paid for three years. My mortgage paid off. That's about forty two grand. No gardening leave. I can get a job when and where I want. And throw my car in too."

"That's preposterous. Six month's salary and you pay the tax, one year's pension premiums, forget the mortgage and the car. The rest I'll live with. But I want an NDA."

"Max, you heard my terms. If you agree them, I'll sign a non-disclosure agreement. If not, I'll walk. I know you can prevent me working but you can't stop my kiss and tell story. I'll tell it to whichever paper wants to pay me the most. I'll get a book deal too. Based on my knowledge of your shenanigans, I'll have no problem finding a publisher."

"You brought the Pearce story to me. I supported you throughout as you made the decisions. And this is my reward! We had a good run. I don't want to stick a gagging order on you. We're sensible men. Surely, we can work this out?"

And they did.

*****

When Miriam Smith was leaving court, Hardy took her elbow. "Can we talk?"

"Yes. What is it? Charles will win. It's all over."

"It's not about the case."

"What then?"

"Not here, Miri. Let's go to Twinings. Have a civilised cup of tea with me."

At the Strand tea shop, Hardy was hesitant. Miriam had not seen this side of him before.

"Spit it out, Hardy, it can't be that bad."

"When we last spoke – not about the case – I was, how shall I say, not as sympatico as I should have been? I want to apologise. I was harsh and uncaring at a time when I should have been the opposite."

"Goodness me, Hardy Burgess eating humble pie. I can hardly believe it."

"Yes, yes, chastise me. I deserve it. Over the weeks since we last spoke, I have been doing some thinking. I can no longer behave like a twenty-something. I need to make sense of this life I have and I want to share it with someone."

"What has got into you, Hardy?"

"I know it has taken a long time for me to come to my senses. I think we made a good team when we were together. I love your mind. I wonder if we might try to give it another go."

"What are you actually talking about? Are you proposing furtive afternoons in a five star hotel bedroom when we aren't on professional duty, naughty weekends in some country retreat, grabbing a day here and a night there?"

"You make it sound so tawdry and cheap."

"Only because it was. I was so infatuated, I let you treat me like dirt. Do you really think I would let you repeat the exercise? Not a chance. When we talked that night, I'd had an awful time in court, my divorce was done as I'd received the decree absolute and I was drunk. I've come to my senses."

Miriam stood and put on her coat. Hardy pleaded with her. "Don't go, Miri, not like this. Next time it will be different, you'll see. I've changed."

"No you haven't. You just feel sorry for yourself. I'm not here to repair you."

With that, Miriam Smith walked out of Hardy Burgess's life.

*****

Alone in his study, Charlie was unable to concentrate, to see his way through. Claire entered the room. "There's a man on the phone. He wants to speak to you. He says his name is Ronnie Bass. Wasn't he your boss at Lloyd's?"

"Yes."

"Speak to him. He sounds pleasant."

Charlie glared at his wife as he took the phone.

"Hello. This is Charles Pearce. How may I help you?"

"Never mind that Charles Pearce bollocks. You know who I am. If I'd wanted to give you up, I'd have done so months ago. I want to see you. I live close by in Beaconsfield. Half eight tonight at The Royal Standard of England? The beer is good."

It was a pleasant, warm evening without an autumnal chill. Charlie and Ronnie took their pints into the beer garden. Ronnie had lost weight and a lot of hair too. But he hadn't changed the manner in which he spoke. Direct, straight to the point.

"What do I call you now? Charlie? Tell me, why'd you bolt like that twenty years ago? It made the rest of us look bad."

"Straight to the point, Ronnie. I admire that. I bolted, as you put it, because you, Harvey Williams and the others constantly got me involved in your scams and I had no doubt I would have been put in the middle of the frame for everything that happened. Deny it if you can." Ronnie was silent. "Be honest, I was headed for the chop."

Ronnie grinned. "Got me there."

"You were good to me and made me wealthy but I made a fortune for you. You were up to all kinds of stuff that was plain wrong and I told you so. And I admit I did wrong things too. The courts may have let you off but you and I know what you and the others did. I wasn't going to spend ten years inside while you and your mates sunned yourselves in Provence."

Ronnie shrugged. "I don't blame you. Different times. Arthur, oops Charlie, I liked you when we met. You had a lot of talent and we did well together. But leaving like you did put me in the shit. You had details in your head that I didn't have. I never understood the computer stuff. I was left like Long John Silver without his wooden leg."

"And without his parrot? Why don't you and I agree, it's all water under the bridge? Anyway, how are you keeping? You're looking trim."

"Old, you mean. Life has had its ups and downs. The Bentley went. So did the Ferrari, the house in Mayfair and the villa in St. Paul de Vence. Chloe scarpered as soon as it hit the fan. But the wife and girls stood by me. We live in a nice enough house here. I potter. I have an insurance brokerage in Beaconsfield. Keeps the wolf from the door but I don't get the buzz from the business, not like I used to."

Ronnie ordered another pint. Charlie just took a half. "Driving," he explained.

"You've really got yourself in the tom tit, haven't you? I've read the papers. It's what I went through twenty years ago. It's bloody awful but it doesn't last. Soon the papers will find another victim. I've no hard feelings against you. You did what you had to do. I just wanted to say I'm a friendly face living nearby."

Charlie was stunned by what he heard. Most people would point out that here was a man he had shafted who was offering an olive branch. "Give me your phone number, Ronnie. I appreciate the offer. But as I expect you will read soon, *The Sentinel* has not won. They can't prove their case. I'm coming out on top for now."

"But will the press leave it there. Eventually you'll get found out. Like I said, I'm a friendly face. One other thing. Harvey Williams."

"Do you still see him?"

"Not if I can help it. I didn't like him in the old days and I don't like him now. He was a heavy investor with another syndicate that wrote a lot of American business. He got caught in the asbestos scandal. He was thrown out of Lloyd's and went broke. He had the bloody cheek to come to me for help when he knew I was on my uppers."

"What did you do?"

"Showed him the door. He was the one who came up with most of the dodgy stuff. I was the idiot. Watch out for him. If he can't blackmail you, he'll try to ruin you. He really is vermin."

"Does he know what you know about me?"

"Not as far as I know but he's not a fool. He may put two and two together one of these days."

"What should I do?" asked Charlie with panic in his voice.

Ronnie clapped him on the shoulder. "That's for you, not me. Stay in touch."

Chapter Twenty-One.

Judge Benton took her seat and greeted the legal teams and parties before her with a 'good morning.' "Are there any applications before I give judgment?" she asked. Both silks shook their heads.

"Very well." The judge set out the circumstances of the case, the events leading to the interim injunction, its breach and the aftermath. She continued.

"The Human Rights Act of 1998 codified the provisions of the European Convention on Human Rights. The Claimants seek a permanent injunction based on their rights under Article 8 of the Act which states: *'Everyone has the right to respect for his private and family life, his home and his correspondence.'* The Defendants assert their actions were within the rights set out in Article 10: *'Freedom of expression: this right shall include freedom to hold opinions and to receive and impart information and ideas without interference by public authority.'*

"Both Articles have equal status under the law so I have to decide whether the claimants' rights to privacy were properly overridden by the public interest right asserted by the defendants. When giving evidence, Mr. Pearce strongly defended his right to privacy. Under cross-examination, he was accused of living for the past twenty years or so under a stolen identity but the defendants were unable to offer proof of the allegation on the balance of probabilities. Therefore, I have ignored this issue.

"By pursuing the claimant after the Vaughan interview, the defendants and other members of the media went on a fishing expedition. They had no knowledge of any of the facts surrounding the earlier part of the claimant's life.

"Furthermore, the defendants indulged in excessive door-stepping, hence I had no hesitation in granting an interim injunction. The defendants defied the injunction of this court, for which they have been punished. I am clear that the prime object of the defendants' actions was to harangue, bully, intimidate and terrify not only Mr. Pearce but his wife and children. Such behaviour is plainly wrong and cannot be approved, condoned or permitted.

"One of Mrs. Smith's closing points, namely the absence of Peregrine Vaughan as a witness for the defence, was highly pertinent. It was his interview which was the catalyst for the door-stepping. He is a columnist for *The Sentinel* and his failure to give evidence must lead to my questioning the motives of *The Sentinel* in pursuing Mr. Pearce and his family.

"Mrs. Smith also noted that Martin Foster, the editor-in-chief, had not given evidence but his proprietor, Max Rankin, told the court that Foster was the man who made the decisions. The court was not given the opportunity to examine the rationale of those decisions. I regard this omission as misguided, an effort by the defendants to ameliorate the damage done to their case during this hearing.

"In conclusion, the defendants have not offered any acceptable evidence or argument to support the assertion that their Article 10 rights overrule Article 8. From the evidence produced to this court, it can be concluded that the defendants operated a strategy motivated by vengeance. My judgment is that the claimants have proved their case.

"Accordingly, I am going to maintain the injunction permanently. *The Sentinel* and other defendants who are subject to the injunction will be barred from approaching Mr. Pearce and Dr Pearce, nor may they approach the Pearce children. In particular the defendants will not congregate at the Pearce house or within a mile radius of the house, save as ordered by me.

"All that remains is for me to award damages to the Pearce family for harassment. By his own admission, Mr. Pearce is a very wealthy man so whatever sum is awarded will make precious little difference to the life of his family. Tempting as it may be to award a vast sum against *The Sentinel* and its shareholders for the intolerant behaviour of its employees, I must bear in mind the interests of justice. For Mr. Pearce and Dr Pearce, I award £20,000 each. For the children, I award £40,000 each to be held in trust until they gain their majority. I leave it to their parents to nominate trustees. It would be wrong for Mr. and Dr Pearce to bear any expense of the litigation. I order costs to the claimant on a full indemnity basis."

Judge Benton left the Court amid pandemonium. "A great judgment," Miriam Smith told Charlie. Max Rankin approached. "Pearce or whatever your bloody name is, my newspaper will not stop its enquiries. We'll find you out and call you out, mark my words."

*****

That night, Charlie sat with Claire. "I told you we would win. *The Sentinel* got handed a red card. The money isn't important. The point is I have been exonerated by the court."

"Just for now. You're still in denial, you're living a lie and so am I. You have a choice. The children and I don't."

"Meaning?"

"I'm not Dr Pearce. I'm Dr Hawkins or is it Dr Aitken, I don't know which. Same for our children. And I don't have a choice about coming clean. Well I do but it would mean betraying you. I'm not willing to do that."

"What do you want, Claire?"

Claire's cheeks were stained with tears. "This case has made me ill. I know deep down I can't keep up the pretence and live with you like nothing has happened. *The Sentinel* knows the truth. They just can't prove it. They won't let it go. One day, maybe this week, this month or even in ten years' time, they will publish the truth about you. Maybe you can live with this. I can't."

There was silence between them. Finally, Charlie whispered, "what do you want me to do?"

"I want you to leave. I want you to go now. I've packed your things. Find a hotel for yourself. Just get out of here. Take time, think things through and do what is right for your family. I can't live with this hanging over me, nor can I live with you."

The last was said as the tears flowed. Claire was devastated.

"I don't understand. We won. They may have found things but they don't have the proof. The case is over. Don't force me out of my home. I'd remind you, I paid for it because I write good novels. There is no Lloyd's money in this house. I did what you wanted me to do all those years ago. Why are you demanding this from me?"

"This isn't about money! My god, I can't understand your thinking. It's about honesty and truthfulness and living with a lie. A big lie. And I was complicit. Why did I go along with you? I guess I loved you and they say love is blind."

"I still don't understand."

"Charlie, you won the case because a newspaper couldn't nail the evidence but one day a journalist will discover the whole truth and when that happens, it will be so much worse. I don't want the children to be around then. Yes, I loved you once but I surely don't now. I don't even like you. Where's your moral compass? Please do as I ask. Just go."

Claire sobbed as she left the room. Charlie sat, stunned. How could she ask him to leave? 'She's kicking me out; I'm losing her and the children. This is the last thing I want,' he told himself. He wrote Claire a note.

"I don't want to go but I will do as you ask. I'm doing this because I love you and the children. I don't want you to feel the way you do and maybe a short absence will make you see things differently. Please don't bar me from the children. I want to see them this weekend. C."

Charlie went upstairs and grabbed two bags. He left the house, got into his car and drove. He had no idea where he was going until he reached Hardy's Mount Street building. Around 11.30 that night, he rang Hardy's doorbell.

Injunction

Chapter Twenty-Two.

Hardy's voice came over the entry-phone. "Who is this?"

"It's Charlie. Sorry I'm here so late. I need to see you."

Seated in the spacious lounge of Hardy's flat, Charlie told him, "I have a story for you. A long story. When I finish, may I impose on your hospitality for tonight? Tomorrow I'll book myself into an hotel. Do you have a parking space I can use?"

One of the perks of being senior partner of VP is that Hardy had a car and driver at his disposal. He no longer owned a car. "By all means, use my parking space in the basement. It's number 6."

Charlie parked his car, brought his cases into the flat and sat, nursing a cognac.

"You are full of surprises. I thought you'd be tucked up with Claire, celebrating a victory. It's not often you see a national newspaper stuffed."

"Is what I tell you still privileged?" Charlie was not smiling.

Hardy caught Charlie's mood as he sipped his cognac. "Yes."

"There's no easy way to tell you this. My real name is Arthur Hawkins."

Hardy stiffened but sat in silence as Charlie took him through the lives of Arthur Hawkins, aka Henry Aitken, aka Charles Pearce. It took almost an hour. Hardy remained quiet for the most part, asking the occasional question for clarification.

Charlie finished by saying, "If I'm to keep my marriage and my children, I have to out myself, to tell the truth. If I don't, Claire won't take me back. My life is meaningless without her and the children. The old Charlie would have asked you to talk her round, to tell her the risks we run if I give myself up.

"But I'm Arthur now. I have to get this out in the open, it has to be unconditional and then I have to hope Claire will take me back, despite the shit that will fall on me."

"This is quite a story. I need time to think through the implications. Let's see how far we can get tonight."

"Okay. My questions: first, will I go to prison, Hardy?"

"For hiding your identity? Maybe there are problems ahead with the Home Office for using a false passport. However, you are a UK citizen, you have paid your taxes and you are entitled to a British passport. I don't see prison as much of a risk area. The American authorities will withdraw your US passport and maybe Lizzie's but she was born in America so there may not be an issue. I assume Claire has a British passport. You and the family may be banned from entering the USA but so what? Maybe you won't sell so many books there but notoriety is never a bar."

"Second: what about *The Sentinel* case?"

"I need to consider the implications of the litigation. The judge may want to revoke the judgment so far as it relates to damages for you. When did Claire know about your past?"

"More than twenty years ago. I told her everything before we were married."

"Well, Claire won't collect damages either. The big problem area is a charge of perjury. From memory, Maynard put a question, suggesting you were Hawkins/Aitken but you did not answer. Miriam Smith objected and the judge called an adjournment. Years ago, Jeffrey Archer was accused of perjury and perverting the course of justice in a libel trial. From memory, he got four years. But let's assume you did not answer a question about your identity. If that's right, I don't see the guilt. But, I am not a criminal law expert. I'll talk to a barrister about this once I've checked the transcript."

"More bloody expense."

"It's necessary."

"Third question: I need to reverse the Aitken change of name and go back to Hawkins. Same for the family. I'll need a new British passport and so will Claire and the kids. Also, new driving licences for Claire and me and all the other official documents. Can your firm get this done?"

"I'm sure we can. I'll have one of my people contact you when you're ready."

"Final question for tonight. What is the best way for me to disclose my true identity?"

"Before I answer that, your publishers spoke with me today. They think it's a good time for you to publish. They don't want another novel, they want something else, your story about the court case. Perhaps it's time for you to write your autobiography. After what you've told me tonight, I doubt this is a good idea but I have to pass it on to you."

"Too soon and too raw for me. I agree with you. Tell them 'no.'"

"Now, disclosure of the truth. I'm just thinking aloud. We need to inform the court. I'll speak with Miriam Smith. She will tell me this needs to happen immediately. But this would clash with what I have in mind. What if you went back on the Peregrine Vaughan show? We could ask Judge Benton to defer any court decision for a day or so."

"What! Do you want to get me crucified? Perry Vaughan. He'll destroy me."

"I don't see it that way. Provided you have legal advice that you did not perjure yourself, you can tell the truth, tell your side of the story on live TV. You will get a lot of sympathy from the public, especially if you admit wrongdoing and show remorse. Tell the viewers how you made amends through your charity donations, that sort of thing.

"I'll make sure the programme is unscripted and goes out live so Vaughan and his people can't edit. He'll be unprepared for what's coming. The programme lasts an hour. My partners will find a PR team for you so when you tell your story, it plays well. It will take about 45 minutes to tell it so Vaughan won't have that much time for questions."

"Hardy, this is an unorthodox approach. I want time to think. I need to talk with Claire and the children. I won't do anything to make their lives worse than it already is."

*****

It was early morning when Max Rankin was awakened by his secretary.

"I'm sorry Mr. Rankin but an emergency board meeting is about to start. The Chairman ordered me to call you and demand your attendance."

Max groaned and looked at his bedside clock. "It's not eight o'clock. Tell the Chairman to do one. You can quote me."

"The Chairman said if you responded in the negative, I was to inform you it would go very badly for you."

"Bugger it! Okay, tell him I'll be there in half an hour."

At 8.35, Max Rankin entered the Board Room. He gestured to the Chairman to vacate his seat. The Chairman, Sir John West, shook his head and pointed to a chair at the other end of the table.

"Max, thank you for joining us. Before you say anything, you are here not to discuss or debate, nor are we willing to listen to one of your diatribes about the uselessness of this Board. Instead, you are here to listen to us."

"Who the fuck do you think you are? All of you, you're here to look after the interests of the shareholders of *The Sentinel*. That's me."

Max paused. He didn't take a seat. Instead, he told the Board, "I am *The Sentinel*. I own it. So, bollocks. I'm having no more of this nonsense. I will have my lawyers sack you all. I can replace you with monkeys from the Regent's Park zoo if I want."

West stood, red in the face. His career in the Royal Navy had taught him plenty about men, if not always about business.

"This is the last time you will address me and my colleagues in this insulting way of yours. If this meeting ends as badly as it has begun, there will be no need to fire us. Look at the papers in the centre of the table. They are resignation letters from all members of this Board."

"Good. I accept. Leave now, all of you."

"You are so bloated with your notions of power, you think you cannot be challenged. You are wrong, misguided and stupid. There are laws and rules with which even you must abide." Max's face went white with anger. "You are so puffed up with your own self-importance, you never really consider, do you? You believe you have absolute power at *The Sentinel* but you need us in place to satisfy Stock Exchange and company law requirements. If we resign en-masse, the Stock Exchange will be informed and trading in *Sentinel* shares will be suspended until a new board is in place. The Stock Exchange will not accept a board of monkeys.

"Your own position at Media Universal is different. If this Board resigns en-masse, MU borrowing covenants will be broken. Both MU and *The Sentinel* have loans from a consortium of some thirty banks. From talks we have held with the three lead banks, they will call in the loans. You don't have sufficient cash on hand to repay them."

"What? You don't know what you're talking about."

"If we resign, the share value of both *The Sentinel* and MU will fall dramatically. It will fall far below the level required under covenants given to the banks. You will have to support the share price."

"Then that is what I'll do."

"But it is illegal for MU group companies to use their cash to support the MU share price. Let me spell it out. You will be committing a crime if group companies buy MU shares to keep the price stable."

"What makes you believe the MU lead lenders would actually do this? They love me. I make money for them."

"You are deluding yourself. You consider this Board as useless but have you thought about how many of us sit on the boards of your lenders. I tell you straight, your lenders are even more fed up with your high-handedness than we are. You behave as if the banks are your servants. You are not untouchable, Max, and the way you run your empire as if it all belonged solely to you has made many want to oppose you. You have many enemies, few friends."

"This is hot air, West. You're crazy."

"Fine. If you don't believe me, call them, see them."

"Enough. Those of you who have conflicts of interest should resign. I'm leaving."

"Fine but your funeral. The resignation letters are there. So are letters to the Stock Exchange and Companies House. A press release will go out straight away. I'm telling you, the banks will call the loans."

"What is really going on here? What do you want?"

"The handling of the Pearce case has tipped us over the edge. Your judgment has been appalling. It has cost millions, not to mention the damage to reputation. You and Foster made really bad decisions without referring to us and the end result was nothing, no Pearce disclosures, no triumph for the newspaper, just the ignominy of a judgment against the newspaper."

"So, spell out exactly what you want?"

West passed a sheet of paper to Rankin. Max didn't like what he read.

"The Board of Directors of *The Sentinel* demands the following:

1. *No more will Max Rankin treat this Board of Directors as mere adjuncts to do his bidding as if he is the sole owner of The Sentinel.*
2. *Mr Rankin will immediately place 25% of his Ordinary and Preference shares in Media Universal and 40% of his Ordinary and Preference shares in The Sentinel into a blind trust. The trustees will be chosen by the Board.*
3. *Mr Rankin will join The Sentinel board as its newspaper director. The board fully accepts that his advice on newspaper matters will be valuable.*
4. *Mr Rankin will agree the appointment of a deputy newspaper director who will be chosen by and answerable to this Board.*
5. *The new editor-in-chief replacing Martin Foster will also be answerable to the Board. However, the Board accepts that in day-to-day matters, it should not challenge the new editor-in-chief's decisions unless such decisions are likely to harm the underlying value and interests of the newspaper or its reputation.*

Injunction

6. *As soon as possible, Mr Rankin and the new editor-in-chief will propose a strategy to recover the newspaper's former good reputation. It will be the sole decision of the Board to approve such strategy.*
7. *This agreement will be confidential and will not be released to any third party. However, the Chairman may impart its content to Media Universal's lead banks."*

"We'll give you an hour to agree our terms."

Max stared at the words, glared at the board and stood. "I'm leaving." As he moved to the boardroom door, he heard the Chairman say, "One hour, Max. The clock is ticking."

Max dashed back to his office. He ordered his secretary to call MU's in-house head of finance. Briefly he explained what had happened and asked, "What are our borrowings?" He was alarmed to be told they were at 110% of the facility.

"Why wasn't I told?" The response was curt. "If you'd bothered to read your e-mails, you would have known." Two messages had been sent to Max within the last week.

No point in speaking to MU's lawyers. By the time he got any worthwhile advice, the bomb would have exploded. He told his secretary to find Connie Strauss and ask her to come straight away. "Make it a polite but urgent request." Within five minutes, Connie sat in Max's office.

"Foster has gone, most of my editors are good journalists but they are time-servers. I now need to listen to a cool head, namely you." Briefly, Max explained what had happened at the Board Meeting.

"Read the note they want me to sign. What do you think I should do? The MU loan facility is maxed out. MU will have serious short term problems if the Board pulls the pin from the grenade they're holding."

"Max, this is way above my pay grade. Shouldn't you be asking your professionals?"

"Not this time. They won't act quickly enough for me to get out of this vice." Max checked his watch. "I have to give my answer in 45 minutes."

"Okay, loads of time!" Max grimaced at Connie's irony. "Off the top of my head, I see three choices. First, you can call them out, although from what you've told me, this is no bluff. They mean business. Second, you can agree their terms but fight the agreement later. You can have your lawyers argue that it was signed under duress, that it's unenforceable, something like that. Third, you can ask them to stay in place but to give you more time to negotiate the terms."

"Makes sense."

"After all, these terms needn't be treated as a threat but as a bargaining chip. Fix a time tomorrow to discuss things with them but not all of them. Try a little divide and rule. Overnight, have your professionals see what they can do. This gives you time to talk to bankers, get a new line of credit to pay down some of the MU facility. I don't know, I'm not a business person."

"You sell yourself short. I'm almost minded to have you go into the meeting for me and mesmerise the Board."

"Thanks but no thanks and no way."

"When this stuff is sorted, we should talk. A promotion is overdue. Do you want to cross the aisle and go from writing to editing? It's more status and a lot more money. I'd want you reporting to me." Max caught a look on Connie's face. "I'm not making a move on you. You're a good-looking girl but this is business. I don't mix the two. I rate you as a journalist and want to give you a chance at the big time."

"May I think about it?"

"Yes, but don't keep me waiting."

"Isn't that what the Board told you?"

"Yes. I should go back. Stay on the Pearce/Hawkins business and see if you can come up with the evidence we need to link Pearce to Hawkins. Unlimited budget."

"What will you do?"

"I'll try your third option. If it doesn't work, probably the second option. I'll not let those shits take my company."

Chapter Twenty-Three.

"Quiet in the Studio." A man holding a clapboard and wearing headphones, with wires seemingly coming from everywhere on his body, stood on the stage and repeated the request for silence. Another man appeared. "I normally warm things up with some stories and jokes before we record but tonight's programme is different. The Vaughan Interview is going out live. Perry asks you not to clap, cheer or boo until the interview is completed." Off stage, a voice called, "two minutes."

The lights went down as the 'On Air' sign came on. Perry Vaughan walked on stage to muted applause. He smiled, made a 'thank you' gesture and took his place in the centre.

"Tonight, my guest is the author, Charles Pearce. About a year ago he came on my show but he stormed out when I tried to question him about his private life. Following the incident, he obtained an injunction against members of the media who were besieging his home. *The Daily Sentinel* challenged the injunction and Mr. Pearce's claim for harassment. Three days ago, the claim was upheld in court. Articles have been published by several newspapers about the case. Mr. Pearce has not commented on any of them.

"This interview takes place at the request of Mr. Pearce. It is unscripted. I have no idea of what he wants to say. He says he wants an opportunity to put his side of the story. Mr. Pearce has imposed no conditions whatsoever on my questions but has asked that his opening statement be given without challenge. I have agreed to this. Ladies and gentlemen, Charles Pearce."

Charlie walked on stage. He was dressed elegantly. His clothes weren't matched by his facial appearance. He looked grey, haggard and weary. The two men sat opposite each other in comfortable leather chairs. A coffee table in between held a jug of water and glasses. Charlie had warned Vaughan he would not shake hands.

"Welcome," said Vaughan. "The last few weeks have been tough for you. Are you angry?"

"Our deal is that you'll let me make an opening statement before questions. Are you reneging again?"

"No, of course not, Mr. Pearce. I just wanted to make you comfortable before our audience and the cameras."

"I am way out of my comfort zone, being here like this. May I start? And you agree, no interruptions?"

"Agreed."

"Ladies and gentlemen," Charlie began. "Mine is a long, painful and complicated story. It began nearly 50 years ago in London's East End. It took me to a successful career in the City of London, followed by time in America. I have lived the last twenty years of my life in Buckinghamshire. My name isn't Charles Pearce. It's Arthur Hawkins."

Watching the show at his Docklands flat, Martin Foster jumped out of his chair and shouted, "Fucking hell, I was right after all. Destroy him, Perry." Max Rankin wasn't watching until he received a call from Connie. "Are you watching Vaughan's show? You're not? Watch it now!" Rankin was soon in ecstasy with what he was seeing.

For forty minutes, Vaughan remained silent as Charlie – now Arthur – relayed the highlights of his life. He did not maximise any hardship he suffered, nor he did not play down his role at Syndicate 4455, nor did he fudge details of his flight from London and his life in America and afterwards in Buckinghamshire. He was, he said, a changed man but it was time to own up to his past.

After forty minutes, Arthur ended by saying, "I brought what has happened on myself. I have no right to be angry. I'm philosophical. The people who have been hurt badly by my actions are my wife and children. I am doing this to start making amends to them."

Vaughan scribbled something on a piece of paper and gave it to a stage hand. He adjusted an ear piece and began his examination.

"May I ask you some questions now? What exactly has happened with your family?"

"Nothing physical. However, litigation like this places enormous strains and pressures on a family dynamic. My wife has been unwell. I've been withdrawn and non-communicative. The children have been damaged by the loss of a happy home. It's me who needs to repair things."

"Yet you say you're not angry?"

"I am angry on behalf of my wife and children. I don't have that right for myself."

Vaughan fiddled with his hearing aid. "What are you listening to," asked Arthur, "and what was on that written note?"

"Nothing," Vaughan replied.

"It wasn't nothing. Look at you. You're red in the face. Come on, tell the truth."

"No, I want to get back to the questions and your truth. Now what you've told us is news. It is new to me, this audience and the viewers. Why did you lie about it in court?"

"Let me be clear, I haven't lied. I didn't lie in court, I didn't lie when I gave evidence and I did not lie to any newspaper."

"But you did not tell the truth in court. For example, you gave evidence as Charles Pearce."

"I did but strictly speaking it wasn't a lie when I gave that evidence."

"What was it then? Were you economical with the truth?"

"Yes, perhaps that's a different way to put it. What I'm saying is nobody asked the question, are you Arthur Hawkins, to which I replied, 'no.' Mr. Vaughan, you are fiddling with your ear piece again. Is someone feeding you questions?"

Vaughan ignored the question. "Okay, that was a legal response. Let's move on. Tell me about your early life."

"Not until you tell me why you need someone to tell you what to ask me. Call yourself a journalist?"

"Please answer my question."

Arthur turned to the audience. "They are not his questions. I've a good mind to ask whoever is posing these questions to come on stage. But I won't. I'll move on. But you might want to explain why this is called the Perry Vaughan show when he's not doing the work. I leave it you, the audience. Do you want me to continue like this?"

There were calls of 'yes' and applause. The audience was moving towards Arthur's side.

"Very well. Let's move on. That's a broad question about my early life. Can you be more precise?"

"I just want to know what you remember from your early days."

Arthur talked about his early life.

"Your mother died when you were ten?"

"Yes, on World Cup Final day. My new baby brother died too. My dad was devastated. I was too young to understand it all. Things were never the same after she died. On my fifteenth birthday, my Dad told me my schooldays were over and I had to make my own way in life. He got me a laboring job in the docks. I didn't want to work there and turned the job down, so he kicked me out of the house."

"You were only fifteen and he cut you off just like that? What did you do?"

"Panic!" There was gentle laughter in the audience. "I helped out in a gym for a few years. The owner, Eddie Grey and his wife, Mary, they were wonderful to me and they gave me a place to stay.

"Eddie found me a job with an insurance company, General Insurance. I was good at maths and I did okay. I was spotted by someone who was connected at Lloyd's and I went to work for Ronnie Bass's syndicate."

"Let's go back a bit. You said you have an unusual mind. What do you mean?"

"I have a photographic and eidetic memory."

"What does that mean?"

"Photographic memory means I have the ability to recall pages of text and numbers. Eidetic means I view visual images from memories. So I have the ability to recall and analyse at the same time."

"I gather this helped with your career at Lloyd's. My research tells me there was an anomaly spotted in the way Syndicate 4455 ran its business. This came out in the criminal trial of the leading underwriter, Ronnie Bass, and others. Was it you who found the anomaly and what was it?"

"Yes. I was first employed to head the back office at 4455. I noticed that several times a year, the syndicate sold on policies to a baby syndicate. This was a syndicate separate from 4455 and owned by the lead underwriter and a few others. The policies were low risk so it was rare for there to be a claim. However, if a risk arose and a claim was made, the policy would be sold back to 4455 which then paid out the claim."

"This must have troubled you."

"Let me put it this way. Whistle-blowers were as unwelcome in those days as they are now. In fact, in many businesses whistle-blowers were not tolerated at all. If I'd blown the whistle, I would have been sacked. The law offered me no protection. The baby syndicate practice was not a breach of Lloyd's rules. So, yes, I guess I was troubled all right, but I knew there was nothing I could do about it. I was no match for those I would have to fight."

"So your conscience was overridden by the desire for personal advancement?"

"That's not fair. I was eighteen years old, scared about earning a living. Who did I have to talk to? The police and the Lloyd's committee would have done nothing. I had no mentor, no close friend who would understand. Eddie Grey was living on the coast and unwell. He would not have really understood my predicament. I was into self-preservation, not self-advancement."

"But when you told the boss, he promoted you."

"Yes. Ronnie Bass was big on loyalty. He already knew I had mathematic abilities which you need as an underwriter. To an extent, the job is like being a bookmaker. You have to assess the odds, the gains and losses. I had these skills. As a boy, one of my after-school jobs was as a runner for a local bookmaker, who took a shine to me and taught me the business, how to settle bets and how to lay-off the odds. What he was doing was not legal but I didn't know and my father didn't care."

"Let's get back to your time at Lloyd's. By 1986, you had made a fortune but you decided to chuck it all up, leave the country. Why?"

"I'll put it this way. A senior working member of 4455 was coming up with all kinds of scams, ways of getting more for himself and others at the expense of non-working members."

"Give me an example."

"Writing a policy that was bound to fail. The insured wanted a risk covered. The risk was almost bound to occur. When it did, the syndicate paid. The insured was actually an off-shore company, owned by a few 4455 members."

"Wasn't this fraud?"

"I was not a criminal lawyer. At the time, the practice was regarded as within Lloyd's rules because it was not expressly banned by those rules. Subsequently, senior members of 4455 were tried in the criminal courts for numerous offences including fraud but they were acquitted of all charges."

"So, instead of facing a criminal prosecution, you fled the country and disappeared."

Arthur took a sip of water. "I don't deny it. I admit I benefitted from some of the unorthodox 4455 practices but most of my money was earned legitimately. Underwriters can earn huge sums of money at Lloyd's without breaking the law. What scared me enough to make me run was that if the police got involved, I knew I would be the scapegoat. The other underwriters would deny knowledge. I would be the only one to go down. There was a paper trail which had my name, not the others, although they were involved just as much and benefitted far more than me."

"Some viewers will think you're just a spiv, a cheat, a man who made his money illegally and ran."

Arthur paused for a while. "I suppose they might. An East End spiv rigging the markets, eh? I'd hardly be the first. My answer is this. It is not fair to judge me by today's standards. These events happened more than twenty years ago. I got involved in practices which were not only within Lloyd's rules, they were evidently permissible by law. But I didn't know."

"Just because others were acquitted doesn't exonerate you, does it?"

"If you're right, then you need to explain why those charged were found not guilty. I was no spiv. You can say non-working names were cheated but in our syndicate, they still got a good return on their investment. Unlike several other syndicates, ours did not write business that put names into bankruptcy. Yes, I ran away but I was only in my twenties and scared out of my wits."

"You lied and cheated your way at Lloyd's and afterwards," snarled Vaughan.

Arthur took a beat. "Just like you are doing tonight, trying to make the audience believe these are your questions. Perry, you were born with the proverbial silver spoon. Your father was a wealthy stockbroker, even before Big Bang. You went to public school and the University of York. You enjoyed all the advantages and privileges. Your first job on the Tunbridge Wells Gazette was arranged by your father. Your rise in journalism has a few murky bits, doesn't it? Do you want me to go into detail? If the tables were turned, if you were in my seat, would you not have to admit things you did of which you are ashamed? My point is we both have baggage."

Vaughan recovered his poise. "We're here to talk about you, not me. There is a year-long gap between you leaving London and turning up in Minnesota. What happened?"

"I had a lot of plastic surgery to change my looks. Recuperation took almost a year."

"Not just your looks. Didn't you have your fingerprints obliterated?"

"Yes."

"All of that must have been painful."

Arthur winced as he recalled his recovery.

"Is this you?" Vaughan asked, producing a picture taken in 1982 at a syndicate function. A blown up version was shown on a screen to the audience.

"Yes, that's me."

"You look very different now. Did you change your looks to escape capture?"

"Partly, yes. But I wanted to look less ugly. Just look at me in that picture. I was twenty-four years old and very unattractive. I rarely managed more than a few dates with a girl. I thought I was repugnant. I needed to look different."

Perry Vaughan had not anticipated that answer. "Your life in Minneapolis/St Paul is unremarkable, so let's go back to your time at Lloyd's."

"Unremarkable to you but not me. I met my wife, our first child, Lizzie, was born and my first novel was published. I turned my life around."

"Maybe but you gave no thought to the people in the UK you cheated."

"No thought? I felt guilt. I made large donations to British and American charities when I was in St Paul. The millions I made at Lloyd's were given to charity, pretty well all of my money. I kept $250,000 back for a while but donated this sum to charity too. Since then, a quarter of the royalties from my books and film earnings have gone to charity. If 4455 syndicate names feel I cheated them, they will no doubt take action against me but I wasn't alone."

"I want to know more about 4455. Were there any schemes where you did not participate?"

"Yes. The ones that were blatant. I took no part."

"Give me an example."

"Okay. Bank du Pays was a Swiss private bank with its office in Geneva. Senior 4455 underwriters bought the bank and became shareholders. I was invited to participate but I declined, despite the advantages. I was given a bearer share certificate for 1% of the bank. I gave away the dividends credited to me. I destroyed the bearer share, which meant I had no right to any profits. The shareholders took unsecured loans from the bank to make high risk investments. There were profits from laundering money. All kinds of illegalities and sharp practices were mentioned to me from which big money could be made. I wanted no part of it. When all came to light, Lloyd's forced 4455 people to sell the bank and make full restitution of loans taken from syndicate funds to buy the bank."

"Do you still fear prosecution for what you did?"

"These events happened more than 20 years ago. I don't know what charges I might face now. Do remember, the prosecutions of syndicate members failed so the police may well have no interest. But I could be wrong. So yes, it's uncomfortable." Arthur shrugged.

"What about civil claims from those you cheated?"

"Cheated is your word. Again, this happened so long ago. The names sued and their claims were settled by both the syndicate and Lloyd's. If I'm sued, I'll have to face it. I don't treat these things lightly."

"Didn't you perjure yourself in the case against *The Sentinel*? Giving evidence, you denied you were Arthur Hawkins. That was a lie."

"We've covered this. I didn't make that denial and my legal advisers have checked the transcripts of the hearing and confirm this."

"I don't understand."

"My lawyers have read the evidence given in court. I was asked the question but I did not deny it. I did not answer it. My lawyers tell me that silence on my part does not amount to perjury."

"Do you worry that the public will turn its back on you and not buy your books?"

"I worry about many things but that would be the least of them. I leave those concerns to my literary agents and publishers. Anyway, I am not writing just now. Instead, I'm trying to mend a broken family."

Vaughan was given a hurry up signal from a floor manager.

"Is it true that Dr Pearce is divorcing you?"

"What a question! I admit my relationship with my wife is under a lot of strain. Our lives are broken. You're asking about a part of my life that is personal to me, Claire and our children. I have said more than enough."

"Do you bear any hatred or resentment towards *The Sentinel*?"

"I'm human. I think door-stepping is wrong, whatever the circumstances. So, yes, I feel sore but I know the journalists were just doing their job, trying to discover my past. I wish it had never happened but it did."

"We have just a minute left. Is there anything you want to say to the audience?"

Arthur paused. He looked directly at the television camera.

"If you still feel I'm not worthwhile, that I'm a chancer, so be it but don't include my family in this. They are innocent. Shun me, criticise me, hate me if you must but not my wife and children, please. Leave them out of whatever is to follow."

"And that, ladies and gentlemen, concludes our programme tonight. My thanks to Arthur Hawkins and to you, the audience."

Injunction

There was a round of applause from the audience which didn't stop when the "Off Air" sign came on. Perry offered his hand to Arthur. "No hard feelings?"

Arthur took the hand and gripped it hard as he moved Vaughan into the studio wings where neither of them would be seen by the audience.

"No hard feelings? Are you mad? You're the reason why my life is a mess. So don't try the jolly Englishman with me. I never played cricket. I didn't have your advantages growing up. I was much too poor. I don't do the sporting goodbye."

"Let my hand go, Arthur. You're hurting me."

As Arthur let go, he stamped hard on Vaughan's right foot. Vaughan stared at Arthur, shocked. Arthur kicked him hard in the privates. Vaughan let out an anguished cry as he crumpled onto the floor in pain.

"Vaughan, you sod. You forgot you can take the boy out of the East End but you can't take the East End out of the boy."

Chapter Twenty-Four.

Arthur stayed with Hardy in Mount Street, at Hardy's insistence. "If you go to an hotel, the press will find you. Here you're safe." After the Vaughan interview, Arthur returned to find Hardy glued to watching BBC's Newsnight.

"Come in. Watch this. Max Rankin's empire is the lead story. Media Universal has been taken over by bankers. Max is suffering collateral damage. He's been stripped of his executive roles and his assets have been frozen. He has huge guarantee liabilities. Looks like he's done for."

"I don't believe it. His house was built with straw?"

"So it seems. I watched you tonight. I thought you did really well. I'd still buy your novels. I shan't be surprised to hear from your publisher with another autobiography request."

"That's an emphatic 'no.' Joe Public has learned more than enough about me. I've better things to do, like repair my family."

"Ah, personal relationships. Overrated in my view. By the way, Claire phoned earlier. She wants you to call her."

"I'll call from my room."

"Before you go, let's see what I can find on the internet about Rankin." Hardy surfed like a pro. He logged onto *The Times*.

"In a startling series of events yesterday, Max Rankin's Media Universal empire tilted, perhaps sufficiently to crash in the coming days. The catalyst was the resignation of the entire Board of Directors of The Sentinel. The Stock Exchange temporarily suspended dealings in The Sentinel's shares. The share value of MU fell sufficiently for the group's leading lenders to call their loans.

"In a deal cobbled together during the day, lenders provided stand-by finance upon terms that The Sentinel's Board resume its duties. However, their price was the resignation by Rankin from all his executive roles. Until MU's share price recovers, Rankin has surrendered all his group shares to the lenders. He will no longer run the business in any way.

"When asked to comment, Rankin told our reporter: 'The men who shafted me today will come to regret it. I am not a busted flush.'"

*****

Claire picked up the receiver on the third ring. "It's me," he said.

"I saw you tonight on the Vaughan Show. It was dramatic. Are you okay?"

"Never mind me. How are you? You sound tired."

"I am. Tomorrow I'm checking back into the clinic. Don't know for how long."

"I'll come home to look after the children."

"No, Charlie, or do I call you Arthur? Mrs. James will take care of everything. You coming back now will send wrong signals to the children. I don't want you back here."

"But you said you and I couldn't have a relationship until I told everything. I've done so and opened myself up to heavens knows what. I did this for you and the children."

"Maybe but I never said things between us would be okay if you did this. I've lived through hell for months because of you. I'm sorry, I don't love you anymore. There is no point in our being together. Our marriage is over. Once I'm better, I'll see a lawyer. I want a divorce."

"No, please no. Claire, I love you very much. I am so sorry you've had to live in fear. I've taken steps to put things right, just as you asked. I know you're exhausted. Can we not talk again when you're feeling better?"

"I don't think so. I've fallen out of love with you. There's nothing there. I'm young enough to find someone else. I want a different life. I'll not be difficult about money and I want you to see the children whenever you like. I'll make sure they don't forget you are their father. But you and me, we're over."

"You said….."

"Goodbye, Charlie."

Arthur stared at his phone. He couldn't believe what had happened. He was just like Max Rankin. Through his own selfish behaviour he had lost everything. For the first time in decades, he cried.

Epilogue: 2021.

My name is Lizzie Edwards. My father is the author, Charles Pearce, whose real name is Arthur Hawkins. Pearce is not a nom de plume. Many years ago, Dad abandoned his career as a Lloyd's underwriter, had extensive plastic surgery, created a brand new identity for himself and re-emerged as a different man, an American citizen. About fifteen years ago, *The Sentinel,* a London newspaper, went after Pearce and, following a brutal court case, Dad told the truth about his identity and early life. My parents' marriage ended. Had the case not happened, I'm convinced my parents would have stayed together. Years later, Dad still loves Mum but she moved on.

By the time the case ended, Dad was a changed man. My brother, sister and I hardly saw him for months. Mum tried to make all kinds of excuses for him. She forgot I had been to the trial to give evidence and saw Dad shredded to pieces as he withdrew from life.

In the January after the case ended, Mum sold our house in Buckinghamshire to escape the unpleasantness from former friends. We moved to Leeds to be close to my grandmother and aunt. Mum was offered a teaching position at Leeds University. My siblings and I went to a local grammar school, where I was lucky to be taught by a former journalist. Mrs. Marchant fired up my interest in writing and searching for truth. She had worked on a local Manchester newspaper and made her life there sound fascinating. "Even if you are just reporting on births, marriages and deaths," she explained, "each one is an individual story which might lead you to who knows where or what."

When I left school, I studied journalism at Sheffield University where the course was led by former journalists. I got my first job at *The Yorkshire Evening Post.* My stories were noticed and one of the national newspapers now wants to employ me. Mum isn't good at practical advice but Dad is. He told me to balance the bright lights of London against the career I was creating in Leeds and to put the wishes of my new husband, Joe, at the top of my list. "This is a decision for both of you. Don't push Joe into something he doesn't want."

After Dad's court case ended, it took Dad almost a year to make his way north to see us. I was shocked when I saw him. He had lost a lot of weight and had aged ten years. He was grey and his eyes were sunken; there was no joie de vivre whatsoever. My brother, sister and I didn't know what to say to him as we sat in a park cafe, sipping hot chocolate.

"I want to start with an apology to you all," Dad told us. "Can you possibly understand that when I told the public who I really was, everything I valued was taken away from me. I was left with nothing except money and what good is that if you have nothing else? Mum had left me, you children went with her, friends abandoned me and my reputation was destroyed. This was no fault of yours or Mum's. It was mine and mine alone but I could not face you. I was unable to look you kids in the eye because I had shattered your lives as a result of my bad decisions. I am very, very sorry for it all. I was wrong to have done what I did and, even worse, I have been selfish by not coming to see you."

"Dad, you're here now. Will it be another year before we see you again?" Harry asked.

"Lizzie, Harry, Amber, this will never happen again. I won't move to Leeds because that would not be fair, even though Mum would not stop me. Instead, I am looking for a place in Harrogate or Knaresborough. Wherever I settle, there will be enough space for you all to stay if you want."

And Dad was as good as his word. He rented a flat in Harrogate and he came every weekend. Mum was happy for us to see him and let us stay with him. He ceased to look quite so grey and smiles started to appear on his face.

That spring, something happened to change everything. Amber had always been a sickly child. She ran out of energy quickly and her favourite thing was to sit quietly and read. Mum had her checked out with the GP once or twice but nothing was discovered. Then, out of the blue, Amber collapsed at school. She was rushed to hospital. Of course, Mum told Dad immediately and he raced up from London. By the time he arrived, Amber had been diagnosed with a faulty heart valve. She needed immediate surgery. A paediatric heart surgeon would perform the surgery at The York Hospital, some thirty miles away from Leeds. This meant Amber would have to stay in hospital on her own unless other arrangements were made. But if Mum was with Amber, who would look after Harry and me?

My parents loved us. We never doubted this, even in Dad's absence. So what he did came as no surprise. He headed straight to York and spoke with Mum. They agreed that Mum ought to be with Harry and me. Dad stayed with Amber. The ward sister, Kyra Jones, was persuaded by Dad to let him sleep in an uncomfortable chair next to Amber's bed. He stayed by her bedside through the surgery and her time in intensive care. He held her hand, nursed her, and talked with her so that Amber knew she wasn't alone. And Mum, Harry and I visited constantly.

Mum brought changes of clothes for Dad and Kyra allowed him to use the staff facilities to shower. After a week, Amber had recovered sufficiently to come home. When she realised that Dad would no longer stay with her, she got angry. "Why not? I want him home with us," she yelled. Mum was delighted to find Amber behaving like a teenager. Mum offered Dad the guest bedroom. He accepted.

I'd love to tell you my parents got back together but that didn't happen. Mum no longer felt that way about Dad and he respected this. I know they must have talked about the changed situation and I guess they decided to be sensible adults, doing the right thing by their children.

Dad came up with an idea which changed my parents' lives. When Amber returned to The York Hospital for a check-up, I went along. Amber wanted me with her. Dad arranged to see the hospital's chief executive. Amber and I watched him go to work. We were so impressed by his persuasive powers.

"Mrs Edwards, thanks for taking time to see me. My family and I are so grateful to your hospital for helping Amber. We'd like to do something in return but it will need your support."

"I'm intrigued. Do go on."

"Sister Kyra Jones was kind enough to make arrangements so I could be with Amber when she needed a parent. I suppose it's not unusual for a child patient to be many miles away from family and friends. Had Sister Jones refused, Amber would have spent hours on her own at night. This cannot be right but it's not a perfect world."

"You're right about the facilities being limited, Mr Hawkins, but we have to prioritise our resources. It's the same throughout the NHS. Not ideal but we manage somehow."

"I think I can help. Take the ward where Amber stayed after she was moved from the Intensive Care Unit. Four beds, open plan, cubicles separated by curtains and no facilities for parents. What if I supplied special chairs to go next to each bed? They are called Recliners. The bottom of the chair extends to a footrest, so that the chair becomes a kind of bed. In each cubicle, you could fit a shelf for books, pictures, CDs and stuff. To prevent the shelf from blocking anything, it can be on a hinge so it lies flat. A small room for parents, where they can microwave food and have a shower, is just a matter of design and space. I know health and safety issues arise but look at the benefits for the families."

"I'm not saying yes or no," said Mrs Edwards, "but come back with details and designs. I'll look into this with you. Our paediatric department is not unaware of these shortcomings. But you will have to provide funding. I have nothing in the budget to help."

Over the next few days, Dad threw himself into the task. He went to Gubbins, a huge furniture manufacturer in Leeds, and talked to the boss. Long story short, Gubbins designed a special Recliner which extended into a single bed. Hospital-approved materials were used. Gubbins supplied some chairs at cost and in exchange, their contribution was acknowledged publicly by the hospital. It got press coverage. Dad wanted his name was kept out of things. No fuss or bother. He was happy that his contribution remained private.

"If my role in this plan gets investigated," he told Mum, "all the coverage will be about my past and the idea will be still-born. Instead, I want you to front the charity. 'Chairman – Dr Claire Richardson' has a good ring to it."

"What else?"

"If you and Amber agree, I'd like to call the charity 'Amber's Room.' I'll get the spade work done. I want a better deal from

Gubbins. They might be supplying thousands of chairs. I know architects who will design the family room. I'll put in seed corn money to start things off. I guess half a million should cover it. We will need people, mostly volunteers. Your University could help. I'll talk to my contacts about funding."

"I'm out of my depth here," Mum told him. "What have you got in mind?"

"We need national and local fundraisers, access to every NHS paediatric department and ward in the UK, communicators, accounts people, who knows what else? I've not done this before. I merely gave to charity. But like Mao said, the march of one thousand miles starts with one step."

Twelve years later, I'm at Buckingham Palace with Mum, Harry and Amber, for Mum's investiture. She has been awarded an OBE "for services to Amber's Room." It's an honour well deserved. It took time to get the charity on people's radar but when it took off, it got so large that she gave up teaching to work for it full time for. She and Dad worked closely together and became better friends.

Dad kept to his word and stayed very much in the background. I asked him how he did this without jealousy or resentment. "Read Harry Truman," he told me. It took me a while to find what Dad was talking about. Truman, reminiscing about the Presidency, said, "it's amazing what you can achieve if you don't mind who gets the credit."

My parents found a raison d'etre which was unrelated to their former lives. It brought them together as friends. Deep down, Dad still hopes he might rekindle Mum's feelings for him but, like he says, "I'm not holding my breath." However, Amber's Room has brought us all closer together. That's worth everything to me."

THE END

Acknowledgments

This is a work of fiction. Any resemblance to any person, living or dead, is entirely coincidental. However, I have borrowed from historic events

This novel required a great deal of research, both in the privacy laws of England in the early years of this century and banking practices. I am greatly indebted to lawyers Marcus Boyd, Simone Pearlman and Anthony Inglese for their patience and for explaining esoteric areas of law to a journeyman. My thanks go to Clive and Jo Moore for providing helpful background about Lloyds of London, as well as relating stories of the antics of that market forty years ago. I am grateful to a Swiss lawyer, who at his request will remain anonymous, for explaining the intricacies of moving money in the 2000s to disguise origin.

Part of the story takes place in the Twin Cities of Minneapolis and St Paul. My wonderful cousins, Ann McCaughan and Jake Zimmerman, were very helpful in reminding me of names and places there.

I needed specialist advice on fingerprinting, which was provided generously by Catherine Tweedy of Keith Boren Consultants. The cover design is the work of Gary White. My thanks to him, not only for his efforts on "Injunction" but also the Driscoll Quartet.

My good mates, Professor Scott Lucas and Baron Danny Finkelstein, took time to read the story and offer comment for the book and back cover. Thank you.

There was quite a family effort bringing this book to fruition. I thank my son-in-law, Matt Leach, who was a huge help, handling details with Amazon Kindle. Their website is not the easiest to navigate. Janet Solomon, my dear sister of indeterminate age, proof read the manuscript and my infinitely better half, Linda, edited the book. Accordingly, if there are mistakes, they are the ones to blame. I am entirely innocent!

As for my daughters, Jessica and Susanna, thank you so much for the words of encouragement, such as, "Dad's writing another bloody book!" I love it that you make me laugh.

Printed in Great Britain
by Amazon